What was happening to her?

She had wanted to rescue Oliver Sullivan from himself, but she had not intended to put herself at risk! She had her new world, filled with jam, and the Summer Fest. Rescuing him had just been part of the new do-gooder philosophy that was supposed to fill up her life.

Only something was going wrong this morning. Because it just felt too right!

So, she deliberately broke the connection between them. She sat back down beside him, deliberately not making contact with his shoulder again.

Then she glanced at Sullivan and was transfixed by the relaxed look on his face as if he was taking simple pleasure in a simple moment, and she realized it wasn't as easy to break connections as she'd thought.

"I haven't felt this way since I was a kid," he said.

"I know what you mean," Sarah said, finally giving in to it and savoring how this closed man was revealing something of himself. What would it hurt to encourage him by revealing something of herself?

The Puppy Rescue

Cara Colter & Katie Meyer

Previously published as *The Cop, the Puppy and Me*
and *Do You Take This Daddy?*

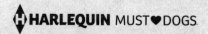

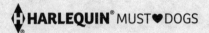

ISBN-13: 978-1-335-98854-6

Recycling programs
for this product may
not exist in your area.

The Puppy Rescue

Copyright © 2020 by Harlequin Books S.A.

The Cop, the Puppy and Me
First published in 2012.
This edition published in 2020.
Copyright © 2012 by Cara Colter

Do You Take This Daddy?
First published in 2016.
This edition published in 2020.
Copyright © 2016 by Katie Meyer

This edition published by arrangement with Harlequin Books S.A.

For questions and comments about the quality of this book,
please contact us at CustomerService@Harlequin.com.

Harlequin Enterprises ULC
22 Adelaide St. West, 40th Floor
Toronto, Ontario M5H 4E3, Canada
www.Harlequin.com

Printed in U.S.A.

CONTENTS

THE COP, THE PUPPY AND ME   7
Cara Colter

DO YOU TAKE THIS DADDY?   205
Katie Meyer

Cara Colter shares her life in beautiful British Columbia, Canada, with her husband, nine horses and one small Pomeranian with a large attitude. She loves to hear from readers, and you can learn more about her and contact her through Facebook.

Books by Cara Colter

Interview with a Tycoon
Meet Me Under the Mistletoe
The Pregnancy Secret
Soldier, Hero...Husband?
Housekeeper Under the Mistletoe
The Wedding Planner's Big Day
Swept into the Tycoon's World
Snowbound with the Single Dad
His Convenient Royal Bride
Cinderella's Prince Under the Mistletoe

Visit the Author Profile page
at Harlequin.com for more titles.

THE COP, THE PUPPY AND ME

Cara Colter

To Rob (again) who loves me through it all.

Chapter 1

Oliver Sullivan—who had been called only Sullivan for so long he hardly remembered his first name—decided he disliked Sarah McDougall just about as much as he'd ever disliked anyone.

And he'd disliked a lot of people.

Meeting dislikable people was a hazard of choosing law enforcement as a profession, not that Ms. McDougall fell into the criminal category.

"Though I have dealt with criminals who were more charming," he muttered to himself. Of course, with criminals he had the advantage of having some authority over them.

All this naked dislike, and Sullivan had yet to even speak to her. His encounters had all been filtered through his voice mail. He'd never seen her, let alone met her, and he would have been only too happy to keep it that way.

But she'd gone to his boss.

Her voice on the phone had been enough to stir his dislike of her and her bulldog-like persistence had cemented it.

Not that her voice was *grating*. It was what she wanted from him that was the problem.

Call me back.

Please.

It's so important.

We have to talk.

Mr. Sullivan, this is urgent.

When he'd managed to totally ignore her, she'd eventually gone to his boss. Sullivan mulled that over with aggravation. Which was worse? The fact that she had gone to his boss? Or the fact that his boss had *ordered* him to comply?

At least go talk to her, the chief had said. *In case you haven't figured it out, you're not in Detroit anymore.*

Oh, Sullivan had figured that out. In about his first five minutes on his new job.

Being a cop in small-town Wisconsin was about as different from being a homicide detective in Detroit as Attila the Hun was different from being Mother Theresa.

"What moment of insanity made me choose Kettle Bend, Wisconsin?" he growled.

Of course his moment of insanity had a name, and her name was Della, his older sister, who had discovered this little pocket of American charm and chosen to come here with her orthodontist husband, Jonathon, to raise her two boys. She'd been trying to convince Sullivan to join their happy family ever since his whole life had gone sideways.

Sullivan shook that off, focused on the town instead. He took in the streets around him with a jaundiced eye.

It looked like the kind of town Walt Disney or Norman Rockwell would have imagined, wide, quiet streets, shaded by enormous trees that he, hard-bitten product of some of Detroit's worst neighborhoods, had no hope of identifying.

Still, there was no missing the newness of the leaves, unfurling in those tender and vibrant shades of spring, the sharp, tangy scent of their newness tickling his nose through his open car window.

Nestled comfortably in the leafy shade were tidy houses, wearing their age and their American flags with equal pride. The houses, for the most part, had a pleasant sameness about them. White with pale yellow trim, or pale yellow with white trim, the odd sage-green and or dove-gray thrown into the mix.

All had deep porches, white picket fences around postage-stamp yards, splashes of spring color in the flower beds lining walkways that welcomed.

But Sullivan refused to be charmed.

He disliked illusions, and he knew this particular illusion to be the most dangerous: that there were places left in the world that were entirely safe and uncomplicated, porch swings and fireflies, cold lemonade on hot summer afternoons.

That there was a place where doors and windows were unlocked, where children rode their bikes unescorted and unafraid to school, where families laughed over board games. That there were places of unsullied innocence, places that whispered the word *home.* He kept trying to warn Della all was probably not as it appeared.

No, behind the windows and doors of those perfect and pretty houses, Sullivan was willing to bet he would uncover all kinds of secrets that belied the picture he was seeing. Behind some of those closed doors were probably booze bottles hidden down toilet tanks. A kid with a crack problem. Unexplained bruises and black eyes.

It was this cynicism that was making him a poor fit for Kettle Bend.

Certainly a poor fit for Sarah McDougall's plans for him.

Her message on his voice mail chimed through his head, making him shudder. *We need a hero, Mr. Sullivan.*

He wasn't about to be anybody's hero. This wasn't how he wanted to be spending his day off. He was about to make one Sarah McDougall very, very sorry she'd gone after this bear in his den.

Checking addresses as he went, Sullivan finally pulled over, stepped out of his car and steeled himself against the sleepy appeal of the street he found himself on. On principle, he rolled up his car window and locked his door. The people of Kettle Bend might want to pretend nothing bad ever happened here, but he wasn't going to trust his new car stereo to that notion.

Then he turned to look at the house that sat at 1716 Lilac Lane.

The house differed from its neighbors very little. It was a shingle-sided, single-story bungalow, painted recently—white, naturally—the trim a deep, crisp shade of olive. Vines—he guessed ivy because that was the only name of a vine that he knew—showed signs of new growth, and would shade the wide porch completely in the heat of summer.

Sullivan passed through an outrageously squeaking gate and under an arbor that he knew would drip the color and fragrance of climbing roses in a few more weeks.

He shrugged off the relief it was not happening now, as if there was something about all this charm that was nattering away at his defenses—not like a battering ram, more like an irritating humming, like being pestered by mosquitoes. The scent of roses would have been just one more thing to add to it.

Peripherally, he made note that the concrete walkway was heaved in places, but lined with an odd variety of spring flowers—deep purple, with a starburst yellow interior.

He noticed only because that was what he did.

Sullivan noticed *everything*. Every detail. It made him a great cop. It hadn't helped him be a better human being, as far as he could tell.

He went up the wide stairs to the front door, crossed the shaded porch to it. Before he rang the bell, he studied the outdoor furnishings.

Old wicker chairs, carefully painted the same olive-green as the house trim, held impossibly cheerful plump cushions, with red and yellow and orange flowers in the pattern. Just as the town painted a picture, so did this porch.

A place of rest. Of comfort. Of safety. Of peace.

"Ha," Sullivan snorted cynically, but was aware of setting his shoulders more firmly against the buzzing of all the pesky details working at convincing him he could maybe try letting this woman down softly. He could try being a nice guy.

"Ha," he said again. So far, subtleness had not worked on her. When you phoned a person sixty-two times and they didn't return your calls that did not mean, *Go to the boss.*

It meant, *Get lost. Go away. Find yourself another hero.*

He turned deliberately away from the invitation of the porch, not prepared to admit for even one small moment, a fraction of a second, that he had imagined himself accepting the invitation.

Rest.

He shook his head, and turned to the door, found the bell—a key type that needed to be turned—and twisted it.

The exterior door was a screen door, white with elaborate carvings around the edges framing the oval of the screen in the middle. The green interior door was open, and he could hear the bell echo through the house.

No one answered, but he figured leaving a door hanging open was an invitation, plain and simple, for prying eyes.

So, unlike the invitation to rest, he took this one, peering in at the house.

The door opened directly into the living room, though a handmade rag rug designated a tiny entry area, and suggested the owner liked order—and wiped feet.

Afternoon sunlight spilled through the open door and through the picture window, slanting across wood floors that were golden with the patina of age.

Two small couches, a shade of sunshine-yellow that matched the interior of the flowers that marched up the front walk, faced each other over a scarred antique coffee table. Again, there was a sense of order: neatly stacked magazines and a vase of those flowers that had lined the walkway, dipping low on slender stems.

Sullivan had not formed a mental picture of his stalker.

Now he did. Single. No evidence—and there was always evidence—of a man in residence.

No children, because there was no sign of toys or mess, though his eyes caught on a wall of framed magazine covers, hung gallery-style, just inside that front door.

They were all covers from a magazine called *To-day's Baby*.

They did nothing to change his initial impression of her. *No life*.

Sullivan was willing to bet the resident of this house was as frumpy as her house was cute. She was no doubt a few pounds too heavy, with frizzy hair and bad makeup, busy making her house look pretty as a picture while she fell into middle-aged decline.

Now that there was nothing left to do on her house—obviously it was magazine photo shoot ready—she'd turned her attention to the town.

Mr. Sullivan, Kettle Bend needs you!

Yeah, right. Kettle Bend needed Oliver Sullivan the way Oliver Sullivan needed a toothache.

He could smell something faintly, drifting through that open door. The scent was sweet. And tart. Home cooking. The sudden, sharp feeling of yearning took him totally by surprise.

He felt it again, like a whisper along his spine. *Rest*.

Again, he shook it off, along with annoying yearnings. He *had* rested. For a whole year. Tying flies and wearing hip waders. It wasn't for him. Too much time for thinking.

Sullivan rang the bell again, impatiently this time.

A cat, a gray puffball with evil green eyes slid out of a hallway, plunked itself in the ray of sunshine and regarded him with slitted dislike, before dismissing him with a lift of its paw and a delicate lick. The cat fit his picture of her life *exactly*.

Still, that cat *knew* he didn't like animals.

Which was what made the whole situation that

had gotten him to this front door even more irritating. A hero? He didn't even like dogs. And so he didn't want to answer the question—not from her and not from the dozens of other reporters and TV stations that were hounding him—why he had risked his life for one.

Sullivan gave the handle of the screen door a firm tug, let the door squeak open a noisy inch or two before releasing it to snap shut again.

Come on. An unlocked door?

It made him feel grim. And determined.

This cozy little world was practically begging for a healthy dose of what he had in abundance.

Cynicism.

He backed off the steps and stood regarding the house.

"She's in the back. Sarah's left that rhubarb a bit too long."

Sullivan started. See? It *had* gotten to him. His guard had been down just enough not to notice that his every move was being monitored by the next-door-neighbor. She was a wizened gnome, ensconced in a deep Adirondack chair.

From under a tuft of cotton-ball hair, her bright black marble eyes regarded him with amused curiosity rather than the deep suspicion a stranger *should* be regarded with.

"You're the new policeman," she said.

So, he wasn't a stranger. There was no anonymity in a small town. Not even on your day off, in jeans and a T-shirt.

He nodded, still a little taken aback by how trust was automatically instilled in him just because he was the new cop on the block.

In Detroit, nine times out of ten, the exact opposite had been true, at least in the hard neighborhoods where he had plied his trade.

"Nice thing you did. With that dog."

Was there one single person on the face of the earth who didn't know? Sullivan was beginning to hate the expression *gone viral* more than any other.

She wouldn't think it was so nice if she knew how often since then he just wished he'd let the damn thing go down the river, raging with spring runoff, instead of jumping in after it.

He thought of it wriggling against him as he lay on the shore of the river afterward, gasping for breath. The puppy, soaked, another layer of freezing on top of his own freezing, had curled up on his exposed skin, right on top of his heart, whimpering and licking him.

Sullivan knew he didn't really wish that he hadn't gone in after it. He just wished that he wished it. And that a person with the cell phone had not recorded his leap into the swollen Kettle River and then posted it on the internet where it seemed the whole world had seen it.

"How is the dog?" she asked.

"Still at the vet," he answered, "but he's going to be fine."

"Has anyone claimed him yet?"

"No."

"Well, I'm sure there will be a long lineup of people who want to adopt him if his owner doesn't show up."

"Oh, yeah," he agreed.

Because of the video, the Kettle Bend Police Department was fielding a dozen calls a day about that dog.

Sullivan followed the narrow concrete path where it curved around the side of the house and then led him down a passageway between houses. Then the path opened into a long, narrow backyard.

There was no word for it.

Except perhaps *enchanting*.

For a moment he stood, breathing it all in: waxy leaves; mature trees; curving flower beds whose dark mounding loam met the crisp edge of freshly cut grass.

There was a sense of having entered a grotto, deeply private.

Sacred.

Sullivan snorted at himself, but a little uneasily this time.

He saw her then.

Crouched beside a fence lined with rows of vigorously growing, elephant-eared plants.

She was totally engrossed in what she was doing, yanking at the thin red stalks of the huge-leafed plants.

It must be the rhubarb her neighbor had mentioned.

She already had a stack of it beside her. Her face

was hidden in the shade of a broad-brimmed hat, the light catching her mouth, where her tongue was caught between her teeth in concentration.

She was wearing a shapeless flowered tank top and white shorts, smudged with dirt, but the long line of strong legs, already beginning to tan, took his breath away.

As he watched, she tugged vigorously on one of the plants. When the stalk parted with the ground, she nearly catapulted over backward. When she righted herself, she went very still, as if she knew, suddenly, she was not alone.

Without getting up, she pivoted slowly on the heels of her feet and looked at him, her head tilted quizzically, possibly aggrieved that he had caught her in a wrestling match with the plant.

Sarah McDougall, if this was her, was certainly not middle-aged. Or frizzy-haired. She was wearing no makeup at all. The feeling of his breath being taken away was complete.

Corkscrew auburn curls escaped from under the brim of her hat and framed an elfin face. A light scattering of freckles danced across a daintily snubbed nose. Her cheekbones and her chin mirrored that image of delicacy.

But it was her eyes that threatened to undo him. He was good at this: at reading eyes. It was harder than people thought. A liar could look you straight in the face without blinking. A murderer could have eyes that looked as soft as suede, as gentle as a fawn's.

But eleven years working one of the toughest homicide squads in the world had honed Sullivan's skills to a point that his sister called him, not without a hint of admiration, scary in his ability to detect what was real about a person.

This woman's eyes were huge and hazel, and stunningly, slayingly gorgeous.

She was, obviously, the all-American girl. Wholesome. Sweet. Probably ridiculously naive.

Case in point: she left her door unlocked and wanted to make *him* a hero!

But instead of that fueling his annoyance at her, instead of remembering his fury that she had called his boss, Sullivan felt a surge of foolish protectiveness.

"You should lock your front door when you work back here," he told her gruffly. Part of him wanted to leave it at that, to turn his back and walk away from her. Because obviously what a girl like that needed to be protected from most was a guy like him.

Who had seen so much darkness it felt as if it had taken up residence inside of him. Darkness that could snuff out the radiance that surrounded her like a halo.

Still, if he left without giving her an opportunity to see that in him, she might pester him, or his boss, endlessly.

So he forced himself to cross the yard until he stood above her, until his shadow passed over the wideness of those eyes.

He rarely shook hands. Keep the barriers up. Establish authority. Don't invite familiarity. Keep your distance.

So it startled him when he wanted to extend a hand to her.

"Sarah McDougall?" he asked, and at her wide-eyed nod, "I'm Sullivan."

The aggrieved look faded from her face. She actually looked thrilled! He was glad he had shoved his hand in his pocket instead of holding it out to her.

"Mr. Sullivan," she said, and scrambled to her feet. "I'm so glad you came. May I call you Oliver?"

"No, you may not. No one calls me Oliver. And it's not Mister," he said, his voice deliberately cold. "It's Officer."

A touch of wariness tinged her gaze. Hadn't she been able to tell from her unanswered pleas that he was a man who deserved her wariness?

"No one calls you Oliver?"

What was she asking that question for? Hadn't he made it eminently clear there was going to be nothing personal between them, not even an invitation to use first names?

"No." His voice had a bit of a snap to it.

Which she clearly did not recognize, or she would have had the sense to back away from the subject.

"Not even your mother?" She raised a skeptical eyebrow. Her looking skeptical was faintly comical, like a budgie bird trying to look aggressive.

"Dead," he snapped. He could see sympathy crowding her eyes, and there was no way he was allowing all that softness to spill out and touch him. His mother had died when he was seventeen years old.

And his father.

Seventeen years ago was a place he did not revisit.

There was no sense her misconstruing his reasons for being here, and there was only one way to approach a person like this.

Brutal bluntness.

"Don't call me anymore," he said, holding her gaze, his voice deliberately low and flat. "I'm not helping you. Not if you call six million times. I'm not any kind of hero. I don't want to be your friend. I don't want to save your town. And don't call my boss again, either. Because you don't want me to be your enemy."

Sullivan saw, astonished at his failure, that his legendary people-reading skills were slightly off-kilter. Because he had thought she would be easily intimidated, that he could make her back down, just like that.

Instead he saw that cute little mouth reset itself in a line that was unmistakably stubborn and that could mean only one thing for him.

Trouble.

Sarah stared up at her unexpected visitor, caught off balance, not just by her tug-of-war with her rhubarb, but also by the fact she'd had a witness to it!

Add to that his unexpected sharpness of tone, his appearance in her yard, his appearance, period, and her feeling of being unbalanced grew.

She'd been totally engrossed in wresting the rhubarb from the ground. Which was what she needed from her house, her yard, her garden and her work.

There was always something that needed to be done, the hard work unending.But her total focus on what she'd been doing had left her vulnerable. Though Sarah suspected that even if you had been expecting this man, had laid out tea things and put on a presentable dress, the feeling you would have when you experienced the rawness of his presence would be one of vulnerability.

The grainy video she had seen—along with millions of other people—had not really prepared her for the reality of him. Though she had already figured out from her unanswered calls that he was not exactly going to be the kind of guy the heroic rescue of a drowning puppy had her wanting him to be.

From thirty seconds of film, from him ripping off his shirt and jumping into the icy water just past where the Kettle River ran under the bridge in downtown Kettle Bend, to lying on the bank after, the pup snuggled into the pebbled flesh of his naked chest, she had jumped to conclusions.

He was courageous. That much was in his eyes. A man afraid of nothing.

But she had thought—a man willing to risk his life for a dog, after all—that he would be gentle and warm.

If his message on his voice mail had been a touch abrupt, she had managed to dismiss that as part of his professional demeanor. But then the fact that he had not returned her increasingly desperate calls?

And now he had been downright rude to her.

Plus, there was nothing warm in those dark eyes. They were cool, assessing. There was a wall so high in them it would be easier to scale Everest.

Sarah felt a quiver of doubt. The reality of Oliver Sullivan versus the fantasy she had been nursing since she had first seen the clip of him did not bode well for her plan, unless he could be tamed, and from looking at him that seemed highly unlikely!

Sullivan was dressed casually, dark denims, a forest-green T-shirt that molded the fullness of his chest, the hard mounds of firm biceps. A hundred other guys in Kettle Bend were wearing the same thing today, but she bet none of them radiated the raw potency that practically shivered in the spring sunshine around him.

He looked like a warrior wearing the disguise of a more civilized man.

He was one of those men who radiated a subtle confidence in his own strength, in his ability to handle whatever came up. It was as if he was ready and waiting for all hell to break loose.

Which was so utterly at odds with the atmosphere in her garden that it might have made her smile, except there was something about the stripping intensity of his expression that made her gulp instead.

Despite astonishing good looks, he had the expression of a man unutterably world-weary, a man who expected the absolute worst from people, and was rarely disappointed.

Still, he *was* unnervingly good-looking. If she could talk him into doing some TV interviews, the camera would love his dark, chocolate hair, short and neat, slashing brows over eyes so dark brown they could have been mistaken for black. He had a strong nose, good cheekbones, wide sensual lips and a devilish little cleft in his chin.

She could not allow herself the luxury of being intimidated by him.

She just couldn't.

Kettle Bend needed him.

Not that she wanted to be thinking of him in the same sentence as the word *need*.

Because he was the kind of man who made a woman aware of things—*needs*—she was sure she had laid to rest.

He was the kind of man whose masculinity was so potent it could make a woman ache for things she had once had, and had no longer. Fevered kisses. Strong arms. Laughter in the night.

He was the kind of man who could almost make a woman entirely forget the terrible price, the pain that you could invite by looking for those things.

Sarah McDougall didn't need anyone looking out for her, thank you very much! It was one of the things she prided herself on.

Fierce independence.

Not needing anyone. Not anymore. Not ever again.

Inheriting this house, and her grandmother's business, Jelly Jeans and Jammies, had allowed her that.

She could *not* back down from him! So, with more confidence than she felt, in defiance of his hostility, she whipped the gardening glove off her hand, wiped it on her shorts just in case, and extended it to him.

Then she held her breath waiting to see if he would take it.

Chapter 2

Officer Oliver Sullivan looked at Sarah's extended hand, clearly annoyed at her effort to make some kind of contact with him.

She knew he debated just walking away now that he had delivered his unfriendly message.

But he didn't. With palpable reluctance, he accepted her hand, and his shake was brief and hard. She kept her face impassive at the jolt that surged, instantaneously, from her fingertips to her elbow. It would be easy to think of rough whiskers scraping a soft cheek, the smell of skin out of the shower.

Easy, too, to feel the tiniest little thrill that her life had had this unexpected moment thrust into it.

Sarah reminded herself, sternly, that her life was full and rich and complete.

She had inherited her grandmother's house in this postcard-pretty town. With it had come a business that provided her a livelihood and that had pulled her back from the brink of despair when her engagement had ended.

Kettle Bend had given her something she had not thought she would ever have again, and that she now could appreciate as that rarest of commodities: contentment.

Okay, in her more honest moments, Sarah knew it was not complete contentment. Sometimes, she felt a little stir of restlessness, a longing for her old life. Not her romance with Michael Talbot. No, sir, she was so over her fiancé's betrayal of her trust, *so* over him.

No, it was elements of her old life as a writer on the popular New York–based *Today's Baby* magazine that created that nebulous longing, that called to her. She had regularly met and interviewed new celebrity moms and dads, been invited to glamorous events, been a sought-after guest at store openings and other events. She had loved being creative.

A man like the one who stood in front of her posed a danger. He could turn a small longing for *something*—excitement, fulfillment—into a complete catastrophe.

Sarah reminded herself, sternly and firmly, that she had already found a solution for her nebulous longings; she was going to chase away her restlessness with a new challenge, a huge one that would occupy her completely. Her new commitment was going to be to the little community that was fading around her.

Her newfound efforts at contentment relied on getting this town back to the way she remembered it being during her childhood summers spent here: vital, the streets overflowing with seasonal visitors, a feeling of endless summer, a hopeful vibrancy in the air.

So, handshake completed, Sarah crossed her arms over her chest, a thin defense against some dark promise—or maybe threat—that swirled like electricity in the air around him.

She wanted him to think she was not rattled.

"I have a great plan for Kettle Bend," she told him. She had interviewed some of the most sought-after people in the world. She would not be intimidated by him. "And you can help make it happen."

He regarded her long and hard, and then the tiniest of smiles tickled the corner of that sinfully sensuous mouth.

She thought she had him. Then…

"No," he said. Simple. Firm. Unshakable, the smile gone from the corner of that mouth as if it had never been.

"But you haven't even heard what I have to say!" Sarah sputtered indignantly.

He actually seemed to consider that for a moment, though his deeply weary sigh was not exactly encouraging.

"Okay," he said after a moment, those dark eyes shielded, unreadable. "Spit it out."

Spit it out? As an invitation to communication, it was somewhat lacking. On the other hand, at least he wasn't walking away. Yet. But his body language indicated the thread that held him here, in her yard, was thin.

"The rescue of the dog was incredible. So courageous."

He failed to look flattered, seemed to be leaning a little more toward the exit, so she rushed on. "I've seen it on the internet."

His expression darkened even more—if that was possible—so she didn't add that she had watched it more than a dozen times, feeling foolishly compelled to watch it again and again for reasons she didn't quite understand.

But she did understand that she was not the only one. The video had captured hearts around the world. As she saw it, the fact he was standing in her yard meant that she had an opportunity to capitalize on that magic ingredient that was drawing people by the thousands to that video.

"I know you haven't been in Kettle Bend very long," Sarah continued. "Didn't you know how cold that water was going to be?"

"If I had known how cold that water was going to be, I would have never jumped in."

That was the kind of answer that wouldn't work *at all* in the event she could talk him into being a participant in her plan to use his newfound notoriety to publicize the town.

Though that possibility seemed more unlikely by the second.

At least he was talking, and not walking.

"You must love dogs," she said, trying, with growing desperation, to find a chink in all that armor.

He didn't answer her, though his chest filled as he drew in a long breath. He ran an impatient hand through the thick, crisp silk of his dark hair.

"What do you want from me?"

Her eyes followed the movement of his hand through his hair, and for a moment the sensation of what she *really* wanted from him nearly swamped her.

Sarah shook it off, an unwanted weakness.

"Your fifteen minutes of fame could be very beneficial to this town," she said, trying, valiantly, and not entirely successfully, not to wonder how his hair would feel beneath her fingertips.

"Whether I like it or not," he commented dryly.

"What's not to like? A few interviews with carefully chosen sources. It would take just the smallest amount of your time," she pressed persuasively.

His look of impatience deepened, and now annoyance layered on top of it. Really, such a sour expression should have made him much less good-looking!

But it didn't.

Still, she tried to focus on the fact that he was still standing here, giving her a chance. Once she explained it all to him, he couldn't help but get on board!

"Do you know what Summer Fest is?" she asked him.

"No. But it sounds perfectly nauseating."

She felt her confidence falter and covered it by glaring at him. Sarah decided cynical was just his default reaction. Who could possibly have anything against summer? Or a festival?

Sarah plunged ahead. "It's a festival for the first four days of July. It starts with a parade and ends with the Fourth of July fireworks. It used to kick off the summer season here in Kettle Bend. It used to set the tone for the whole summer."

She waited for him to ask what had happened, but he only looked bored, raising an eyebrow at her.

"It was canceled, five years ago. The cancellation has been just one more thing that has contributed to Kettle Bend fading away, losing its vibrancy, like a favorite old couch that needs recovering. It's not the same place I used to visit as a child."

"Visit?" It rattled her that he seemed not to be showing the slightest interest in a single word she said, but he picked up on that immediately. "So you're not a local, either?"

Either. A bond between them. *Play it.*

"No, I grew up in New York. But my mother was from here, originally. I used to spend summers. And where are you from? What brings you to Kettle Bend?"

"Momentary insanity," he muttered.

He certainly wasn't giving anything away, but he wasn't walking away, either, so Sarah prattled on, trying to engage him. "This is my grandmother's house. She left it to me when she died. Along with her jam business. Jelly Jeans and Jammies. You might have heard of it. It's very popular around town."

Sarah was not sure she had engaged him. His expression was impossible to read. She had felt encouraged that he showed a slight interest in her. Now, she was suspicious. Sullivan was one of those men who found out things about people, all the while revealing nothing of himself.

"Look, Miss McDougall—"

She noticed he did not use her first name, and knew, despite that brief show of interest, he was keeping his distance from her in every way he could.

"—not that any of this has anything to do with me, but nothing feels or looks the same to an adult as it does to a child."

How had he managed, in a single line, to make her feel hopelessly naive, as if she was chasing something that didn't exist?

What if he was right?

Damn him. That's what these brimming-with-confidence-and-cynicism men did. Made everyone doubt themselves. Their hopes and dreams.

Well, she wasn't giving her hopes and dreams into the care of another man. Michael Talbot had already taught her that lesson, thank you very much.

When she'd first heard the rumor about Mike, her fiancé and editor in chief of *Today's Baby*, and a flirty little freelancer named Trina, Sarah had refused to believe it. But then she had seen them together in a café, something too cozy about the way they were leaning into each other to confirm what she wanted to believe, that Mike and Trina's relationship was strictly business.

Her dreams of a nice little house, filled with babies of her own, had been dashed in a flash.

No accusation, just, *I saw you and Trina today*.

The look of shame that had crossed Mike's face had said it all, without him saying a single word.

Now, Sarah had a replacement dream, so much safer. A town to revitalize.

"Yes, it does have something to do with you!"

"I don't see how."

"Because I've been put in charge of Summer Fest. I've been given one chance to bring it back, to prove how good it is for this town," she explained.

"Good luck with that."

"I've got no budget for promotion. But I bet your phone has been ringing off the hook since the clip of the rescue was shown on the national evening news." She read the answer in his face. "*The A.M. Show*, *Good Night, America*, *The Way We See It*, *Morning Chat with Barb*—they're all calling you, aren't they?"

His arms had now folded across the immenseness of his chest, and he was rocking back on his heels, watching her with narrowed eyes.

"They're begging you for a follow-up," she guessed. She wasn't the only one who had been able to see that this man and that dog would make good television.

"You'll be happy to know I'm not answering their calls, either," he said dryly.

"I am not happy to know that! If you could just say yes to a few interviews and mention the town and Summer Fest. If you could just say how wonderful Kettle Bend is and invite everybody to come for July 1. You could tell them that you're going to be the grand marshal of the parade!"

It had all come out in a blurt.

"The grand marshal of the parade," he repeated, stunned.

She probably should have left that part until later. But then she realized, shocked, he had not repeated his out-and-out no.

He seemed to realize it, too. "No," he said flatly.

She rushed on as if he hadn't spoken. "I don't have a hope of reaching millions of people with no publicity budget. But, Oli—Mr.—Officer Sullivan—you do. You could single-handedly bring Summer Fest back to Kettle Bend!"

"No," he said again, no hesitation this time.

"There is more to being a cop in a small town than arresting poor old Henrietta Delafield for stealing lipsticks from the Kettle Mug and Drug."

"Mug and Drug," he repeated dryly, "that sounds like my old beat in Detroit."

Despite the stoniness of his expression, Sarah allowed herself to feel the smallest stirring of hope. He had a sense of humor! And, he had finally revealed something about himself. He was starting to care for his new town, despite that hard-bitten exterior.

She beamed at him.

He backed away from her.

"Let me think about it," he said with such patent insincerity she could have wept.

Sarah saw it for what it was, an escape mechanism. He was slipping away from her. She had been so sure, all this time, when she'd hounded him with message after message, that when he actually heard her brilliant idea, when he knew how good it would be for the town, he would *want* to do it.

"There's no time to think," she said. "You're the hot topic *now*." She hesitated. "Officer Sullivan, I'm begging you."

"I don't like being impulsive." His tone made it evident he *scorned* being the hot topic and was unmoved by begging.

"But you jumped in the river after that dog. Does it get more impulsive than that?"

"A momentary lapse," he said brusquely. "I said I'll think about it."

"That means no," she said, desolately.

"Okay, then, no."

There was something about the set of his shoulders, the line around his mouth, the look in his eyes that he had made up his mind absolutely. He wasn't *ever* going to think about it, and he wasn't *ever* going to change his mind. She could talk until she was blue in the face, leave four thousand more messages on his voice mail, go to his boss again.

But his mind was made up. Like the wall in his eyes, it would be easier to climb Everest than to change it.

"Excuse me," she said tautly. She bent and picked up her rhubarb, as if it could provide some kind of shield against him, and then shoved by him. She headed for the back door of her house before she did the unthinkable.

You did not cry in front of a man as hard-hearted as that one.

Something in his face, as she glanced back, made her feel as if her disappointment was transparent to him. She was all done being vulnerable. Had she begged? She hoped she hadn't begged!

"You should try the Jelly Jeans and Jammies Crabbies Jelly," she shot over her shoulder at him. "It's made out of crab apples. My grandmother swore it was a cure for crankiness."

She opened her back screen door and let it slam behind her. The back door led into a small vestibule and then her kitchen.

She was greeted by the sharp tang of the batch of rhubarb jam she had made yesterday. Every counter and every surface in the entire kitchen was covered with the rhubarb she needed to make more jam today.

Because this was the time of year her grandmother always made her Spring Fling jam, which she had claimed brought a feeling of friskiness, cured the sourness of old heartaches and brought new hope.

But given the conversation she had just had, and looking at the sticky messes that remained from yesterday, and the mountains of rhubarb that needed to be dealt with today, hope was not exactly what Sarah felt.

And she certainly did not want to think of all the connotations friskiness could have after meeting a man like that one!

Seeing no counter space left, she dumped her rhubarb on the floor and surveyed her kitchen.

All this rhubarb had to be washed. Some of it had already gotten tough and would have to be peeled. It had to be chopped and then cooked, along with all the other top secret ingredients, in a pot so huge Sarah wondered if her grandmother could have possibly acquired it from cannibals. Then, she had to prepare the jars and the labels. Then finally deliver the finished product to all her grandmother's faithful customers.

She felt exhausted just thinking about it. An unguarded thought crept in.

Was this the life she really wanted?

Her grandmother had run this little business until she was eighty-seven years old. She had never seemed overwhelmed by it. Or tired.

Sarah realized she was just having an off moment in her new life.

That was the problem with a man like Oliver Sullivan putting in a surprise appearance in your backyard.

It made you question the kind of life you *really* wanted.

It made you wonder if there were some kinds of lonely no amount of activity—or devotion to a cause—could ever fill.

Annoyed with herself, Sarah stepped over the rhubarb to the cabinet where she kept her telephone book.

Okay. He wasn't going to help her. It was probably a good thing. She had to look at the bright side. Her life would have tangled a bit too much with his had he agreed to use his newfound fame to the good of the town.

She could do it herself.

"WGIV Radio, how can I direct your call?"

"Tally Hukas, please."

After she hung up from talking to Tally, Sarah wondered why she felt the tiniest little tickle of guilt. It was not her job to protect Officer Oliver Sullivan from his own nastiness.

"And so, folks," Sarah's voice came over the radio, in that cheerful tone, "if you can spare some time to help our resurrected Summer Fest be the best ever, give me a call. Remember, Kettle Bend needs you!"

Sullivan snapped off the radio.

He had been so right in his assessment of Sarah McDougall: she was trouble.

This time, she hadn't gone to his boss. Oh, no, she'd gone to the whole town as a special guest on the Tally Hukas radio show, locally produced here in Kettle Bend. She'd lost no time doing it, either. He'd been at her house only yesterday.

Despite that wholesome, wouldn't-hurt-a-flea look of hers, Sarah had lost no time in throwing him under the bus. Announcing to the whole town how she'd had this bright idea to promote the summer festival—namely him—and he'd said no.

Ah, well, the thing she didn't get was that he didn't care if he was the town villain. He would actually be more comfortable in that role than the one she wanted him to play!

The thing *he* didn't get was how he had thought about her long after he'd left her house yesterday. Unless he was mistaken, there had been tears, three seconds from being shed, sparkling in her eyes when she had pushed by him.

But this was something she should know when she was trying to find a town hero: an unlikely choice was a man unmoved by tears. In his line of work, he'd seen way too many of them: following a knock on the door in the middle of the night; following a confession, outpourings of remorse; following that moment when he presented what he had, and the noose closed. He had them. No escape.

If you didn't harden your heart to it all, you would drown in other people's tragedy.

He'd *had* to hurt Sarah. No choice. It was the only

way to get someone like her to back off. Still, hearing her voice over the radio, he'd tried to stir himself to annoyance.

He was reluctant to admit it was actually something else her husky tone caused in him.

A faint longing. The same faint longing he had felt on her porch and when the scent from her kitchen had tickled his nose.

What *was* that?

Rest.

Sheesh, he was a cop in a teeny tiny town. How much more restful could it get?

Besides, in his experience, relationships weren't restful. That was the last thing they were! Full of ups and downs, and ins and outs, and highs and lows.

Sullivan had been married once, briefly. It had not survived the grueling demands of his rookie year on the homicide squad. The final straw had been someone inconveniently getting themselves killed when he was supposed to be at his wife's sister's wedding.

He'd come home to an apartment emptied of all her belongings and most of his.

What had he felt at that moment?

Relief.

A sense that now, finally, he could truly give one hundred percent to the career that was more than a job. An obsession. Finding the bad guy possessed him. It wasn't a time clock and a paycheck. It was a life's mission.

He started, suddenly realizing it was that little

troublemaker who had triggered these thoughts about relationships!

He was happy when his phone rang, so he didn't have to contemplate what—*if*—that meant something worrisome.

Besides, his discipline was legendary—as was his comfortably solitary lifestyle—and he was not thinking of Sarah McDougall in terms of the "R" word. He refused.

He glanced at the caller ID window.

His boss. That hadn't taken long. Sullivan debated not answering, but saw no purpose in putting off the inevitable.

He held the phone away from his ear so the volume of his chief's displeasure didn't deafen him.

"Yes, sir, I got it. I'm cleaning all the cars."

He held the phone away from his ear again. "Yeah. I got it. I'm on Henrietta Delafield duty. Every single time. Yes, sir."

He listened again. "I'm sure you will call me back if you think of anything else. I'm looking forward to it. No, sir. I'm not being sarcastic. Drunk tank duty, too. Got it."

Sullivan extricated himself from the call before the chief thought of any more ways to make his life miserable.

He got out of his car. Through the open screen door of Della's house—a house so like Sarah's it should have spooked him—he could hear his nephews, Jet, four, and Ralf, eighteen and half months, running wild. He climbed the steps, and tugged the door.

Unlocked.

He went inside and stepped over an overturned basket of laundry and a plastic tricycle. His sister had once been a total neat freak, her need for order triggered by the death of their parents, just as it had triggered his need for control.

He supposed that meant the mess was a good thing, and he was happy for her, moving on, having a normal life, despite it all.

Sullivan found his sister in her kitchen. The two boys pushed by him, first Jet at a dead run, chortling, tormenting Ralf by holding Ralf's teddy bear high out of his brother's reach. Ralf toddled after him, determined, not understanding the futility of his determination was fueling his brother's glee.

Della started when she turned from a cookie sheet, still steaming from the oven, and saw Sullivan standing in her kitchen door well. "You scared me."

"You told me to come at five. For dinner."

"I lost track of time."

"You're lucky it was me. You should lock the door," he told her.

She gave him a look that in no way appreciated his brotherly concern for her. In fact, her look left him in no doubt that she had tuned into the Tally Hukas show for the afternoon.

"All Sarah McDougall is trying to do is help the town," Della said accusingly.

Jet raced by, cackling, toy high. Sullivan snagged

it from him, and gave it to Ralf. Blessedly, the decibel level was instantly reduced to something that would not cause permanent damage to the human ear.

Sullivan's eyes caught on a neatly bagged package of chocolate chip cookies on the counter. His sister usually sent him home with a goodie bag after she provided him with a home-cooked meal.

"Are those for me?" he asked hopefully, hoping she would take the hint that he didn't want to talk about Sarah McDougall.

His sister had never been one to take hints.

"Not now, they aren't," she said sharply.

"Come on, Della. The chief is already punishing me," he groaned.

"How?" she said, skeptical, apparently, that the chief could come up with a suitable enough punishment for Sullivan refusing to do his part to revitalize the town.

"Let's just say it looks like there's a lot of puke in my future."

"Humph." She was a woman who dealt with puke on a nearly daily basis. She was not impressed. She took the bagged cookies and put them out of sight. "I'm going to donate these to the bake sale in support of Summer Fest."

"Come on, Della."

"No, *you* come on. Kettle Bend is your new home. Sarah's right. It needs *something*. People to care. Everyone's so selfish. Me. Me. Me. Indifferent to their larger world. What happened to Kennedy? *Think not what your country can do for you, but what you can do for your country?"*

"We're talking about a summer festival, not the future of our nation," he reminded her, but he felt the smallest niggle of something astonishing. Was it *guilt?*

"We're talking about an attitude! Change starts small!"

His sister was given to these rants now that she had children and she felt responsible for making good citizens of the world.

Casting a glance at Jet, who was using sweet talk to rewin his brother's trust and therefore get close to Bubba the bear, Sullivan saw it as a monumental task she had undertaken. With a crow of delight, Jet took the bear. She obviously had some way to go.

If she was going to work on Sullivan, too, her mission was definitely doomed.

"Why on earth wouldn't you do a few interviews if it would help the town out?" Della pressed him.

"I'm not convinced four days of summer merriment *will* help the town out," he said patiently. "I haven't been here long, but it seems to me what Kettle Bend needs is jobs."

"At least Summer Fest is an effort," Della said stubbornly. "It would bring in people and money."

"Temporarily."

"It's better than nothing. And one person acting on an idea might lead other people to action."

Sullivan considered his sister's words and the earnest look on her face. Had he been too quick to say no? Strangely, the chief going after him had not even begun to change his mind. But his sister looking at him with disapproval was something else.

It was also the wrong time to remember the tears sparkling behind Sarah McDougall's astonishing eyes.

But that's what he thought of.

"I don't like dealing with the press," he said finally. "They always manage to twist what you say. After the Algard case, if I never do another interview again it will be too soon."

Something shifted in his sister's face as he referred to the case that had finished him as a detective. Maybe even as a human being.

At any other time he might have taken advantage of her sympathy to get hold of those cookies. But it was suddenly there between them, the darkness that he had seen that separated him from this world of cookies and children's laughter that she inhabited.

They had faced the darkness, together, once before. Their parents had been murdered in a case of mistaken identity.

Della had been the one who had held what remained of their family—her and him—together.

She was the one who had kept him on the right track when it would have been so easy to let everything fall apart.

Only then, when she had made sure he finished school, had she chosen to flee her former life, the big city, the ugliness of human lives lost to violence.

And what had he done? Immersed himself in it.

"How could they twist what you had to say about saving a dog?" she asked, but her voice was softer.

"I don't present well," he said. "I come across as cold. Heartless."

"No, you don't." But she said it with a trace of doubtfulness.

"It's going to come out that I don't even like dogs."

"So you'll come across as a guy who cares only about himself. Self-centered," she concluded.

"Colossally," he agreed.

"One hundred percent pure guy."

They both laughed, her reluctantly, but still coming around. Not enough to take the cookies out of the cupboard, though. He made a little bet with himself that he'd have those cookies by the time he left here.

Wouldn't that surprise the troublemaker? That he could be charming if he chose to be?

There it was. He was thinking about *her* again. And he didn't like it one little bit. Not one.

"You should think about it," his sister persisted.

It occurred to him that if he dealt with the press, his life would be uncomfortable for a few minutes.

If he didn't appease his sister—and his boss— his life could be miserable for a lot longer than that.

"*I* think," Della said, having given him ten seconds or so to think about it, "that you should say yes."

"For the good of the town," he said a little sourly.

"For your own good, too."

There was something about his sister that always

required him to be a better man. And then there was a truth that she, and she alone, knew.

He would do anything for her.

Yet she never took advantage of that. She rarely asked him for anything.

Sullivan sighed heavily. He had a feeling he was being pushed in a direction that he did not want to go in.

At all.

Chapter 3

The phone couldn't have rung at a worse moment. Sarah was trying to shovel her latest batch of rhubarb jam into jars. How had her grandmother done this without getting jam everywhere? It was dripping down the outside of the jars, ruining the labels. She had managed to get sticky globs everywhere, including her hair!

Frisky? Sarah felt utterly exhausted.

Her phone had been ringing more than normal because of the free time on the Tally Hukas radio show yesterday, but still, she had the thought she had had every single time her phone had rung since she moved here to Kettle Bend.

She hoped it was Mike. She hoped he was phoning to beg her forgiveness. She hoped he was phoning to beg her to come back!

"I can't wait to tell him no," Sarah said, wiping goo off her hand before picking up the receiver.

Her ex-fiancé begging her forgiveness would go a long way in erasing the sourness of a heartache!

"Miss McDougall?"

It was definitely not her philandering ex-fiancé calling—Sarah would recognize that voice anywhere! She froze, licked a tiny trace of rhubarb jam off her wrist. Her heart was pounding unreasonably.

The jam seemed a little too tart.

Just like him.

"Oliver?" she said. She used his first name deliberately, hoping to aggravate him. No doubt, he was not calling voluntarily. Forced into it by the notoriety he had come into yesterday as a result of that radio show.

She enjoyed the sensation of having the upper hand.

But she also liked the way his name sounded on her lips. She had liked his name ever since she'd seen that video on the internet, and heard his name for the first time.

And this just in, fantastic footage out of Kettle Bend, Wisconsin, of Officer Oliver Sullivan...

His silence satisfied her. Then the silence was shattered by the shriek of a baby. For a stunned moment, she allowed that Oliver Sullivan might be married. There had been no ring on his finger. But lots of men did not wear rings. Especially if their line of work might make wearing them a hazard.

Sarah considered the downward swoop of her stomach with amazement. Why would she feel *bereft* if Oliver Sullivan was married?

"I'm having an emergency," he said, after a moment. "I've tried everything. I can't stop the baby from crying."

"Wh-wh-what baby?"

He had her off balance, again. He was supposed to be caving to pressure, begging her to let him do some interviews!

"My nephew, Ralf. My sister takes pity on my bachelor state—"

Bachelor state. How silly that it felt as if the light was going back on in her world!

Her world, she reminded herself sternly, was jam and Summer Fest.

"—and has me over for dinner when I'm off. But she's had a family emergency last night. Her husband was in a car accident on his way home from work. She had to leave suddenly. I don't want to call her at the hospital and tell her the baby won't stop crying. She's got enough on her plate already."

Sarah felt a faint thrill of vindication. She had just *known* this kind of man was lurking behind that remote facade he presented. The kind of man who would rescue a dog. Who would shield his sister from more anxiety.

"How is your brother-in-law?"

"Jonathon is fine. The injury is not life-threatening. It's just a complicated fracture that needs surgery. It's serious enough that she's not leaving him."

He would be like that, too, Sarah thought with a shiver. Fiercely devoted. If he ever allowed anything or anyone to get by his guard. Which seemed unlikely. Except this phone call would have seemed unlikely, too—yet here it was.

"And here I am," he said. His voice was unreasonably sexy. "Jet, get down from there! With a four-year-old nephew who is climbing the curtains and hanging off the rod. And with a baby who won't stop crying. Not knowing who to call."

Sarah was surprised to hear, beyond the sexiness, the faintest note of something else in his voice. Panic? Surely not?

"And why call me?" she asked, softly. Imagining he might say, *I saw something in your face I could not forget. You are the kind of woman a man dreams of having children with. Did you know you have a tender beauty in your eyes?*

"Your front door was open when I came by to see you the other day. I saw the framed magazines on your wall. I figured you must be some kind of expert on babies. Though, Ralf's not *today's* baby, exactly. He's eighteen months old."

"Oh." Again, not what she'd expected.

"Ah, also, I figured I had a bargaining chip with you."

"A bargaining chip?"

"You want me to do a few interviews. You have

the credentials of a baby expert. Maybe we could work a trade."

It wasn't begging exactly, but it was a stunning capitulation.

Still, it was so far from her fantasy of what he might say that she burst out laughing. "I have to warn you, my knowledge of babies is pretty much theoretical." *Sadly.*

"You're *not* an expert on babies?"

"I worked for that magazine for four years. I was a writer. I interviewed new moms and wrote how-to articles." Now she felt like she was applying for a job. And one she was rather startled to find that she wanted, too!

She deliberately left out info about how many nursery remodels she had done features on, thinking he would dismiss that as frivolous. She also did not mention she knew at least a dozen remedies for diaper rash, thinking that would just make him hang up the phone! She was a hair away from having Oliver Sullivan on her team.

"Were any of those how-to articles on crying babies?" he asked. She had been right. That was desperation in his voice.

Sarah stifled a giggle at how easily a little scrap of humanity could bring a big man to his knees.

"Dozens," she said. "I've done dozens of articles on crying babies."

"He's been crying for two hours."

"Babies are very sensitive to tension," she said.

"Mine?" he asked, incredulously.

"Possibly just something in his mother's tone before she left, a change in routine, now her absence and his daddy not coming home. He knows something is amiss."

"You *are* an expert! Can you help a guy out, Sarah?"

Instead of gloating that it was his turn to beg, she focused on something else, entirely.

Not Miss McDougall. *Sarah.* Her heart feeling as if it were melting should at least serve as a warning that this was a very bad idea.

But he'd said he would do the interviews! For the good of the town, she had to suck it up.

"What do you want me to do?"

"Come over."

Suddenly it felt as if she was playing with fire. She was *way* too happy to be talking to him, and it wasn't just because their arrangement was going to be good for the town, either.

Don't go over there, she warned herself. She could make suggestions over the phone. She could protect herself from whatever dumb thing her heart was doing right now.

Beating in double time.

Sarah caught a glimpse of herself in the mirror over the kitchen sink. She was blushing crazily, like a preteen girl getting her first call from a boy. She had her new life to think about. She had the new *her* to think about—independent, not susceptible to the painful foibles of the human heart.

She, Sarah McDougall, had learned her lessons!

She heard a crash and a howl. "What was that?"

"The living room curtains just came down. My nephew Jet was attached to them."

"I'll be right there."

"Really?"

"Really."

He gave her the address.

"Bring some of that jam," he suggested, "Crabbies, right? The one your grandmother said relieved crankiness. If ever a guy needed it, it's this one."

"You or the baby?"

"Both," he said ruefully.

Sarah knew she should not be so flattered that he seemed to remember every single thing she had said to him.

"Could you hurry?"

If she didn't hurry she would have an opportunity to make a better second impression on Oliver Sullivan. She could do her hair and her makeup. She could throw on something flirty and fabulous. But the baby in the background, his little voice hoarse, hiccuping his distress, did seem to give the situation a sense of urgency.

Plus, she did not want to give in to that urge to make Sullivan find her attractive. The situation she was heading into was dangerous enough without the complication of attraction between them.

Five minutes later, she shut her door, trying very hard not to acknowledge how happy she was to be escaping from her sticky jam jars.

Moments later, Sarah arrived at the door of a

charming little bungalow that was very much like hers, at least on the outside.

When Sullivan came to the door, she realized trying to halt that particular complication—attraction—would be like trying to hold back the tide.

The man was glorious.

A few days ago, he had been all icy composure. Today, the man who came to the door was every bit as compelling as the one she had seen in the video with the puppy.

His dark chocolate hair was mussed. His sculpted face was shadowed with unshaven whiskers. The remoteness of his dark eyes was layered with exhaustion, a compelling kind of vulnerability. His shirt had damp tear blotches on it.

And in his arms was a baby.

A distraught baby, to be sure, but even so, there was something breathtaking about the contrast between such a strong man, and the baby in his arms. His muscled arm curved around the baby's behind, holding him firmly into the broadness of his chest.

For all that he was exhausted, there was something in Sullivan's stance that said it all. This baby, fragile, vulnerable, needy, was safe with him. It would come to no harm on his watch.

A little boy squeezed between Sullivan's legs and the screen door, and pushed on it. When it gave way, he gave a little whoop of freedom, which was short-lived when his uncle freed a hand, snatched his collar and pulled him back in the house. He would come to no harm on his uncle's watch, either.

The little boy, like a wind-up toy that had hit an obstacle, changed direction and darted off down a hallway.

"Come in," he invited over the howling of the baby and the screeching of his other nephew echoing from deep within the house.

She had known coming here was entering a danger zone like none she had ever known. Seeing Oliver Sullivan standing there, with that baby in his arms, confirmed it.

He still looked every inch a warrior, strong, *ready*, formidable.

But she suspected his exhaustion, his sudden immersion into a battle of a totally different sort, one he was obviously ill-prepared to deal with, had him as close to surrender as she would ever find him.

Surrender to what? she asked herself. *Being vulnerable. Attraction. Being human.*

Run, she told herself.

But running would look foolish and she didn't want to look foolish to him. Some despicably traitorous part of her wanted to look as attractive to him as he did to her.

Perhaps she could look at this as a test of her resolve. This was a test of how deeply committed she was to a life of giving her heart only to something inanimate, that could not hurt her, like a town.

Taking a deep breath, Sarah stepped in the open door. The air had a scorched smell to it.

As if the devil had been hard at work, creating

a perfect potion to tempt her away from the life she had chosen for herself.

The baby was part of that potion, adorable, radiating sweetness despite the lustiness of his howls. He twisted his head and regarded her solemnly. His face was blotchy from crying. His voice was a croak of indignation.

"Hello, sweetie," she said softly.

The baby stopped, mid caterwaul, and regarded her with both suspicion and hope.

"Mama," he whispered.

"I know, baby. You miss your Mommy, don't you?"

A thumb went into a mouth and he slurped thoughtfully, nodded, squeezed out a few additional tears, then reached out both pudgy arms for her.

Sullivan said a word under his breath that you weren't supposed to say around babies and passed the child to her.

Sarah slid her bag off her shoulder onto the floor, then took the surprising weight of the baby in her arms. As if seeing Sullivan holding the baby hadn't been bad enough, experiencing the baby's warm, cuddly body pressed against her breast increased the squishy feeling inside of her.

"His name is Ralf," Sullivan said, his voice low, unintentionally sensual, the voice of a man afraid to speak in fear of getting the baby going again.

"Hello, Ralf, I'm Sarah."

"Want Mama." Sarah stepped over an overturned tricycle into a living room that had been ransacked. The curtain bar was up on one side and ripped down on the other. Books had been pulled off the shelves and scattered. A diaper sack had fallen over and was spilling its contents onto the floor. She cleared a jumble of toys off the couch and sank down on it, pressing the baby into her shoulder.

"Of course you want your mama," she said soothingly. "She'll be home as soon as she can. Does he still take a bottle?" she asked Sullivan.

"A bottle of what?" he asked, baffled.

"Rye whiskey," she teased with a shake of her head. "Go check the fridge and see if there are any baby bottles in there."

"There are!" he called, a moment later, with relief. "I've just been feeding him that baby gruel stuff. I didn't know he still took a bottle."

"Okay, heat it up in the microwave for a few seconds and bring it here."

He galloped in with the bottle.

"Did you test it to make sure it's not too hot?"

Sullivan looked at her as if her request was untenable. He glanced at the bottle, grimaced, then lifted it, a soldier prepared to do what needed to be done.

"No!" she said, just in time. "You test it on your wrist!"

"Oh." With relief, he shook a few drops of the milk in the bottle onto his wrist. His wrist was large, and square and strong, making her ultra-aware of the sizzling masculine appeal of him.

He handed her the bottle a little sheepishly. "See? An expert. I knew you'd know what to do."

Shaking her head, she took the bottle from him,

nestled Ralf in the crook of her arm and put the bottle to his lips.

With an aggrieved look at his uncle and a sigh, he nestled more deeply into her, wrapped his lips against the bottle and began to make the cutest little *slurp-slurp* sound. The tiny slurping sounds grew farther and farther apart.

Within seconds the baby was asleep.

Sullivan was staring at her as if she had parted the sea.

"I can't believe that."

"He was exhausted, ready to go no matter what."

"I owe you big-time."

"Yes, you do."

His gratitude was colossally short-lived. He folded his arms over his stained chest and rocked back on his heels. "Three interviews. No parade marshal."

"I see I should have driven my bargain while he was screaming," she said ruefully. But inside she savored her victory. He was going to do it! He was going to help her save Kettle Bend by making it the best Summer Fest the town had ever had.

"I have to warn you, I'm not good at interviews. I have a talent for saying exactly the wrong thing," he said ruefully.

"Luckily for you, in my past life, I've interviewed tons of people. I know the kind of questions they'll ask you. Why don't I come up with a list, and we can do a practice run?"

What did that have to do with getting away from this man as quickly as possible?

The little boy, Jet, came back in, tucked himself behind his uncle's leg and peered out at her.

"I'm Sarah," she said.

"I'm hungry."

"Hello, hungry."

"Sullivan burned supper."

"He doesn't call you Uncle Oliver?" Sarah asked, surprised.

"I told you no one calls me Oliver."

"Who's Oliver?" Jet asked with a scowl, and then repeated, a little more stridently, "I'm hungry!"

"What's your favorite thing to eat?" she asked him.

"Mac and cheese. He burned it."

"How about your second favorite thing?" A picture of her cooking dinner for them crowded her mind. It occurred to her it was way too cozy. If attraction could be complicated, what would sharing such a domestic scene be?

She pictured washing dishes with Sullivan and then felt annoyed with herself. Is this what her life had become that she could find washing dishes with a man romantic?

Of course, she thought, as she slid the man in question a look, there wasn't much she could do with him that wouldn't feel romantic.

Which was a big problem.

"My second favorite food is Hombre hamburgers!" Jet crowed.

Sarah felt a twinge of regret that was far larger than her twinge of relief. Hombre's was a favorite

Kettle Bend eatery just a few blocks away. It was a plan for supper that didn't need to include her.

"That sounds like a perfect solution for supper," Sarah said brightly to Sullivan. "You can pop the baby in the stroller, and he'll sleep all the way there."

She stood, a bit clumsily with the baby in arms. "It looks like your emergency is over, Oliver."

"Who's Oliver?" Jet demanded again.

She held out the sleeping baby. Sullivan took him, reluctantly.

"Don't go," he pleaded. "He's going to wake up sometime."

"Well, I can't stay all night."

The blush moved up her cheeks like fire, as if she had propositioned him. Or he her.

He had the audacity to look amused by it.

"No, but walk down to Hombre's with us. I'll buy you a hamburger. It's the least I can do," he wheedled.

Oh, boy. Sitting across the table from him in a restaurant would be worse than doing dishes with him. A fantasy of a happy family crowded her mind.

Of course, if her own family was anything to go by, that's exactly what happy families were. A fantasy.

One she had believed in, despite her upbringing. Or maybe because of it. One that had made her so needy for love that she had fallen for the wrong person.

She could feel that neediness in her still, and knew that was the demon she needed to fight.

"The least you can do is for me is four interviews," she said.

"Three," he replied.

"Four, if I join you at Hombre's."

What was she doing? She couldn't play at happy families with this man. She couldn't. What had made her say that, when she already knew she had to get herself out that door and away from him? Her new life was wavering in front of her like a distant mirage on a scorching desert day.

The look of amusement around his eyes deepened.

It made him more attractive than ever, even though he didn't smile. Good grief, she hoped he wouldn't smile. She'd be lost.

"I have to say that's the first time anyone has ever made me bargain with them to go on a date."

She stared at him. "A date?" she squeaked, and then forced herself to regain her composure. He was just that type of man. No, he would not have to bargain with women to go on dates with him. They would throw themselves at his feet for the opportunity.

She had been weak like that, once, but she was no more.

"I don't do dates," she said crisply.

She saw way too much register in his eyes, as if she had laid out every pathetic detail of her broken engagement to him.

"I didn't mean a *date* date." Was his tone almost gentle? Somehow, from the moment she'd first seen him risk his life for the dog, she had known there was a gentle side to him. But to see it in his eyes now and know it was pity? She hated that!

Of course he hadn't asked her on a *date*. She could feel herself squirm at the very assumption she'd made.

"Four interviews if you come to Hombre's. Not on a date. How would a date be possible with these munchkins watching our every move?" he teased.

Dumb to wonder what he would consider a date, then. Obviously it would involve something that he wouldn't want his nephews to see!

Her eyes moved involuntarily to his lips. Would he kiss on the first date? Even allowing herself to ponder the question seemed weak and juvenile. He was obviously a mature man, somewhat hardened and certainly cynical. Possibly he would expect quite a bit more than a kiss on a first date.

She had to stop this, right now. The conjecture was making her feel as if she was burning up, coming down with a fever.

He could take his nephews to Hombre's by himself.

But he might need me, a voice inside her quibbled.

No, that wasn't the truth at all. The truth was, Sarah wanted to spend more time with him.

She tried to tell herself it was because anything would be better than going back to that jam. But she knew it was more, something leaping in the air between them, that baby creating moments of vulnerability in her that were bringing barriers down that needed to be up!

Sullivan was looking at her so intently she thought she would melt.

"Uh, maybe you'd want to do something with your hair," he said after a moment. "I think it has something in it." He reached over and touched it.

His touch was so brief. But it made her aware of a very real danger of the awareness that sizzled in the air between them.

Or maybe not. Mortified, she watched as he looked at the blob on his finger, and then sniffed it. Then he put it to his lips and tasted.

And smiled.

That smile was just as devastating as Sarah had known it would be.

She felt weak from how it changed him, the guarded look swept from his face, revealing a hint of the light that he kept well hidden inside himself.

"It's jam," he said. "Crabbies?"

"No. Crabbies is made from crab apples. This is rhubarb. My grandmother called it Spring Fling." She blushed again when she said it, as if she had said something off-color and provocative.

"So, if Crabbies can cure crankiness, what can a Spring Fling do?" he asked and raised a wicked eyebrow at her.

What could a spring fling do? Somehow Sarah didn't want to tell him abut the promised friskiness of the jam. Or of its promised properties to erase the sourness of a heartache and herald in new hope.

"It's just jam," she said, "it can't *do* anything."

"Not a bad hair pomade, though," he said seriously.

She laughed, reluctantly, and he laughed, too. If his smile had been devastating to her carefully laid plans for her new life, his laughter was downright dangerous.

It revealed something so *real* about him. It intrigued her. It made her wonder why he was so guarded, so closed off, so deliberately unapproachable.

It made her want to rescue him from himself. It occurred to her it was the first time since her breakup that she had allowed herself to feel curious about a man.

It seemed new hope had crept into her life whether she wanted it or not.

And she did want it.

Just not from this source! People—particularly *men*—were too unpredictable. Mike had already taught her that.

Even before Mike, her father had ripped apart her own family. She would forget the lessons she had learned from the men in her life at her own peril.

Hadn't Michael Talbot *seemed* totally decent? Reliable? Even a touch staid? Exactly the kind of man one could count on building a life with?

Hadn't her father seemed like that, too? A partner in a law firm, the epitome of success by any standard?

But this man who stood before her was nothing like Mike. And nothing like her father, either. Oliver Sullivan seemed full of contradictions and dark mysteries. Something in him was deeply wounded.

It would be a mistake to think you could fix something like that without getting hurt yourself.

"I can't possibly take the children to Hombre's with you," she said quickly before she could change her mind. "Not possibly. Three interviews will be just fine. More than enough. I'll call you with the details when I've set it up."

She turned and bolted from the house, aware of his curious eyes on her, but not daring to look back.

Chapter 4

So, she didn't date, Sullivan thought, watching Sarah scurry down his sister's sidewalk and get in her car. She drove away with haste, a quick shoulder check, and a spin of tires.

That whole incident had been very telling for a man who read people with such stripping accuracy.

Sarah McDougall didn't date.

She was as cute as a button, refreshingly natural, obviously single and in the prime of her life. She probably had guys falling at her feet. And she didn't date?

Plus, she was devoting herself to what could very well be a lost cause, the rebirth of Kettle Bend through its Summer Fest. But at least, he saw with clarity, it was a cause that couldn't hurt her.

Heartbreak, he told himself. She'd suffered a heartbreak.

And from the way she looked holding that baby? Like a Madonna, completely serene, completely fulfilled. Her heartbreak hadn't done one little thing to cure her of what she really wanted. Her longings had been written in the tender expression on her face, in the little smile, in her unconscious sigh as that baby had settled against her.

Sarah McDougall wanted a family. Babies. Security.

She'd been wise to leave.

And he'd been wise to let her. Their life goals were at cross purposes. His was to do his job and do it well. His kind of work did not lend itself to the kind of cozy life she craved. It required a hard man who was prepared to do hard things.

People, including her, wanted to believe something else because of the video of him rescuing the puppy. But Sullivan knew himself—and his limitations—extremely well.

Sarah's life goal—no matter what she had convinced herself—had been written all over her when she'd had that baby pressed to her breast.

The other thing he could tell about her was that she was one of those naive people who believed she could use the force of her will to mold a happy world. Her devotion to Summer Fest was proof of that.

He was pretty sure he could kill her illusions in about ten minutes. Not deliberately. It was just the dark cynicism he'd developed for dealing with a tough, cold, hard world. If her illusions made her happy, even if they were hopelessly naive, he should just leave her alone with them.

Their lives would tangle once more because he'd agreed to do the interviews. Then he would put her behind him. Along with this strange yearning he felt every time he saw her.

Rest.

"I don't need a rest," he said out loud, annoyed. The baby woke up with a sputter and Jet raced by, his mother's lipstick streaked across his face like war paint.

"Except from that."

The next day, Sarah called him on his cell phone. He was at work, but it was an exceptionally quiet morning, even for Kettle Bend. It would have been a good morning to start cleaning cars, but somehow he wasn't. So far, some foolish sense of pride had prevented him from telling the chief he'd agreed to do the interviews, after all.

Sullivan registered, a little uneasily, that he felt happy to hear her voice.

"How's your brother-in-law?"

She would ask that first, a tenderness in her, an ability to care and to love deeply. Busy making her own happy world, whether she would admit to it or not.

Which meant he had to put a red warning flag beside her in his mind. Oh, wait, he'd already done that! So he shouldn't be all that happy to hear from her. But he could not deny that he was.

He tried to tell himself that between Sarah and cleaning cars, she was the clear winner. It didn't *mean* anything.

"The surgery went well. No complications. He'll be in the hospital a little longer, but my sister got home late last night."

Silence. He could tell that she wanted to ask him how the baby had been, and if they'd gone for their supper at Hombre's after all.

But she didn't. Evidently all her warning flags were waving, too.

Which was a good thing. A very good thing.

He could hear her trying to keep the distance in her voice when she asked if they could meet. She had set up the interviews and, as promised, would run a few potential questions by him.

That was perfect. She was all business. It would be good to get it over with and put his very short Sarah McDougall chapter behind him.

"Do you want me to come by your place?" he asked.

"Uh, no."

He felt relieved. There was something about her place, the coziness of those yellow sofas facing each other over drooping flowers that would not lend itself to the barriers he felt were essential to keep up between them.

"I'm in a jam. Literally," Sarah said.

He heard something in her voice that gave him

pause. "You don't really like making jam, do you?" he asked quietly.

He could have kicked himself. A question like that was personal! It had nothing to do with keeping barriers up. It was as if he'd said to her, *You're not fulfilled. How come? What's up? What's getting in the way of your happy fantasy?*

The question, he told himself firmly, was what was up with him, not her!

Luckily, his question actually seemed to succeed at putting a barrier up, not taking one down.

"What would make you say that?" she asked defensively. "I happen to *love* my grandmother's business. I *love* making jam."

Leave it.

But he didn't. His *uh-huh* was loaded with disbelief.

"I do!"

A woman, if there ever was one, who was made to say *I do.* To believe in forever after.

Talking about jam, he reminded himself firmly, furious that his mind had gone there.

He could tell she was fuming. Well, it wasn't his fault that he was pretty good at reading most people, and really good at reading her in particular. Besides, fuming was good. Barriers up!

"So, where do you want to meet?" he asked.

Her voice was cool. "How about Winston's Church Hill Coffee Shoppe? What's your schedule like? Could you do it in half an hour?"

Winston's was always loud. And crowded. Very

public. A good choice. He wished she had picked Grady's, which had booths and better coffee.

"Winston's would be the best," she said, as if she had read his mind. "It'll be crowded. It'll go through town like wildfire that you met me there. It might undo some of the damage to your popularity the radio show caused."

Yeah, Winston's was the town rumor mill, not that Sullivan gave a fig about popularity.

He was working. He was in uniform. That might be a good thing. There was nothing like a uniform to keep his distance from people.

She was already there when he walked into the coffee shop, bent over some papers, her tongue caught between her teeth in concentration.

He hesitated for a moment, studying her.

Sarah didn't look like she had looked yesterday at his sister's, or the way she had looked in her garden, either.

She was wearing a sundress the color of her sofa, summer-afternoon yellow. It hugged the slenderness of her curves, showed off skin already faintly sun-kissed, brought his eye to a little gold heart that winked at the vulnerable hollow of her throat.

She'd done something to her hair, too. The curls had been tamed, straightened, and her hair hung in a glossy wave to the swell of shoulders that were naked save for the thin strap of the dress.

When she glanced up, he saw that she had put on makeup and that her eyes looked dazzling. But not as dazzling as her freshly glossed lips.

It worried him that all this might be for him.

But as soon as he joined her, he saw this was her barrier, as much as his uniform was his.

She was here as a professional woman.

Sarah wore that role with an ease and comfort that was very telling.

Though he'd decided he wasn't going to try and tell her anything anymore. She was a little too touchy. It was none of his business that she was trying to run from the very things that gave her the most satisfaction.

Babies.

Her career.

There was no reason the two things could not co-exist, he thought.

Not that it was any of his concern.

She got down to business right away.

"You'll be happy to know we're just going to do one interview."

We're.

"I've arranged for you to do one interview, which will be taped with the local television station. The news anchor, Bradley Moore, will do it, and then they'll send it to their national affiliates."

He was impressed. She was a professional. "Perfect."

"I think you should wear your uniform." Her eyes drifted over him, and despite his determination to untangle their lives after this task was completed, he was more than a little pleased by what he saw.

She liked a man in uniform.

"So, just pretend I'm the person interviewing you."

A waitress came by and filled his coffee cup without asking him.

"So, Officer Sullivan," Sarah said, putting on her interviewer hat, "what did you do before you came to Kettle Bend?"

"I was a homicide detective in Detroit."

"Couldn't you elaborate?" she prodded him.

"No, I couldn't."

She dropped the interviewer hat. "But it's a perfect opportunity to introduce the charms of Kettle Bend to the conversation. You could say that you tired of the coldly impersonal life in the big city and chose the warmth and friendliness of Kettle Bend instead."

"To tell you the truth I had no objection to the coldly impersonal life in Detroit. I could go get my groceries without someone telling me there was a car illegally parked on their block. Or worse, asking me about that blasted dog," he said caustically.

"You can't call him *that blasted dog*," she said, horrified. "Why did you move here if you liked your coldly impersonal life so much?"

He shocked himself by saying, "I burned out," and then, irritated at himself for saying it, and annoyed at the warmly curious look in her expression, he changed the subject.

"I don't like dogs," he said. It might as well come out. It might as well come out as a way of keeping her at bay. He took a sip of his coffee and watched her closely over the lip of the mug to see what her response to that would be.

"You can't say you don't like dogs!" she said. "What kind of person doesn't like dogs?"

Perfect. The kind of person little Sarah McDougall should be very cautious of.

"I'm not the warm and fuzzy type," he warned her. "And that does not translate well in interviews. I'm not going to lie about liking dogs. I'm not going to lie about anything."

"I'm not asking you to lie!" she protested.

"That's good."

"Okay," she said, determined, looking at her notes. "So, you don't like dogs. I'm sure you could gloss over that without *lying*. Something like, *there are dog people and cat people. I'm a cat person.* Maybe that would make your leap into the river seem even more heroic."

"I'm getting a headache," he said. "And I don't like cats, either."

"Horses?" she said, hopefully.

"I'm not an animal person."

"Not an animal person," she repeated, faintly distressed.

"There are animal people and not animal people. I'm in the 'not' category."

"Why wouldn't you like animals?" she asked.

Don't tell her the truth. But he couldn't help himself. "I don't like neediness. I don't want anything relying on me. I don't want to become attached to anything." He didn't have to elaborate. In fact, he ordered himself not to elaborate. Then… "I don't want to love anything."

They both sat there in shocked silence.

"But why?" she finally ventured.

Don't say it. She doesn't have to know. There is no reason for her to know.

"My parents were killed when I was seventeen." He *hated* himself for saying it. Why was he admitting all this stuff to her? It felt as if she were pulling his insides out of him without really trying, just looking at him with those warm, understanding eyes.

Sullivan pulled back into damage-control mode as quickly as he could. "That had better not come out in the interview. I don't want any sympathy. From anyone."

Her mouth had opened as if she was going to say something sympathetic. She correctly interpreted his glare, and her mouth closed slowly. But she couldn't do anything about her eyes.

They had softened to a shade of gold that reminded him of the setting sun, gentle, caressing, not simply sympathetic, somehow. Sharing his pain with him.

He shrugged uncomfortably. "Don't worry. I'm not going to say in public that I don't like dogs because I don't want to get attached to anything. I'm not even sure why I said it to you."

He was already very sorry he had.

He glanced at his watch, a hint for her to move on, and was unreasonably grateful when she did.

"So what are you going to say when or if you're

asked why you jumped in the river to save the dog?" she asked curiously.

"Momentary insanity?" He looked at her face, and sighed. "I'll say I thought it probably belonged to the kid I'd seen riding his bike across the bridge earlier, and that I didn't want him to lose his dog."

"Oh," she said, pleased, "that's nice."

Nice. She wasn't getting it. Oliver Sullivan was not *nice.*

"As it turned out," he said gruffly, "the puppy didn't belong to him. They still haven't found the owner. The dog's going up for adoption next week if he isn't claimed."

"That would be good to mention. That would bring a lot of attention to Kettle Bend."

"Believe me, it already has. The police station had a call from Germany last week asking about the dog."

"If you can say that, that would be wonderful! People in Germany interested in Kettle Bend! An international angle!"

"I'll try to work it in," he said. Her enthusiasm should have been annoying. Instead, it seemed as cute as her sunshine-yellow dress. She seemed to have an absolute gift for making his mind go places it did not want to go, breaking down barriers that he had thought were high and fortified.

"Now," she tapped her pencil against her lips, "how could you work in Summer Fest?"

He groaned, and not entirely because of the mention of Summer Fest. She had drawn his attention to her lips, which were full and plump.

Kissable.

"I don't understand your cynicism about it," she said, pursing those delicious lips now.

"I'm cynical about everything." He covered his fascination with her lips by taking a swig of his coffee.

"No, you're not."

Oh, Sarah, do yourself a favor and do not believe the best in me.

"Look," he said, "I think it's naive to believe a little festival can do much for a town. I don't understand exactly what you think it's going to do for Kettle Bend."

"It's going to bring back the summer visitors. It's going to revitalize things. It's going to bring in some much-needed money. It's going to put us on the map again, as a destination. All those people who come here are going to realize what a great place this would be to come live."

Let her have her illusions, Sullivan ordered himself. But he didn't. In fact, he suddenly felt as if he was done with illusions. Like the one that he would ever taste those delectable lips.

His cynicism, his dark history, could put out that light that radiated off of her in about three seconds.

"You know, Sarah, I haven't been here long, but this town is suffering because some of its major employers are gone. The factories are shut down. How can it be a great place to live if there are no jobs here? What Kettle Bend really needs is jobs. Real jobs. Permanent jobs."

"Your sister and her family moved here," she said defensively.

"Jonathon has to commute to Madison. He keeps an apartment close to work for the days he's too tired to drive home. He makes a lot of sacrifices so my sister can have her fantasy of small-town life. I think his accident probably resulted from the fatigue of the constant commuting."

"Did you tell your sister that?" she asked, clearly horrified.

"I did." Unfortunately. So he was still off the cookie list, even though he had told his sister he would do the interviews arranged by Sarah, after all.

"You shouldn't have said that to your sister."

"No practice runs about what to say in real life," he said, putting unnecessary emphasis on *real life*.

She flinched. He covered his remorse by taking a sip of coffee.

"Summer Fest is going to help Kettle Bend," she said stubbornly.

"I've done a bit of checking. It was cancelled because there was no way of measuring whether the output of money could be justified by a temporary influx of visitors."

"I'm being very careful with the budget I've been given. I'm supplementing it with several fundraisers," she said.

"I know. My sister is donating *my* cookies to the bake sale." The very thought soured him. Well, that and the fact Sarah McDougall, with her kind eyes and her sunshiny dress, had ferreted information out of him that he was in no way ready to divulge.

"You know what I think?" He knew he was about to be a little nasty.

He also knew this was more about his lapse—his confiding in her—than it was about Summer Fest. He had to get his walls back up before she crashed right through them and found herself in a land where she didn't want to be.

He needed her to know, beyond a shadow of a doubt, he didn't want or need her sympathy. He wanted to drive what remained of that gentle look out of her eyes.

The kind of look that could make a hard man soft.

A strong man weak.

The kind of look that made a man who had lost faith in any kind of goodness feel just a smidgen of doubt about his own solitary stance.

"What do you think?" But she asked tentatively, something in him making her wary. As well it should.

"You think immersing yourself in Summer Fest is going to help you get over your heartbreak," he said.

She stiffened. He was relieved to see that look— as if her heart was big enough to hold all her own troubles and his too—evaporating from her eyes.

"What heartbreak?" she said warily.

"A girl like you doesn't come to a town like this unless you're trying to outrun something."

"That's not true!" she sputtered.

He looked at her coolly. Maybe it was because she'd somehow made him blurt out his own truth that he needed to show her he could see hers. No, it wasn't that complicated.

He was trying to drive her away.

Before he became *attached*.

"You know, Summer Fest can't make you feel the way you felt when you came here as a kid. No matter how successful it is."

"How do you know what I felt as a kid?" she asked in a shrill whisper.

He snorted. "You felt as if your every dream could come true. You were full of hope and romantic illusions."

She stared at him, two little twin spots of anger growing bright on her cheeks. Then she got up abruptly. She tossed her neatly printed sheet of questions at him.

"Here. You look at these questions yourself. I'm sure you can come up with some answers that won't manage to offend every single person who watches you on television."

He'd made her very angry. He'd hurt her. In the long run that was only a good thing.

Because there was something about her that made a guy want to say way too much, reveal way too much.

There was something about her that made a man wonder what his life could have been like if he had been dealt a different deck, or chosen a different road.

He watched her through the window, walking away from the coffee shop, her hips swishing with anger, the yellow dress swirling around her slender legs.

He picked up the papers she had tossed down, pulled on his cap and pulled the brim low over his eyes.

His uniform, his job, had always been a shield that protected him. How was it she had broken right through it, without half trying?

And why was it, that even though he had succeeded in driving her off, she had succeeded in piquing his curiosity, too? He had uncovered some truth about her, but it felt like it wasn't enough.

As a former detective he had all kinds of ways of finding things out about people without their ever knowing he had....

Sarah was furious. "Of all the smug, bigheaded, supercilious, self-important jerks," she muttered to herself, walking fast away from the café, her head high. "How dare he?"

It had really started with the phone call.

You don't really like making jam, do you?

Then it had just gone all downhill from there.

You think immersing yourself in Summer Fest is going to help you get over your heartbreak.

It was humiliating that somehow he knew that she'd had a heartbreak, as if she were some pathetic cat lady whose life tragedies were apparent to all! It was particularly nasty that he'd had the bad manners to call her on it.

And telling her that she was using Summer Fest to try and recapture the dreams of her youth was mean.

Oliver Sullivan was just plain *mean*.

She hoped he blew the interviews. She hoped the whole world hated him as much as she did! At this moment, she was too angry to care if it damaged Summer Fest!

She stomped into her house, and slammed the door extra hard when the smell of cooked rhubarb hit her.

She went and ripped off the gorgeous little sun-dress that she had always loved, and put on old clothes that wouldn't be ruined by making jam all afternoon. She had loved putting on that dress again!

Then suddenly it hit her.

The enormity of the thought made her sink down on her bed.

With a meow of pure contentment her cat, Sushi, found her lap and settled on it.

He'd done it on purpose. Oliver Sullivan had made her mad on purpose.

And he'd done it because he'd given something to her. He had trusted her with parts of himself. He had told her things he was not accustomed to re-vealing. He'd come out from behind his barriers for a little while.

And then he had gone into full retreat!

He'd succeeded, though. She bet he was feeling mighty pleased with himself right now because he'd managed to drive her away.

Sitting there on her bed she contemplated the

loneliness of Sullivan's world. At least she had her cat. At least she wasn't so damaged she couldn't even get attached to an animal.

And she was making a ton of friends here in her adopted town. She adored her neighbors, she was developing friendships with many of the volunteers on the Summer Fest committees.

He had chosen a world and a job that could isolate him.

"I'm going in after him," she said out loud, shocking herself. Where had that come from?

She contemplated the absolute insanity of it, and then laughed out loud. She didn't care if it felt insane.

Sarah felt alive. Something she had not felt since Mike had driven the spike of betrayal right through her heart.

It was something she had not felt when she moved to her grandmother's house. She had certainly not felt it stirring endless pots of jam. And Summer Fest had not made her feel like this, either.

She felt *needed*.

She felt like she could put her petty need to protect herself on hold.

She felt that she had a mission, a man to save from himself, to rescue. He had shown her that brief glimpse of himself for a reason. She was not going to turn her back on him. She was not going to leave him in that dark, lonely place.

And she knew exactly how she was going to do it, too.

"I'm going to use the puppy."

Sushi gave a shrill meow of pure betrayal and jumped off her lap.

Sarah's confidence had dwindled somewhat by the time she arrived at Sullivan's house, unannounced. Obviously, if she called him to warn him of her arrival with the dog, he would just say no.

Of course, there was plenty of potential for him to just say no, regardless.

She was also beginning to understand why Sullivan did not like dogs. Sarah's experience with dogs was very limited. The charm of the adorable cuteness of the puppy—soulful eyes, huge paws, curly black hair—wore off in about five seconds.

The puppy was rambunctious. His greeting this morning when he had been let out of his kennel in his temporary quarters at the vet's office had been way too enthusiastic.

He was gigantic, the vet said, probably some Newfoundland or Bouvier blood—and possibly a combination of both—making him so large even though he was only about four months old.

He had nearly knocked Sarah off her feet with his joy in seeing her. Her yoga pants—picked because they were both flattering and appropriate for an outing with a dog—now had a large snag running from thigh to calf.

The puppy flung himself against the leash, nearly pulling her shoulder out of the socket. Once in her car, he had found a box of tissue in the backseat and shredded it entirely on the short drive to Sullivan's house.

Sullivan had insinuated she didn't have a clue about real life.

The puppy seemed determined to prove him correct. *Real* puppies were not fun like fantasy puppies.

So, Sarah was already questioning the wisdom of the idea that had seemed so perfect in the sanctuary of her bedroom.

The puppy was reminding her that reality and fantasy were often on a collision course.

Still, she was here now, and there was no turning back. So, ignoring the beating of her heart, unwrapping the leash from around her legs for at least the twentieth time, she went up the stairs.

Sullivan's house was not like her house. And not like his sister's. There were no flowers, there was no swing on the porch.

Everything was in order, and it was immaculate, but there was nothing welcoming about his house. There were no planters, no rugs, no porch furniture, no screen door in front of the storm door.

Because he doesn't welcome anybody, she reminded herself. He pushes away. That's why she was here.

With a renewed sense of mission, she took a deep breath, ordered the dog to sit, and was ignored, and then rang Sullivan's doorbell.

He didn't answer, and she rang it again.

Just when she thought the whole idea was a bust—he wasn't home, despite her careful and clever ferreting out of his schedule—she heard a noise inside the house. He was in there. He'd probably peered out the window, seen it was her and decided not to answer his door.

She rang the bell again. And again. Then gave the door a frustrated kick. As a result, she nearly fell inside when his door was suddenly flung open.

Oliver Sullivan stood in front of her, wearing only a towel, his naked chest beaded with water, his dark hair plastered against his head like melted chocolate.

Sarah gulped as his eyes swept her, coolly, took in the dog, and then he planted his legs far apart and folded his muscled arms across the masculine magnificence of his deep, deep chest.

The whiteness of the towel, riding low and knotted at his hip, made his skin seem golden and sensuous. Steam was rising off his heated body.

That first day he had appeared in her garden, she had foolishly imagined how his skin would smell fresh out of the shower.

But again, she could see fantasy and reality were on a collision course.

Because his scent was better than anything she could have ever, ever imagined. It was heady, masculine, crisp, clean. His scent tickled her nostrils like bubbles from freshly uncorked champagne.

It occurred to her she had been very, very wrong to come here. Her reasoning had been flawed.

Because Sarah had never seen a man less in need of rescuing than this one.

He was totally self-reliant, totally strong, totally sure of himself.

And he was nearly naked.

Which made her the exact opposite of all those things! She dropped her eyes, which didn't help one little bit. Staring at the perfect cut of his water-slicked naked legs, she felt totally weak and unsure of herself.

She forced herself to look back at his face. His gaze was unyielding. She opened her mouth, and not a single sound came out.

The puppy, however, was not paralyzed. With an ecstatic yelp of recognition, it yanked free of the leash, and hurled itself at Sullivan. It jumped up on its back legs, scrabbled at his naked chest with his front paws, whining, begging for affection and attention.

One of those frantically waving paws clawed down the washboard of perfect abs and caught in the towel.

Before Sarah's horrified eyes, the dog yanked his paw free of where it had become entangled in the towel. That scrap of white terry cloth was ripped from Sullivan's waist and floated to the ground.

Chapter 5

Sarah kept her eyes glued on the puddle of white towel on the porch floor.

Sullivan said three words in a row, universal expressions of extreme masculine displeasure. Then, thankfully, his feet backed out of her line of vision. It was really the wrong time to think he had very sexy feet!

The dog's feet also left her line of vision, Sullivan using him as some sort of shield as he backed into his house.

The front door slammed closed.

Sarah dared to lift her eyes. She wanted to bolt off the porch and go home, crawl into bed and pull the covers over her head.

Rescue Oliver Sullivan? Was she crazy? She

needed to get out of here before she was faced with the full repercussions of her impulsiveness!

But there was the little question of the dog she had brought. She was going to have to face the music. Tempting as it was, she couldn't just dump the dog here—at the mercy of a man who had admitted he didn't like dogs—and run home.

With nothing to sit on, she settled on the steps, chin in hands, trying to think of anything but that startling moment when the towel had fallen.

The door swished open a few minutes later, and Sarah scrambled to her feet and turned to face him. He had put on a pair of jeans, but his chest was still bare. And so were his sexy feet.

Wordlessly, he passed her the dog's leash, folded his arms over his chest and raised an eyebrow at her.

She didn't know what had happened in the house, but Sullivan had obviously proved himself the dominant member of the pack. The dog was subdued. It sat quietly, eyes glued adoringly on him.

"What do you want?"

Was there an unfortunate emphasis on *you* as if he would have rather seen anyone else on his door—vacuum cleaner salesman, Girl Scouts with cookies, old women with religious tracts?

"Um," Sarah said, tucking a loose strand of hair behind her ear, and making a pattern on his porch with her sneaker, "the TV station asked if you could bring the dog to your interview."

"I must have missed the memo where you sched-

uled the interview," he said, not making this easy
for her.

"It's actually scheduled for tomorrow, at 6:00 p.m.
but given how you feel about dogs, I thought maybe
you and the dog should bond a little first."

"Bond," he said flatly.

"I didn't want it to be obvious to the viewers during the interview that you didn't like dogs."

"Bond," he repeated. "With a dog."

"Would you?" she asked hopefully. She dared
glance up at him. She was encouraged to see he
had not just gone back into his house and slammed
the door. "There's a dog park in Westside. I thought
maybe you could go and throw a stick for him. Just
so that you look like buddies for the interview."

"Look like buddies," he said, his voice still flat,
his arms crossed, his body language completely un-
inviting, "with a dog."

She nodded, but nothing in the stern lines of his
face gave her any reason to hope.

"That's nutty," he said.

Suddenly she remembered why she was here! Just
because she had nearly seen him totally naked was
no reason to get off track. He was desperately alone
in the world! She was here to save him from himself.

"So what if it's nutty?" she said, lifting her chin.
"Does everything have to be sane? Does everything
have to be on a schedule? Does everything have to
be under your control?"

Coming from her, who had always been the perfect one, that was quite funny. But he didn't have to

know it was out of character for her. Besides, what had all her efforts to be perfect ever gotten her?

She had spent so much time and effort and energy trying to be the perfect daughter. And then the perfect fiancée. What had it made her?

Perfectly forgettable. Perfectly disposable.

"You sound like my sister," he said, not happily.

"Can't you be spontaneous?"

He glared at her. "I can be as spontaneous as the next guy."

"So prove it. For the greater good," she reminded him.

"Please don't say it. Please."

"What?"

"Kettle Bend needs you."

"I won't say it. But come to the dog park. One hour. It's really part of your agreement to participate in the interview. I've even got it down from four interviews to one. I helped you out in your moment of need. With your nephews."

She had used every argument she had. He seemed unmoved by all of them.

"I think your being the cause of my public nakedness should clear all my debts."

"Nobody saw you," she said hastily. "And I didn't look!"

His lips twitched. Something shifted, ever so slightly. Whatever it was, it was far more dangerous than his remoteness.

"Were you tempted?" he asked softly.

She stared at him. His eyes were wicked. This was the problem with deciding to rescue a man like him.

It was akin to a naive virgin boarding a pirate vessel and demanding the captain lay down his sword for her because she thought she knew what was best for him.

It was a dangerous game she was playing, and the mocking look on his face made her very aware of it.

She took a step backward. "Sorry," she said. "Obviously this was a bad idea. One of my many. According to you." She bolted to the bottom of the steps, then stopped to unwrap the leash from around her ankles.

"Oh, wait a minute."

She turned back to him. He ran a hand through his hair, looked away from her and then looked back at her. "Okay. An hour. To bond with the dog."

Sullivan closed his bedroom door, leaned on it and drew in a deep breath. Sarah McDougall was in his living room. With a dog. Waiting for him to throw on a shirt so they could go bond.

Him and the dog, or him and her?

"You could have said no," he told himself.

But as she had pointed out, it would be unreasonable for him to say no when she had come so willingly to his rescue when Jet had been destroying his sister's house, and Ralf had put on his marathon crying jag.

Who cares if he appeared unreasonable?

She'd seen him naked. And not under the pleasant

kind of circumstances that might have been normal for a gal to see a guy naked, either. That was a good enough reason to say no.

But her face when he'd asked her if she'd been tempted to peek at him had been so funny. He *liked* teasing her.

Besides, after their interview in the coffee shop, where she had left in a fit of pique, it had taken a certain amount of bravery for her to show up here.

Also, he'd since given in to that desire to probe her secrets. Not surprisingly, she was every bit as wholesome as she appeared to be. She'd never even had a traffic ticket.

Sarah wasn't a member of any social networking website, which was both disappointing in terms of a fact-finding mission and revealing in terms of the type of person she was.

But there were plenty of other ways to find out things about a person. An internet search of her name had brought up the Summer Fest website. The four-day extravaganza of small-town activity—games, picnics, bandstand events—seemed like more, way more, than one person could take on.

But he wasn't interested in her recent activities. So he'd followed the thread to articles she had written for *Today's Baby*.

He read three or four of her articles, amazed that, despite the content, they held his interest completely. As a writer, Sarah was funny, original and talented. Which meant he'd been entirely correct in assuming some personal catastrophe had made her leave her successful life in New York behind.

Knowing those little tidbits of information about her made it difficult to send her away now.

She'd had disappointments in her life. It was possible, given the unrealistic scope of Summer Fest, she was setting herself up for another one.

So, as much as Sullivan thought spending time with Sarah McDougall had all kinds of potential for catastrophe, he could not help but admire her bravery. No matter how much he wanted to keep his distance from her, he couldn't throw that bravery back in her face.

He had been aware he'd hurt her at the coffee shop, maybe said too much and too harshly.

And so when he'd come back to his door after pulling on his jeans, with every intention of repeating the first message he'd ever given her, *leave me alone*, he'd been stunned to find he couldn't do it.

Those eyes on his face, embarrassed, eager, hopeful, ultimately brave.

Trusting something in him. Something he had lost sight of in himself a long, long time ago.

"This is really dumb, Sullivan," he told himself after he'd put on a shirt and some socks and some shoes, and opened his bedroom door to rejoin her.

He came down the hallway and saw her perched on the edge of his couch. Today she was wearing some kind of stretch pants that molded her rather extraordinary legs and derriere. She had on a T-shirt—with a cause, of course, breast cancer research, because she was the kind of girl who was going to save the world. Her curly hair had been tamed again, today, pulled back into a ponytail. Once again she didn't have on any makeup. He could see a faint scattering of freckles across her nose.

She looked about twelve years old.

It reminded him again, that there was something about her, despite her heartaches, that was fresh and innocent, eager about the world.

Which was part of what made saying *yes* to an outing with her so damned dumb, even if it was fun to tease her. Even if it was hard to say no to the brave part of her that trusted him.

He should have sucked it up and done what needed to be done.

But he hadn't.

So now he might as well just give himself over to the mistake and make sure it was a glorious one.

She turned to him with a faint smile. "What's your decor inspiration? Al Capone's prison cell?"

He realized she was bringing elements of the unexpected into his carefully controlled world and it was unexpectedly refreshing. Despite himself, he wanted to see what would happen next.

How much damage could she do to his world in an hour, after all?

And how much damage could *he* do to *her* in just an hour? He'd give himself that. Like a gift, an hour with her, just enjoying her, enjoying the spontaneity of it, since she had challenged him about his ability to be spontaneous.

Who knew? He might even enjoy the dog.

Then he'd give her the gift of never doing it again.

"Al Capone had naked girl pictures in his prison cell," he told her, straight-faced.

A faint blush moved up her cheeks. He liked that. Who blushed anymore?

"You can't know that," she said firmly.

"It's an educated guess."

"I think we've had quite enough naked stuff for one day." She had a prim look on her face, like a schoolteacher.

He was astonished when, this time, the blush was his. He turned quickly from her and opened the door.

"Walking or driving?" he asked.

"Walking. He's not car-trained." She did stop at her car, though, and retrieved a large handbag from it. Her car was somehow exactly what he had known it would be: a little red Bug. Evidence of the dog and the tissue box filled the backseat, though.

After watching her struggle down the sidewalk with the dog for a few minutes, Sullivan realized the dog wasn't trained in any way, shape or form. He took the leash from her.

"Let me do that."

He did not miss her smile of satisfaction. Bonding-101 taking place according to her schedule of sunshine and light.

The funny thing was, he did feel a little twinge of pure optimism. It was a beautiful day. He liked walking with her, their shoulders nearly touching, her ponytail swinging in the breeze, her scent as light and happy as the day.

"For practicality purposes, we should name the dog," she said. "Just for today."

Sullivan cast her a glance. Oh, she was trying to wiggle by his every defense. Naming the dog would be dangerously close to encouraging an attachment to it. He could see clearly, she was that kind of girl.

If you gave her an inch, she would want a mile!

"He doesn't need a name for an hour outing."

"Just something simple, like Pal or Buddy."

"No."

"It's practical. What are we going to say at the dog park after we throw him a stick? Fetch, black-dog-with-big-feet?"

"Okay," he conceded. "It."

"We're not calling him It."

We're.

"K-9, then."

"That's not very personal," she argued.

"It's more personal than It."

That earned him a little punch on his shoulder. The smallest of gestures, and yet strangely intimate, playful, an invitation to cross a bridge from acquaintances to something more.

Don't do it, he ordered himself, but he switched the dog leash to his other hand, and gave her shoulder a nudge with his own fist.

He was rewarded with a giggle as pure as a mountain brook tumbling over rocks.

There were no other dogs at the dog park, which

he thought was probably a good thing given that K-9 was very badly behaved. She said she was disappointed that K-9 wasn't going to make any friends.

He wasn't at all sure dogs made friends. He could say something about her Disneyland town and her rose-colored vision of the world, remind her of his cynicism, remind her of how different they were.

But, surprised at himself, he chose not to.

One hour. He could be a nice guy for one hour.

Sarah was rummaging in the bag and came out with a bright pink Frisbee. He could object to the color, but why bother? It was only an hour.

He took the Frisbee from her when she offered it to him, waved it in front of K-9's nose and then tossed it. The dog looked after the Frisbee, then wandered off to pee on a shrub.

"No friends, and he doesn't know how to play," she said sadly.

For a moment, Sullivan was tempted to say on the scale of human tragedy, it hardly rated. It could be the story of his own life. But again, he refrained. Instead, he went after the Frisbee and tossed it back at her.

Sarah leapt in the air, clapped her hands at it, and missed catching it by a mile. But when she jumped up like that he caught a glimpse of the world's cutest belly button. He made her jump even higher for the Frisbee the next time!

She couldn't throw, and she couldn't catch, either.

But she was game. Running after the Frisbee, jumping, throwing herself on the ground after it, making wild throws back at him. Her enthusiasm for life could be contagious! And if it was only for an hour, why not?

"Has anybody ever told you, you have the athletic talent of a fence post?" he asked her solemnly.

"In different words, I'm afraid I've been told that many times." There was something about the way she said it, even though her tone was flippant, that made him think someone somewhere had either told her, or made her feel, she didn't measure up.

There was no reason for him to take that on, or to try and do something about it, except that he had promised himself that for an hour he could manage to be a good guy. And that might include teaching her to throw a Frisbee. The world changed in small ways, after all, as much as large ones.

Isn't that what his sister had tried to tell him about Summer Fest?

He brought the Frisbee over to her, and gave it to her. "No, don't throw it. Not yet."

He went and stood behind her, leaned into her, reached around her and tucked her close to him with one arm wrapped around the firmness of her tummy. Sullivan took her throwing arm with his own.

She had stiffened with surprise at his closeness, at his touch.

"Relax," he told her. She took a deep breath, tried, but it was as if her whole body was humming with tension. Awareness.

So was his. He was not sure what he had expected, but what he felt with her back pressed into his chest was a sense of her overwhelming sweetness, her enticing femininity. She seemed small and fragile, which made him feel big and strong.

Stop it, he warned himself. He was not going to give in to the pull of age-old instincts. He thought he should have evolved past, *Me, Tarzan, you, Jane*.

"Concentrate," he said, and she thought he meant her, but he didn't.

He guided her arm with his arm. "See?" he said softly, close to her ear, "It's a flick of the wrist. Arm all the way in to your stomach, like this, then out. Release, right there."

She missed the *right there* part by a full second. He went and retrieved the Frisbee. He contemplated how he felt.

The physical contact with her made him aware of how alone he had become in the world. Aside from the occasional hug from his sister, and being climbed all over by his nephews, when was the last time he had touched someone?

There was an obvious reason why he hadn't. Once you let that particular barrier down, it would be extremely hard to get it back up. To ignore the part of him that ached for a little softness, a little closeness, a little company.

The smart thing to do would be to back off, to coach Sarah from a distance. But Sullivan reminded himself that if he was going to make a mistake he planned to make it glorious in its scope and utter wrongness.

So he went and conducted the whole exercise all over again.

He allowed himself the pure enjoyment of a man who was doing something once. He became aware of her different scents—one coming from her hair, another from her skin, both light and deliciously fragrant.

Sullivan allowed himself to savor their differences—the way she felt, like melting butter, within the circle of his arms. He could see little wisps of golden auburn hair escaping her ponytail and dancing along the nape of her slender neck. His arms around her felt so gloriously wrong, and as right as anything had ever felt in his life.

He liked *accidentally* rubbing his whiskers against the tender lobe of her ear, then watching her flub that throw hilariously.

He liked how the nervous thrumming of her body was giving way to something softer and more supple.

After a dozen or so attempts, Sarah finally managed a half-decent Frisbee toss. The pink disc sailed through the air in a perfect arc.

Neither of them noticed. She leaned back into him and sighed, finally fully relaxed. He took her weight, easily, rested his chin on the top of her head, and breathed in the moment. He folded his arms over the tiny swell of her tummy, and they just stood like that for a moment, aware of each other, comfortable with each other at the same time.

The park suddenly looked different, as if each thing in it was lit from within. He could see individual leaves trembling on branches, the richness of the loam. The sky seemed so intensely blue it made his eyes ache.

As he watched the dog, cavorting, joyous, and felt Sarah sink deeper into him, he felt as if he had been asleep for a long time and was only now awakening.

The moment had a purity, and Sullivan felt contentment. He was aware of not having felt like this for a long, long time. Maybe not ever.

The dog suddenly seemed to catch on to the game. He retrieved the Frisbee and brought it back to them, wiggled in front of them, his tail fanning the air furiously.

"Look," Sarah said softly, "he knows he's our dog."

Sullivan could point out it was not *their* dog. But she had turned and looked over her shoulder at him, and there was something shining in her face that didn't give him the heart to do it, to steal the utter purity of this moment from her.

In fact, what he wanted to do was kiss her. To touch those lips with his own, to taste her while he was in this state of heightened awareness. He wanted to deepen the sense of connection they had.

But sanity prevailed. Wouldn't that make everything way too complicated? He wanted a glorious mistake, but he didn't want to hurt her. Not her heart. Her past heartbreak was already written all over her.

Instead, amazed by the discipline it took, Oliver gently released her and backed away from her. Afraid he had become transparent, he turned quickly away.

It was time to go home.

But he had used every ounce of discipline he had to release her. There was none left to do what needed to be done. So, he went to get the Frisbee from the dog.

Sarah watched as Sullivan broke away from her, drank in the expression on his face as if she were dying of thirst and he was a long, cool drink of water.

She contemplated what had just happened between them. Her skin was still tingling where he had stood at her back, and she felt a chill where his warmth had just been.

He had nearly kissed her. She had seen the clearness of his eyes grow smoky with longing, she had felt some minute change ripple through the muscles in his arms and chest. She had leaned toward him, feeling her raw need for him in every fiber of her being.

Was it that need, telegraphed through her own eyes, her own body language, that had made him change his mind? Had she puckered her lips in anticipation of a kiss? Oh! She hoped she had not puckered!

"Hey, give that here!"

Sarah watched, and despite her disappointment at not being kissed, she could not help but smile.

The dog had apparently decided he liked playing Frisbee, after all. Only he invented his own version of the game, darting away whenever Sullivan got close to him.

That moment of exquisite physical tension and awareness was gone. But it seemed, suddenly and delightfully, like a new moment awaited. With a shout of exuberance, Sarah threw herself into that moment, and joined in the chase after the dog.

Sullivan was as natural an athlete as she was not. He was also in peak physical condition.

As if chasing the dog wasn't leaving her breathless enough, watching Sullivan unleash his power almost stopped her heart beating, too.

He was a beautifully made man, totally at ease with his body, totally confident in his abilities. It was hard not to be awed by this demonstration of pure strength and agility, Sullivan chasing after the dog, stopping on a hair, turning in midair, leaping and tackling. As he played, something came alive in his face that was at least as awe-inspiring as his show of physical prowess. Some finely held tension left him, and his face relaxed into lines of boyish delight.

What haunted him? What made this the first moment that she had seen the grimness that lingered in his eyes, that sternness around the line of his mouth, disappear completely?

"Sarah, I'm herding him toward you. Grab the Frisbee as he goes by!"

She let go of wondering what was in his past and gave herself to what he was in this moment. But of course the dog leapt easily out of her grasp, earning her a fake scowl from Sullivan.

"You have to cut him off, not jump out of his way. He's a puppy, not a herd of elephants."

"Yes, sir," she said, giving him a mock salute and jumping out of the puppy's too rambunctious path as he catapulted by her again.

"I fear you are hopeless," he growled, and then he threw back his head and laughed as she made a mistimed grab at the Frisbee when the dog came by again.

Sarah found herself laughing, too, as they both took up a frenzied pursuit of the delighted dog. She realized the moment of closeness they had experienced didn't seem to evaporate just because they had physically disengaged from it. Instead, as they chased the dog, their comfort with each other seemed to grow, as did the fun and camaraderie shimmering in the air, carrying on their shouts of laughter, the dog's happy barks.

Finally, the dog collapsed and surrendered the Frisbee. Sullivan snatched it from him, and then collapsed on the ground too, his head on the puppy's back. He patted the ground beside him in invitation, and of course she could not resist. She went and lay down, her head resting on the dog alongside his, her shoulder touching Sullivan's shoulder, her breath coming in huffs and puffs.

Clouds floated in a perfect sky.

"I see a pot of gold," she said, pointing at a cloud. "Do you?" Of course, seeing that was a reflection of the way she was feeling. Abundant. Full.

He squinted at it. "You would," he said, but tolerantly.

"What do you see?"

"You don't want to know."

"Yes, I do."

"A pile of poo."

She burst out laughing. "That's awful."

"That is just one example of how differently you and I see life."

He said it carelessly, and casually. But it reminded her that they seemed to be at cross-purposes. He wanted the barriers up. She wanted them down.

But she had a feeling she had won this round. She slapped him on the shoulder. "Don't be such a grump."

He looked astounded, glanced at his shoulder where she had smacked him, and then he actually smiled. "Oh, I see a force-feeding of a full serving of Crabbies in my future."

Future.

She was determined not to ruin this perfect moment by even thinking of that!

She was getting way too used to that smile, and how it made him look so boyish and handsome, as if he had never had a care in the world. It would be way too easy to start picturing her world with him in it.

What was happening to her? She had wanted to rescue Oliver Sullivan from himself, but she had not intended to put herself at risk! She had her new world, filled with jam and Summer Fest. Rescuing him had just been part of the new do-gooder philosophy that was supposed to fill up her life.

Only something was going wrong this morning. Because it just felt too right!

So she deliberately broke the connection between them. She retrieved her bag, pulled out water bottles. She sat back down beside him, deliberately not making contact with his shoulder again. She got her pant legs soaked trying to get the dog to drink out of one.

Then she glanced at Sullivan and was transfixed by the relaxed look on his face, taking simple pleasure of a simple moment, and she realized it wasn't as easy to break connections as she'd thought.

"I haven't felt this way since I was a kid," he said.

"I know what you mean," Sarah said, finally giving in to it, and savoring how this closed man was revealing something of himself. What would it hurt to encourage him by revealing something of herself?

"When I worked for the magazine, the girls and I would go on all these fantastic trips. We spent a weekend shopping in San Francisco. Once we went skiing in the Alps. I feel as if we were trying to manufacture the feeling that I'm feeling right now."

She stopped, embarrassed by her attempts to explain her surprise at the exhilaration that had come from something so simple as chasing a misbehaved puppy around a park.

But was this glowing feeling inside of her from the activity? Or from being with him?

He reached over and gave her shoulder a squeeze that said, *I get it. I feel the same.*

She turned her head and gazed at his face. Really, it was mission accomplished. She had set out to rescue him from darkness and she had done it.

The echoes of his laughter were still on his face. They would probably be in her heart forever.

It would be greedy—and ultimately foolish—to want more.

But she did.

The hour he had promised her had been up half an hour ago. He'd bonded with the dog. He'd no doubt do great at that interview, the dog clearly worshipped him and it would show.

It had been more than she had hoped for.

For an hour or so, laughing and playing in the sunshine, with his arms around her, and chasing that fool dog, Sarah had seen Oliver Sullivan at his best, unguarded. He had been carefree. Happy.

"How come you haven't felt this way since you were a boy?" she asked, not wanting to know, *having* to know.

He hesitated, and then he said, "I entered law enforcement really young. I had the intensity of focus, the drive, the motivation, that made me a perfect fit for homicide. But dealing with violence on a daily basis is a really, really tough thing. Dealing with what people are capable of doing to each other is soul-shattering."

Sarah thought of the grimness in his eyes, the lines around his mouth, and was so glad she had been part of making that go away, even if it was just for a little while. Even if it cost her some peace of mind of her own.

He continued softly, "If people tell you they get

used to it? They're either lying or terrible at their jobs. You never get used to it."

"Is that why you came here, to Kettle Bend, instead?"

He was silent for a very long time. He moved his hand off her shoulder. "I caught a really bad case. The worst of my career. When it was done, I just couldn't do it anymore."

"Do you need to talk about it?" she asked softly.

He snorted derisively, leapt to his feet. "No, I don't need to talk about it. And if I did, I wouldn't pick you."

For a moment, she felt wounded. But then she saw something else in his face, and his stance.

It wasn't that he was not trusting her. It was that he was protecting her from what he had seen and done.

"I took a year off," he said. "That's good enough."

She had a feeling it wasn't. That he carried some dark burden inside himself that it would do him nothing but good to unload. But his face was now as closed as it had been open a few minutes ago.

"So, what did you do for a year?" she asked him, pulling the dog's head into her lap, scratching his ears, not wanting those moments of closeness between them to disappear, hoping she could get him talking again. Even if somehow it was opening her up in ways that would cost her.

"I rented a cabin outside of Missoula, Montana, and went fishing."

"Did it help?"

"As an experiment, I would say it failed. Miserably."

"Why?" she asked.

"I'd say I had too much me time. Hour after hour, day after day, with only my own dreary company. It was time to get back to work. Della had moved here. She wanted me to come, too. I thought something different would be good."

"And has it been?"

"I miss the intensity of working as a detective in Detroit. I miss the anonymity. I miss using skills I spent a lot of years developing. On the other hand, I sleep at night. I get to watch my nephews grow up. And small towns have a certain hokey charm that I'm finding hard to resist."

But she had a feeling, from the way his eyes rested on her, he wasn't just talking about small towns having a certain charm that was hard to resist.

Though she hoped hers wasn't hokey!

Still, she could not help but feel thrilled. Sarah knew that today had been a part of that. Today, he had shared his life with someone outside of the small, safe circle of Della and her family. It had allowed him to get out of himself. To engage. To feel a reprieve from the yawning abyss of apartness that separated him from his fellow man. And she'd been part of that!

The problem with that? It was hard to let go of.

"I have to meet with the Summer Fest committees this afternoon," she said, not looking at him. She ordered herself to let go.

To say to herself, *Do-gooder, mission accomplished. Go back to your life.*

That was the problem with messing with this kind of power. Regaining control was not that simple.

Because she heard herself saying, her tone deliberately casual, "You know, in terms of the interview tomorrow, maybe you should come. It would give you a real feeling for the community spirit that is building. It might give you some ideas how to work Summer Fest into the discussion at the television station."

After his lecture to her about all the things Summer Fest was not going to do for her, she was nervous even bringing it up. She felt the potential for rejection, braced herself for it. Sullivan was probably way better at exercising control than she was.

He stared at her as if he couldn't believe she was going to try for another hour of his time.

She saw the battle on his face.

And then she saw him lose, just as she had done.

Because he ran a hand through the thick crispness of his hair and gave in, just a little.

"I have to admit I've been just a little curious about how you are going to pull off the whole Summer Fest thing. It seems like a rather large and ambitious undertaking for a woman who can't even throw a Frisbee."

She looked at him now, stunned. "You'll come?"

"Sure," he said with a shrug, as if it meant nothing at all, as if he had not just conceded a major battle to her. "I wouldn't mind seeing what you're up to, Sarah McDougall."

Chapter 6

"I can't believe you talked him into coming," Mabel Winston, chair of the Summer Fest Market Place committee, said.

Sarah let her eyes drift to where Sullivan was in deep discussion with Fred Henry, head of the Fourth of July fireworks team, and Barry Bushnell, head of organizing the opening day parade. She felt a little shiver of pure appreciation.

"He's even better in real life than he was on the video," Maryanne Swarinsky, who was in charge of the Fourth of July Picnic Committee, said in a hushed tone.

The whispered comment echoed Sarah's thoughts exactly. Oliver Sullivan was simply a man who had a commanding presence. It was more than his physical stature, and it was more than the fact he was a policeman.

He radiated a confidence in his ability to handle whatever life threw at him. He was *that* man, the one you wanted with you when the ship went down, or the building burst into flames. The one who would be coolly composed if bullets were flying in the air around him, if he had his back against the wall and the barbarians were rushing at him with their swords drawn.

But he had shared with her that he did not feel he had handled something life had thrown at him. Sarah shivered again, thinking how truly terrible it must be. *Wishing* she had been able to relieve him of some of that burden.

But she had noticed, as soon as he had entered the room, there had been a sudden stillness. Then all the men had gravitated to him and all the women had nearly swooned.

"Just look at the way that dog is glued to him," Candy McPherson, who was running the old-fashioned games day, said. "You know, maybe we should have a dog show. Just a few categories. Cutest dog. Cutest owner. That sort of thing."

There was no doubt, from her tone, that Candy had already picked the cutest owner.

"We already have six events planned over the four days," Sarah said. "That's more than enough. Maybe we'll look at some kind of dog event for next year."

Candy looked stubborn. "I could fit it into the games day, somehow."

"Is he going to take the dog?" Maryanne asked her.

Sarah glanced over at Sullivan again. The dog, worn out from his morning activities, or just plain worn out from adoring his hero, snoozed contentedly, his head on Sullivan's feet.

Sarah was amazed by what she was seeing in Sullivan. She wasn't sure what she had expected when he met the committee members. Cynicism, possibly. Remoteness, certainly.

But the playful morning with the dog seemed to have lightened him up. Sullivan looked relaxed and open.

Or maybe it was just hard to keep yourself at a distance when you were surrounded by people like these: open, friendly, giving by nature.

Unaware how intently he was being watched, Sullivan reached down and gave the dog's belly a little tickle.

"In terms of the free publicity we're getting from him and the dog," Sarah said thoughtfully, "wouldn't that be a fantastic outcome? If he kept the dog? A feel-good story with a great ending like that would bring nothing but positive to Kettle Bend."

"Talk him into it," Candy said.

Sarah smiled a little wryly. "If ever there was a man you couldn't talk into anything, it's that one, right there."

"I don't know," Mabel said. "You talked him into coming here."

Suddenly, all the women were looking at her so intently, considering her influence over that powerful man. She could tell there was curiosity and conjecture about the nature of her relationship with the handsome policeman.

Feeling herself blushing, Sarah said, "Let's get back to business, shall we?"

An hour later, she was trying to pry Sullivan away from them.

Finally, they were back out on the street, the dog padding along beside them as if it was the most natural thing in the world for the three of them to be together as a unit.

"I have to admit, Sarah," Sullivan said, "I thought you were being way too ambitious with this whole Summer Fest thing. But those people in there are really committed to you. You've built a solid team. I think, maybe, you're going to pull this off."

"Maybe?" she chided him. She stopped, planted her hands on her hips, and glared at him. Of course, it was all a ruse to hide how much she enjoyed his praise.

"Don't hit my shoulder," he begged, covering it up in mock fear with his hand. "I'll already be sporting bruises from you."

"Take it back, then," she said. "Say, *Sarah McDougall's Summer Fest is going to be an unmitigated success.*"

He laughed then. "Sarah McDougall, there is something infectious about your enthusiasm. You're even starting to get to me."

"Yippee!" she said.

His laughter deepened and made things so easy

between them. She was astonished that this side of him, easygoing, relaxed, so easy to be around, was lasting. She loved how his laughter made her feel. Like the world was a good place, full to the brim with excitement and potential.

"I'm starving," he said.

She realized the hour she had promised him he would be away had now stretched late into the day. It was time to let him go.

"You want to go grab a bite to eat?"

Could it be possible he didn't want to let her go, either? Amazed at the joy in her heart, Sarah said, "I'd like that."

Like chasing the dog around the park, sitting at an outdoor table with him was really just the most ordinary of things. A guy and a gal and their dog enjoying a warm spring afternoon by having lunch on main street.

Except it wasn't *their* dog.

And they weren't really a guy and a gal in the way it probably looked like they were.

Although it felt like they were.

How could such an ordinary thing—sitting outside under an umbrella, eating French fries, feeding morsels of their hamburgers to the dog—make her feel so tingly? So wonderful and alive and happy?

Probably because the man sharing the table with her was about as far from ordinary as you could get.

They talked of small things. The ideas for Summer Fest, the weather, his brother-in-law Jonathon's recovery.

Then, out of the blue, he said, "Tell me about your job in New York."

"Oh," she said, uncomfortably, "that's in the past."

"That seems like a shame."

"What does that mean?"

"I went on the internet and read a couple of your stories for the magazine."

"You read stories by me?" she asked, astounded.

He shrugged. "Slow night for hockey."

"You read stories about babies?" she said skeptically, but something was hammering in her heart. She was flattered. Who had ever showed that much interest in anything she did?

"Don't read too much into it," he said. "Once a detective, always a snoop."

"Why would you go to the trouble?"

"Curiosity."

Oliver Sullivan was curious about her?

He took a sip of his coffee and looked at her intently. "You are really a very good writer."

"I was okay at it."

"No, actually, you were better than okay. Tell me why you decided to leave that world."

"I already did tell you that. My grandmother left me a house and a business. It was time for a change."

"That's the part that interests me."

"It's not interesting," she said evasively. But now she could see the detective in him. He was trying to find out something, and she had a feeling he would not be content until he did.

He was trying to confirm the heartbreak part of

the scenario he had guessed at, when he had made her so angry and she had stormed away from the café. Now, Sarah would just as soon end the day on the bright note that they had sustained so far.

"Let me be the judge of whether it's interesting or not," he said silkily. "Why did you leave the magazine and New York? Aside from the convenient fact you were left a house and a business. If you were perfectly happy, you could have just sold them both and stayed where you were."

Her flattery was quickly being replaced by a feeling of being trapped. "Were you good at interrogations?" she demanded.

"Excellent," he said, not with any kind of ego, simply stating a fact.

"Curiosity killed the cat," she told him snippily.

"I'll take my chances."

"Why do you care?" she asked, her voice a little shrill.

"It's a mystery. That's what I do. Solve mysteries. Indulge me. I'm compulsive."

"I don't see anything mysterious about it."

"Beautiful, extremely talented young woman leaves the excitement of a big city and a flourishing career. She leaves behind shopping trips in San Francisco, and skiing in Switzerland. And for what? To live the life of a nun in Kettle Bend, Wisconsin, devoting herself to unlikely causes, such as saving the town."

She could argue she had already told him she had

more fun today than skiing in Switzerland. She could argue her cause was *not* unlikely.

Instead her mind focused, with outrage, on only one part of his statement.

"A nun?" she squeaked.

"A guess. I didn't mean a nun as in saying the rosary and walking the stations of the cross. I meant, like, er, celibate."

"Huh. That shows what you know. I happened to see a naked man just this morning."

He choked on his coffee. "Touché," he said, lifting the mug to her.

"I had no idea I was appearing pathetic."

"Anything but. Which is why I'm so curious. The boyfriends should be coming out of the woodwork."

"What makes you think they aren't?"

"You don't have the look of a woman who's been kissed. And often. And by someone who knows how." He smiled and sipped his coffee.

Sarah stared at him. "How can you argue with a man who can paraphrase Rhett Butler from *Gone with the Wind*?" she asked.

"Besides, you've already told me on more than one occasion. No dating. You're obviously aiming for cynicism in the love department."

She was simply unused to a man who paid such close attention to everything she said!

"Okay, here is the pathetic truth. I was engaged to be married. While I was picking venues, pricing flowers, shopping for wedding dresses, and daydreaming about babies in bassinettes, my fiancé was having a fling with a freelancer."

"The dog," he said quietly, and then to *their* dog, "Sorry, no offense."

Really, she had said quite enough. But something about the steadiness of his gaze encouraged her to go on, to spill it all.

"He was an editor at the magazine. I caught the occasional rumor about him and Trina."

"Which you chose to ignore," Sullivan guessed.

"It seemed like the noble thing to do! To ignore malicious office gossip. I actually put it down to jealousy, as if certain people could not stand my happiness."

He shook his head. "An optimist thinks that light at the end of the tunnel is the sun," he said. "A cynic knows it's a train."

"It was a train," she agreed sadly. "I saw them together having coffee. It could have been business. I wanted to believe it was business, but there was just something about it. They just seemed a little too cozy, leaning in toward each other, so intent they never even saw me walking by the window. So I confronted him. Right until the moment I saw his face, I held out hope there would be an explanation for it. It was really just too awkward after that. I couldn't stay on the magazine and see him every day."

He was quiet, watching her intently.

"There? You wanted to know about my tawdry past, and now you do. You were right. I moved here to lick my wounds. I moved here because I felt I couldn't hold my head up in the office anymore. Are you happy?"

"Actually, I'd be happy if I could meet him, just once."

"And do what?" she asked, wide-eyed.

He shrugged, but there was something so fierce and so protective in his glance at her that a shiver went up and down her spine.

After a moment, Sullivan said, "You know what really bugs me? It's that you felt you couldn't hold your head up. As if *you'd* done something wrong."

"I was naive!"

"That's not a criminal offense."

"From the expert on criminal offenses," she said, trying to maintain some sense of humor, some sense of dignity now that she'd laid herself bare before him.

"You understand that it's entirely about him, right? It has nothing to do with you?"

"It has everything to do with me. My whole life went down the drain!"

"The career you chose to let go of, apparently, probably not your best decision ever. But him? You were lucky you saw them together. You were saved from making a horrible mistake."

That was true. If she had not found out, would he have carried on, married her anyway?

It occurred to her, if she had married Mike, she might not be sitting here.

Even leaving her career—which Sullivan said was not her best decision—if she had not done that, she would not be sitting here.

Across from him.

Falling in love with the way the sun looked on his hair, and the way his hands closed around a coffee cup, and the way his eyes were so intent on her.

"I'm going to guess you started telling yourself all kinds of lies after it happened," he said. "Like that you weren't pretty enough. Or interesting enough. Somehow, you made it your fault, didn't you?"

Falling in love with the way he had of saying things, of making things that had been foggy suddenly very, very clear.

"It's one hundred percent about him, Sarah. He's a snake. You didn't deserve that."

"Well, whether I deserved it or not, it made me cynical. Confirmed my cynicism about love and happy ever after."

He laughed softly. "You may think you are cynical, and you may want to be cynical, but, Sarah, take it from one who has that particular flaw of human nature down to an art form, you aren't."

"Well, about matters of the heart I am cynical."

"You didn't come from one of those postcard families, did you?"

Falling in love with the way he *saw* her, and stripped her of the secrets that held her prisoner.

"What makes you say that?"

"Something you said when we were playing Frisbee. I got the impression you'd been told once too often you didn't measure up."

Sarah gulped. He really did see way, way too

much. He read people and situations with an almost terrifying accuracy.

Yet there was something very freeing about being seen.

"If you'd had proper support through your breakup, you'd probably still be in New York writing. You probably wouldn't have decided to love a town instead of a man quite so quickly."

She stared at him, but then sighed, resigned to the fact he could read her so clearly.

"I actually did think I had a perfect family," she confessed, and confession felt good, even though she had already said more than enough for one day! "Except for the fact my father seemed to want a boy, it was a fairly happy childhood."

"Personally, I think that's a pretty big fact," he said, "but go on."

"When I was eleven, my mother discovered my father was having an affair. They tried to patch it up, but the trust was gone. There were two bitter years of fighting and sniping and accusations."

"And you'd come spend summers at Grandma's house, and dream of the perfect family," he guessed softly.

"I'd plot how to fix the one I had," she admitted with a reluctant smile. "It didn't work. When my dad finally did leave, he never looked back. He remarried and his new family—two little boys—was everything to him. You wouldn't have even known he had a daughter from a previous relationship. His idea of parenting was support cheques and a card on my birthday. Despite his neglect, according to my mother, I started looking to replace him the minute he left. Then I did find one just like him—and nearly married him, too. Amazing, huh?"

"Not so amazing," he said softly.

She was suddenly embarrassed that she had said so much, revealed so much about herself, even if it did feel good to be so transparent. "It's a good thing I never committed any crimes," she said. "You'd have a full signed confession in front of you!"

The talk turned to lighter things, and finally Sullivan called for the bill, giving her *a look* when she offered to pay half of it.

As they walked back to his house, he charmed her with a funny story about his nephew Jet.

As grateful as she was for the change of subject, Sarah was aware of feeling dissatisfied.

He had uncovered her deepest secrets with ease, made her feel backed into a corner until she had no choice but to spit it out. Well, maybe that wasn't so surprising. That's what detectives did, right?

But now, after hinting this morning at the dissatisfactions that had brought him to Kettle Bend, he was giving nothing in return. In a way, he was keeping his distance just as effectively with the small talk as he had been with his remoteness.

Sarah bet he'd used charm plenty of times to avoid any intimacy in his life!

So, now they stood on his front porch, and Sarah was stunned by what time it was. "Shoot. I missed the vet's office. They're closed in a few minutes. I won't be able to get the dog back there in time."

She hadn't done it on purpose, but maybe the dog could wheedle by the defenses that she could not.

"Could you take him?" she asked. "Just for to-night? You have to pick him up for the interview to-morrow, anyway."

He shrugged. "Sure. No big deal."

Somehow she could not bear to say goodbye. Not like this. Not with him knowing everything there was to know about her in all its humiliating detail, and her knowing close to nothing about him.

"Are you from one of those good families?" she asked. "Or were you, before your parents died?"

He stared off into the distance for a minute. "Yeah," he finally said, slowly, "I was. I mean, it wasn't the Cleavers. We were a working-class fam-ily in a tough Detroit neighborhood. There was never enough money. Sometimes we didn't even have enough food. But there was always enough love."

He suddenly looked so sad.

"How did your mom and dad die?"

She blurted it out. Maybe because a dog getting by his defenses was not really a rescue at all.

Sarah watched him. She could tell he was blind-sided by the question. It was taking a chance.

But it just felt as if she had to move deeper.

Now he looked as if he might not answer. As if giving himself over to the simple intimacies of shar-ing a sun-filled morning with her and the dog had been enough of a stress on his system for one day.

As if his peek into her life by going to the meetings and probing into her history at the outdoor café had been more than enough for one day.

But how was it any kind of intimacy if it was not shared? If it was a one-way street?

She held her breath, pleading inwardly for this breakthrough. For his trust. To offer him the kind of freedom from his past that he had just offered her.

"They were murdered," he said, finally, reluctantly, quietly.

She felt the shock of it ripple along her spine, felt the dark violence of it overlay the beauty of the day.

Then she realized that this dark violence must overlay him every single day of his life.

All day she had been watching him change, sensing his barriers go down. She had watched as he became more engaged, more spontaneous, more open. She had seen him reach out, take her secrets from her, expose them to the light of day, their power evaporated as the sun hit them.

But her secrets suddenly seemed petty, so tiny and tawdry in comparison to his tragic revelation.

The look on his face now reminded Sarah that the bond between them was tenuous, that he might, in fact, still be looking for an excuse to break it.

So even though she wanted to say something, to ask questions, or to say she was sorry, some deep, deep instinct warned her not to.

Instead, she laid her hand across the strength of his wrist, lightly, tenderly, inviting him to trust.

After a long moment, he said, "It was a case of

being in the wrong place at the wrong time. Mistaken identity. A gang shooting gone terribly wrong."

Her hand remained on his wrist, unmoving. Her eyes on his face, drinking in his pain, feeling as if she could take it from him, as if she could share his burden.

Suddenly he yanked his wrist out from under her hand, muttering, "It happened a long time ago."

It might be a long time ago, but it was the answer to everything. Why he had chosen the profession he chose—and more. It was the key to why he chose to walk alone.

She knew he had just given her an incredible gift by trusting her with this part of himself.

"Thank you for telling me," she said quietly.

He looked annoyed. Not with her. But with himself. As if he had shown an unacceptable lack of judgment for sharing this. A weakness.

But she saw something else entirely. She saw a man who was incredibly courageous. Oliver Sullivan had tried to take on something—or maybe everything—that was terribly wrong in the world.

But he had sacrificed some part of himself in his relentless pursuit of right. He had immersed himself so totally in the darkness of the human heart that he really did believe every light at the end of a tunnel was a train.

She had been right to come after him.

But now she could see if she had thought finding out about him would create closeness, the exact opposite was true.

He fitted his key in his door, shoved the dog inside without looking back at her. "I have to go."

Retreating. Saying no to the day and to what her hand on his wrist had offered. Saying he could carry his burdens by himself.

Even if it killed him.

Just when she thought he was going to leave without even saying goodbye, he turned back to her suddenly, took a step toward her and then stood above her, looked down at her with dark eyes, smoky with longing. He took his finger and tilted her chin up. And dropped his head over hers and kissed her.

His lips touching her lips were incredible. He tasted of things that were real—rain and raging rivers—and things that were strong and unbreakable—mountain peaks and granite canyons.

He tasted not of heaven, as she had thought he would, but of something so much better. Earth: magnificent, abundant, mysterious, life-giving, *attainable to mere mortals*.

She could feel a fire stirring to life in her belly. She thought she had doused that particular flame, but now she could see that wasn't quite right.

No, that wasn't right at all.

It was as if every kiss and every passionate moment Sarah had experienced before this one had been the cheapest of imitations. Not real at all.

She told herself it was a hello kind of kiss, a door opening, something beginning between them. That's what she thought she tasted on his lips: realness, and strength and the utter spring freshness of new beginning.

But when his lips left hers, she opened her eyes, reluctantly. He took a step back from her and she read a different truth entirely in his eyes.

His eyes were suddenly both shadowed and shuttered.

It hadn't been hello at all. It had been goodbye.

Then he straightened and smiled slightly, that cynical my-heart-is-made-of-stone smile.

"Sarah," he said softly, "you've got your hands full trying to save this town. Don't you even try to save me."

Then he turned and walked through his open door. He was alone, even though the dog was with him. He was the gunfighter leaving town.

Not needing anyone or anything. Not a woman and not a dog.

She was humiliated that she had been so transparent.

But then she realized, buried in there somewhere, in those soft words, had been an admission.

He hadn't said he didn't need saving.

He had just warned her not to try.

It seemed to her, suddenly, that in her whole life she had never been spontaneous, she had never done what her heart wanted her to do.

She'd always backed down from the desires of her heart, so afraid of being let down, of being disappointed, that she had not even spoken them, let alone acted on them.

Sarah had always chosen the safe way, the conservative way, the don't-rock-the-boat way. She had never broken the rules. She had worked hard at being the proverbial good girl.

Where had that gotten her? Had it ever earned her the love and approval she had been so desperate for?

No.

Except this morning, for once in her life, Sarah had done what she wanted to do, not what she *should* do. Because she *should* have obeyed his boundaries. But instead, she had marched up the steps of Oliver Sullivan's house with that dog, an act of instinct, as brave as she had ever been.

And today she had *lived.*

Somehow, after that, after having *lived* so completely, having experienced exhilaration in such simplicity, life was never going to be the same.

Taking a deep breath, even though she was quivering inside, Sarah decided she wasn't backing down now. With every ounce of courage she possessed, she crossed the threshold into his house, where Sullivan stood by his open door, just getting ready to shut it.

Tentatively, she reached out, touched his face. She felt the roughness of a new growth of whiskers under the tenderness of her palm. She touched the stern line of his mouth with her fingertips.

Something shifted in his face. She could clearly see the struggle there.

When she saw that struggle, she sighed, and pulled herself in close to him. She wrapped her arms around the solidness of his neck and pressed herself against the length of him.

She could feel the absolute strength of him, the soft heat radiating off his body. She could hear the beat of his heart quickening beneath his shirt. She could smell the rich, seductive aroma of him.

She held on tight, waiting to see if he would recoil from her, reject her as she had been rejected by her father. As she had been rejected when a man she'd thought she had loved, whom she had planned her future with, had cavalierly given himself to another.

Would Oliver Sullivan reject her?

Or would he surrender?

She was terrified of finding out.

But she was even more terrified of walking away without having the courage to explore what might have been.

Chapter 7

Sullivan felt the delicious curve of Sarah's body pressed against the length of him. If there was a word that was not in his vocabulary, it was this one.

Rest.

From the moment he had first met her, everything about her had told him she would offer him this.

A place in the world where he could rest.

Where he could lay down his shield, and share his burdens, and rest his weary, weary heart. Where he could find peace.

He had tried to send her away, he had tried to save her from himself. And instead of going, she had seen right through him, to what he needed most of all.

He was taken by her bravery all over again. And

by his own lack of it. Because he should have refused what she was offering him and he could not.

Instead, he kissed the top of her head and pulled her in close to him. She stirred against him and looked up at him, and there were tears shining in her eyes.

So, instead of doing what he needed to do—putting her away from him and shutting the door on her—he touched his fingers to her tears and then touched those fingers to his lips.

"Don't cry, sweet Sarah," he said softly. "Please don't cry."

He realized he wasn't nearly as hardened to tears as he had thought he was. Because he wanted never to be the reason for her tears.

"What do you want?" he asked, into her hair.

"I want this day to never end," she said.

He thought maybe he couldn't give her everything she wanted. In fact, he knew he could not give her the dreams that shone in her eyes: a perfect family, behind a white picket fence.

She was a nice girl who deserved a nice life. He did not perceive himself as any kind of nice person. Giving someone a nice life, given the darkness of his own soul, was probably out of the question.

But he could probably give her this one thing: a day that never ended. When he had first met her, he had thought he could spare ten minutes for her. Then this morning, he'd thought an hour with her would not pose any kind of threat to either of them.

Now, he considered. He could give her himself for the rest of the day.

He stood back from his door, inviting her in. "I hope you like hockey, then."

"Adore it," she said.

"Sure you do," he said skeptically. "Who's playing tonight?"

"The Canucks and the Red Wings, Game Two of the Stanley Cup Final."

He stared at her. Oh, boy. She was going to be a girl to contend with.

"Hey," she said, "you're looking at the girl who tried desperately to be the boy her father wanted."

"Do you know how to make popcorn, too?"

At her nod, he muttered, "I'm lost," and was rewarded with the lightness of her laughter filling up a house that had never been anything but empty.

And threatening to fill up a man who had never been anything but that, either.

The question *Where is this all going?* tried to claw by his lowered defenses. The question *How can this end well?* tried to force its way past the loveliness of her laughter.

He ignored them both. It was only the rest of the day, a few hours out of his life and hers.

What was so wrong with just living one moment at a time, anyway? Perhaps, one moment leading into another could get out of hand. Maybe it was a little out of hand already.

But it was nothing he could not bring back under his control the minute he chose to.

So they learned together that feeding popcorn to a large dog in a small room was a bad idea. He learned she knew more about hockey than anyone else of his acquaintance. She insisted on staying until one minute past midnight, so she could say their day together had never ended. And he learned a woman falling asleep against your chest was one of the sweetest things that could happen to you.

Bringing things back under his control was obviously not as simple as choosing to do it. Because as he watched her putting on her shoes, giving the dog a last pet, he heard himself say, "Do you want to come to the TV station with me tomorrow?"

She beamed at him as if he'd offered her dinner for two at the fanciest restaurant in the area.

He watched her little red Bug drive away into the night and some form of sanity tried to return. One day was clearly becoming two.

After that he would extricate himself from this whole mess he'd gotten himself into.

The next day, the interview for television went extremely well. The dog behaved, the questions were easy to answer and he managed to mention Kettle Bend and Summer Fest at nearly every turn.

Sarah was waiting in the wings, her face aglow with approval. It was a light that a man could warm himself in for a long, long time.

"I thought you said you weren't good at interviews," she teased.

"I guess it's different when you don't have a whole city howling for a crime to be solved, eager for someone to throw under the bus if an investigation isn't moving fast enough or moves in the wrong direction."

She wasn't just listening, she was drinking him in.

"Do you want to come to my place?" she asked. "We could order a pizza and watch Game Three together."

She wouldn't meet his eyes, so shy and fearful of asking him, that he did not have the heart to say no.

Besides, one day had already become two, so why not just give himself over to it?

The living room of her house was as he remembered it. A sweet, tart aroma permeated the whole place.

Sullivan remembered smelling it that first day.

And it reminded him of things gone from his life: cooking, warm kitchens, good smells. Home.

Rest.

Thankfully, before he could get too caught up in that, the dog spotted her cat and went on a rampage, under the coffee table, over the couch and through the door to her kitchen.

He finally cornered the dog in the kitchen, where he was howling his dismay that the cat had disappeared out the cat door. Sullivan stopped and surveyed Sarah's kitchen, astounded. *Could anything be further from* rest *than this?*

He went back into the living room. Sarah was bent over, picking up flowers that had been knocked off the coffee table out of the puddles on the floor. Her delectable little derriere pointed in the air was some-what of a distraction.

"Um, what's with the kitchen?"

She turned and looked at him, blushed red. Because she knew he'd been sneaking a peek at her backside or because Little Susie Homemaker did not like getting caught with a mess in her perfect life?

"It's my new decorating theme," she said, a touch defensively. "I call it Titanic, After the Sinking."

"It's more like Bomb Goes Off in the Rhubarb Patch." He turned back and looked at the kitchen. Every counter was covered in rhubarb, some of it wilted. There were pots stacked in the sink and over-flowing it. In an apparent attempt to prolong its life, some of the rhubarb was stuck, stalks down, in buckets full of water.

"Just shut the door," she pleaded.

"Is that rhubarb on the *ceiling*?"

She came and stood beside him with her rescued flowers. "I had a little accident with the pressure cooker."

"People can be killed by those things!" he said, his tone a little more strident than he wanted.

"I just thought I could expedite the jam-making process. As you can see, I'm a little behind."

He turned and looked at her. He saw by the slump of her shoulders that she *hated* making jam. And he also saw that this was, at least in part, his fault. She'd been out with him when she clearly should have been making her jam.

So he closed the kitchen door, partly to protect the

cat and partly to protect her from whatever it was she hated so much. They ordered a pizza and watched hockey—and learned you shouldn't feed all-dressed pizza to a large dog in a small room.

After the game, he really knew it was time for him to go.

But in a way, whether he wanted it or not, she had rescued him from his life. Only for a few days, it was going to be over soon, he told himself firmly, but he wanted to do something for her.

"Let's tackle that rhubarb together," he said.

Her mouth fell open. "Oliver, that's not necessary. I can manage."

Oliver. Why did she insist on calling him that? And why did it feel so right off her lips? Part of this sensation of homecoming.

Yes, he owed her something.

"Sure, you can manage," he said. "Just fit in a few thousand jars of rhubarb jam between saving the town, and—" And what? *Saving me.* "—and everything else," he finished lamely.

"I only have a couple of dozen orders left to fill," she said. "And then I hoped to have some ready for the Market Place at Summer Fest, but if that doesn't happen it's okay."

But it wasn't really okay.

She was putting her livelihood on hold for the town. And for him.

He could help her with this. Repay his depts. Then *adiós, amiga.* He would have given her—and himself—two days, one hour and ten minutes.

"Show me to your recipe," he said.

"No, I—"

"Don't argue with me."

She looked at him stubbornly. It occurred to him he actually *liked* arguing with her.

She folded her arms over her chest. "I can argue with you if I want."

"Yes," he said, "you can. But I have to warn you, there will be repercussions."

"Such as?" she said, unintimidated.

"Such as my tea-towel snapping is world class."

"Your what?"

"Let me demonstrate." He took a tea towel from where it hung over her oven handle. He spun it, and then flicked it. The air cracked with the sound. He spun it again, moved toward her, then snapped it in the general direction of that delectable little backside.

"Hey!"

But she was running, and then they were darting around her kitchen island, and in and out of the buckets of rhubarb. They'd forgotten to shut the door, so the puppy joined in, not sure what he was chasing, but thrilled to be part of the game.

On her way by the stove, she grabbed her own tea towel, spinning while running. Then she turned and faced him, got off a pretty good crack at him. Laughing, he swiveled around, and they reversed their wild chase through her kitchen.

Finally, gasping for breath, choking on laughter, they stopped. She surrendered.

She showed him her grandmother's recipe.

"'Spring Fling,'" he read. Then he read the rest, and looked up at her with a wry smile. "You think this works?"

"Of course not!"

He looked back at the recipe. "No wonder you hate making jam," he said. "Sixty-two cups of rhubarb, finely chopped? You'd have to eat a couple of jars of the stuff first. You know, so you felt good and frisky."

"I don't hate making jam," she said stubbornly. "And I used up all my frisky being chased around the kitchen."

"Yes, you *do* hate making jam." He was willing to bet he could coax the frisky part out of her, too.

But he wasn't going to. He was going to be a Boy Scout doing his good deed for the day.

Whether or not she hated making jam, another truth was soon apparent to him. He really did like the playful interactions with her. Friskiness aside, it was fun bantering. Bugging her. Chasing her around the kitchen until the dog was wild and she was helpless with laughter.

He really did like arguing with her about what was finely chopped and what was not. About training dogs. About whether or not to try the pressure cooker again.

It was two o'clock in the morning when he stood at her front door, putting on his coat and shoes. He doubted he would ever feel free of the smell of cooking rhubarb.

"Do you have to work tomorrow?" she asked, concerned.

"Yeah, I start really early. Five-thirty. It's okay. I'm used to rough hours."

"I can't believe it! All that jam, done. And the most fun I've ever had doing it, too."

Then she blushed.

And he realized he had never left a woman's house at two in the morning with *nothing* happening.

Except thirty-two pint jars of jam sitting neatly on a counter, glowing like jewels. Except chasing her around the kitchen, snapping a tea towel at her behind. Except standing shoulder to shoulder, washing and drying that mountain of pots.

Oh, something *was* happening, all right. It felt like he was being cured of the sourness of old heartaches. It felt as if he was feeling new hope.

Dangerous ways to feel.

He hadn't even eaten any of that blasted jam! Unless the taste test off the shared spoon counted. Unless licking that little splotch off the inside of her wrist counted. It was the best damned jam he'd ever tasted, but he was well aware that what he was feeling didn't have a thing to do with the jam.

It was the circumstances that had made it so sweet and so tart. If coming home had a taste, that would be it.

He straightened, looked at her, and just could not resist.

He beckoned her into the circle of his arms, tilted

her chin up and touched his lips to hers. Then he deepened the kiss.

And found out he had been wrong about the taste of coming home.

It was not in her jam.

It was in her lips.

She took a step back from him. He could see the question in her eyes.

She bent and took the dog's ears in both her hands, and planted a kiss right on the tip of his black nose.

When she straightened, she looked Sullivan right in the eye.

"I think it's time to give the dog a real name," she said.

It jolted him. Because it wasn't really about giving the dog a name. It was about whether or not he could commit.

It was about his phobia to attachment.

It was about where this was all going.

He didn't answer her, and he could see the disappointment in her face.

He'd always known he was bound to disappoint her. The truth? Sarah McDougall didn't really know the first thing about him.

Now might be the time to tell her. He was damaged. He had failed at a relationship before. She'd made a poor choice in a man before, and he would be a worse choice.

But even telling her the details of his life and of his past implied this was all going somewhere, and he was determined that it wasn't.

So when Sarah said, "Do you want to meet after work tomorrow? We can walk the dog-without-the-name."

He knew he had to say no. He *knew* it. But he didn't. The new hope that had sprung up in him, unbidden, wouldn't let him.

"Why don't you meet me at my place around four?" he said. "Don't come earlier. I don't want to get caught in the shower again." And he realized he liked to make her blush nearly as much as he liked to argue with her.

But she wasn't letting him have the upper hand completely. She smiled sweetly and said, "I'm going to make a list of names for the dog."

As he walked away from her, Sullivan realized two days were becoming three. His legendary discipline was failing him at every turn. No, not at every turn. Maybe it was to convince himself he was still in control that he decided right then and there that he was never going to name that dog.

"Trey, Timothy, Taurus, Towanda…"

"Towanda?"

"I just threw that in to see if you were paying attention. I'm already at T and I find it hard to believe you haven't liked one single name for the dog," she commented.

"Sarah, I'm not keeping him. It doesn't make sense to name him. That will be up to the people who get him."

He said he wasn't keeping the dog, but Sarah didn't believe him.

The three of them had spent lots of time together over the last week. That dog belonged with Oliver Sullivan and he knew it! He was just being stubborn.

And he was certainly that. Stubborn. Strong.

But what most people would not know was that he was also funny. Unexpectedly tender. Gentle. Intelligent. Playful.

Sarah slid a look at him. They were walking the dog by the river, Oliver's idea, to get the dog over his fear of water.

She watched him throw a stick into the water, and felt her heart soar at the look on his face when the dog refused to fetch. Determined. Curious. Open. Tender.

What was happening to her? And then, just like that, she knew.

She wasn't just in love with things about him: the way his hair fell over his eye, the way his smile could light up her whole world, the way he could make making a walk along the river or making jam an adventure in being alive.

She was falling in love with Oliver Sullivan.

She contemplated that thought and waited for a feeling of terror to overtake her. Instead a feeling of exuberance filled her.

Life had never been better. Ever since the interview that he had done, reservations for accommodations during Summer Fest were pouring into the town. The committees were going full steam ahead, and final details were in place for most of the activities and events.

Every booth was sold out for Market Place.

In the last week, Sarah had seen Oliver every day. They had walked the dog. One day they rented bikes and rode the entire river path, the dog bounding along beside them, a reflection of the joy in the air. The most ordinary of things—making popcorn and watching hockey—became infused with the most extraordinary light.

They had exchanged tentative kisses that were growing deeper and more passionate with each passing day.

They held hands openly.

When they watched TV he put his arm over her shoulder, pulled her in tight to him. Sometimes he would take her hand, kiss it, blow on where the kiss had been, and laugh when she tried to shake off the shivers that went up and down her spine.

But that had nothing on the quivers she felt every single time she saw him. Her first glimpse of him in a day always felt as if her heart had been closed, like a fist, and now it opened, waiting, expecting to be filled.

And he never disappointed.

As she watched, he threw a stick in the water again for the dog. Spring runoff was finished. The river was shallow and mellow.

The dog whined, watched it plaintively, and then went and hid behind Oliver's leg, peeking out at the stick drifting lazily down the river. She watched the stick go, thinking about currents, how you could be caught in one before you knew it. You started out drifting lazily along, and then what?

He sighed, and scratched the dog's ears. "Aw, hells bells," he said. "Maybe I am keeping him." Then he turned and looked at her, gauging something.

"My sister invited us over for dinner tomorrow. Are you game?"

She stared at him. He might be keeping the dog. His sister had invited *them* for dinner. Everything was changing and deepening in the most exciting and terrifying of ways.

"Did you tell your sister about me?" she asked, something pounding in her chest. She knew from the way he looked when he talked about Della that his sister was the most important person in his world. What would it mean if he had talked to her about Sarah?

He looked sheepish. "Nah. She saw us riding bikes along the river path. She said she nearly drove into the river she was so shocked to see me on a bike. She thinks I don't know how to have fun. What do you think of that?"

"She doesn't know you at all."

He laughed. "She doesn't know what I've become in the last little while."

His eyes rested on hers with *that* look in them. The one that made her insides feel as if they were turning to goo, the one that made her heart feel as if it was expanding mightily, the one that stirred embers within her to flame.

"I'd love to go for dinner with you at your sister's house," she said.

He nodded, looked out at the river. "That's what I was afraid of."

She knew then that he felt it, too. They were caught in something as powerful as the current of that river.

"Where do you think that stick will end up?" she asked him.

It was a dot now in the distance. She thought of it ending up in a green field a long way away, a child picking it up and throwing it again. Maybe it would make it to the ocean, drift out to sea, end up in a foreign land. The possibilities, for the stick and for her life, seemed infinite and exciting.

"Probably going to go over a waterfall," he said, "and be pulverized."

Sarah felt the smallest chill.

"I have to go," she said reluctantly. "Committee meetings. Are you coming?"

"No, I better go get ready for work."

Still, it amazed her how often he did come, it amazed her how quickly and effortlessly he won the respect of his neighbors, how he belonged.

She was aware that, more and more, they were seen as a couple and couldn't suppress the thrill it gave her.

She walked into the meeting feeling as if she was still trembling from the lingering kiss he had planted on her all-too-willing lips down there by the river before they said goodbye.

* * *

"Oooh, look who's in love," Candy teased her.

Sarah had only just discovered it herself and felt embarrassed that she was telegraphing it to the whole town.

"I'm not in love," she protested, but weakly.

Candy just laughed. "Talk about a perfect ending to the story! Drowning dog brings beautiful couple together. And then they keep the dog!"

"Oh, stop, we're nowhere near a couple."

"Look, when you go to Hombre's on a Saturday night in Kettle Bend, and order one milkshake with two straws? That's official."

"You heard about that?" Sarah said.

"I even know what you were wearing."

"Stop it. You don't!"

"White safari-style shirt, black capris, and the whole outfit saved from being completely boring by candy-floss pink ballet-style shoes."

"Oh my God."

"That's small towns, Sarah. Everybody knows everything, usually before you know it yourself. So, you can tell me you're not in love all you want. The glow in your cheeks and the sparkle in your eyes are telling me something quite different. Have you named the dog yet?"

"No." But suddenly it felt so big, that she had to tell someone. She leaned toward Candy. "But I think he *is* going to keep him."

Candy laughed. "I never had a doubt! Like I said, the perfect happy ending."

* * *

The next night, Sarah met Della and Jonathon for the first time. Della had made spaghetti, and if Sarah was worried about awkward moments, she needn't have been.

Between Jet and Ralf chasing the dog through the house, and then making spaghetti the messiest meal ever, she was not sure she had ever laughed so hard.

Sarah was astounded by the level of comfort she felt in this house. Because Oliver had brought her, she was, no questions asked, part of an inner circle she had always longed to belong to.

Family.

Sarah marveled at the feeling of closeness. There was plenty of good-natured kidding around the table, but no put-downs. Oliver and Jonathon had an easy rapport, and he and Della obviously shared a remarkable bond.

Della asked her brother to put the kids to bed, while she and her husband did the dishes.

"You go with him, too, Sarah."

They went into the boys' bedroom together. There was a single bed on one side of the room and a crib on the other.

With the baby nuzzled against her chest, Jet propped up the pillows on his bed. Impossibly they all squeezed onto Jet's skinny little bed, she on one side of the little boy, and Oliver on the other. The dog tried to join them, and looked stubborn when Oliver told him no. Then he tried to crawl under the bed, and they all clung to the rocking surface until the dog figured out he wouldn't fit, and sulkily settled at the end of the bed instead.

Finally, everyone was settled and Jet carefully chose a book.

"This one," he said, and Oliver took the book from him.

Oliver was a great reader. With his nephew snuggled under his arm, they all listened raptly as the story unfolded. Within seconds the baby fell asleep, melting into the softness of her chest.

She stole a look at Oliver and felt a yearning so strong it was like getting caught in a current that you had no hope of fighting against.

If you had no hope of fighting against it, why not just relax and enjoy the ride?

She let his rich voice wash over her. She let the sensory experience flood into her: his dark head bent over his nephew's, his hand turning the pages.

After her relationship with Mike, she had tried to convince herself she could live without this.

Now she knew she could not. This was what she wanted.

No, it was more than that.

This was what she *needed*. This was the life she had to have for herself.

When the story was done, Oliver took the sleeping baby from her, settled him in his crib, Ralf's little rear pointed at the ceiling, his thumb in his mouth.

For a moment, they stood there, together, frozen in a moment of perfection.

Then they joined Della and Jonathon on the back deck sipping coffee and watching the stars come out.

"I never saw the stars in Detroit," Della said, and Sarah was aware of how the other woman's hand crept into her husband's.

Jonathon's leg was still in a cast, but if he had any resentment toward Della for the fact he worked so far away, it certainly didn't show. He looked like a man overjoyed to give his wife the stars. Who would drive a hundred miles a day to do it for her.

The conversation was easy.

Sarah simply loved watching Oliver with his sister. Playful, teasing, protective. This was the real Oliver, with no guards up.

Later, she and Della sat at the table, the men had moved away to the back of the yard, the tips of cigars winking against the blackness of the night.

"How come you call your brother Sullivan?" Sarah asked.

"To tell you the truth, I'm amazed he lets you call him Oliver."

"Why?"

"He's never really been called Oliver. Even in school, he was always called Sullivan, or Sully."

"Even by you?"

"Threatened to cut my pigtails off while I slept if I ever told anyone his name was Oliver."

"Why?"

"Who knows? Somebody must have teased him. The school had produced *Oliver Twist* and he was probably tired of hearing *Consider yourself at home*."

For a moment, Sarah heard the jingle inside her head. *Consider yourself at home. Consider yourself one of the family…*

The feeling she had wanted her whole life. And had felt, for the first time, in the past few days.

"My dad always called him a nickname, Sun, *s-u-n*, not *s-o-n*. He said the day Oliver was born the sun came out in his life and never went back down. I was Rainbow, for the same reason."

Sarah felt the love of it, the closeness of this family, felt the full impact of the tragedy that had disrupted their lives.

"My mom called him Oliver," Della continued softly. "She was the only one who ever did. After she died, he seemed even more sensitive to people calling him that. I think it reminds him of all he lost that night. Which is why it surprises me that you call him that." Her voice trailed off, and she studied Sarah.

"Oh," Della said, and her eyes widened.

"Oh, what?"

"You're just good for him, that's all. I couldn't believe that was him, when I saw you guys riding your bikes by the river." Della looked out over the yard, a small, satisfied smile playing across her pretty face. Contented. "Denise wasn't good for him. Thank God they never had kids."

"Denise?" Sarah asked, startled.

Della looked surprised. "Oh! I would have thought he'd told you about his ex-wife. I'm sorry. I shouldn't have mentioned it.

Oliver had been married? And he had never told

her? Sarah felt the shock of it. Oliver knew everything there was to know about her. Everything. He knew about her childhood and her father's philandering and her poor choice of a man to share her future and dreams with.

Over the past days she had told him about dead pets, disastrous dates, her senior prom and her favorite movie of all time.

How was it she felt so close to him, and yet, when she thought about it, he still had revealed relatively little about himself?

A wife in his past? Sarah felt stunned. When she had first seen him with his nephews, she had concluded he was a man who would be fiercely devoted when he decided to commit.

Getting to know him, she had concluded he would be a man who would take *forever* seriously, a man incapable of breaking a vow.

She felt the wrongness of her conclusions slide up and down her spine, reminding her she had been wrong once before.

She had been wrong about Mike, not listening to the subtle clues he had given of his growing dissatisfaction with their relationship.

Hadn't Oliver been giving her clues, too? Not naming the dog, for one. For another, he had told her point-blank he was attachmentphobic.

Why had she chosen to ignore all that?

Charmed, obviously, by *this*. By being invited to meet his family. By long walks with the dog. By making rhubarb jam together and watching hockey.

So charmed she had deliberately not seen the truth?

Suddenly, in the quiet of the night, they heard a cell phone ring.

"I hope he doesn't answer that," his sister said.

But they both heard Oliver say hello, and Della sighed. "I'll bet it has something to do with work. And I bet he'll go." She turned and looked hard at Sarah. "How will you feel about that? Because that's what finished Denise."

Denise again.

Sarah was suddenly uncertain that it even mattered how she felt about it! But she answered, anyway, a little stiffness in her voice, "I've figured out his work isn't what he does. It's who he is."

Della didn't seem to hear the stiffness. She gave her a smile that until that moment had been reserved just for Oliver, and then she gave Sarah a quick, hard hug that renewed her longing to be part of a unit called family.

But had that very longing made her blind? Just as it had before?

Chapter 8

Sullivan listened to the voice on the phone. "You heard *what*?"

From the porch, he could hear his sister and Sarah laughing, and turned his back away from the compelling sound of it.

Della adored Sarah. He could tell. Is that why he had brought her here? Obviously bringing a girl to his sister's was a big step.

Akin to posting banns at the church, now that he thought about it.

Why hadn't he thought about that before? It was unlike him not to think situations completely through. Why hadn't he thought that both his sister and Sarah were going to read things into his arrival here with her that he might not have intended?

In that moment when they had climbed into that tiny bed, on either side of Jet, Sarah with the sleepy baby cuddled into her chest, he had seen that same look on her face that he recognized from the first time she had held Ralf.

Whether she knew it or not, this is what she wanted out of life.

But what had shocked him, what had come out of left field and whacked him up the side of his head was this thought: *it was what he wanted, too.*

Suddenly, he knew what terrible weakness had allowed him to not think things through, to bring her to his sister's.

He had fallen in love with Sarah McDougall.

It was just wrong. He had nothing to bring to a relationship. He had seen and experienced too much darkness. Not just seen it, sought it out. It had seeped into him, like drinking toxic waste. It had made him hard and cold and cynical, as ready to believe bad about his fellow man as Sarah was ready to see the good.

A girl like Sarah needed a guy like his brother-in-law, Jonathon. One of those uncomplicated, regular, reliable guys, with no dark past. Jonathon was a third-generation orthodontist. Jonathon had learned as soon as he started breathing what family was all about: safety, security, happiness, routines, traditions.

Sullivan and Della had learned those things, too. But the difference was they both knew how those things could be ripped from you.

Jonathon knew Della's history, but he didn't *feel* it.

Jonathon didn't really believe that your whole life could be shattered in the blink of an eye. He didn't carry the knowledge that a man could not really control his world. Sullivan carried that knowledge deep inside himself like a festering wound.

Jonathon naively believed that his strength and his character and his ability to provide were enough to protect his family.

And Della? His sister was courageous enough to have embraced love even knowing life made no promises, even knowing happily-ever-after was not always the outcome, not even if that's what you wanted the most.

Sullivan did not kid himself that he had anything approaching his sister's courage.

"Thanks for calling," Sullivan said, and clicked off the phone.

"Everything all right?" Jonathon asked.

"Not really," Sullivan said. He had known what had to be done before the phone call. He had known as soon as he had sat on that bed beside Sarah, reading stories to his nephews. He had known as soon as he acknowledged the truth.

He had to say goodbye to her.

The phone call had just given him a way to do it. Bradley Moore had found out Sullivan was keeping the dog.

Only one person in the world had known that. One.

His anger was real. But this was the part he couldn't let her see.

He wasn't really angry at her. No, Sullivan was angry with himself. For letting this little slip of a woman slide by his defenses. For letting things develop between them when he had absolutely no right to do that, when he had nothing to bring to the table. He'd buried his parents and failed at one marriage already. In his final case as a homicide detective he had seen—and done—things that he could not forget.

This is what he brought to the table.

An inability to trust life.

Sarah sharing a deeply personal moment of his life with Bradley Moore, using it to her advantage, only confirmed what he already knew.

He couldn't really trust anyone.

Least of all himself.

Walking up from the back of the yard, toward the light, toward the warmth and laughter of the two women on the back deck, felt like the longest walk of his life.

Sarah turned and watched him coming across the yard, something troubled in her face as he came into the circle of the backyard light. As if she knew something was shifting in him, between them.

He had come to like how Sarah looked at him, lighting up as if the sun had come up in her world. The way she was looking at him now, tentatively, as if she was trying to decide something, made him aware he was already missing that other look, the one a man could find himself living for.

But a man had to deserve that. He would have to prove himself worthy of it every day.

A man would want to protect her from anything bad ever happening.

And because of what he had dealt with every single day of his working life, Sullivan knew that was an impossible task. He could not even protect her from himself, let alone forces out of his control.

Well, yes, he could protect her from himself. By doing what needed to be done. He took a deep breath and walked up the stairs.

"Sarah, we have to go." He heard the tightness in his own voice.

So did Della. So did Sarah. He saw it register, instantly, with both of them that something was wrong. He hardened himself to the concern on their faces.

"Sorry, Della. A nice night, thank you."

He whistled for the dog, who came groggily out of the boys' room. When it looked like Sarah intended to linger over goodbyes, he cut her short, took her by the elbow and hustled her out to the car.

It occurred to Sarah that the coldness wafting off Oliver like a fast-approaching Arctic front was being directed at her. She jerked her arm away from him. She wasn't exactly feeling warm and fuzzy toward him, either.

"What is wrong with you?" she demanded.

"Get in the car." He opened the back door and the dog slid in, looking as apprehensive as she felt.

He drove silently, his mouth set in a firm line. She glanced at his face once, then looked out the window.

His expression reminded her of their first meeting. The barriers were up. *Do not cross.*

Sarah folded her arms over her chest and decided she did not have the least interest in mollifying him. Or prying the reason for his bad mood out of him! Let him stew!

Still, because his bad temper was crackling in the air around him despite his silence—or maybe because of it—her heart was racing. It felt as if the current she had been caught in was moving faster and not in a nice way. Swirling with dark secrets and things unsaid, moving them toward the rapids that could break everything apart.

Finally, he pulled up in front of her house.

His voice tight, he said, "That call I took at Della's was from Bradley Moore, the news anchor who did the follow-up story."

"I know who Bradley Moore is," she said.

"Of course you do," he said silkily.

"What does that mean?" she exclaimed.

"He said with Summer Fest just around the corner, how would I like to do one more interview?"

"That's good, isn't it?"

"No, it isn't. He wants to talk to me about my decision to adopt the dog. I've only told one person in the whole world I was thinking of taking that dog," he said quietly. "You couldn't wait to turn that to your advantage, could you? Your stupid festival meant more to you than protecting my privacy."

"How could you even say that?" Sarah asked, stunned. She hardly knew what to address first, she felt so bewildered by the change in him.

Her stupid festival?

"The facts speak for themselves. You were the only one who knew and now Bradley Moore knows."

It was his detective's voice, hard, cool, filled with deductive reasoning that she found hateful since it was finding *her* guilty without a trial.

Candy had told Bradley, Sarah thought, sickly. But how dare this man think the worst of her? After all the times they had spent together, he had to know her better than that! He had to.

But obviously, he, who guarded his own secrets so carefully, didn't have a clue who she really was. Any more than she had a clue who *he* really was!

Bewilderment and shock were fueling her own sense of betrayal and anger.

"The facts do speak for themselves," she said, tightly. "And I've been mulling over a discovery of my own. Like the fact you have an ex-wife. When did you plan on telling me that?"

If she had expected shock in his features, she was disappointed. He looked cold and uncaring, his features closed to her.

"I didn't see any reason for you to know that," he shot back. "I don't really like wallowing in my failures."

"Is that how you saw the things I confided in you?" she asked, incensed. "Wallowing in my failures? I saw it as building trust. Apparently that was a one-way street!"

"Which was probably wise on my part, given where trusting you has gotten me! Imagine if I'd told you about my ex-wife, and the reason I left my job in Detroit. I'd probably be reading about my very worst moments in a sad story designed to bring more people to Summer Fest!" he accused.

"You are the most arrogant, pigheaded moron of a man I have ever met!"

"I already knew those things about myself. You're the only one who's surprised."

Sarah got out of the car regally. She was shaking she was so angry. She was aware they had squabbled in the past. Enjoyed lively arguments. This was different. This was their first real fight.

"Don't forget to take *your* dog with you," he said tightly.

"I can't have a dog," she said. "I have a cat."

"I'm sure they'll sort it out."

Should she read something into that? That things could get sorted out? That if creatures as opposite as a cat and a dog could work it out, so could they?

Still too angry to even cry, Sarah opened the back door and called the dog out.

"Towanda, come here."

Inwardly she begged for him to comment that he didn't like the name. That he didn't approve.

But he just sat there like a stone.

She slammed his car door with a little more force than was necessary, and watched Oliver drive away.

Only when he was completely out of sight, did she finally burst into tears. The dog whined, and licked her hand, then got up and pulled hard on the leash, trying pathetically, heartbreakingly, to do exactly what she wanted to do.

To follow Oliver down whatever road he took her on.

"Have some pride, girl," she told herself fiercely.

He would figure it out. That it wasn't her who had told Bradley. He would come around. He would tell her about his ex-wife, and why he had left his job in Detroit.

Sarah tried to convince herself it was an important part of their developing relationship to have a real disagreement, to see how they worked through things.

Soon she would know if they could pop out the other side of the rapids and float back onto a more peaceful stretch of water. He would apologize for jumping to conclusions about who had leaked his secret to Bradley. He would open up about his life before her, confide in her and tell her about his previous marriage, tell her about what had made him leave his job.

Failures, he had called them.

She hated the sympathy that tugged at her breast when she thought of him using those words.

He was a man who would not like to fail. At all. At anything.

She was sure he would feel better once he confided in her. She was also sure that something deep and real had happened between them and that he would not be able to resist coming to her.

But as days turned to a week, Sarah began to face the possibility that while she was waiting for them to come through the rapids, he was seeing them as already over the falls.

Pulverized.

There was plenty of proof in her house that things did not always work out. That opposites could not always find common ground. The dog and cat hated each other. If Sarah had contemplated that she might keep the puppy herself, a reminder of those sunshiny days of early summer with Oliver, a house full of destroyed furniture and broken glass from dog-chase-cat fracases was convincing her it was not a good idea.

Maybe remembering Oliver wasn't going to be such a good idea, either. There was no explaining the depth of her anguish when she would go to bed at night, contemplating that one more day had passed. He had not phoned. He was not going to phone.

Or bump into her by accident.

Or show up at her door with flowers and an apology.

It was over.

Sarah did the only thing she knew how to do to dull the sharp edges of the emptiness he had left in her life.

She buried herself in work, in relentless activity. She walked the dog six times a day, carefully avoiding places she and Oliver had taken him. If she hoped it would drain off the puppy's energy so he would give up on tormenting the cat, she was wrong.

She began to produce jam like a maniac, trying to ignore the fact that her kitchen had become a painful place, memories of them running around the island, snapping towels at each other crowded into every corner.

She attended every committee meeting, monitoring the progress of every function. She was helping build floats and stands for the marketplace. She was putting up colorful banners on the parade route and picking up programs from the printer.

Despite the smile she pasted to her face, she felt sure everyone knew something was wrong, and everyone, thankfully, was too kind to say anything.

After spending the days trying to exhaust herself, every night with jars of freshly canned jam lining her cupboard, and the exhausted dog snoozing at her feet, Sarah sorted through the mountains of new requests delivered to her house from Kettle Bend City Hall.

It seemed all the world had watched the clip of Oliver rescuing that dog, and at least half the world his follow-up interview where he said the dog had not yet been claimed.

Now everybody wanted to adopt the dog. How was it that sorting through all these requests had fallen on *her*?

"Possession is nine tenths of the law," the city hall clerk had said, dropping off a sack of mail.

Some of it was addressed only to Kettle Bend, Wisconsin. Feeling responsible for finding the perfect home for the dog, since she could not keep him, Sarah forced herself to read every single letter, even though it was ultimately as heartbreaking as the fact she had not heard from Oliver.

She, who was trying desperately to regain her cynicism about dreams coming true, seemed to be having the reality of her dream shoved in her face routinely. These perfect, loving families were everywhere.

They were in small towns and in big cities, on farms and on ranches and living beside lakes or in the mountains.

Photos fell out of some the letters. One sent a photo of the dog who had died and they missed so terribly. She read heart-wrenching letters from children saying how much they wanted that dog. She looked at crayon drawings of dogs. A dog bone fell out of one fat envelope.

She had to make a decision, for the dog's own good. He wasn't getting any younger. He was in his formative stage. He needed a good home. One without a cat!

But in her mind, though there were obviously many homes that fit her picture of perfection, in her heart he was Oliver's dog. She couldn't even stick with calling him Towanda, not just because it didn't really suit him, and not just because it would not be fair to name the dog in a burst of mean-spiritedness.

She could not name the dog, because in her heart it was Oliver's job to name him.

But she also knew she could not keep the dog from the family it deserved for much longer.

When Barry Bushnell called, frantic because the parade was days away and they still had not agreed on a grand marshal for the parade, Sarah gave up on her dream that Oliver would come around.

She had always, in the back of her mind, thought she could convince him to be the parade marshal.

She had always, in the back of her mind, felt she could convince him to love her.

What kind of love was that? Where you had to convince someone to love you?

To Barry, she said, "Let's make the dog the grand marshal of the parade. He's the one who got us all the publicity. Visitors would love to see him. And," she steeled herself, "on the final day of the festival, right after the fireworks, we'll announce what family the dog is going to."

"Brilliant," Barry breathed with satisfaction. "Absolutely brilliant."

But if it was so brilliant, Sarah wondered, why did she feel so bereft?

In fact, going into the final frenzy of activity before the parade, Sarah was aware that Summer Fest was going to succeed beyond her wildest dreams. Accommodations in the town were booked solid. The crowd was arriving along the parade route in record numbers.

With all this growing evidence of her success, she was all too aware that she was plagued by a sense of emptiness.

On parade morning, the committee begged her to ride on the town float. But she didn't want to. Instead, she managed to lose herself in the crowd along the parade route and watched, emotionless, as the opening band came through, followed by a troop of clowns on motorcycles.

It was a perfect, cloudless day, not too hot yet. The streets had been cleaned to sparkling. Fresh flower baskets hung from light posts. Stores had decorated their windows.

Kettle Bend had never looked better.

She looked at the people crowding the parade route around her. It was just as she had planned it. Families together, children shrieking their delight at the antics of the clowns, grandmothers tapping their toes in time to the music of the passing bands. Candy apples and cotton candy—both Summer Fest fundraisers—were selling by the ton.

But as she looked at the Kettle Bend float, Sarah was aware of fighting a desire to weep. All the people she had worked with to make this day a reality were on that float, smiling, waving. She had become so close to these people. How was it she felt so sad?

The truth hit her. You could not make a town your family.

She had learned that at Della's house. *That* was what a family felt like. There was simply no replacement for it. Love had perils. Love hurt.

And in the end, wasn't it worth it? Didn't it make you become everything you were ever meant to be?

Sarah felt the hair on the back of her neck rise, and she sought out the reason.

Standing behind her, and a little to the left, she saw Oliver. She was pretty sure he had not seen her.

Like her, he had chosen to blend into the crowd.

He was not in uniform, he had a ball cap pulled low over his eyes, and sunglasses on.

He did not want to be recognized.

He did not want to play the role of hero.

He had never wanted to do that. She had thrust it upon him. She had thrust a whole life upon him that he had not wanted.

But maybe she had not completely thrust things on him. Why was he here today? Watching a parade did not seem an activity he would choose for himself.

Was it possible he missed the sense of belonging he'd felt when he'd joined her in the committee rooms? Was it possible he had read in the paper the dog would be the parade marshal? Was it possible he was reluctantly curious to see how it had all turned out?

Was it possible he wanted to see how it had turned out for her?

Of course, that would imply he cared, and the silence of her telephone implied something else.

Still, she could not tear her eyes away from him.

When a great shout of approval went up from the crowd around her, followed by thunderous applause, she glanced only briefly back at the parade route.

The dog was happily ensconced in the backseat of a white convertible, tongue lolling and tail flapping. The mayor was beside him, one arm around him, the other waving. The crowd went wild.

Then the dog spotted Oliver and jumped to his back legs, front paws over the side of the car, ready to leap. The mayor was caught by surprise, but managed to catch the dog's collar just in time. He pulled him back onto the seat beside him.

Sarah watched Oliver's face. She felt what was left of her heart break in two when she saw him watching the dog.

He took off his sunglasses and she could see the absolute truth in the darkness of his eyes. The memory of every single time they had ever spent together flashed across his face. She could see them throwing that pink Frisbee, feeding the dog popcorn that first night they had watched hockey together, and pizza the second.

In Oliver's eyes, she saw them chasing one another around the kitchen island, walking by the river, the dog cowering when he threw the stick into the water. In his eyes, she saw that last night they had spent together, saw them on the bed with his two nephews, the bed heaving up as the dog tried to get underneath it.

Oliver suddenly glanced over and saw her watching him. He held her gaze for a moment, defiant, daring her to *know* what she had seen. His expression became schooled, giving away nothing. And then he slipped the sunglasses back over his eyes, turned and disappeared into the crowd.

She stood there for a moment, frozen by what she had just seen.

The truth.

And she knew, as she had always known, that loving Oliver was going to require bravery from her. She could not hide from the potential of rejection, from the possibility of being hurt.

That day she had gone up the steps with the dog, she had found the place inside her that was brave.

She knew it was there. She was going to have to try again. Laying everything she had on the line this time. She could not hold anything back. She could not protect herself from potential hurt, from the possibility of pain.

Real love had to go in there and get him.

But for now she had to let him go. The Market Place was opening right after the parade, and she had her booth to get ready.

Without staying to watch the rest of the parade, she, like Oliver slipped into the crowd.

The Market Place was both exhausting and rewarding. Throngs moved through it. Sarah had samples of jam for tasting on crackers, and between keeping her sample tray filled and putting sold jars of jam in bags, she could barely keep up.

A man stood in front of her. Good-looking. Well-dressed. She offered him the sample plate, turned to help another customer.

When she turned back, he pressed a card into her hand. "Call me," he said, and smiled.

Once, she would have been intrigued by that kind of invitation. Now, she just gave him a tired smile and slipped the card into her pocket.

She actually was able to laugh at herself when she took the card out of her pocket later that night.

The name Gray Hedley rose off it, finely embossed. Underneath was the well-known logo for Smackers Jam.

Misreading men again, she chided herself. *Whatever he wanted, it probably was not a date.*

It seemed like a very long time ago, a lifetime ago, that she had mistaken another man's invitation for a date.

It was time.

It was time to find out if there was anything at all in her world left to hope for. When she had seen Oliver's face this morning at the parade, she had dared to think there was.

Now, dialing his number with trembling fingers, she was just not so sure.

She knew he had call display, and so she was both astonished and pleased when he answered.

He'd known it was her, and he had answered anyway.

"Hello, Oliver."

"Sarah."

Her whole being shivered from the way her name sounded on his lips. There was no anger there, not now. Something else. Something he was trying to hide.

"Congratulations on a successful first day of Summer Fest." His voice was impersonal. Polite. But guarded.

But she knew that the fact he'd even answered the phone when he had known it was her was some kind of victory.

She felt like she had so much to tell him. She felt

the terrible loneliness of not having someone to share her triumphs and truths with.

"Oliver," she said quietly, firmly. "We need to talk."

Silence.

And then, "All right." Chilly. Giving away nothing.

Yet for him, just saying "all right" was a surrender. She hung up the phone and dared to feel a flicker of hope. That flicker felt like a light winking in the distance, guiding a traveler, weary and cold, toward home.

Chapter 9

Sullivan watched as Sarah came up his front walk. She had brought the dog with her. He wished he had thought to tell her not to bring the dog.

On the other hand, she might read into it what he least wanted her to read. It was what he had known all along.

She might know then that he had become attached and she might guess the truth.

Attachments made a man weak. Love didn't make a man strong. It made him long for what he knew the world could not give, a way to hang on to those feelings forever. There was no forever.

Not for him. Over the course of his career he had seen it way too many times. Love lying shattered.

Maybe for her, if she found the right guy, like

his sister had found Jonathon, maybe there would be hope for Sarah. She could believe in love if she wanted. Yes, a nice orthodontist would be perfect for her. He should ask Jonathon to find her one.

Never mind that the thought of her with someone else made Sullivan feel sick to his stomach. That's what needed to be done.

He had always been that man. The one who did what needed to be done.

And he would do it again now.

He would send her away from him, back into the world where she belonged, where she could dream her secret dreams of wedding dresses and picket fences, babes against her breast.

The lie had not driven her away, the lie that he was angry with her about word getting out to Bradley Moore that he was going to keep the dog.

The lie had not done it. He'd thought it had. One day without her becoming another, the emptiness of his life made rawly apparent by her absence.

Then, always the brave one, she had phoned.

So he had no choice left. He had to count on the truth to do what the lie had not. He would show Sarah who he really was and it would scare her right back into her little jam-filled world.

He couldn't think, not right now, *but she doesn't like making jam*. He could not think one thing that would make him weak when he needed strength as he had never ever needed it before.

He opened the door before she knocked.

He hoped what he felt didn't show on his face.

She couldn't know that he loved her little pink dress with the purple polka dots on it. She couldn't know that he wanted to smell her hair one last time. She couldn't know he had to hold back from scratching the dog behind its ears.

She could *never* know his heart welcomed her.

Sullivan took a step back from the truth that shone naked in her face. A truth more frightening to him than any truth about himself that he could tell her.

Just in case he'd got it wrong, just in case he had misread that look on her face, she said it.

She stepped toward him, looked into his face, and he hoped his expression was cold and unyielding. But if it was, it didn't faze her.

Sarah did what he'd come to expect her to do. She did the bravest thing of all. She made herself vulnerable to him.

"I've missed you so much," she said with quiet intensity.

I've missed you, too. It has felt like my heart was cut in two. But he said nothing, hoping it would stop her.

But she plunged on, searching his face desperately for a response. "Oliver, I love you."

I love you, too. So much I am not going to do what I want to do.

Because what he wanted was to lay his weapons at her feet. Surrender to it. He wanted to gather her in his arms and kiss every inch of her uplifted face.

But loving her, really loving her, meant he had to

let her go. He had to frighten her off once and for all. She deserved so much better than him.

"You'd better come in," he said and stepped back from the door, holding it open for her as she passed him. The dog was exuberant in his greeting, and that desire to lay it all down nearly collapsed him. Instead, he drew in a deep breath and followed her into the living room.

Seeing her there, on his couch, reminded him of the first time she had come in. The towel at his feet. Accusing him of taking his decorating lessons from Al Capone. Making her blush. The day that never ended.

He contemplated what to do next. Offer her a drink? No, that was part of the weakness, prolonging the moment of truth. This was not a social call. This was an ending, and the sooner he got it over with the better for both of them.

He sat across from her in his armchair. "I need to tell you some things."

She nodded, *eagerly*, that's how damn naive she was.

"I was married. In my early twenties. It lasted about as long as a Hollywood wedding with none of the glamour. I didn't tell you, because, frankly, I didn't see the point. I might share my history with someone I planned to have a future with. Otherwise, no."

He saw a tiny victory. She flinched. Some of the bravery leached from her face, replaced with uncertainty.

"You already told me your fiancé had a mistress. Well, I had one, too. That's what destroyed my marriage."

Her mouth dropped open with disbelief. Maybe he should just let her believe that, but then he remembered his truth would be enough to scare her off. He didn't need to make anything up or embellish anything.

"My mistress wasn't a woman," he said quietly. "It was my job. The work I did was not work to me. It was a calling that was worse than a mistress. It was demanding, it took everything I had to give it, and when I thought I had nothing left, it would ask for more. I was young, my wife was young. She had a right to expect she would come first, and she didn't. The work came first.

"This was the part she didn't get. For me, it was never just another violent ending. It was never just another body. It was never just another homicide. It was never just a job.

"It was dreams shattered. It was families changed forever. It was the mother who has been waiting all night for news of her son, and the young wife, pregnant with a child, who fell to the floor howling when she found out her husband was dead.

"To me finding who did it was my life. Nothing else. That's how I honored those who had gone. I found out who did it when I could. I lived with the agony of it when I couldn't."

He gathered himself, glanced at her, frowned at what he saw. She was leaning toward him, her eyes soft on his face, obviously not getting what he was trying to tell her at all.

"But don't you think," she asked him, "that devotion to your calling was because of what happened to your parents? Wasn't every single case about finding who destroyed your family? Wasn't every single case trying to make something change that you never could?"

He stared at her. But if he looked at her too long, he would get lost in her eyes, he would forget what he wanted to do. He didn't want her insights. He didn't want her understanding. He wanted her to get that he lived in a different world than her. That she couldn't come over, and he couldn't go back.

"I've lived and breathed in a world so violent and so ugly it would steal the heart out of you."

Despite the fact she looked sympathetic, she did not look convinced that the world he had moved in could steal her heart. But that was because she was impossibly naive!

"I'm trying to tell you, each case is like a scar for me. Each one took a piece of me, and each one left something inside of me, too. Do you know how many cases I've been on?"

She shook her head, wide-eyed.

"Two hundred and twelve. That's a lot of scars, Sarah."

A mistake to say her name.

Because she took it as an invitation. She left the couch and came and sat on the arm of his chair, one hand resting on his shoulder, the other stroking his hair.

"Some people," she said slowly, "say a painting without shadows is incomplete. Maybe it's the same for a person without scars."

"I'm trying to tell you, you don't know me."

"All right," she said gently. "Tell me more, then."

Something was shifting. He wasn't scaring her off, and yet the words were fighting with each other to get out of him, like water bursting through a broken dam.

"On my last case in Detroit," he continued, relentlessly, needing to say all of it, "after thinking I knew the darkness of the human heart inside out and backward, I found out how dark my own heart was. In that last case, I came face-to-face with my own darkness."

He paused, glanced at her. All that softness. *Don't tell her*, he said to himself. *Spare her the supreme ugliness*. Just kick her out and tell her not to come back.

But he'd already tried that. From the very beginning he had tried to discourage her interest. The only weapon he had left was the truth, and he had to use it. He could not stop now. He was nearly there.

"It started like so many of them. Neighbors heard shots. Cops arrived, knew right away to call us as soon as they stepped in the door.

"You know what they found?"

She shook her head.

"A whole family, dead. The Algards wiped from

the face of the earth. Mommy. Daddy. Five-year-old, three-year-old, two-year-old."

"Oh, Oliver," she said, and pressed her fist into her mouth. If he hoped she was finally starting to get it, the look in her eyes told him he was mistaken. She didn't get it! She still thought she could take some part of it, absolve him.

Why did it feel as if she was? Ah, well, she had not heard the whole sordid tale yet.

"We got it all wrong," he said softly. "We thought it was a gang war. We thought who else could do something like this? We thought they were sending a message to the whole community. Don't cross us, we run the show. Then a high-ranking gang member came to me, ridiculously young, given his status. But when I looked at that boy, I was so aware if Della hadn't saved me from that lifestyle, he would have been me.

"That kid was smart and savvy and a little cocky. Luke. Unapologetic about his affiliations. Said he'd been looking for a family all his life, a place where he could belong, and his gang was it. I can remember his exact words. *We're all just soldiers, man. Lots of kids gettin' sent over to the land of sand, killing people for less than what I kill people for.*

"And then Luke told me his gang didn't kill the Algards. He was disgusted that we would think his gang killed babies, and I had offended his sense of honor. He told me I was looking in the wrong place, and he was going to find out who did it. And you know what? He did. He had contacts and inside channels and the power to intimidate in that community that I could never have. It was humbling how fast he found the truth.

"According to Luke's information, it wasn't a gang thing at all. The perp was my adult male victim's brother. It was a family squabble gone stupidly, insanely, irrevocably wrong.

"Luke said, *I can look after it.* And that's when I found out what a thin, almost invisible line can divide good and bad. That's when I found out the darkness was in me, too. Because I wanted vengeance for that family. For those babies gunned down before they ever knew one thing good. No first day of school. No visit from the tooth fairy. No first kiss, or prom, or graduation, or wedding. I didn't want to trust the outcome to the system. Two hundred and eleven previous cases. I knew, firsthand, things did not always go the way I wanted them to.

"*Twenty-four hours*, he told me. He told me if I hadn't looked after it in twenty-four hours, he would."

"You let him," she whispered, horrified.

Oliver laughed, and it sounded ragged in his own ears. "No, I didn't. I did the right thing. I brought in the brother. Complete confession. He killed his brother in a fit of rage over an argument. And do you know why he killed the rest of them, why he shot those little babies? Because they saw him do it. That's all. Because even that two-year-old baby knew her uncle had killed her daddy."

"So, you did the right thing," she prodded him.

"I guess that depends on how you look at it. Things did not go the way I wanted them to. He walked free and I could not stop thinking of those tiny, defenseless bodies. And thinking about him out on the streets. I could not stop thinking about the opportunity I'd passed on to have things looked after. Up until that point, I'd always felt like the cowboy, always felt like I was on the side of the righteous. But suddenly everything seemed muddy. Then it got worse.

"Within hours of beating the system, the brother faced street justice and it was swift and violent. I knew exactly who killed him. So I did my job. I brought in Luke. And it twisted my world up even further when he did not walk free. He was twenty-three years old and he got life in prison.

"You know what he said to me? *Worth it. We're all just soldiers.* Well, that was the end of me. I felt turned inside out. Who was the good guy? Who was the bad guy? I felt as if I had failed at everything I ever put my hand to. I failed as a cop, I failed as a husband, I failed as a son."

"Failed? You?" She sounded incredulous, still wanting to believe the best of him even though she had now heard the worst. She was still sitting way too close to him. Why hadn't she moved? Couldn't she see he was a man who had lost his moral compass? Who had lost his faith that good could triumph over evil?

"This is what people who have never been exposed to violence don't know. You think about it all the time. You think, *What could I have done to make it different?*"

"You can't possibly believe you could have protected the whole world!"

"No," he said sadly. "You are exactly right. That is the conclusion I have come to. This is what you need to know about me, Sarah McDougall. Other people have a simple faith. They believe if you are good only good things happen to you. They find comfort in believing something bigger runs the show. But I know it's all random, and that a man has no hope against that randomness.

"And that's why I can't be with you, Sarah, why I can't accept the gift of love you have offered me, or ever love you back. Because, despite having taken a few hard knocks yourself, you're still so damned determined to find good. You're a nice girl and I've walked too long with darkness to have anything nice left in me. In time, my darkness will snuff out your light, Sarah. In time, it will."

There, he had said it all. He waited for her to move, to get up off the chair, go to the door, walk out it and not look back.

Inwardly he pleaded that she would take the dog with her.

And then he felt her hand, cool and comforting on the back of his neck. He made himself look at her. But he did not see goodbye in her face. He was nearly blinded by what he saw there.

He had tried so hard to let her go. But she wasn't going. In her face, in the softness of her expression, in the endless compassion of her eyes, he saw what he had been looking for for such a very long time.

Rest.

Sarah stared at the ravaged face of the man she loved. Suddenly she understood the universal appeal of that video she had seen of him jumping in the river to save the dog. She understood exactly why that clip had gone viral, why so many people had watched it.

This man, the one who claimed not to believe in goodness, was the rarest of men. Here was a man willing to live his truth, a man prepared to give his life to protect someone—or something—weaker, vulnerable, in mortal danger.

She saw so clearly that ever since the death of his parents, Oliver had pitted himself against everything wrong in the world. He had given his whole life trying to protect everyone and everything.

No wonder he felt like a failure.

Could he not see that was just too big a job for one man?

With tears in her eyes, she saw another truth. Shining around him. He was willing to give up his life—any chance he had of happiness or love—to protect her from what he thought he was.

And the fact he would do that? It meant he was not what he thought he was. He was not even close.

"I have to tell you something, Oliver Sullivan," she said, and she could hear the strength and certainty in her own voice.

"What's that?"

He had folded his arms over the mightiness of his chest. He had furrowed his brows at her and frowned.

He looked like the warrior that he was.

But it was time for that warrior to come home.

"You are wrong," she said softly. "You are so damned wrong."

"About?"

"The darkness putting out the light. It's the other way around. It has always been the other way around. The light chases away the darkness. Love wins. In the end, love always wins."

"You're hopelessly naive," he snarled.

But she wasn't afraid. She was standing in the light right now. It was pouring out of her.

More importantly, it was pouring out of this good, good man who had given his whole life to trying to protect others and who had not taken one thing for himself.

Well, if it was the last thing she did, she intended to be Oliver Sullivan's one thing.

"I've lived it," he said, his voice tortured. "Sarah, I've lived it. It's not true. Love does not always win."

"Really?" she said softly. "What is this, if it's not love winning?"

She touched his neck, looked into his raised face, and then dropped off the arm of the chair right onto his lap.

"I love you," she said fiercely. "I love every thing about you and I am never, ever going to stop. I've come to get you, Oliver Sullivan. And that *is* love winning."

"You're being foolish," he said gruffly. He did not hold her, but he did not push her away, either.

"You think I would care about you less because of what you just told me?" she laughed. "You're the fool! Oliver, I care about you *more*."

She felt his eyes on her face, searching, and she knew the instant he found truth there. His body suddenly relaxed, and he pulled her deep against him, burying his face in the curve of her neck.

She ran her fingers, tenderly, thought the thickness of his hair, touched her lips to his beautiful forehead, to each of his closed eyes.

"Let me carry it with you," she whispered. "Let me."

After the longest time, she felt him shudder against her, heard him whisper, "Okay."

And she finally let her tears of joy chase down her cheeks and mingle with his.

"Jelly," Oliver called, "Jam. Best you've ever eaten. Cures heartaches!"

"You can't say that!" Sarah chided him, but she was laughing.

He was helping her with her booth at the Market Place. It was the last day of Summer Fest. He had spent every minute since he had told her his truth with Sarah, something in him opening, like a flower after the rain.

They could not bear to say goodbye to one another.

They could not get enough of each other.

Last night, they had even fallen asleep together on her couch, words growing huskier and huskier as they had gotten more tired, finally sleeping with unspoken words on their lips. When he had woken this morning, with her head on his shoulder, her sleepy eyes on his, her hair in a wild tangle of curls, it had felt as if he was in heaven.

So Oliver Sullivan was selling jam—he'd donned an apron to get a rise out of Sarah—and he was having the time of his life. He didn't just sell jam. What was the fun of that? No, he hawked it like an old-time peddler with a magic elixir.

He moved amongst the crowd. He stood on the table. He kissed babies and old ladies.

He was alive.

How could it be that selling jam at a humble little booth set up in what was usually a school yard field could feel as if he was standing on top of a mountain? As if all the world was spread out before him, in all its magnificence, put there just for his enjoyment?

It could feel like that because she was beside him.

Sarah.

Who had listened quietly to his every secret and not been warned off. Who had set him free.

That's what he felt right now. Free.

As if aloneness had been his prison and she had broken him out. As if carrying all those burdens had been like carrying a five-hundred-pound stone around with him, and she, little Sarah, who probably weighed a hundred pounds or so, had been the one strong enough to lift it off of him.

"Excuse me, ma'am? If you'll buy a single jar of the jelly, I will show you how I can walk on my hands."

"Oliver!"

But the lady bought jam, and he walked on his hands, and Sarah laughed and applauded with everyone else. Plus, it attracted quite a crowd, and then they were sold out of jam.

"Come on, sweetheart," he said, putting the Closed sign up on her little booth. "We probably have time to win the three-legged race."

Later, lying in a heap with her underneath him, their legs bound together, nearly choking he was laughing so hard, he wondered if this is what it felt to be a teenager, because he never really had been.

The death of his parents had cast a shadow over the part of his life when he should have been laughing with girls, and stealing kisses, and feeling his heart pound hopefully at the way a certain girl's hand felt in his.

To Oliver Sullivan, it was an unbelievable blessing that he was actually getting to experience a part of life that had been lost to him.

The falling-in-love part.

Because that's what had been happening from the minute he met Sarah. He had been falling for her.

And fighting it.

Now, to just experience it, to not fight it, made him feel on fire with life.

Somehow he and Sarah managed to find their feet, and lurched across the finish line dead last. But the crowd applauded as if they had come first when he kissed her and they did not come up for air for a long, long time!

"I think we could probably win the egg and spoon race," he decided.

"I doubt it," she said.

"Let's try anyway. I like the ending part when we lose."

"Me, too."

Laughing like young children, hands intertwined they ran to the starting line.

For supper, they bought hamburgers with heaps of fried onions and then had cotton candy for dessert. They rode the Ferris wheel, and he kissed her silly when it got stuck at the top.

Then, as the sun set, they went back to his house, briefly, and changed into warmer clothes and grabbed their blankets.

And their dog.

They joined the town on the banks of the Kettle River. People had blankets and lawn chairs set up everywhere. There were families there with little babies and young children. There were young lovers. There were giggling gaggles of girls. Young boys sipped beer from bottles, until they saw him, and then they put it away.

He and Sarah and their dog lay back on their blanket, and as the night cooled they pulled another tight around themselves.

The fireworks started.

It was exactly how he felt inside: exploding with beauty and excitement.

The dog was terrified, and had to get in the blankets with them, his warm body all quivery and slithery.

Sarah, one arm around the dog, leaning into Oliver, looked skyward, her expression one of complete enchantment. When he looked at her face, he saw her truth. He saw in her face she would always believe good things could happen if you wanted it badly enough.

And who was he to say she was wrong? She'd made this happen, hadn't she? The whole town and an unimaginable number of visitors were all sitting here on this warm night enjoying the breathtaking magic of the fireworks because of her. Because she had believed in a vision, trusted in a dream.

She had rescued him, too. Because she had believed in something it would have been so much wiser for her to let go of.

His way had not brought him one iota of happiness. Not one. Being guarded and cynical, expecting the worst? What had that brought him?

He was going to try it her way.

In fact, he knew he was going to try it her way for a very, very long time.

A firework exploded into a million fragments of light above them, and those fragments of light were doubled when they reflected on the quiet black surface of the river.

"I'm going to name the dog," he decided in a quiet place between the boom of the fireworks being set off.

She turned and looked at him, a smile tickling across those gorgeous, kissable lips.

"Moses," he decided.

"I love that. But why Moses?"

"Because I found him floating in the river. Because he led me out of the wilderness, to the promised land."

"What promised land?"

"You."

Right on cue, fireworks exploded in the sky above them, a waterfall of bright sparks of green and blue and red cascading through the sky.

She stared at him, and then she bit her lip, and her eyes sparkled with tears. She reached up and touched his face with such tenderness, such love, and he was humbled.

He knew he would not go back from this place to the place he had been before. He might be strong, but he wasn't strong enough to survive a life that did not include Sarah in it.

"Marry me," he murmured, as the sparks of the firework faded and drifted back toward earth.

Her face was lit by those dying lights.

"Yes," she whispered.

As their lips joined, the sky exploded, once again, into light and sound above them. It was the finale: shooting higher, the sky filling with a frenzy of light and sound and smoke. And as the sound died, the fireworks disintegrated into pinwheels of fiery gold that drifted down through the black sky toward the black water.

Silence followed, and then thunderous applause and cheering.

To Oliver it felt as if the whole earth celebrating this moment. This miracle.

Of the right man and the right woman coming together and having the courage to say yes to what was being offered them.

Maybe all of creation did celebrate the moment when that magnificent force that survived all else, that triumphed over all else, that force that was at the heart of everything, showed itself in the way one man and one woman looked at each other. Maybe it did.

Epilogue

Sarah came into the house, and smiled when she heard the sound. Banging. Cursing. More banging.

She followed the sound up the stairs to the room at the end of the hallway.

She gasped at what she saw. Where there had been worn carpet this morning, now there was hardwood.

Curtains with purple giraffes and green lions cavorting across them were hung on a only slightly bent rod.

Oliver sat on the floor, instructions spread out in front of him, tongue caught between his teeth, crib in a million pieces on the ground. Moses watched from one corner where Sushi had him trapped. She lifted her paw delicately to let the dog know who was boss, and his expression was one of long suffering as he flopped his tail at Sarah in greeting.

Oliver looked up at her. He had sawdust in his hair, and a smudge on his face. His smile did what it had been doing since the moment she said *I do*.

It turned her insides to goo.

"You know," he said, looking back at his instructions, trying to fit a round peg into a square hole, "I remember once I thought home was about rest. I was sadly mistaken. I haven't had a moment's rest since we bought this old junk heap." But he said it with such affection. And it was true. Everywhere in the house they had purchased together was his mark.

He had torn down every wall downstairs to give them a bright, open modern space that was the envy of the entire neighborhood, and especially his sister Della, who lived two doors down.

Oliver was not a natural carpenter or handyman. Sometimes he had to do things two or three times to get them right, sometimes even more. His work around the house involved much effort, cursing, pondering, trying, ripping down, rethinking and then trying again.

The fact that he loved it so, when he was quite terrible at it, made Sarah's heart feel so tender it almost hurt. This man, who had hated failure so much, had become so confident in himself—and in her unconditional love for him—that he failed regularly and shrugged it off with good humor.

That's what love had done for him. Made him so much better, so accepting of his own humanity.

She cherished that about him.

"You didn't have to start on the nursery just yet," Sarah said, and came in and ruffled his hair, flicked some of the sawdust from it. She had never tired of the way that thick hair felt under her fingertips. "We only found out we were pregnant two days ago."

"Ah, well, you know the saying. Don't put off until tomorrow what you can do today. I've been asked to consult on that case in Green Bay. You know me. Once I get going on that." He shook his head with good-humored acceptance of his tendency toward obsession.

She knew him and loved this part of him, still trying to make all that was wrong in the world right. But there was a difference now. Now, he came back into the light after he had spent time dealing with darkness. And let her love heal him.

"What if things don't go right?" she asked, tentatively. "It's a first baby. That's why I thought maybe you should hold off—" she gestured uncertainly around the room "—on all this."

He turned and grinned at her, that smile sweeping away her fears. "Everything is going to be fine," he told her, and his voice was so steady and so confident that she believed him.

Sarah marveled at the fact that Oliver, who had once had so many problems believing life could bring good, was already committed to a good outcome. He already saw a baby in this room and he already loved it with his whole heart and soul.

"I love the curtains. Where did you find that fabric?" She went and touched it, felt teary that he could pick such a thing, that he could know it was just right. Then again, teary was the order of the day!

"Is the rod a little crooked?" he asked, cocking his head at it.

"Um, maybe just a hair."

"I'll fix it later. I got the fabric at Babyland."

"You went to Babyland?" she asked, incredulous that her husband had visited the new store on main street.

"Why so surprised?"

"It hardly seems like a place the state's most consulted expert on homicide would hang out. Or the new deputy chief. There's probably some kind of cop rule against it. You are going to be teased unmercifully."

"Just don't tell your big-mouth friend, Candy, or Bradley Moore will be calling for the inside scoop on the new deputy chief. Could you hand me that wrench?"

She wandered back over, handed it to him. "Oliver?"

"Huh?"

"Are we going to the parade tomorrow?"

"Oh, yeah. The parade, the picnic, the fireworks." He slid a look at her. "Are you disappointed by the new format?"

This year by unanimous vote, Summer Fest had been made a one-day event, all on the Fourth of July.

"No," Sarah said. "I know the four days just cost too much money, and it was too hard to get volunteers to run all the events. I know my great idea was given a fair trial, two years in a row, and it didn't even come close to saving the town, Oliver. You don't have to be gentle with me."

"Ah, Sarah, you still saved the town."

"I did not!"

But she had saved *him*. Somehow, inside herself she had found the courage to rescue Oliver Sullivan. Maybe even in a larger world, in the bigger picture, she had only thought she was rescuing the town, that thought leading her to where she really needed to be.

"I don't know," Oliver said. "When you sold out Jelly Jeans and Jammies to Smackers and they bought the old factory on Mill Street, they brought a lot of work and money to this town. Eighty employees, at last count. And you know, those articles you write for *Travel* and *Small Town Charm* do more than their fair share of mentioning Kettle Bend. No wonder we have a Babyland on the main street! No wonder Jonathon is opening an office here."

"And then," she said, "there's our most famous citizen."

Moses gazed at her adoringly, looked like he might come over, and then cast a look at the cat, and decided against it. He flopped his tail again.

Moses still got fan mail, he and Oliver were still asked to do follow-up interviews. That whole incident at the river somehow had captured people's hearts and minds and imaginations.

Why?

Sarah thought it stood for good things happening in a world where currents could take you by surprise and sweep you away. It stood for good coming from bad.

It let the world know there were still men who would sacrifice themselves for those who needed them.

And who had needed Oliver more than her?

That was the most wonderful irony in all of it. She had thought she was rescuing him.

In fact, he had rescued her.

The past two years had been beyond anything she could have ever dreamed for herself. Sarah woke in the morning with a song in her heart.

"I'm the luckiest woman in the world," Sarah said, "that you fell in love with me."

She had his full attention. He did that little thing he did. He took her hand, kissed it and then blew on where his lips had been.

"Oh, you are so wrong. I never fell in love with you, Mrs. Sullivan."

"Fine time to tell me now that you've got me knocked up," she teased. She loved more than anything else these moments between them. Ordinary, but not ordinary. The best moments of all. When it seemed like nothing was happening, and yet everything was.

"Love isn't something you fall into," Oliver said, letting go of her hand and eyeing the instructions. He frowned at the crib panel that was definitely on upside down, and possibly backward, too.

He abandoned it suddenly, got up, swept her into

his arms and kissed her until she couldn't breathe. Then, looking deep into her eyes, he said, "Love is a choice. It's a daily choice of how to live."

Live love.

He rested his hand on her stomach. There wasn't even a baby bump there yet. She touched his face, relaxed against him, and was sure she felt the new life stir within her.

There was a pure exhilaration in the simplicity of the shared moment that rose within her, and headed like an arrow into the dazzling future.

* * * * *

Katie Meyer is a Florida native with a firm belief in happy endings. A former veterinary technician and dog trainer, she now spends her days homeschooling her children, writing and snuggling with her pets. Her guilty pleasures include good chocolate, *Downton Abbey* and cheap champagne. Preferably all at once. She looks to her parents' whirlwind romance and her own happy marriage for her romantic inspiration.

Books by Katie Meyer

Harlequin Special Edition

Proposals in Paradise

A Wedding Worth Waiting For

Paradise Animal Clinic

Do You Take This Daddy?
A Valentine for the Veterinarian
The Puppy Proposal

Visit the Author Profile page
at Harlequin.com for more titles.

DO YOU TAKE THIS DADDY?

Katie Meyer

This book is dedicated to

My husband,
for the countless weekends he took kid duty so
I could write. (And for never mentioning all the book
purchases that show up on our bank statement.)

A big thank-you also to the Romance Divas
and all my writing friends who helped me
wrangle this book into submission.

And as always, my gratitude goes to my agent,
editors and the entire Harlequin team.
I couldn't do it without them.

Chapter 1

It definitely wasn't the worst honeymoon on record, Noah James decided. That honor belonged to the unhappily married couple behind him, who had already argued about everything from who got the window seat to what where to make dinner reservations when they landed. Sure, he might be flying solo on the way to what should have been his honeymoon, but there were some good points of being jilted practically at the altar. Like two weeks in Paradise, Florida, stretching out in front of him, with no one to answer to other than himself. Unlike the newlyweds in the next row, he could eat when he wanted, go where he wanted, and do his own thing.

It wasn't as if his heart had been broken, although his ego had taken a pretty good beating. Dating Angela had been a mistake from the beginning. But breaking up with her wasn't an option, not after she'd shown him the test with the two pink lines. In that instant, his stomach had dropped and his world had turned upside down. Just like that, Angela went from a fling to a fiancée. She might not have been what he'd hoped for in a bride, but there was no way he was going to miss out on raising his child.

He'd been there to hear the heartbeat, chugging along. He'd squinted at the ultrasound pictures, unable to understand any of it but overwhelmed all the same. And he'd been there to feel the first kicks, the first tiny movements of his unborn son. Except it hadn't been his son at all.

Two days ago, Angela had disappeared, leaving her ring and a note after helping herself to a good portion of his available cash. Her written apology had been brief, as if she'd eaten the last cookie rather than torn apart his life. Some other guy was the father-to-be, and he'd been nothing but an easy mark for yet another gold digger.

He probably should have been embarrassed, but more than anything he just felt empty inside. Not that he missed Angela. The spoiled socialite had seemed fun at first, but her true colors had eventually come out and he was nothing but grateful to have avoided being legally bound to her. But losing his son, or what he thought was his son, had left him aimless and confused.

Finding out it was too late to get refunds on anything had given him the excuse he needed to get out of town, and away from prying eyes. He'd turned what should have been their honeymoon into a bachelor's vacation. He'd get his head on straight and come back to Atlanta ready to focus on his work. His art had suffered during the constant storm of his relationship, and it was time to recommit to it, while the name Noah James still meant something in the art world. Otherwise he'd have an ex-career to go with his ex-fiancée.

"Sir, would you care for a cocktail?" The flight attendant waited expectantly, a bevy of liquor bottles and mixers on her cart.

"I don't think so. Water will be fine." He'd never been a drinker, and ten thousand feet in the air seemed like a poor place to take up the practice. The pretty attendant started to hand him a plastic bottle, but had to move aside to let a mother carrying a fussy baby past. The child stared at him with big blue eyes while chewing intently on a drool covered fist, and Noah's gut clenched.

"I'm so sorry," the frazzled mother apologized. "He's teething, and walking the aisles is the only thing that seems to calm him."

Noah forced a smile. "It's fine." He even waved at the little guy as the mom turned to go back the way she came, and was rewarded with a gummy grin that cut right to his heart, stirring up the pain he'd tried to bury.

Maybe he'd have that cocktail after all. "Miss, could you switch that to a whiskey and coke?"

* * *

Noah meant to have one drink, just to take the edge off. He certainly hadn't planned on getting drunk. But seeing that baby had reminded him a bit too much of the mess his life had turned into, and before he knew it he had an impressive collection of tiny liquor bottles covering his seat tray. Which meant he was most definitely drunk. Or whatever came after that. Snookered? Wasn't that what the British called it? He was pretty sure he'd heard that on *Sherlock* once. Whatever you wanted to call it, it felt pretty amazing. The only problem was he was finding it just a wee bit difficult to walk. Also, he'd planned on renting a car while at the airport, but driving was most definitely out of the question. Luckily, a very nice security guard had been on hand to pour him into a cab.

Now that car was stopped in a gravel driveway fronting a three-story wood-framed building. Hanging from the wraparound porch was a sign, identifying it as the historic Sandpiper Inn. The perfect location for a destination wedding or honeymoon, at least according to the brochure he'd memorized. Hopefully it was also a decent place to sleep off a binge.

The driver unloaded Noah's suitcase from the trunk, and happily accepted the crush of bills he gave him for a tip. It was probably too much, but he was in no shape to do the math, and it wasn't like money was an issue.

No, his issues were far more complicated.

The most pressing being the way the ground kept shifting under his feet. Clutching his bag, he tried to navigate the wide, whitewashed stairs leading to the front door.

Tried, and failed.

Two steps up, and he was on his butt. At least, with all the liquid courage he'd imbibed, it didn't hurt. In fact, everything felt a bit numb. Maybe he should just stay put until he sobered up a bit. He'd planned on relaxing and might as well start now.

"Hey, are you all right down there?"

He looked around. No one. Man, was he starting to hallucinate?

"Do you need some help?"

This time, he managed to focus his not-so-steady vision in the direction of the voice. Up on the porch, sitting on a cushioned bench, was the most amazing woman he'd ever seen. She had short, close-cropped brown hair framing an elfin face. Her large brown eyes were too big for the rest of her, and were currently zeroed in on him, and his not-so-stable perch on the steps.

"You're gorgeous." Oops. He was pretty sure he just said that out loud.

Her laugh confirmed that yes, he had. Stupid alcohol.

"Are you drunk?" She stood up and started down the stairs towards him. Her legs were long and lean, sprinkled with the same freckles that dotted her nose. She stopped beside him, and he nearly toppled over trying to look directly up at her.

"Could you not be so tall?" he asked, politely, he thought.

"Sure." She chuckled again and sat down on the steps next to him. "You are drunk, aren't you?"

"I guess so." He might as well admit it. "See, the thing is, I don't drink."

She eyed him skeptically. "Right."

"I mean, I don't normally drink. But today I did. A lot, I think."

"Yeah, I think that's a safe guess." She smirked. "Well, you'll sober up, I imagine, but you can't do it here. Jillian sent me to keep an eye out for some guests who booked the honeymoon suite, so she could give them a special welcome. And I don't think a drunk guy collapsed on the steps is quite the welcome she had in mind."

"No worries," he reassured her. "That's me. I'm the couple you're looking for." He stuck out a hand for her to shake. She took it, eyeing him curiously. "Noah James."

"Mollie Post, nice to meet you." She looked past him onto the path below. "But where's your wife? Is she taking a walk on the beach or something?"

"She's not coming." The buzz must be wearing off, because that sounded pathetic even to him.

"What do you mean, she's not coming? You can't have a honeymoon without the bride."

She probably thought he was confused because of the whole drunk thing. But on this particular point he was perfectly clear. "Then call this a first. No bride. No wedding, for that matter. She took off before the rehearsal dinner." The pleasant numbness from earlier was replaced by a pounding in his head.

Her mouth dropped open. "Wow, that sucks."

Her frank acknowledgment did more than all the softly worded platitudes he'd heard in the past week. "Yeah, it does suck. But I figured it could suck back home, where everyone kept asking me if I was okay every two minutes. Or it could suck here, on the beach, with a margarita in my hand." His stomach lurched. "Although, I think I'll skip the margaritas."

Mollie watched the newcomer with fascination. She didn't care much for alcohol herself, but she wasn't bothered by his blatant drunkenness. He seemed harmless enough, and Nic and Jillian were right inside. Besides, he looked like he needed a friend. So she sat on the sun warmed steps with him, watching a flock of white ibises pick their way across the lawn.

He was certainly nice enough to look at, a long, lean body and slightly curly brown hair that was just a shade too long. His face was almost beautiful, with high cheekbones. But it was his eyes that really got to her, dark and hooded; they were the kind of eyes that saw things other people didn't. The eyes of an old soul, her Granny would have said. She wondered what his story was.

"You're staring."

"So? You're interesting to look at."

He blinked, and then let out a hoot of laughter. "Do you always say just what you're thinking?"

"Pretty much. I'm told I have no filter." She shrugged. "I tried, for a while, to learn to say the right things. But it never really stuck."

"I'm glad it didn't. Not many people are willing, or able, to be that honest. It's a good thing."

"Most people don't think so. My fifth grade catechism teacher found it particularly upsetting." She winked conspiratorially. "She smelled funny."

He winced. "You told her that?"

"I thought she'd want to know. Turns out, not so much. People are funny that way. Most of the time, they don't want the truth."

"Yeah, well sometimes the truth is painful." He stretched, sprawling his lanky legs in front of him.

"Oops. Sorry. Yeah, I guess you've had your share of truth for the time being, huh?"

"You have no idea."

"So tell me." She stood up. "We can get some dinner, get you some water to flush out the booze, and you can tell me how you ended up on your non-honeymoon." Gossip usually wasn't her thing, but he looked like he could use someone to talk to. And she never had been able to turn her back on a stray.

His boyish grin was a startling contrast to his soulful eyes. "Did you just ask me out on a date?"

She hadn't, had she? "No, I don't date. But I'm hungry, you need to eat something to soak up the rest of the alcohol and I want to hear your story. New friends having dinner, not a date."

"You don't date at all?" He squinted at her, as if

he expected to see some kind of physical sign to explain her celibacy.

"It's a long story, and I'm starving. Ask me again later."

"Shouldn't I get checked in first?"

"That depends. Can you make it up the steps yet?"

He looked up and shook his head. "Good point. Dinner it is. Where's your car?"

She wasn't one to let common sense interfere with an adventure, but even she had limits. "No car—we're going to walk. There's a place just down the beach path." A popular place for an evening stroll, with plenty of people around just in case her instincts about him were wrong.

"Afraid to be alone with me?"

Caution was part of it. Her parents might think she was naive, but she knew not to get into a car with someone she'd just met, even if she was the one driving. But there was another, more pressing reason.

"I'm just afraid you might puke in my car."

Noah would have laughed, but she looked pretty serious. And who could blame her? Luckily, he wasn't feeling nauseated, just weak and dehydrated. And more than a little foolish. He couldn't remember the last time he'd had more than a single beer. And yet he here was, too messed up to drive, being led around like a child. In other circumstances, he would have been humiliated. But even after seeing him at his weakest, Mollie hadn't given him a hard time. Sure, she'd laughed at him, but in a teasing way that had him laughing along with her.

She'd walked down those steps and treated him like a friend, not a stranger. He'd grown up always being the new kid, and even as an adult he usually felt like an outsider. His art had opened some doors, but having new money wasn't the same as fitting in. If anything, he felt even more awkward now, shoved into a rarified world, than he had when he was an army brat, bouncing from place to place. People might be more polite to his face now that he'd made something of himself, but celebrity hadn't bought him any true friends. Being welcomed and accepted right off the bat, that was something new.

They walked for about fifteen minutes along a gravel path that started behind the Sandpiper and ran alongside the dunes, and although they'd passed plenty of other walkers he hadn't seen anything that looked like a restaurant. "Where are you taking me, anyway?"

She winked. "Afraid I'm going to kidnap you?"

"Afraid, no. Hoping, yes."

She grinned. "Sorry, no such luck. But how do you feel about Cuban food?"

"I don't think I've ever tried it, but I'm hungry enough to eat anything." His stomach growled as if to emphasize his point.

"Well, then, you're in luck. We're almost there."

Another minute of walking brought them to their destination, which was more of a roadside stand than a real restaurant. A simple wooden structure, the walls were covered in a brightly colored mural, except for right above the order window where a menu board advertised the specials. There were a few tables scattered in front, topped with brightly colored umbrellas, and wafting on the breeze was the most amazing smell. "I think I'm about to start drooling."

She smiled. "Best Cuban food for miles, and coffee that will make you think you've died and gone to heaven."

Looking at her had him thinking he was already there. She'd blown him away from the beginning and it wasn't a case of beer goggles. In fact, the more he sobered up, the better she looked. She was tiny, at least eight inches shorter than his own six feet, with a slender, birdlike build. But it was her face that captivated him, the bone structure so fine it looked like she'd been sculpted by an artist's hand.

"I'll have the *ropa vieja*, and he needs a *medianoche* with a side of *maduros*. Oh, and a colada and a bottle of water." The man behind the window nodded, writing down the order.

He nudged her to the side, and got out his wallet. "Let me buy, please."

She motioned him forward. "Be my guest."

He paid what seemed like way too little and accepted a bag stuffed with food and the bottle of water in exchange. Mollie grabbed a full Styrofoam cup and two smaller, empty plastic ones. They picked a table farther back from the path and sat down facing each other.

'Okay, so tell me what I just paid for."

"My company?" At his pointed look, she took pity on him and started opening packages. "I got the *ropa vieja*. It's shredded beef, and it comes with rice. Your *medianoche* is a pork sandwich on a soft, sweet bread." She unwrapped it for him while she talked. "The name means midnight, because it's usually eaten when you are out partying and drinking. I figured it would be perfect for soaking up the last of the alcohol. The *maduros* are fried sweet plantains, and the colada is kind of like espresso, but with sugar."

Coffee sounded amazing. He reached for it, only to have her block him, putting her hand over the cup.

"First some food and water, then coffee."

"Anyone ever tell you you're kind of bossy?"

"All the time." She dug into her food, closing her eyes in bliss. "This is so good. How's your sandwich?"

He took an experimental bite. The salty pork and pickles vied with the cheese and mustard for top billing in his mouth. "Amazing." He took another bite, considering. "The bread's a bit like the challah my grandmother used to make. I like it."

"Challah? Are you Jewish, then?"

"My *bubbe* was, and my mom. My dad's Catholic. One item on a long list of things they disagreed on. I'm the only person I know that had to go to both confirmation classes and Hebrew school. Religion was just one more way to fight with each other without actually getting divorced."

"Wow. That's kind of crazy." She snagged another

plantain from the bag. "The weirdest thing my parents ever did was putting up the Christmas tree the day before Thanksgiving one year, instead of the day after."

"They sound very…sane."

"If by sane, you mean utterly normal and conforming, yes. I'm definitely the black sheep of the family."

"That sounds better than the constant fighting at my house. Maybe we should trade."

Finishing his sandwich, he tentatively tried one of the plantains. Slightly crisp on the outside, soft on the inside, and sweeter than he'd expected. He quickly grabbed another before Mollie could finish off the container.

When he couldn't fit in another bite, he stretched and looked around. The haze of his earlier imbibing was gone, and he realized that although the restaurant itself was modest, the scenery was spectacular. Dunes stretched for what seemed like miles, and beyond them he could see the deep blue of the ocean. Sprawling trees dotted the landscape, with huge green leaves the size of dinner plates. "What are those trees with the giant leaves? The ones growing right in the sand?"

"They're called sea grapes. Those big leaves help block any light from the town that might disturb nesting sea turtles. In the summer they grow these berries that look almost like grapes that the birds go nuts for. And of course the roots help stabilize the dunes, so they don't just blow away." She poured coffee into the two small cups. "It's beautiful, but there's a lot of strength there, too."

Somehow, he had a feeling the same could be said about her.

Mollie wasn't blind; she'd noticed the way he looked at her. She just wasn't sure what to do about it. She should probably just walk him back to the Sandpiper, then go home and clean her house or something. That would be the practical thing to do. Of course, as the black sheep of he family, practical wasn't really her speed. Despite her mother's best efforts to the contrary. No, Mollie believed in going with her gut, and her gut was saying it was way to early to say good night. "How do you feel about a swim?"

He looked down at his faded T-shirt and jeans. "Now? I'm not exactly dressed for it."

"Not here, back at the Sandpiper. I'm assuming you packed a bathing suit?"

He grinned. "What, no skinny-dipping on the first date?"

Oh, boy. He was cute and he had a sense of humor. And was totally on the rebound. She was in deep trouble. But in for a penny, in for a pound. "I'll take that as a yes. I've got one in the car, so while you get checked in I can duck into Jillian's room and change."

"Jillian?"

"Jillian Caruso. She and her husband, Nic, own

the Sandpiper. They have a private suite on the first floor."

"Ah, when I made the reservations, Nic mentioned he'd gotten married recently." He stood and collected their trash, disposing of it in the labeled bin. "I don't think I would want to live where I worked, with the public just a few doors away all the time."

"Yeah, it's not ideal. But they're building a separate house on the property, so they can have some privacy. Plus, with the baby coming, they'll need the space."

His smile faded at the mention of a child.

"What, don't you like kids?"

"Actually, I do. Up until a few days ago, I thought I was having one."

She sat back down on the picnic bench. "Excuse me?"

He rubbed a hand across the stubble on his jaw. "My ex-fiancée is pregnant—she's due in a month."

"But it's not your baby?"

He shook his head. "When she ran out on me, she left me a note. It said she couldn't go through with the wedding and that I shouldn't try to find her. Of course, she might have said that last part because of the money she took out of my account before she left." Shoving his hands in his pockets, he started back towards the Sandpiper. "She also admitted the baby wasn't mine."

Shell-shocked, Mollie just sat there for a minute, watching him walk away. Getting dumped was bad enough, but this was like something out of a daytime talk show. Belatedly getting to her feet, she ran to catch up with him.

What did you say after an admission like that? Maybe it was better not to say anything. He was a stranger and probably didn't need some random girl poking into his life. On the other hand, sometimes it was easier to talk about the hard things with someone you didn't know. And she wasn't good at keeping quiet anyway. "Do you believe her?"

He sighed, looking out over the water as if the answer to her question could be found along the horizon. "I don't know. I guess I have to. I don't even know where she went, and I don't know why she'd lie about it. Not that I understand much about why she did what she did. We never should have been together in the first place. She was a friend of a friend, no one I knew well, and it didn't take long to figure out we had nothing in common. But by then she was pregnant, and in the shock of it all I made a bad situation worse and proposed." A harsh laugh escaped. "It seemed like the honorable thing to do, you know? But the more I got to know her, the less I could picture us married. We spent the last several months living mostly separate lives. At least she had the guts to realize it wouldn't work. I was too stubborn to admit it."

"Because you thought she was pregnant with your child."

"Exactly. As much as I wasn't in love with her, I wanted to be there for my son." He stopped, and a hint of a smile touched his lips. "I was there when they did the ultrasound. It's a boy."

"So what do you do now?"

"There's not much I can do. I hired an investigator. If he finds her, I'll get a court order for a DNA test. But he doesn't sound very hopeful."

"That sucks."

He rubbed a hand through his hair, shoving it back in a burst of frustration. "Yeah, it does. But I couldn't just sit around my apartment, feeling sorry for myself. I was going to go crazy."

"So you came here."

He shrugged. "I still had the tickets and it was too late to get a refund."

She walked beside him in silence, feeling his betrayal and confusion. Maybe she'd only known him a couple of hours, but there had been an instant connection as soon as she'd seen him on the stairs at the inn. He was like a wild animal that'd been abused, beautiful and proud but hurting inside. She couldn't fix his life, but maybe she could help him forget a bit, at least while he was here. Sometimes a distraction was almost as good as a cure.

At the Sandpiper, she stopped in the gravel lot to retrieve her bathing suit. She unlocked the trunk and swung her backpack over her shoulder before taking the path to the front door.

"Does everyone in Florida keep an emergency bathing suit in their car? The way people up north keep blankets in theirs?"

"Not everyone. But I do, in case I want to go for a swim after work or on my lunch break."

Noah's single suitcase was on the covered porch where the cab driver had left it. He grabbed it with one hand and held the door for her with the other. "Wait, you go to the beach on your lunch break?"

"Sure, it's only five minutes from the clinic I work at. I can change, have a half-hour swim, then eat a sandwich in the car on the way back to work."

He shook his head and smiled. "No wonder they call this place Paradise."

Mollie left Noah at the front desk with Jillian while she went to change into her suit. Ducking into the master suite, she noticed the new hardwood flooring in the halls and fresh paint on the walls. Nic was doing a great job restoring the old inn. Of course, she was happy that Jillian had such an incredible place to live, but the whole idea of marriage and babies seemed so grown-up and responsible. She wasn't ready for all that yet. She'd seen what raising a family had done to her mother's dreams—her professional dance career had ended before it really began—and Mollie wasn't going to let that happen to her.

Which was why she didn't date. Dating led to relationships—first comes love, then comes marriage, then comes Mollie with a baby carriage. No, thank you. She had things she wanted to accomplish, and getting sucked into the mommy track wasn't in the plans.

Jillian poked her head around the door. "Hey, I just checked in a Noah James. He said you two are heading to the beach?"

"Yeah, we're going to get in a swim before dark."

Jillian's eyebrows rose. "You know he was supposed to be here on his honeymoon, right? He's on the rebound, hard-core."

Mollie rolled her eyes. "I'm not sleeping with the guy—we're just going swimming. I found him on the front steps earlier, and we ended up getting a bite to eat at Rolando's. He seemed like he could use some cheering up." She reached back to adjust the tie of her bikini top, torn between sharing his story with her friend and protecting his privacy.

Jillian's expression softened. "Yeah, I guess he does. I don't know very much about him—he dealt with Nic when he made the reservations. They know each other, though, from some welding project he worked on for Caruso Hotels. Nic says he's a good guy, but still, be careful, okay? I know you never turn away a stray, but you don't want to get wrapped up in that level of drama."

Be careful. Safety first. Look before you leap. Why did everyone feel the need to say things like that to her? She was twenty-six, not twelve. She was getting tired of everyone she knew treating her like she couldn't handle herself just because she led her life a little differently. So what if she ate sushi for breakfast sometimes or preferred thrift-store T-shirts to business casual? And yeah, she had daydreamed and doodled her way through high school, but not everyone could be the straight-A student her sister was. She'd graduated just the same, and if her choice to focus on the arts rather than something practical was a risk, it was one she was willing to take. Her goal was to live life without regrets, to follow whatever adventure came along.

Maybe that's why she'd been so ready to take a chance and invite Noah to dinner. A small rebellion against all the caution signs surrounding her. Or maybe he was just that intriguing. Whatever it was, she wasn't backing off. Her gut told her he needed a friend right now, and despite what everyone seemed to think, her gut was usually right.

"We're going for a swim, not robbing a bank. I'll only be a stone's throw from your back door. Heck, you can send Nic to find us if we aren't back in a few hours." She threw the backpack on her shoulder and headed for the door.

"I might just do that." She grinned. "But in the meantime, he's lucky to have you to introduce him to Paradise Isle. He couldn't ask for a better tour guide."

"Well, when you've never been anywhere else, you get a good appreciation for a place." She shrugged. "But thanks. I'll see you later."

She found Noah waiting for her out back. Nothing like watching a man's mouth fall open to boost the ego. She didn't have the curves of a supermodel, but her new push-up bikini top seemed to be working just fine. "You can put your tongue back in your mouth now."

He chuckled. "I'll apologize for staring if you want, but it would be a lie."

She understood his predicament. She was doing some ogling herself, taking in all six-foot something of him. She'd known he was tall and broad-shouldered, but she hadn't anticipated all the lean, tanned muscles he'd been hiding under his street clothes. Jillian was right—this man was no stray.

"Shall we?" He gestured for her to pass, and she padded down the sandy wooden steps, the boards still warm from the heat of the day. Summer had barely started, but the temperatures were already in the eighties. At the bottom she paused for him to take off his shoes; she'd stashed hers in her backpack when she changed.

"You can just leave your shoes next to the steps. No one will touch them."

He didn't argue, and she gave him a mental bonus point. Not all guys tolerated being told what to do. The sand was hot under their feet, but when they neared the water it phased it out. "Just so you know, the water is still pretty cold this early in the year. By August it will be like bathwater, but for now it's a bit bracing." Then, grabbing his hand, she pulled him in with her.

"Whoa, you weren't kidding. This is freezing." He stopped her when they were about chest deep. Well, chest deep for her; he was significantly taller.

"You'll get used to it." She released his hand and leaned back to let herself float, her body rocked by the calm swells. Nothing was better than this. It was that magical time of evening when the day was over but night hadn't quite taken hold yet. The sky was an abstract ballet of colors dancing in the light, changing minute by minute as the sun dropped. If she had to be stuck in one place forever, Paradise Isle wasn't a bad choice. But she didn't plan on staying stuck.

Turning her head, she could see Noah floating beside her, as mesmerized by the view as she was. Moving on instinct, she reached out and took his hand, sucking in a breath at the buzz of attraction that sparked between them. She'd meant to show him a bit of the peace that Paradise had to offer. Instead, he was creating his own version of chaos in her world.

The cold Atlantic water had washed away the last lingering effects of the alcohol, leaving Noah feeling more clear-headed than he had in days. Maybe longer. Everything had gone haywire the minute he'd met Angela. At first her need for excitement had been fun, the constant parties a way to let loose after the months of work he'd put into his latest project. But then the drama started. Late-night fights over nothing, constant demands for attention. She thought that a man of his fame, who had been touted as one of Atlanta's most eligible bachelors, would live an extravagant life and spend lots of money, preferably on her. His modest lifestyle had been a shock, and any attraction had faded quickly, on both their parts. But the drama had lingered until the final day, with fights over everything from what car he drove to where they were going to live.

Mollie tugged at his hand. "You aren't brooding over there, are you?"

"Are you kidding? I'm literally in Paradise, hanging out with a beautiful woman, watching the sun set. What do I have to brood about?"

She blushed at his compliment, a faint pink creeping across her face. He liked that behind her boldness, there was an innocence about her, too. There was no cunning or guile with her. "How long have you lived here?"

"All my life," she answered easily. "Actually, I was born on the mainland, at Palmetto Hospital, but only because the Paradise Medical Center wasn't built yet. I've been an islander since I was a few days old."

"Seriously?" He couldn't imagine living in one place your whole life.

"Yeah, I'm a native. How about you—where are you from?"

He never knew how to answer that question. "Everywhere. Nowhere."

She stood, wiping at the water dripping down her face. "That's not an answer."

He stood, too, a full head above her. "I'm not trying to be evasive. I just don't have a good answer. I was born in Colorado, but I've lived in more places than I can remember. Dad's army, so we moved every few years. I think the longest I stayed in one place was four years, and that was in college."

She tilted her head, considering him with those big brown eyes that seemed to see more than they should. "Was it hard? Moving all the time?"

A dozen different goodbyes flashed through his head. "Yeah. It was hard."

She ran a hand up his arm, her fingers leaving a trail of saltwater and awareness. "I'm sorry." Her voice was as warm as her touch, drawing him in.

"Don't be. I had just as many hellos as goodbyes." He moved closer until he could feel her slick skin pressed against him.

She tipped her chin up, her gaze locked on his. "Well then, I guess we could consider this a hello."

He could make a joke, laugh it off and swim back. He probably should. He hadn't so much as looked at another woman since he met Angela, even though they'd had separate bedrooms for the past six months. But there was a single drop of water clinging to Mollie's lip and he just had to have a taste.

Slowly, giving her time to stop him, he leaned down and pressed his lips to hers. She tasted of salt water and sweetness, like the taffy he'd had at a carnival as a kid. She floated in his arms as they kissed, the waves washing against them while he feasted on her mouth. He wanted more, to take her right there, to feel her from the inside out while the first stars of the night peaked through the sky.

Mollie pulled away, leaving him with her taste clinging to his lips. "This is crazy."

"It doesn't feel crazy." It felt incredible.

"Despite the fact that you're on the rebound and I don't date?"

"Well, yeah, aside from that. Are you sure you don't date?" She was pretty and fun and could have her pick of guys. So why was she off the market?

She nodded, bobbing in the water. "Very sure. No offense, but men have a way of getting in a woman's way when it comes to a career. I've got too much I want to do to risk getting distracted by a relationship."

She had a good point, but something in him wanted to try to change her mind. Maybe it was the months of celibacy talking or the need to forget all the crazy parts of his life, at least for a few minutes. Whatever it was, he didn't want to say goodbye, not yet. "I don't know, distractions can be fun."

She shivered. The sun had fully set now, and the air was no longer warm enough to make up for the cold water. "Nice try, but I don't even know you."

"Sure you do. You know I'm a military brat, my parents are crazy, and I can't hold my liquor. What more is there?"

She splashed him. "I mean, I don't know where you live, what you do for a living, if you have any pets, that kind of thing."

"To be fair, I don't know any of that about you, either. But I'm willing to keep making out anyway." His body didn't care about any of that stuff. And the rest of him was too spellbound to think straight.

"How very generous of you." She was shivering again.

Taking her hand again, he waded up to the shore. He wrapped her in one of the soft, oversize towels they had left there and then rubbed himself down.

"You're like ice. We need to get you into some dry clothes."

She rolled her eyes. "One minute you're acting like you want me out of my clothes, the next you want me to put more on. I can't win with you."

"Very funny. Come on." He led the way to the steps and onto the deck, then held the door for her to go inside."

She hesitated. "I'm not going up to your room with you."

He hadn't expected she would. But he wasn't ready to let her walk out of his life yet, either. "Mollie—"

"No, wait, I've been thinking. You said you want to get your mind off things while you're here, right?"

"Yeah, I guess. But that doesn't mean I expect you to—"

She smacked him. "Get your mind out of the gutter. No, I was going to say, why don't you let me show you around while you're here, be your personal vacation guide?"

Was she serious? "What about your work, or whatever?" He didn't know what she did, but she must have some kind of responsibilities.

"I've actually already got the week off from school and work."

"School?" He'd thought she was in her midtwenties, just a bit younger than him.

She shrugged. "I take college classes at night, and I arranged my vacation hours at work to match up with the break between the fall and summer semesters. So I've got the time." She blinked those big eyes at him. "I'm not suggesting anything, well, romantic—I'm not looking for a relationship, and I don't do one-night stands. But I'd like to be your friend while you're here. If you're interested."

Interested in spending a week in Paradise in the company of a beautiful woman? "I can't think of anything I'd like better."

Mollie sipped her coffee and checked the kitschy black-and-white cat clock hanging on her living room wall. It was almost nine o'clock; Noah should be there any minute. As if on cue, she heard a car pull into the driveway. Nerves flopping in her stomach, she quickly smeared on some tinted lip gloss. Makeup so wasn't her thing, but after that kiss last night, soft lips seemed more of a priority than they had before. Not that she was planning to kiss him again. Still, better safe than sorry.

She opened the door before he could knock and was struck again by that feeling of awareness that had tickled her senses from the first time she saw him. It was a bit like the tingle before a lightning storm, a warning of the heat and power to come.

He was dressed casually, in a pair of cargo shorts and a gray army T-shirt, and had a bag from Sandcastle Bakery in his hand. "Ooh, breakfast?"

"If you consider a variety of sugary pastries

breakfast, then yes. I had the cabdriver stop on the way here."

"That's the very best kind of breakfast. Let me get some plates." She led him into her tiny kitchen and handed him the plates. "Do you want coffee or orange juice?"

"As a Florida tourist, I think I'm required to at least try the orange juice."

"Good point." She poured a glass for him, and then motioned to the back door. "We can eat on the patio."

He reached the door before she did and started to open it, only to slam it closed again.

That was odd. "What are you doing?"

He swallowed hard. "This is going to sound crazy, but do you have bears around here?"

"What? No way. They see them over near Orlando and Ocala, but we don't have bears on the island." A thought occurred to her. "Wait, you haven't been drinking again, have you?" If he had some kind of problem, she needed to know now.

"No, I'm telling you, there's something out there in the bushes. Something big."

Realization dawned. Oops.

"Yeah, about that…" She pushed past him and opened the door, letting out a whistle.

"Are you crazy?"

"Hey, I'm not the one seeing imaginary bears." She pointed and he peered around her. Out of the bushes came her large, but not quite bear-sized, dog.

"Holy cow, what is that? And why does he only have three legs?"

"That's Baby, and you be nice to him. He might be big, but he's sensitive."

Noah's eyes widened. "He's yours?"

"It's more that I'm his. But don't worry. He's a total sweetie. He just looks intimidating, right, boy?" The massive dog trotted over on and sniffed the bakery bag.

"If I give him the donuts, will it keep him from eating me?" To his credit, Noah hadn't retreated back into the house, but his color looked a bit pale.

"He's not going to eat you. And he's not allowed any donuts. He's on a diet."

"So you're saying he's hungry? Great. That's just great."

She shook her head. "I can't believe you're afraid of dogs."

"That's not a dog," he protested. "Beagles are dogs. Cocker spaniels are dogs. That's a—"

"Mastiff. An English mastiff, to be exact. And he wouldn't hurt a fly, so stop acting like he's the big bad wolf. You're going to hurt his feelings." She rubbed the big dog's head and took the pastries from Noah. Immediately, the dog left him and followed her, nosing hopefully at the bag. "I said no. You already had your breakfast, and Cassie says if you don't lose weight you're going to end up with arthritis. Go lie down."

Chastised, the oversize canine shambled off to lie in the grass. She put the bag on the bright blue picnic table and sat in one of the mismatched chairs. Noah cautiously joined her, keeping his attention on the now-snoozing beast. "So, what happened to his other leg? And who is Cassie, some kind of doggie-diet guru?"

"Cassie's my boss. She's a veterinarian. She and her father own the clinic I work at. As for Baby, a rescue group we work with brought him in when he was just a puppy. He'd been hit by a car over in Cocoa Beach and one of the volunteers found him. We fixed him up, and when no one claimed him I got to bring him home."

"So you work at a veterinary clinic? Are you some kind of animal nurse or something?"

She finished the bite of donut she was chewing. "No, that would be Jillian. She's the veterinary technician. I'm the receptionist. Oh, and I teach obedience classes on the weekends."

"Is that what you always wanted to do, work with animals?"

"Not as a career, no. I do like the dog-training part of it—I don't want to give that up. But working in an office, any office, for the rest of my life would suffocate me eventually."

"Well, what are you going to school for?"

"I'm only going part-time, but I'm a photography major, much to my parents' disappointment." She grimaced. "They're glad I finally went back to school, but they think I should do something practical, like accounting."

"But that puts you right back in the office all day."

"Exactly."

"Okay, so forget them. What do you want to do?"

Right this second, what she wanted to do was to lick the powdered sugar off his lips. But that probably wasn't the answer he was looking for. "What I'd love to do is travel, take pictures, maybe work for a magazine. I want to make a name for myself as a nature photographer. But as my parents have repeatedly pointed out, art isn't exactly a practical career choice."

"Photography, huh? Can I see some of your pictures?"

She hesitated. She always felt so vulnerable, showing her work to a new person. And with him, for whatever reason, the nerves were multiplied.

"Please? You show me yours, I'll show you mine."

If that was a pickup line, it was awful. "Show me what?"

"My sculptures. Well, photos of them. I might have some on my phone of the most recent one, or you can just look it up online."

"Excuse me?" Sculpture. Her stomach dropped. Oh no. He couldn't be. She pulled her cell phone out of her pocket and started frantically typing. At the top of the search results was Noah James, metal sculpture artist. She clicked on the link and there he was, in a photo taken at the grand opening of the Caruso Hotel in Las Vegas. Behind him was the sculpture the hotel had commissioned for the lobby, an abstract swirl of metal twining at least ten feet high.

She held the phone out and showed him the photo. "You made that? Jillian told me you were a welder!"

"I did make that, and I am a welder."

She shook her head in frustration. "No, you're not. I mean, I'm sure welding is involved, but you're one of the most famous metal artists in the country." Hadn't a celebrity magazine included him as one of its sexiest men alive last year? She remembered only because he'd been the only artist in a list of politicians, actors, and pop stars. But he'd had a beard then; no wonder she hadn't recognized him right away. That, and well, famous people didn't tend to show up in small towns like Paradise. She looked down at the screen again, trying to understand how the man sitting across from her could be the man in the article. "This says your last sculpture sold for almost a quarter of a million dollars! I thought you welded rebar for building foundations or something. Why didn't you tell me?" She tossed the phone down, and covered her face with her hands. "Oh my God, I made out with Noah James. *The* Noah James." Holy crap. Girls like her did not go around kissing famous millionaires. So much for him being a stray in need of a helping hand.

He reached over to pry her hands away. "I didn't tell you because it didn't matter. I'm still the same pathetic guy you found on the steps yesterday."

She rolled her eyes. "You might be the same guy, but from where I sit your bank account just got a lot bigger. For crying out loud, I fed you food from a roadside stand." She paused, considering. "Although, I will say, I feel better now about making you pay for dinner."

* * *

He hoped his financial status wasn't going to change things for her. He was happier here, eating donuts from a sack than he'd ever been at fancy galas or exhibitions. A few high-dollar sales hadn't changed who he was or what he wanted. And right now, he wanted to see her photos. He'd bet money she was better than she thought she was. Her house and garden reflected an innate understanding of color and light. Even her mismatched furniture showed an artistic flair. "So, are you going to show me some of your work, or not?"

She looked at him. "After finding out you're a famous artist? No way. My ego isn't ready for that kind of scrutiny, not this early in the morning."

Eager as he was, pressing her would probably do more harm than good. "Fine, then let's get started with whatever's first on the tour. What are we doing today? Swimming, Jet Skiing, sightseeing?"

She shook her head. "Nope, today we're fishing."

"You mean, with worms and stuff?" He hadn't been fishing in years, and had never really enjoyed it. Sitting on the edge of some muddy pond doing nothing for hours on end didn't sound like much fun. Of course, he'd never had her for company before.

"No worms. You'll have fun, guaranteed, or your money back."

"Easy to say when I'm not paying you anything anyway."

She winked. "Exactly. And if we want to actually catch anything, we need to hurry. Once it really heats up, the fish stop biting." She stood and gathered their breakfast remains. "Baby, come on. Time to go."

The big dog stood and shook himself, then loped over, panting and wagging his tail.

"He's going with us?"

"Oh yeah, he loves to fish. He goes nuts when he sees the poles. We can't leave him behind."

Of course not. That would be crazy. After all, who wouldn't want to spend their vacation fishing with a moose-sized three-legged dog? He eyeballed him again. "Does he even fit in the car?"

"Sure he does, but the longer we stand here talking about it, the less time we have to actually fish."

That had kind of been the point. But he'd asked her to give him the real island experience and if that meant fishing, well, then, he'd fish. Fishing with her would be better than doing pretty much anything without her. "By all means, let's go then."

She stacked the dishes in the sink, then came back out and locked the door. A small detached garage was beside the house, and she ducked into it, telling him to wait. A minute later she was back with two fishing poles, a long leash, a bulky camera bag and what must be a tackle box. Setting the box down, she snapped the leash on Baby and handed it to him. "You take him, I'll carry our gear."

He recognized the challenge in her suggestion, and took the leash. It wasn't like he was afraid of dogs. He'd just never met one that looked like it could eat him whole and still have room for dessert. Following Mollie around to the front of the house, he kept a tight hold on the leash and a close eye on the dog.

He had to admit, it was pretty impressive how well the dog managed on three legs. Unlike most people, he didn't seem to care that he wasn't quite perfect. He just was happy to be alive. When Noah stopped in the driveway beside Mollie's little hatchback, Baby moved closer, bumping Noah's hip with his massive head. Getting the hint, Noah gave the dog a cautious scratch and was rewarded with a tail wag forceful enough to knock over a small child.

Mollie secured the poles to a roof rack, and then took the leash and loaded the dog into the cargo area. Noah watched with fascination as Baby wedged himself into a comfortable position, then proceeded to shut his eyes as if the whole process had exhausted him. By the time Noah was buckled into the passenger seat, there were loud snores coming from the backseat.

Mollie started the car. "I still can't believe you're a famous artist."

"And I can't believe you're still thinking about that. I'm just me, and this is like any other fishing trip, okay? Just you, me and Baby. Which, by the way, is a ridiculous name for a hundred-pound dog."

"He's almost two hundred pounds, actually." She grinned. "I thought the name might help him seem less intimidating."

"It didn't work."

"Hey, I saw you petting him. Admit it, you like him."

"Fine, yes, I like him. What concerns me is how he feels about me."

She laughed. "I see your point. But you don't have to worry, you're pretty easy to like."

The drive to the marina was quiet, other than Baby's snoring. Inside her head, though, chaos reigned. Was she crazy to be spending more time with Noah? Safety wasn't her concern; between Baby and her years of martial arts training, she wasn't worried about him trying anything. But how could she keep things fun and casual when every minute around him had her liking him more? And not in a platonic, let's-be-friends way. Not even close. But even if she was willing to break her no-dating rule, in a few days he'd be headed back to his real life, and she wasn't interested in being someone's vacation fling. Not to mention he was on the rebound. No matter how she looked at it, anything other than friendship would just be asking to get hurt.

He broke the silence first. "Do you go fishing a lot?"

"Not as much as I'd like. Between work and school, it's hard to find the time. But I try to go out at least every few weeks, usually with my dad." Which reminded her—she really ought to make an effort to go see him and her mom while she was off this week. She made a mental note to call them as she turned into the parking lot of the marina. Boats of all sizes and shapes dotted the water, from beat-up fishing vessels to sleek yachts. There were quite a few houseboats, too, some that were bigger than her own home.

"What are those garage-like buildings?" Noah pointed to a row of open fronted warehouses where boats were stacked four high in individual slots.

"Those are dry racks. People pay to have their boats stored there to protect them from the elements. The marina uses a big forklift to move them in and out."

"Valet service for your boat?"

She smiled. "I've never heard it put quite that way, but yeah, basically." Getting out of the car, she checked that she had everything and let Baby out of the back. "Let's head up to the marina store. I want to get some bottled water and we're going to need bait."

"So what's the deal? Are we renting a boat here?"

"Nope, my Dad has one stored here. Well, I guess it's the family boat, but he and I are the only ones that take it out. My sister is a workaholic and doesn't make it down here much. And Mom likes to tag along, but she won't take it out by herself."

With Noah carrying the gear this time, she walked with Baby, waving at a few of the people down on the docks. They passed the restrooms and a covered picnic area, and then the pool.

Noah turned to take it all in. "I always thought a marina was like a parking lot for boats, but it almost seems like a campground or something."

"Well, it's kind of both. Most people just store their boats here, but some live off them. For them, this is a neighborhood of sorts. And even the day trippers sometimes like to get a drink or something to eat at the restaurant."

"I wonder what that's like, living on a boat."

"I've thought about trying it, but haven't had the guts or the money to actually do it." She shrugged her shoulders. "Maybe someday, though."

They reached the small bait-and-tackle store along the waterfront, and she reminded Baby to behave.

"You can bring the dog inside?"

"Everyone here knows Baby. They'd give me hell if I didn't bring him in." Once inside, she walked past the rows of shiny lures and the displays of custom-made rods to the coolers in the back. "You grab us some water and ice. I'll get the bait." She picked out a package of frozen shrimp and some squid. Usually she went with live bait, but given Noah's lack-luster reaction to the idea of a fishing trip, the frozen stuff might be a better way to ease him into the experience.

Taking everything up to the register, she paid while Baby was fawned over by Frank, the owner. "How's my favorite pup?"

"She's doing great, thanks. How are you and Marie?"

"Oh, we're good." His smile crinkled the lines on his face. "The grandkids were down last week and about wore us out."

"And I'm sure you can't wait for them to come back again." The elderly couple doted on their grand-children, and the feeling was mutual. The kids were often underfoot around the marina, enjoying the fresh air whenever they had a school break.

"You got that right." He tipped his head toward Noah, who was inspecting some handmade boat models. "Who's the fella?"

"Oh, he's one of Jillian and Nic's guests, someone Nic knows from work. I'm just showing him around a bit." In a small town like Paradise, it was better to stop any rumors before they started.

"Mmm-hmm. Well, you just make sure he treats you right. You never know with those tourist types. At least you've got Baby here to keep an eye on things."

She had no doubt the loyal dog would defend her from an attack, but what she really needed was protection from herself and the growing attraction she felt every time Noah was around. She wasn't about to explain that to Frank, though, so she just nodded and headed for the door.

"Hey, don't forget me," Noah called, putting down the replica sailboat he'd wandered over to.

Forget him? She hadn't stopped thinking about him since she saw him on the steps of the Sandpiper. No, the only thing she was in danger of forgetting was her common sense.

Noah followed Mollie out of the dimness of the bait shop, squinting against the harsh glare of the sun. Taking one of the plastic bags from her, he matched her pace down one of the long docks extending over the blue-green water. "Which boat is yours?"

She pointed to a midsize vessel about halfway down, a picture of an orange and the words *Main Squeeze* emblazoned on the hull.

"Cute name."

She rolled her eyes. "That was Dad's attempt to suck up to my mom. He was trying to get her to like the boat more."

"Did it work?"

"Nope. I mean, I'm sure she appreciated the gesture, but she'd rather stay on dry land and fuss with her plants. The garden is her happy place."

"And the water is yours?"

"One of them. I'm not real picky. Anywhere outside works for me."

"And anywhere you can snap off some good shots?" He nodded to the camera bag she'd pulled from the car, now hanging from her shoulder.

A quick smile of acknowledgment was replaced with a grimace as she stepped onto the deck, absorbing the movement of the sea like a seasoned sailor. "Someone must have left some bait on board." Her nose crinkled, her freckles bunching up as she made room for him to join her. "Sorry, I'll rinse out the bait wells if you'll keep an eye on Baby."

At the sound of his name, the dog stood up from where he'd been sprawled on the warm wood planks of the dock, leaping across the gap between the dock and boat with much more grace than Noah expected from the oversize amputee. "Show-off."

Switching the bags to his left hand, he braced his right on the post beside him and swung down, a bit more clumsily than the dog but without falling on his butt, thankfully. Being out of his element was one thing; making a fool of himself was another.

Baby sat calmly a few feet from his mistress, not needing any minding that Noah could see. Mollie had her back turned, a hose in her hand as she bent over the bait wells hidden inside a set of bench seats. He wasn't quite sure what she was doing, but he wasn't going to distract her as long as he had such a nice view. Long, tanned legs ended in a trim bottom with just the right amount of curves, displayed nicely in a ripped pair of cutoffs that had him looking at denim with new appreciation.

"There, that's better." Mollie stood up, tossing the short hose back onto the dock. Kicking off her flip flops, she stepped up onto the gunwale, stretching to reach the spigot sticking out from a mooring post.

"Careful!" His breath caught at the way she was leaning out so far over the edge—and not just because of the way her tank top was riding up.

Ignoring his warning, she turned the water off and then hung the hose up neatly on the hook next to it. "Relax. I'm not going to fall overboard. I promise."

As if to prove her point, she balanced for a minute, hands free, before hopping down beside him. "See, totally safe."

She might not be worried about drowning, but with her standing only inches away neither one of them was safe. She was close enough to taste, and he'd like nothing better than to kiss that cocky grin off her face. But she'd set the ground rules, and he wasn't enough of a jerk to break them. He hoped.

Backing up, he put some breathing room between them. "All right, so, what do we have to do now? Tell me how I can help, and don't say watch the dog—he obviously doesn't need a babysitter."

Amusement flashed in her eyes. "You caught on to that, huh?"

"That you were just giving me a job to salve my ego and keep me out of the way? Yeah."

Unrepentant, she shrugged a shoulder. "Well, I really didn't need you to do anything, and a lot of guys would get offended if I did everything myself and didn't let them help."

"Are you kidding? I'm on my vacation. Or honeymoon, whatever. I think my ego can handle sitting here and watching a pretty lady take care of things. But," he added, more seriously, "I'd love to learn, so maybe you can explain what you're doing, and then next time I really can be of some help."

"You've got a deal." She took the bags from him and dumped ice into a cooler located under yet another seat, stowed the drinks, and then put the frozen bags of bait in the now clean bait wells. "No ice on these. We want them to thaw a bit so we can use them. If we were using live bait, we could fill these compartments with seawater, and then turn on the air pump to keep the water oxygenated."

"So noted. Drinks and bait separate, and live bait should be kept live." He leaned his weight against the tall captain's chair, enjoying watching Mollie work. "So what's next?" She was an excellent teacher, and he was definitely an eager student.

"Next you get out of my seat so I can start the boat." She gave him a gentle nudge with her elbow, and even that contact was enough to have his body reacting in ways that were not particularly appropriate. Glad he'd worn baggy shorts, he eased past her, careful not to let their bodies touch.

She inserted a normal looking key attached to a bright orange foam keychain and the engine rumbled to life. "We'll let it idle for a bit while I text my dad our float plan. Then we'll untie the lines and be on our way."

"Float plan?"

"It's like a flight plan, but for boating. Whenever any of us go out, we let someone know when we are leaving, where we plan to go and when we should be back."

"That's smart of you." He relaxed a bit; he should have known she'd take the proper precautions. As impulsive as she claimed to be she also had a level head on her shoulders.

Mollie stared for a minute before seeming to accept his compliment at face value. "Thanks. All right, now, time to cast off. I'm going to untie this line, if you want to get the other one."

Pleased that she'd given him a job, no matter how small, he carefully unwound the rough rope from the anvil-shaped metal cleat bolted to the dock. As soon as he was done, Mollie pushed off, freeing the small craft from its moorings before returning to the captain's seat. A minute later they were slowly motoring out of the marina towards the Intracoastal Waterway.

Looking back at Mollie, a peaceful smile on her face, the breeze blowing her hair as she effortlessly steered the boat through the channel, he couldn't help but think it might not be just the fish in danger of being hooked.

Mollie focused on steering the boat down the center of the channel, pretending that whatever this feeling was that sparked around Noah was nothing more than the normal response to being around someone as famous as him. Of course, it, whatever it was, had started before she'd known his identity. Which would mean it was something else entirely, something more primitive, more basic.

She certainly felt more primal, more aware of her own body around him. Cutoffs and a tank top had never felt so revealing, not that he'd done or said anything inappropriate. He was sticking to the terms of her agreement, but that didn't stop the air from almost crackling when they touched. Not that she planned on touching him again, but the boat was only so big and casual contact was hard to avoid.

"What's that?" Noah broke into her musings, pointing to a large wooden platform perched atop a post at the water's edge.

"A nesting platform. The power company builds them for the osprey, to try to keep them from nesting on utility poles. If you keep an eye out, you should see a few with actual nests on them. The ospreys around here are a bit unusual in that they don't migrate, so the breeding season goes on all year."

"They live in Paradise, literally." He gestured out over the clear water towards the picturesque sandy shore. "I wouldn't want to migrate, either. What could be better than this?"

"Adventure? New things, new places, new people? Stores that stay open past nine p.m.?"

"Whoa, where did that come from?" Noah's eyes crinkled in concern, his lazy slouch against the railing belying the edge beneath his words. "I thought you loved this place. Isn't that why you're showing me around? So I can see how great it is?"

Mollie bit back a defensive retort; it wasn't Noah's fault she felt so conflicted. Taking a few deep breaths of the salty humid air, she tried again. "I do love it here. I can't imagine a better place to grow up, or anywhere else ever being home."

"But?" He raised an eyebrow, waiting for her to continue.

"But I want more!" She felt her cheeks heat at the outburst. Great, now she sounded like a spoiled brat. "That sounds awful, doesn't it?"

He grinned. "Not awful. Just sounds like you have a bit of wanderlust, that's all. Nothing wrong with wanting to travel a bit, strike out on your own."

"You get it." He put her rambling thoughts into words so easily it was like he could read her mind. "My family, my friends… They think I'm crazy to want to leave, I don't even have anywhere in particular I want to go. I guess I just don't want to end up tied down like my mom did."

Noah waited for her to explain, not pushing, but letting her know he was listening if she wanted to share. Funny how it was so much easier to talk about this stuff with a near-stranger than her friends.

"My mom was a dancer, a talented one. She had a chance to go to New York and dance with a major company. I've seen the newspaper clippings, the old programs—she has a whole scrapbook full. She could have been famous."

"What happened?"

"She met my dad." And that had been the beginning of the end when it came to her mother's dancing career. "They fell in love, one thing led to another and a year later she had a ring, a mortgage and a baby. By the time I came along, she had given up on it completely. Once Dani and I were old enough for school, she started working at my father's law office as a secretary. She's never done anything else."

"Does she regret leaving dance?"

"She says she doesn't." Mollie shrugged. What else could she say? That she wished she'd never given up her career to have kids? Not exactly something you could tell your daughter. "She says she's happy, that having a family was always her real dream."

"But that's not what you want." It was a statement, not a question.

She shook her head. "I don't know if I ever will. I'm not like her. I can't even think about it. I want some adventure in my life, a chance to test my limits, make my mark on the world. I can't do that if I never leave the island."

"So then go, chase your dreams."

"What, just pick up and leave? Now?"

"Why not?" he challenged.

"Because... I'm not ready yet. I'm going to leave, at some point. But right now there's school, and my job, my family—"

"Those are excuses, not reasons." She started to argue, but he held up a tanned hand, silencing her. "You could apply to school somewhere else, transfer your credits. Or take a semester off. There are jobs everywhere. And your family, assuming everyone is in good health, isn't going to wither up and die if you leave the zip code. As far as I can see, there's nothing keeping you here, assuming you really want to leave, that is."

"Of course I do." Didn't she? She wasn't making excuses; she was waiting for the right time.

"Then trust me. Just do it. Do whatever it is that makes you happy, that makes you whole."

He made it sound so easy. "Is that what you're doing?"

He was silent for a moment. Maybe she was getting too personal, too heavy, but he'd started it. Hadn't he?

"I don't know." His eyes were clouded, as if he were seeing something other than the water and mangroves around them. "In some ways I always have, if only out of self-preservation. There wasn't much point in trying to impress my parents. Even if I'd made one happy, the other would have disapproved, just on principle. And I moved too often to make any real friends, let alone worry about impressing them. I guess that was the only good thing about growing up in chaos—you learn to rely on yourself."

"And now?"

"I don't know. For a little while, I had thought maybe it was time to reach out, build some real relationships. Maybe even settle down with someone special." He looked out over the water, his body tense. "Obviously, that didn't work out very well, and honestly, I don't think I've got it in me to try anymore."

Noah knew his words sounded cold, but there was no point in lying to her. He was done pretending, done trying to be someone he wasn't. He'd done that with Angela, and that hadn't done anyone any good. Besides, Mollie had said she was known for telling it like it is; the least he could do was return the favor. Even if it wasn't what she wanted to hear.

She seemed to consider his words as she scanned the horizon. "So you're just a lone wolf, huh?" She didn't seem upset by the idea; her shoulders were still relaxed, her limbs loose, as she steered the boat away from the main channel and into a narrower, winding section of water. Of course, why should she be? He was just one more temporary tourist to her; his views on life didn't have any importance for her.

"Yup, didn't you hear me out howling at the moon last night?"

She rolled her eyes. "I'll keep that in mind. Not sure I'm ready to break from the pack though. When I go—and I will go—I want to do it right. I don't want to have to come crawling back, tail between my legs, as it were."

"Being prepared is good," he conceded. "But there's a fine line between planning and procrastination. When I'm working on a big project, I sometimes find myself bogged down in the details, sketching out every angle when I need to just jump in and trust the details will work themselves out." He flashed her a grin. "But enough philosophy. Tell me about this place."

She'd slowed the boat while he was talking, nosing them into a quiet cove surrounded by a dense thicket of low-slung trees, their bare roots making a tangle above and below the clear water. It was like something out of a movie, exotic and yet somehow peaceful, too.

"Well, it's my favorite fishing spot. Other than that, what do you want to know?"

"For starters, what are those?" He pointed to the alien-looking trees that surrounded them. "I didn't know trees could grow in water like that, let alone salt water."

"Mangroves." She turned the engine to idle and went to the front of the boat, lifting the heavy anchor and tossing it in with a splash before he could offer to do it for her. "Red mangroves, specifically. Those freaky-looking roots keep them from drowning. Kind of like a house on stilts. And they act like a nursery for all sorts of baby fish, protecting them from bigger predators."

"And where there are fish, there are things that eat fish." As if to punctuate his words, a pair of pelicans flopped to a landing atop the nearest bunch of trees.

Mollie followed his gaze, and chuckled. "Exactly. That's why the birds hang out here, and it's why we're here. Should be enough for all of us. Grab a pole, and I'll help you get a line in the water."

"Don't think I can handle baiting my own hook?" He tried to look offended.

"Can you?"

"Um, maybe? Honestly, that was never my favorite part as a kid." He probably should be embarrassed by that but he wasn't. He didn't feel the urge to pretend or to try to fit in around Mollie. The sheer relief of just being himself in a place where no one cared who he was or wanted anything from him made the whole trip seem worthwhile. He might not be having the typical honeymoon, but he was definitely having a good time. Even if he didn't know how to put a frozen shrimp on a hook.

Mollie did, though. Sitting on the seat closest to the bait well, she took the sleek black rod with its brass fittings and braced it between her knees, a sight that was way more erotic than it should be. Then she swiftly threaded the hook through a partially thawed shrimp in a figure-eight type motion. "There you go. Now, how about a quick lesson in casting?"

"Sure." He stood and followed to the side of the

boat farthest from the mangroves. "I thought you said the fish like to hide in the tree roots?"

"The little ones do, but getting your line trapped in the trees is a huge pain. Most of the time it snaps, and then a bird can get tangled in whatever is left in the branches." She patted him on the back. "Don't worry. There are plenty of fish on this side of the boat, too. Now, take the pole in your right hand, like this."

She quickly showed him how to hold the pole with one finger securing the line before releasing the wire bail that controlled the reel. He imitated her movements, finding that the muscle memory built from those trips as a kid was still there.

"Good, now just bring the tip of the pole back. No, not so stiff...that's it, you've got it!"

Without even really thinking, he released the line just as the pole swung overhead and his hook sailed out to land right in the middle of the cove. Hot damn, it was like riding a bike, you never really forgot. Thank heavens for muscle memory.

Mollie beamed, her smile as bright as the Florida sun overhead. "Great cast! You'll be a fisherman yet."

"I have to catch something first."

"You will—I have faith in you. Besides, you have an excellent teacher."

Her words proved prophetic, and what seemed like only minutes later he felt a tug on his line. The current? Or something more. A second later a harder tug gave him his answer. "I think I've got something!"

"Ooh, awesome! Keep reeling. Let's see what you got."

He had no intention of stopping; he was having too much fun. Seconds ticked by with the turning of the reel as he brought the fish closer to the boat. When it broke the water, Mollie leaned out and grabbed the line, handing him his prize, a sleek white and silver speckled fish.

"You did it! That's a spotted trout, and if it's big enough to be legal it's our dinner tonight."

He was grinning like a fool, but he didn't care. He was on a boat in Paradise, he'd caught a fish and he had a beautiful woman smiling at him. Simple pleasures, sure, but often those were the best kind.

Mollie couldn't take her eyes off of Noah. His bronze skin was shining in the bright sun, his hair ruffled by the breeze, and he was standing there like every proud fisherman before him, except he wasn't every fisherman. He was a famous artist. And yet that didn't matter, not out here. In his T-shirt and flip flops, he looked…perfect.

"So, is he big enough?"

Right, focus on the task at hand, Mollie. You're fishing, for heaven's sake; since when do you get all girly when you could be fishing?

"I'll grab the ruler, just a sec." Digging in the tackle box, she found the same folding ruler she'd used for her own first fish and measured carefully. "Fourteen inches. That's an inch under legal. Looks like he's gotta go back. Need some help unhooking him?"

"No, let me try." His brows furrowed in concentration as he carefully eased the hook back out. "Did it. See, I'm a quick learner."

"It helps that you're good with your hands." His eyes widened at the remark. "I mean, with sculpting and—oh, hell, you know what I mean. Just put the fish back in the water and pretend I didn't say that, okay?" She knew from long experience that the best way to get past one of her ill-thought-out remarks was to just acknowledge it and move on.

Smirking, he did as she instructed, proving once again he could follow instructions. If only her tongue would do the same. "Ready to try again?"

"Sure, but I'll bait it myself this time. You haven't even gotten a line in the water yet. I can fend for myself."

"Thanks." She quickly baited her own hook and cast out into her favorite spot, watching him out of the corner of her eye. He was managing fine, which was no surprise. He really was good with his hands, which despite her protest to the contrary had her thinking about all the other ways he could use them.

Damn, she needed to cool off before she did something crazy, like make a move on him. She never did that. Guys were not interested in skinny brunettes with fish slime on their hands; they wanted blonde bombshells who got manicures and wore sundresses. Her own cutoffs were getting so frayed she'd need to throw them out soon, and her tank top was faded and plain. Her biggest nod to fashion was her extensive collection of bathing suits. It's not that she disliked shopping as much as she figured she was never going to look like a supermodel, so why bother?

Noah might make her feel good about herself, but she needed to remember she was still a small-town tomboy who probably smelled like bait. And even if he was interested, he was leaving in a week. She respected herself too much to be just an upgrade on some guy's vacation package. She needed to treat him like all the other guys she knew, a buddy, someone to have some laughs with. She could do that. She just needed to put things back in perspective.

Thankfully, when it came to perspective, she had a secret weapon. Putting her pole in one of the rod holders, she retrieved her camera bag from where she'd stowed it earlier. Her Canon Rebel was secondhand, but worked better than a lot of the newer models she'd seen tourists carrying. More importantly, she'd spent enough time with it to learn all its quirks, until it had the same familiar comfort as a favorite pair of slippers.

Noah was watching his line with the intensity of a lion stalking its prey, and she was able to snap several shots of him before he noticed.

"I wondered how long it would take you to get that thing out."

"Sorry, I don't usually sneak photos of people like that. You just looked so…." Gorgeous? Distracting? "Focused," she finished. "I can get rid of it if you want, but it's a good shot."

He shrugged. "If it's good, keep it."

It was good, she knew without looking. She'd felt that tingle that said the shot was exactly how she wanted it to be. "Thanks. And I promise I'll give you a heads-up if I aim your way again."

Glancing at her still slack line, she moved to the bow. There was an anhinga perched on a partially sinking tree stump drying its wings, just begging to be photographed. Stretching out on her belly, she steadied the camera, letting her world shrink down to the size of her viewfinder. Shot after shot, the hypnotic sound of the shutter clearing her mind. By the time the gangly bird flew off, she had a cramp in her neck and could feel the sting of a sunburn starting. No telling how long she'd been there; hopefully Noah wasn't too bored. So much for being a fun tour guide.

She rolled over and saw him reeling in his line, Baby asleep at his feet. A minute later, he pulled up a small fish, deftly snagging it in one hand. "Are these things good to eat?"

"Oh, yeah, that's a mangrove snapper, but he's a bit too small."

"I figured, but this is the third one I've caught. The first two were bigger, but I wasn't sure what they were or if I should keep them, so I let them go. Guess I'll send this one back to his buddies." He deftly released the fish, unconcernedly watching it swim away.

"Two more? You should have said something!"

"I didn't want to break your concentration. I hate it when people interrupt me when I'm working."

She shook her head. "I appreciate that, but I'm supposed to be helping you. You could have kept those bigger ones for dinner tonight."

"I'm fine. There was nothing pressing I needed. Besides, we can still have a fish dinner."

"I don't think so." She eyed the sun, now directly overhead. "It's getting too hot to catch much now. We'd have to stay out until nearly dark if we wanted to have a chance, and I didn't bring enough food or water for that."

"You forget, there's more than one way to skin a cat. Er, fish." He winked. "Trust me. Be at the Sandpiper at six and I'll show you."

Noah stepped out of the shower and wrapped a towel around his waist. After the fishing trip this morning, he'd taken a walk on the beach, then ordered room service for lunch, staying in his room to work on some sketches and catch up on email. He'd also used part of the afternoon to track down the area's best seafood restaurant. Initially he'd approached Nic, but the hotel proprietor had deferred to his wife, explaining that Jillian had lived on the island far longer and was the better source of information.

She'd been exactly that, and he now had a reservation for two at a place called Pete's Crab Shack and instructions to bring back a slice of key lime pie. It seemed the mother-to-be had a craving for it. Hopefully the place was as good as they had hyped it to be; he wanted to do something nice for Mollie after all the time she'd spent with him this morning.

He'd had a really good time, far better than he'd expected. She'd impressed him with her knowledge of the plants and wildlife they'd seen, but mostly he'd just enjoyed being around her. He liked that she didn't need him to entertain her every minute; she didn't hang on his every word or try to flatter him. In fact, although she probably wouldn't admit it, she'd been so relaxed around him she'd forgotten he was there. Another guy might be offended, but he knew what it was like to get caught up in the moment. And having a bit of quiet time to himself had been just fine, too.

Pulling a pair of casual but neatly pressed khakis and a lightweight button-down shirt from the closet, he dressed and wondered what Mollie would be wearing. So far he'd only seen her in casual clothes; would she dress up tonight? Not that it mattered; she'd look great in a paper bag. She didn't need to fuss with her appearance to be a knockout; between her fine bone structure and those Bette Davis eyes she was already there. It really was too bad she'd insisted on things staying platonic. A vacation fling with someone like her would give him memories for a lifetime.

But she had every right to draw the line, and the part of him not located below the belt respected her for doing it. She was right, he wasn't sticking around, and she deserved way better than a quick roll in the sand with the likes of him. She deserved someone with a lot less baggage and a lot more permanence.

Tonight, though, tonight she was his, if only for

dinner. Grabbing his wallet, he strode out of the room, locking the door and pocketing the old-fashioned key. One more sign that the Sandpiper was sticking to its historical roots. Everything in Paradise was that way—modern enough to be functional, but with a 1950s, wholesome vibe he'd never thought to see outside of a *Leave It to Beaver* rerun. As a kid, this was the kind of place he had wanted to live. Now, it was a great place to regroup and recover.

Downstairs he avoided the cluster of travelers in the lobby, ducking out the side door instead. The humidity slapped at him as soon as he stepped onto the deck, but the temperature had dropped a bit and the forecast was for a balmy evening. Even so, the whitewashed porch offered an extra measure of comfort. The wide roof protected him from the still-warm sun and oversize paddle fans provided a constant breeze. Rambling his way past comfortable-looking patio chairs and baskets of vividly blooming orchids, he made his way to the front steps where he'd first met Mollie, just twenty-four hours ago.

And there she was, walking up the path in a pair of black jeans that looked painted on and a halter top held up by the thinnest of straps. One good tug and... well, he wasn't going to think about that. There was enough skin showing already to make him a bit weak in the knees as he descended the steps to meet her.

"I'm a little early," she apologized, "but I couldn't wait any longer—I'm starving."

"Well, then, let's get going." He kept pace with her across the parking lot, wedging himself into her tiny car. "I think I could get very used to being chauffeured around, although I'd request a bigger limo next time."

"Hey, beggars can't be choosers, and if you think I'm waiting around for a cab, you've lost your mind. I need food, stat, and you promised me a fish dinner."

"I did. We have reservations at Pete's Crab Shack. Jillian recommended it."

She glanced over at him in surprise. "I didn't think Pete's took reservations."

An uneasy feeling settled in his gut. "Is it not good? I told Jillian I wanted the best. If there's somewhere else you'd rather go, just name it."

Pulling out of the lot, she grinned. "No, Pete's is great, and it really does have the best seafood anywhere on the island. It's just not the kind of place you make reservations at." Chuckling, she patted his leg, sending heat straight to his groin. "I can't imagine what they thought when you called."

"Probably that I'm some pretentious out-of-towner who doesn't know how to blend in with the locals. Guess they're right."

"Hey, I'm flattered by the thought, even if it was unnecessary. And if we *had* needed reservations, I'd be glad you called."

"You're saying it's the thought that counts?"

"Something like that, yeah."

"Well, that's something. So, if this isn't the kind of place that takes reservations, what kind of place is it?"

She slowed and turned into a crowded parking lot. "You tell me."

* * *

Mollie parked the car and tried to see the restaurant through Noah's eyes. She hadn't lied—Pete's really did serve great food—but right about now he was probably kicking himself for his choice in venue. It sounded like he'd been expecting something fancy, and well, Pete's wasn't. Maybe she should have warned him, but she refused to be embarrassed.

The weathered wooden structure was perched precariously along the dunes, looking like one good storm would tumble it right into the sea. Outdoor wooden picnic benches made up most of the seating, with a tiny indoor dining room that was mostly used by senior citizens and out-of-towners.

Noah got out of the car and scanned the building. "When Jillian told me the name, I kind of thought *shack* was a euphemism."

"Nope." She elbowed him as she walked by, heading for an open table in the back where they'd be able to see the ocean. "Thirty years ago, Pete started with a three-wall shack and a grill. He's changed a few things, kept up with the code requirements, but that's about it."

Sitting down, she handed him a plastic menu from the bucket sitting on the table. He took it, his eyes widening as he read the selections.

"Ginger curry mahi-mahi served over coconut rice, a snapper BLT with a citrus beurre blanc sauce, fish tacos with mango salsa—"

"Like I said, the best seafood in town." She grinned at his enthusiasm; Pete's had that effect on people.

"And let that be a reminder not to judge a book by its cover."

"So noted." He set the menu down and held her gaze. "And for the record, I'm glad that we aren't at some stuffy restaurant with white linen tablecloths. I never know what fork to use."

"I don't buy it. No way you grew up with a military father and didn't learn basic table etiquette. But I'll agree that this is way better. I tend to avoid any place that expects me to wear high heels, just on principle."

"So I shouldn't expect any formal events this week?"

"Not in Paradise. You'd have to go south to Palm Beach or Miami to get that kind of scene." Was that what he'd expected on this trip? Was he bored already? "You could always get a rental car and shift your vacation there. I'm sure Nic would give you a partial refund, given the circumstances." It made sense that someone used to running in artistic circles would be bored in such a small town, but darned if she wasn't disappointed at the thought of him leaving so soon.

"Hey, who said anything about leaving?" He shifted, stretching his legs out under the table. "I'm more than comfortable right here. Unless you're trying to get rid of me?"

Relief flooded her body—and she wasn't going to analyze why. "Sorry, I guess I was getting ahead of myself, jumping to conclusions. I do that sometimes. In good news, I'm told by my friends that you get used to it." She flagged down a waitress, ready to order and restore some normalcy to the evening. "So, do you know what you want?"

He looked deliberately at her. "Everything looks good."

Wow. Heat rose on her cheeks to match the heat in his voice. Keeping her cool around him wasn't going to be easy if he kept this up. "Limit yourself to the menu, big guy."

There, see, she could handle herself. Setting her own menu aside, she waited for him to order.

"I'll have the fish tacos and one of the local beers, whichever you recommend." Turning to Mollie, he grinned ruefully. "Only one beer, I promise. You don't have to worry about getting me up the hotel steps tonight."

"Good. But I'll have an iced tea, just to be on the safe side. Designated driver and all that. And the crab cakes with a side of conch fritters, please."

"You got it. I'll be back with your drinks in a minute." The waitress left, and Mollie took a long breath, wondering what to say now. Funny how she hadn't had any problem talking to him on the boat or the beach, but tonight felt more like a date, which was stupid. All because he'd made reservations. No guy she'd eaten with had ever called to make reservations or taken her anywhere they were needed. Her contact with the male of the species had been limited to a shared pizza during a Dolphins game or a hot dog on the beach. That Noah had wanted to do something special, even if it hadn't worked out that way, had her off balance and unsure.

"So, what's next on the agenda for tomorrow?"

"Well, you choose—water or land?"

"We were on the water today, so I say land. Mix it up a bit."

"Okay, I'll pick you up at eight—the Sandpiper is on the way."

"On the way to where? What did I just agree to do? And why so early?"

Just then the waitress arrived with their drinks, and Mollie used the interruption to draw out the suspense, taking a sip of her tea as Noah eyed her warily.

"So? Out with it. Alligator wrestling? What?"

"Well, there are a few alligators…"

His eyebrows rose, and she realized she liked teasing him. Probably because he was such a good sport. "I'm friends with some people over at the Paradise Wildlife Rehab Center. I already asked, and they said I could bring you by any time for a behind-the-scenes tour."

"Rehab center, is that for sick animals or something?"

"Pretty much, yes." She watched him sip from his beer, relaxed once again. "They take in sick or injured wildlife, and volunteers help care for the animals until they are well enough to be released."

"Let me guess, you're one of the volunteers."

"Guilty as charged. I'm only there a few times a month, though. A lot of people do more. I just help with some of the permanent residents, the ones that couldn't be released. I leave the medical stuff to Jillian and Cassie."

"So college student, receptionist, photographer and now wildlife rehabilitator. Is there anything you can't do?"

The waitress returned with their food, saving Mollie from a response. Because she was beginning worry that the one thing she couldn't do was resist him.

Noah dug into the basket in front of him, his appetite heightened by the fresh, salt-tinged air of the island. One bite of the tangy, sweet tacos had his taste buds begging him to sell his apartment and move to Paradise, ASAP. He'd eaten in some fancy digs over the years, but this place was amazing. Or maybe he was just more able to appreciate it, given the company.

"So, tell me more about yourself. You said you have a sister?"

She licked a stray drop of tartar sauce off her finger, making him stiffen in his seat. "One older sister. She's a lawyer like our dad. Very by the book, always got perfect grades, had a scholarship to college, that kind of thing."

"And your parents expected you to do the same?" he guessed.

"At first they did. I think they're finally starting to realize that just isn't me. At least I hope so, 'cause it's never going to happen."

She offered him what he assumed was a conch

fritter, and he accepted, biting into the spicy fried confection while she talked.

"But you can see how my—what was it they called it…unconventionalism?—would be unsettling compared to all that."

"Sounds like I might have gotten off easy as an only child. I always wanted a sibling, but I think you've convinced me otherwise."

She bit her lip, a habit that was quickly driving him insane.

"It isn't all bad. Dani can't help being who she is, and she always stuck up for me when we were growing up. She's just naturally driven."

"Right, and you're just a total slacker, what with school and your job and volunteering—"

"None of which have long-term potential, according to the most recent lecture from my father. But really, it's okay. They just worry."

Maybe so, but they didn't sound very supportive. "Still, it has to be hard, knowing you aren't living up to their expectations. Even if their expectations are all wrong for you. I know my military father sure as hell didn't expect his son to become an artist, that's for sure."

Mollie's eyes sparked in indignation. "Doesn't he know how amazing your work is? How amazing you are?"

She was sexy when she was pissed, all hot and bothered on his behalf. She'd be fiery like that in bed, too, no doubt about it. Too bad that idea had been tabled. Draining his beer, he reminded himself that it was his crappy relationship skills that had gotten him into this situation in the first place; he didn't need things to go from bad to worse by scaring off the first person to make him laugh in a long time. "I appreciate the compliment, but my father, like yours, has his own definition of success. But forget about them. How about we order some dessert and take it back to the inn? I'm under orders to bring back some key lime pie for Jillian. Might as well pack up something for everyone."

"Distracting me with dessert?"

"Maybe. Is it working?" He'd certainly rather discuss that than his family life.

"Is there a woman it wouldn't work on?"

"A woman on a diet?"

"Lucky for me, I tend towards bony, not plump, because their key lime pie really is the best. We should get a whole pie or maybe two, given how strong Jillian's cravings can be. That way, you and I can share one, and Nic can fight Jillian for part of hers."

Her hearty appetite was just one more thing he liked about her. And no matter what she said, she wasn't bony. Just slender, with a hint of curves that seduced the eye rather than shouting their presence. A level of nuance that appealed to the man and the artist.

It was driving him crazy not to touch her, but he'd promised to keep his hands to himself, and he was a man of his word. The question was, could he handle being around her like this, day after day, without driving himself crazy in the process? A week was starting to seem like a very long time.

Frustrated, he ordered two key lime pies and paid the bill, insisting meals were included in her nonexistent tour-guide salary. That had gotten another laugh out of her, a laugh that he was finding as addicting as everything else about her. On the drive home, she pointed out more of natural beauty of the island, but the only beauty he was interested in was sitting right there in the driver's seat. Being this close, he could smell the coconut and vanilla scent he already associated with her; hell, he could practically taste her. And he wanted to taste her.

By the time they arrived at the hotel, he knew he wasn't going to be able to keep this up, not with the rules she'd set in place. Maybe that made him weak, but she was too potent a drug for him resist. Jaw clamped tight, he walked with her up the steps of the inn, carrying the pies and listening to her chatter about their plans for tomorrow. Plans he was going to have to break. Maybe he would rent a car, drive somewhere else, out of reach of temptation. Or maybe he'd just take an earlier flight home, and forget the whole idea of a solo honeymoon.

"Noah, did you hear me?" Mollie had stopped in front of the carved wooden doors and was staring at him, face turned up to the moonlight and looking like the fairy sprite he'd imagined her to be at their first meeting. Something not quite real, and definitely not of the same world as him.

"I'm sorry, I was just… Can we sit down?" He

gestured to a love seat tucked into a corner of the porch between two potted palms.

"Um, sure." She looked down at the pies he was holding. "Should we take these in first?"

"No, just let me do this, please." He needed to say this while his brain was still in control of his libido. Sitting on the edge of the cushion, he looked out over the railing, knowing that if he faced her he'd never be able to stick to his good intentions. "I don't think we should go to the rehab center tomorrow."

Mollie shrugged beside him. "That's fine. We can do something else. Kite boarding, maybe? Or snorkeling? What did you have in mind?"

"No, I mean we shouldn't do anything together. It was really nice of you to offer to be my tour guide, but I don't think it's a good idea to continue." He took a step back towards the stairs; he needed to leave before this got even more awkward.

"What?" Mollie jumped up to stand in front of him, her arms out as if she could physically block him in. He'd have laughed if he wasn't feeling so sick about the whole thing. "What made you change your mind? Because I thought we were having a good time here." Her tone was angry, but he could see the hurt in her eyes. "Was I wrong about that?"

"Damn it, no, you weren't wrong. That's the problem."

She cocked her head, looking at him like he'd grown a second head. "Let me get this straight. You want to cancel our agreement because you're having too good a time? Are you feeling guilty because you were supposed to be here with your ex? Because there's nothing wrong with enjoying yourself, having a little fun."

"No, it's not about guilt." He ran a hand through his hair, trying to figure out how to explain things without sounding like a hormone-crazed teenager. "It's a bit more basic than that. The bald truth is… I'm attracted to you."

She grinned, her shoulders relaxing. "Okay, well, I think you're attractive, too. I mean, we had that great kiss and all. Obviously there is some chemistry. But I thought we decided that was a bad idea, that we'd just ignore that and have fun as friends."

"We did. I promised to keep things platonic, and I intend to stick to that promise. Which is why I can't see you anymore." He paused, needing her to understand. "Sweetheart, I'm at the point where ignoring it isn't an option anymore. So I'm backing out now, before I do something I regret."

"Something you regret?" she parroted his words back to him slowly, as if trying them on for size. "Like what?"

Fisting his hands in his pockets, it took every last bit of his control to keep from showing her exactly what he meant. "Like kissing you silly, right here in the moonlight, where anyone could see."

She froze, her pupils dilating at his words. "Which we agreed was a mistake. Neither of us is looking for a relationship, and you're leaving soon anyway."

He nodded. Even if he did feel like a creep, it was better to be honest.

"So, now I'm supposed to thank you for your honesty and let you leave."

"Something like that."

She bit her lip, worrying at it, and he had to clench his jaw to keep from groaning at the sight. "Then we have a problem, because I've never been very good at doing what I'm supposed to do."

Mollie meant to give Noah time to digest what she'd said, to let him respond. But he looked way too good, and the night was only so long. So she took matters into her own hands and climbed up onto his lap, straddling him on the floral couch.

"What do you think you're doing?" He wasn't moving, but she could feel the tension vibrating through him, feel how much he wanted this.

"I'm making a mistake," she whispered, lowering herself closer to his mouth. "A really good mistake."

At the first touch of lips, she felt the dam inside him burst, and all the energy he'd had vibrating below the surface was suddenly focused directly on her. His mouth fed on hers like he was a starving man and she was the last morsel of food on earth. He tasted and teased with his tongue, and all she could think was *more*. She needed more.

Her hands wove through his hair as she settled farther onto his lap, pressing herself against him as they kissed. He gripped her hips and held her in place, pinning their bodics together. Her eyes closed, Mollie ran her hands down his chest, needing to touch more of him.

Sensing her need, he leaned back to give her more access. Now she could work her hands under his shirt, skimming the muscles honed by hard work and heavy welding tools. She wasn't a virgin; she'd had her share of fumblings on the beach with boys that were more curious than passionate. But Noah was no boy; he was all hard, hot man. And he wanted her just as much as she wanted him. He didn't see her as a problem to be fixed or an issue to be dealt with. He saw her as a woman, and that alone was enough to have her ready to take him upstairs.

He was thinking along the same lines if his hands kneading her ass were any indication. Pulling away from his mouth, she worked tiny kisses up his jaw, nipping the delicate skin just below his ear. "We should go to your room," she whispered as he moved one big hand under her shirt.

"What?" he muttered, his fingers working the clasp of her bra.

"Your room. We should go there before Jillian or Nic finds us naked on the patio."

Her words finally seemed to penetrate, and he stilled, breathing hard. A moment later, he lifted her off of him onto the other side of the couch.

"Noah? Are you okay?"

"Yes… No. I'm sorry. I can't take you up to my room."

"What?" She hadn't imagined that kiss—he wanted her, she knew he did. She'd felt it, felt him. "Are you worried about Jillian or Nic? Trust me, they don't care. And the rooms are soundproof."

At that comment he froze, and she saw his eyes go dark. But then he shook his head and stood, turning his back to her as he leaned on the railing, catching his breath.

Straightening her shirt, Mollie walked over to stand alongside him. "Hey, you're going to have to make up your mind here. First, you say you're too attracted to be friends, then we're kissing like the world's going to end, then you're pushing me away." She bumped him with her shoulder. "You're kind of giving mixed signals here, but if you're expecting me to apologize for that kiss, I'm not going to."

He grinned, his features softening with the movement. "You'd better not. That was possibly the best kiss of my life."

"Just possibly? Should we try again to make sure?" This was totally out of her norm, but hey, go big or go home. She was up for another try as long as he wasn't going to flash hot and cold again.

Gripping the balcony, he sighed. "I'm sorry. I know I'm not making much sense here. But believe me. I want you in every single way."

Her toes curled at the intensity of his voice. "But?"

"But like you said before, casual sex isn't a good idea. I learned that lesson the hard way. Not that you're anything like Angela," he hastened to correct, "but sex can have consequences. Consequences that neither of us is in a place to deal with right now."

He really looked at her then, and she saw the determination in his eyes as well as the longing. She sighed. He was right. Damn it. She hated when common sense kept her from having fun. "Then where does that leave us?" Her stomach clenched; she wasn't sure what answer she wanted to hear, but she knew he'd be honest with her. He'd proven that to her.

"Well," he drawled, trailing a finger from her cheek down to her lips. "There's just friends, and there's making love, and there's all whole lot of space in between. Maybe we can play it by ear, and find our way down the middle?"

She shivered, fighting the urge to lean into him. She needed to get this straight. She was in uncharted waters and didn't want to run aground on some hidden reef. "So you're saying we'd be…what? Dating? And then what?"

He sobered. "And then I leave. But I've got until the end of the week, and I'd like to spend it with you. And I don't want to be fighting the urge to kiss you the whole time."

So, this was it. She could take what he was offering for now, and then he'd be gone. Or she could say goodbye to him now, and never see him again. Put that way, it really wasn't even a choice. "So are you going to kiss me again, or what?"

Noah did kiss her, thoroughly and with great pleasure. Having Mollie in his arms, with the stars above and sound of the waves crashing in the background, was definitely a high point of his vacation. Hell, a high point of his life. But at some point a light had turned on inside and Mollie had insisted they needed to take Jillian her pie. He had offered to buy the woman a dozen of them tomorrow if they could stay outside making out, but Mollie had just laughed and dragged him inside.

So now he was eating pie at the big wooden table in the Sandpiper kitchen with way too many people. Well, just Jillian and Nic, but that was two too many, as far as he was concerned.

"This is exactly what the baby wanted. Thank you, Noah." Jillian scraped the last bite off of her plate and reached for another slice. "But I'm holding you responsible when you have to roll me out of here at nine months. I have zero self-control when it comes to sweets right now."

"Eat what you want," Nic responded, placing a glass of milk in front of her. "You barely picked at dinner and didn't have much more at lunch. Besides," he said with a wink, "I like you a little plump."

Jillian smacked his shoulder, but her laugh tempered the rebuke. In truth she looked beautiful, and everyone in the room knew it.

"Please, at least you have an excuse." Mollie dug a fork into the pie that she and he were sharing, forgoing cutting a slice to eat directly from the pan. "I'm only eating for one and I'm pretty sure I've outpaced you."

Her innocent comment had him wondering what she would look like, heavy with child. He pushed the ridiculous thought away, but not before longing hit him solidly in the gut. But this time it wasn't for the marriage and family he'd lost. This was a new fantasy, one that centered on the slip of a woman sitting beside him. He gulped from a glass of ice water, suddenly realizing that sex wasn't the only way to complicate things. Feelings did that, too.

Needing to change the subject, Noah looked to Nic across the table. "So, I hear you were born into the hotel industry, more or less."

"That's right. My father made hotels his business before I was born. When I got out of college, I joined him, working my way up the ladder. But by the time I came to Paradise I was ready for a change."

Noah tipped his head. "Doesn't seem like you got too far away from the family business. You stayed in hotels, just on a smaller scale."

Nic grinned. "I figured it made sense to play to my strengths. But the big change is that now I'm in one place, setting down roots. Before, I lived out of my suitcase more than my apartment. Every time I got a new hotel just how I wanted it, I'd have to leave and move on to the next one. Now, when I fix something, make it better, I get to stick around and enjoy it."

"Is that what made you quit and buy this place? You wanted to settle down?" He ate another bite of pie, following Mollie's example and taking right from the tin.

"Basically. Buying the Sandpiper was my wedding gift to Jillian."

"Caruso Hotels was going to tear it down," Jillian broke in. "Nic knew how important this place was to me, so he bought it himself instead."

"And I'm going to be paying the bank for it for

quite some time," he replied shaking his head ruefully, but gripping his wife's hand where it lay on the table. The love between them was obvious, the kind of love that overcame whatever obstacles it encountered.

"It was a wonderful thing to do, and I'll never forget it." Jillian fanned her eyes in a vain attempt to stem the tears that were spilling onto her cheeks. "I'm sorry, it's the hormones. I cry over everything now."

Mollie got up and got Jillian a tissue from the box on the counter. "Hey, no crying. It all worked out okay. The Sandpiper is still here, better than ever. And now you've got your own home being built, and it's all going to be picture-perfect. You and Cassie have everything so wrapped up I may have to run off and join the circus just to even things out."

Jillian giggled, her tears forgotten, and he had a sneaking suspicion that had been Mollie's goal. "You will not. You're going to find your own guy and settle down, too. And I'm going to say 'I told you so' when it happens."

Mollie made a gagging noise, causing every to join in on the laughter. But Noah wondered how much of what she said was for comedy's sake. She'd said before she wanted adventure. Well, he knew a bit about that. He'd been known to pick up and move just because he'd gotten tired of the color of his apartment walls, and unlike Nic, he'd enjoyed the constant variety. Maybe he and Mollie didn't have to end things when she left; maybe they could have some adventures together. She could come see him in Atlanta, or he could close up the studio for a while and take her on an extended trip somewhere, show her some of his favorite places. He wasn't quite ready to go there yet, but it was something to keep in mind.

Jillian stood, a hand pressed to her lower back as she angled her way upright. "You two are welcome to keep chatting, but it's past my bedtime." She started for the private section of the inn. "Oh, and Mollie, could you give me a hand for a second? I need your opinion on the curtains for the nursery."

Mollie followed Jillian down the hall, far enough to be out of earshot of the men. "All right, we both know I have zero opinions when it comes to curtains, so what's up?"

"That wasn't very believable, huh?"

"Not at all. But seriously, is everything okay? You're scaring me." Was there something wrong with the baby, something she did want to make public?

"I'm fine." Jillian smoothed down the front of her maternity shirt, a small smile lifting her lips as she rubbed her rounded belly. "It's you I'm worried about."

"Me?"

"Yes, you. The chemistry between you and Noah was so thick I could have served it with the pie. What's going on with you guys?"

What *was* going on with them? "It's…complicated. But it's fine. I've got it under control. Just a little summer fling with a hot guy. After all, not all of us are ready to get married and have our two point five children."

Jillian blanched, tears threatening to return.

Crap. "Oh, Jillian, I'm sorry! I didn't mean it that way. I'm happy for you, I really am. And for Cassie. But I'm in a different place, and I'd like you to be happy for me, too." Wanting to kick herself for making her friend cry, she gave her a hug. "Everything is going to be fine, I promise."

Jillian nodded and gestured towards the kitchen. "Well, then, go get him. And make sure you tell me every detail once this fling of yours is over. As an old, matronly lady, I need to live vicariously through you."

"It's a deal. We'll have a girls' night after he leaves—you, me and Cassie. I promise." Impulsively, she gave her one last squeeze, then hurried back to find Noah and Nic bonding over some single-malt scotch, telling stories about their travels. Nic didn't have a lot of guy friends in the area yet; it was nice to see him finding someone to talk to.

"Hey, boys, I'm off." Standing on her toes she reached up to give Noah a goodnight kiss. The open display of affection had Nic choking on his whiskey—apparently he wasn't as insightful as his wife and hadn't picked up on the aforementioned chemistry. "Don't keep him up too late, Nic. I'm picking Noah up at eight, and if he's hungover, I'll know who to blame."

She needn't have worried. Noah was standing on the steps waiting for her when she pulled up the next morning, looking rested and ready to work in a pair of jeans and a surf shirt she suspected he'd purchased just for this trip. Better yet, he had a cup of coffee in each hand. A sexy man bearing caffeine—did it get any better than that?

Idling in front of the inn, she accepted the travel mug he handed her as he got in. The bold flavor rolled over her tongue, waking her much more thoroughly than her alarm clock and a five-minute shower had. By the time they reached the turn-off to the rehab center, she was fully caffeinated and ready to go.

Her small car bumped over the hills and ruts in the gravel road, banging Noah's knees against the dash. "You've have got to get a bigger car. If not for my sake, then for Baby's."

"Baby's fine. He likes my car." She darted a glance to the rearview mirror and checked that the big doofus really was fine. He had his head poked forward, trying to catch the breeze from Noah's open window, drooling all over the rear seat. She'd have to hit the car wash again. And look into protective seat covers—waterproof ones.

"He'd like a big SUV better," Noah mumbled, rubbing his battered leg as best he could, given the close confines. "Thank goodness everywhere on Paradise Isle is a short drive."

She rolled her eyes at him and parked in the small, shaded lot. Directly in front of them was the main hospital and office building, their first destination of the morning. "Okay, everyone out. We'll leave

Baby in the office. They love him here, but he has a tendency to spook the animals."

"Shocking."

She elbowed him. "I told you before, it's not his fault he's big. But you're right, he is a bit intimidating. Luckily the office staff knows he's nothing but a big teddy bear."

Mollie led the way into the simple wooden building, pointing out a small, tasteful plaque with the Sandpiper Inn logo near the door. "They had to put on a new roof a few months ago, and the Sandpiper donated most of the materials. Nic actually came out and helped with the installation, as well. Some of the animal enclosures are sponsored by other local businesses."

There weren't many people in the office at this hour, or really any hour. It was a bare-bones kind of operation. But Tara, an intern from the University of Florida, and Dylan, the director, were already hard at work, bent over a spreadsheet that, she was willing to guess showed too little money coming in and too much going out. It was always that way, but somehow Dylan managed to make it work. He had an MBA from Harvard and a magic touch when it came to soliciting donations. His charm and good looks didn't hurt, of course. Once upon a time, she'd had a crush on him, but he'd never seen her as anything but a friend. Now, looking at the bleach-blond hair spilling over his blue eyes, she didn't feel anything. No, it was the dark, brooding artist beside her that had her heart racing and her girly parts keeping time.

Baby, however, still had a thing for the guy, and was currently trying to squirm his considerable girth in between Dylan and his cheap metal desk. The scrape of aluminum on terrazzo flooring made it clear Baby wasn't taking no for an answer.

"Baby, stop that! Have a little dignity, for heaven's sake."

Ignoring her, the big pooch flopped down in the space he'd created, rolling over to beg a belly rub. Unfazed, Dylan, who'd known Baby almost as long as Mollie had, just leaned down and scratched the dog while continuing to pore over the numbers in front of him. "Hi, Dylan, sorry to interrupt." She gave a pointed look at Baby. "But I wanted to see if there was anything you need me to do while I'm here."

He looked up from his desk, as if finally noticing her. "Hey, I didn't think you were on the schedule today."

"I'm not. But I'm giving Noah here a tour, and figured I might as lend a hand if you needed it."

"That's right. You did say you might bring someone by. Sorry, it's been a bit crazy here. Not that that's any different than usual." He stood, extending a tanned hand to Noah. "Nice to meet you."

Mollie watched the two men shake hands and nearly sighed. They were both beautiful specimens of the male gender, one blond, one dark, both simmering with testosterone and some undeniable quality that made men so interesting. But only one of them made her toes tingle when he looked at her.

Which, given the circumstances, was one too many. Still, she couldn't help but hope that he'd see some of what she saw in this place, that he'd get why she came here week after week. Too often, she was the odd one out, the misfit, but here the animals accepted her for who she was. No one else in her life did that.

Except for Noah.

Damn, she was in serious trouble.

Noah shook the proffered hand, then looked around the room. The floors were bare, and the office furniture the staff used was thrift-store chic at best, but there were some hand-carved chairs for visitors and an amazing array of framed wildlife photos lining the walls, each with a name plaque beneath it. "Mollie says you do some good work here."

The taller man shook his head. "Not me—I just try to keep the roof from caving in, sometimes literally. Our volunteers do all the real work. Like Mollie, she's our official, but unpaid, photographer. The framed prints and postcards she lets us sell raise quite a bit of money, and she took all the photos on the website, too."

So she was the one behind the gorgeous pictures hanging on the walls. Still listening, he moved in to get a closer look, a germ of an idea forming in his head.

"She also developed an operational conditioning program that's she's teaching to all the other volunteers. We're incredibly lucky to have someone of her skill here."

Mollie blushed. "I do some clicker training with the animals and taught the other staff how. It's not rocket science."

"What's clicker training?"

"It's a form of operant conditioning," Dylan explained. "It uses positive reinforcement to get the animal to offer the behavior you're looking for without stressing them out. Lots of trainers do it, with domestic and zoo animals, but some are better than others. Mollie's one of the best. Speaking of which..." He grabbed a sticky note off his desk. "Since you're here, could you swing by Simba's enclosure? He's refusing to go into the holding area, and Krissy can't get in there to clean. I was going to try to make it down there myself in a bit..."

"But you've got your hands full. No problem, I'm on it." She swiped a lanyard off a peg in the wall and waved goodbye to Tara. Dylan was already back at work and didn't seem to notice them leaving. Noah would be offended, but he wasn't exactly a people-pleaser himself when he was working. He understood intensity first hand. As did Mollie, who was already halfway out of the room, intent on helping Simba, whoever that was.

Following her to the back door of the office, he was amused to see that Baby had positioned himself directly under Dylan's desk and was now operating as a living footrest. The big beast was so docile he was practically inert.

The rest of the building seemed to be a combination of an animal hospital and wildlife cafeteria. Chrome cages, several holding injured wildlife, lined the walls. He spotted a pelican with a bandaged wing, a turtle with a cracked shell held together with what looked like modeling clay, and a very small squirrel. Other cages had towels draped across their fronts, perhaps to shade the more nocturnal species from the bright fluorescent lighting. The back wall, where Mollie had headed, held a long chrome counter top and a large sink. Under the counter were several small refrigerators as well as storage cabinets he assumed held dry goods or other equipment. A teenage boy with red hair and freckles was busy chopping up vegetables, while another boy, shorter and rounder, weighed out the food and placed it in metal dishes.

"Hey, Andy, Tom, how's it going?" Mollie greeted the boys, then dug into one of the refrigerators, pulling out a baggie of what looked like chopped meat.

"Hi, Mollie," the stockier boy replied, a big grin on his face. His friend just nodded, his face blushing nearly as red as his hair. He wondered if Mollie knew they had the hots for her and realized immediately she'd never show it if she did. She wouldn't want to embarrass them like that. "I heard Simba's giving Krissy a hard time again. You going to help her?"

Mollie held up the baggie. "I'm going to try. If not, we'll just leave that cage for tomorrow. No one goes in there, okay?" She waited until both boys had nodded their understanding before leading him out the back door onto a mulch covered path.

"So, what's a Simba?" Images from *The Lion King*

flashed in his head as they passed by wooden and steel habitats housing an assortment of wildlife.

"Simba is a very beautiful, very traumatized Florida panther. He was being held as a pet illegally until Fish and Wildlife got a tip from a neighbor." Her stride quickened in visible agitation. "The man who owned him had starved him and used a Taser on him. He was terrified of people when he came here, and sometimes he still gets panicked." She stopped at a large, fenced-in area, anger and pain radiating off of her. "I don't understand how anyone can be that cruel."

He kept his silence; as far as he was concerned, jail was too good for someone that abused animals. But saying that wasn't going to help, so he just squeezed her hand in sympathy.

Beyond the fence a shadow moved, and he caught his breath. There, only a few yards away, a big tawny cat paced from one end of his territory to the other, eyes darting as if looking for danger. That such a large, powerful predator could be so anxious was just wrong; he could see why Mollie was so angry. It was disgusting the way some people treated animals.

Mollie wasn't showing her anger now, though. She'd turned it off somehow, exuding a calm confidence as she climbed over the low railing along the path and worked her way right up to the fence.

Oh hell, she wasn't going in there with the panther—was she? He'd learned to trust her judgment over the past few days, but every protective instinct in his body was screaming for him to stop her. But if he said something, she'd know he doubted her, and that would make him as bad as all the other people who had tried to control her life. He couldn't—he wouldn't—do that. Fisting his hands in his pockets to keep from grabbing her back to safety, he waited and prayed he'd made the right choice.

Chapter 2

Mollie could sense Noah's tension as she approached the big cat, but she couldn't stop to reassure him right now. All her focus was on Simba and on convincing him she wasn't a threat. She'd been working with him off and on for months, and although he'd filled out and healed physically, mentally he still had scars. Which meant she would *not* be going in the enclosure with him. Simba's training was done via protected contact—panther on one side of the fence, her on the other.

"Hey, big boy. What's wrong, having a bad day?" She kept her voice low, her movements slow and measured. When she finally reached the fence, she slid down into a sitting position and watched him, hoping he'd stop his pacing long enough to recognize her as the friend she was. At first, he ignored her, his eyes clouded with past pain. But she kept up a steady stream of chatter, telling him about Noah, about her job, anything she could think of. It was the tone that mattered, not the words. At this point she wasn't training, just connecting. A brain can't learn when it's overwhelmed by stress or fear, so she needed to wait for a signal that he'd downgraded from anxious to cautious.

Finally, the big cat stopped his patrolling and truly looked at her, one ear twitching in recognition. This was it; he was ready to work. Reaching into the baggie she'd set beside her, she threaded a piece of meat onto the end of a long stick. "Kebabs, panther style," she whispered to Noah. His stifled chuckle had her watching Simba for a reaction, but the cat was now more concerned with the meat than stranger danger.

His whiskers twitching, Simba scented the air.

"That's it, big guy, you know the drill. Come to Mama."

A few seconds passed without movement. Maybe he wasn't going to do it today. She could try again tomorrow, but damn it, she didn't want to give up. Not yet.

Then, as if moving in slow motion, he took a single cautious step towards her.

Click! She used the noisemaker around her neck to mark the behavior and threaded the meat-on-a-stick through the holes in the fence as far as she could. Simba had to move even closer to reach it, so she clicked again and gave him another reward. The familiar game seemed to ease the old anxieties, and within minutes he was close enough for her to feel his warm breath on her face.

She heard Noah stand up, and waved him back. "It's fine," she reassured him, using much the same tone as she had with the panther. "The fence will hold." Besides, Simba wasn't looking to cause any trouble now. He was smart, and now that he'd settled down was more than happy to work for his food.

She took out the collapsible targeting stick she carried in her pocket, extending it the full eighteen inches of length. A rubber ball on the end acted as a focus point, and the second she offered it to him he turned and touched it with his nose. Another click, another chunk of meat. "Good boy. Now let's make it a little harder." She slowly stood up, discreetly stretching out the kinks before offering the target again, this time several feet higher. Without missing a beat, the big cat put his massive paws up on the fence to reach it. Click and reward.

Moving several steps to the right, she repeated the targeting game a few more times. Only when the cat was eagerly moving wherever she directed him did she move towards the holding area built against the back of the enclosure. This was where the keepers put the animals when they needed to clean or otherwise work in the larger part of the habitat. It kept the animals out of trouble and the keepers safe—if you could get the animal in there. Which was why Mollie had worked with all the volunteers to teach them the targeting routine she was putting Simba through now. Most of the staff and animals had picked it up pretty quickly, but some, like Simba, took a little more time and patience.

Krissy was pretty new and had probably rushed this morning, not recognizing Simba's agitation. Luckily, now he was cooperating, and she was able to take baby steps, clicking and rewarding the whole way, right up to the entrance of the holding pen. This was the real test. After being kept in a small cage for so long by his former owner, he preferred the open. But his enclosure needed to be cleaned and restocked for his own good.

She held her breath and moved to the gate of the smaller structure, the target held where Simba would have to enter the pen in order reach it. Biting her lip, her hand shook slightly, making the red ball waver. Simba paused, and she silently urged him on, cheering for him in her head. Then, as if it had been his own idea all along, he padded in and touched the target, letting Mollie close the gate behind him before accepting the rest of the meat as his reward.

"You did it!" She pumped her fist, wishing she could hug the silly beast.

"He did. And you did—that was amazing." Noah was grinning ear to ear, and without thinking she wrapped her arms around him, giving him the celebratory hug she wished she could give Simba.

Noah hugged Mollie, letting his initial concern and admiration heat into something more primal. There was no way he could have that tight body pressed against him without reacting. She felt his response and looked up, surprise flashing in her eyes before she pulled his head down for the kiss they both wanted. He let her take control, holding himself back as she explored his mouth, fisting his hands in her shirt to keep them still. His heart was pounding hard in his ears when she finally lifted her head and smiled at him.

"So, what do you think?"

"I think that we should do that more often," he teased.

She gave him a half-hearted push. "No, about Simba. Isn't he gorgeous?"

"I don't know, I think you've got him beat, looks-wise. But he is impressive. You about gave me a heart attack when you walked up to the fence like that."

"Sorry." She shrugged. "I should have warned you what to expect. But trust me, I'm not going to put myself in any danger."

"Good." His shoulders relaxed a bit.

"If Simba hurt me, who knows what would happen to him? I couldn't take that chance."

"Wait, you didn't go in there because you were afraid for him, not yourself?" Her logic was giving him an ulcer. "He could kill you with one swipe of his claws."

She tensed, her eyes narrowing at him. "He's not a bad animal, and it's not his fault what happened to him. This is his chance at a better life, and I'm not going to do anything to screw it up."

Noah shook his head. "Fine. Whatever your reasons, I'm just glad you're going to be safe. I don't want to turn on the evening news one day and find out you got eaten by an alligator or something."

"I promise," she swore, tracing a cross on her chest with her finger. "Now, time for the real work. It shouldn't take me too long to clean out his enclosure—you're welcome to take a walk and check out the other animals. I can come find you when I'm done."

She thought he was going to go play tourist while she sweated and did manual labor? He hadn't planned on scooping panther poop on his vacation, but he also wasn't going to sit by and let a women half his size do all the heavy lifting. "I'll help. Just show me what to do."

Forty-five minutes later, he'd scooped, scraped and hosed down the enclosure. Mollie, in turn, had scrubbed out the giant water bowl, fetched Simba's meal and vitamins from the main building, and placed what she called enrichment objects, basically industrial-sized cat toys as far as he could tell, all around the enclosure. She'd even scrambled up a tree to hang a rope from a low branch. The last step had involved them hiding the cat's food all around the enclosure—inside hollow logs, under piles of branches and even hanging from what looked like an oversize clothespin on the rope she'd put up. He was hot, sweaty, and probably smelled like panther poop and raw meat, but the look of satisfaction on Mollie's face made it all worth it.

"Done. Now we just have to let him back in."

"As long as we're getting out first, that's fine." He led the way back out, carrying the cleaning supplies and empty food bucket while she made sure the lock was secure, then watched her slide back the gate that had kept the oversize cat contained.

Wasting no time, Simba loped back out, but instead of pacing this time he circled more methodically, sniffing around until he discovered one of the hidden food caches. "He looks happy."

Mollie smiled, rocking back on her heels as she watched. "He does, doesn't he? Thank you for letting me take the time to do this and for helping with all the cleaning. You didn't have to do that."

"I know, but I wanted to." She'd put a spell on him, just as she'd done with the wild animal in there. Like the panther, he'd been hurt and licking his wounds when he met her, his head full of anger and betrayal. But she'd seen past that and had accepted him right where he was. From the start, her easy manner and natural confidence had seeped under his skin, winning him over before he'd even thought to protect himself. Her boss had said she was the best, and given how quickly she'd wrapped him around her little finger, he believed it.

Something about her just eased the ragged edges deep inside, soothing him when he hadn't realized he needed soothing. Like the panther, he'd come to Paradise wary, but none of that had mattered once he looked into Mollie's eyes.

He was in trouble, no way around it. Wanting something this badly meant being vulnerable, meant hurting. He'd learned never to hold on too tight, to wish too hard—too many moves and too many broken promises littered his past to believe otherwise. But today, standing in the sunshine with a sprite of a woman, surrounded by wounded and healed animals, it was a little too easy to believe in second chances and happily-ever-afters.

"Everything okay?" She squinted up at him, her innocence and beauty nearly knocking him out. "I was thinking we'd get this stuff put away, wash up, and then I'd give you that tour. No more mucking out cages, I promise."

He'd shovel crap all day, if that's what she wanted to do. "I'd like that. But then I'm taking you to lunch. Maybe kebabs… I'm having an odd craving for them all of a sudden."

He got the laugh he was going for and spent the rest of the morning being introduced to an incredible assortment of native Florida wildlife. The alligators he'd expected, as well as a variety of other animals—opossums, armadillos, bobcats, raccoons, pelicans and even a bald eagle that was missing part of a wing. All looked happy, despite being either too injured or too traumatized to survive on their own. Just like Baby, who had handled the transition to three legs better than some people handled a broken fingernail. He knew that part of the ability to push on, heal and survive was due to their innate resilience.

But he was beginning to think that it was more than that. They couldn't have recovered without the help of people like Mollie, without a support system.

Relying on others hadn't made them weak; it had given them strength. He'd spent a lifetime keeping people at a distance in an attempt to protect himself. Hell, he'd even kept his fiancée at arm's length.

Of course, just because he was ready to let down his guard and start reaching didn't mean Mollie felt the same way. She'd told him from the beginning she was looking to spread her wings, not get tied down. If he wanted any kind of chance at all, he needed to back off and let her take the lead.

Mollie was relieved to see that Baby hadn't caused any problems in the office since they left him. Not that he was a bad dog—she'd worked hard on his training—but his size alone could lead to issues in small, enclosed spaces. He had a habit of knocking things over with his tail, which was tabletop height, not to mention his tendency to move furniture just by leaning on it. But today he'd just napped, opening one eye lazily when she called his name, then insisting on giving a slobbery goodbye to everyone in the room before following her and Noah back to the car.

She loaded him up, then blasted the AC in a vain attempt to cool off. Noah looked just as sweaty, but in that sexy way that only worked on men. Women just got gross. Not the look she was going for. "Minor problem. I know you said you wanted to go to lunch, but we can't take Baby inside a restaurant, and it's too hot to sit outside. Maybe I should just drop you off at the inn? Or we could go drop Baby off, and then find somewhere to eat."

Noah's stomach growled in response. "I'm too hungry to wait that long. Why don't we pick up something to go, then take it back to the inn? Assuming Baby can come in there, of course."

"He can. It's practically his second home. And he loves to play with Murphy. But are you sure you're okay with takeout?"

"I'm sure. Let's just go get it before I die of starvation, okay?"

"Okay."

In the end, Mollie ran into a local deli while Noah stayed in the air-conditioned car with the dog. Five minutes later and they were back at the inn, Baby nearly tripping over his own feet in his mad dash up the stairs.

"Do you want to eat in the kitchen or on the porch? It's cooler inside, but we might have more privacy out here."

Noah headed for the front door, carrying the bags from the deli. "Cool sounds good right now, and I don't mind sharing. Besides, Baby is dying to get inside."

The mastiff was sitting in front of the door, whimpering in a very unmasculine way.

"Move over, and I'll open the door." She gently nudged the dog out of the way with her foot and opened the front door, leading Noah through the main lobby into the kitchen, Baby impatiently bringing up the rear.

A loud woof sounded from the back of the inn, and then a blur of black and white fur whizzed into the room. Ecstatic, Baby returned the greeting, then set to sniffing every inch of the smaller dog.

Noah found a rope toy and tried to instigate a three-way game of tug while Mollie spread out the food on the counter. "We've got smoked fish dip and crackers, club sandwiches, pasta salad, fruit, and rolls. Oh, and some cookies for dessert."

"Sounds good, I'll have some of everything." Leaving the dogs to play, he washed up and joined her at the counter, heaping a plate with, as he'd said, everything. He reached across her for a second cookie, his arm brushing her chest just enough to shift her appetite from food to him. Oblivious, he shoved the cookie in his mouth, leaning one hip against the counter.

"Dessert first?"

"Is that a problem?" he asked, one crumb sticking to corner of his mouth.

"Nope." She stood on her tiptoes and licked it off, watching his eyes go cloudy with desire. "Life is short. You have to enjoy it while you can."

He growled in agreement, then lifted her onto the counter, trapping her with his body. Her legs wrapped around his waist as he feasted on her mouth. Chocolate and sin, that's what he tasted like. She let herself get swept up in the moment, her hands tangling in his soft hair, his gripping her bottom, holding her in place. Not that she wanted to escape; there was nowhere else she wanted to be. Unless it was in a bed, naked. Just the thought of Noah naked had her whimpering.

"I don't mind you two making out on my kitchen counter, but the least you could have done is let me know you there was food."

Mollie pulled back enough to look over Noah's shoulder and saw Jillian filling a plate. "Oops. Sorry. There are cookies, too, but you'd better grab one before Noah eats them all."

Noah rested his forehead on Mollie's, his breathing ragged. "Jillian, I'll buy you one hundred cookies if you leave right now."

Mollie put her hands on his chest, appreciating the hard pecs under his shirt even as she tried in vain to push him away. "Sorry, but it's her house. Now let me down so I can get my lunch."

Noah obliged, lifting her off the counter as if she weighed nothing, then letting her slide down the front of his body where she could feel the evidence of his frustration. She loved that she had that power over him, but the chemistry between them was going to make her crazy if they didn't take a step back and cool off. She had some photos she needed to edit; maybe it would be a good idea to take a break from each other for the afternoon, get some perspective. Otherwise she was liable to do something stupid, like seduce him past the line he'd drawn or confess her undying love. Which was insane, because they'd just met, and people didn't fall in love that fast. She just liked him. A lot. And, you know, wanted to jump his bones on the kitchen counter.

"You going to eat?" Jillian was already tucking

into her food, sitting next to Noah at the same table they'd eaten the pie at the night before.

"Of course, do I ever turn down a meal?" She put a scoop of fish dip and a handful of crackers on her plate, along with some fruit. The cookies were gone, damn it. She plopped down on the other side of Jillian, who was barely picking at her food. "Hey, I thought you were hungry?"

"I thought so, too." She gave a rueful smile. "I just don't feel quite right. I thought a snack would help, but maybe not."

Mollie sat up straight, tension shooting down her spine. "Should we call the doctor? Does Nic know? Are you having contractions, headaches, what?"

Jillian held up a hand. "Whoa, slow down. No contractions. At least, I don't think so. I'm just tired and probably a little overheated. I spent most of the morning cleaning out the big flower garden over by the gazebo. Once I cool off a bit more, I'll be fine."

"You what?" Mollie dropped her fork with a clatter. "It's nearly a hundred degrees out there today, not to mention the humidity! You could have cooked that kid working outside like that."

Jillian smiled, but it didn't reach her eyes. "I doubt that. But I will admit it wore me out more than I realized. I promise to be more careful. Now, can I eat my lunch in peace or are you going to yell at me some more?"

"I don't know," Mollie answered honestly. The thought of something going wrong with Jillian's pregnancy had her insides all twisted up.

"Here, drink this." Noah set a large glass of ice water on the table in front of Jillian. "And when that's done, drink another. Dehydration can be serious during pregnancy."

Jillian shot Mollie a look, but didn't say anything other than a brief thank-you. She must be wondering how a single guy like Noah had a working knowledge of pregnancy, but she was too polite to ask. And Noah didn't look interested in sharing the details of his almost-baby. Yet another reminder why this vacation fling was destined to burn out. He was on the rebound in more ways than one, and if she didn't keep her feet under her she was going to wind up in a world of hurt. It was definitely time to put some distance between them.

She was about to say something about needing to leave when Jillian gasped, her knuckles turning white where she gripped the edge of the table.

"What, what is it?"

"I think… I think I had a contraction." Fear and pain tinged her voice. "But it's too early for contractions."

Mollie panicked for one small moment. Then she turned and ran down the hall, shouting for Nic, her feet slapping on the tile in rhythm with her jacked-up pulse.

"What?" Nic glared at her from his office doorway. "I'm trying to get some work done, if you don't mind."

"It's Jillian—she's in labor!"

Chapter 3

Noah shifted in a too-small plastic chair, watching Mollie pace the waiting room. He probably shouldn't even be here. He wasn't family, wasn't even really a friend, just a paying guest. But he'd given Mollie a ride, not wanting her to get behind the wheel in her agitated condition and knowing she'd be stranded at the hospital if she'd ridden with Jillian and Nic. An hour ago, he'd convinced her to grab a quick dinner in the cafeteria, but otherwise she'd spent the hours since they got here wearing a trench in the linoleum. It was enough to give him a headache. That, and the constant coming and going of families with new babies. A maternity-ward waiting area wasn't exactly on his top places to visit right now. Seeing the excitement was like having salt poured in a wound, one he wasn't sure how to mend. How did you get over losing a child you never really had?

Probably by moving on, getting back to who you were. Which wasn't a father or a family man. He didn't even have houseplants, never knowing when he'd decide to pick up and take off. He'd probably have messed it up anyway. But damn, he'd wanted to try.

The double doors at the end of the hall swung open, and a tired but grinning Nic walked out. "The contractions stopped. She's not dilated at all, and the baby's fine." He collapsed into the chair across from Noah. "She was just dehydrated and has what they called an irritable uterus. Not preterm labor."

"Oh, thank God." Mollie had tears in her eyes, but she forced a smile. "So everything is okay, really okay?"

"Everything is fine. They're going to keep her overnight, just so they can keep the IV going and monitor things, and she can go home in the morning. No bed rest or anything, but no more working in the heat, either."

Mollie pulled out her phone. "I'll call Cassie and let her know everything is okay. She wanted to come down but Alex was working and Emma was already in bed. And Nic, tell Jillian not to worry about work tomorrow. I'll cover for her."

"Thanks. She was already making noises about going straight to the clinic in the morning."

Mollie just rolled her eyes while listening to whoever was on the other end of the phone—her boss, Cassie, no doubt. It was good to see a group of friends sticking together and helping each other out, even if it meant he'd be on his own tomorrow. He'd kept to himself too much to make those kinds of connections in his own life, but when was he going to do what he could to change that? In the meantime, he'd get some sketching done and spend some time just chilling on the beach. If he really wanted to see Mollie, he could always take her to dinner or something. He could certainly wait until then.

He didn't even make it past lunch. Just before noon, he borrowed Nic's car and headed to the Paradise Animal Clinic, following the directions the couple had given him. He'd felt stupid asking for the favor, but that hadn't stopped him from doing it. Hopefully Mollie would be interested in going to lunch with him and not think he was some lovesick fool who couldn't stay away from her for more than a few hours. Even if it was the truth.

He pulled into a small lot in front of a cheery yellow building and told himself he was just a friend stopping by. A friend that had tossed and turned in bed all night thinking about her.

Inside he was met with the smell of disinfectant and wet dog, but at least the air was comfortably cool. An older woman was at the front desk, her gray hair cut in an efficient bob that matched the quick movement of her fingers across the keyboard in front of her. There was no one else in the waiting room, so he approached and waited for her to look up.

"Hello, can I help you?"

"Yes, I'm looking for Mollie. Is she available?"

"Who shall I say is asking for her?" The woman reminded him more of a butler than a receptionist, but Noah played along.

"Noah, Noah James. I was hoping to take her to lunch."

She frowned. "She didn't mention anything about that, but I'll let her know you're here."

Noah tried to look casual as he waited for her to fetch Mollie. He really should have called first. But that would have given her a chance to say no, and he wasn't risking that.

"Noah!" Mollie popped through a swinging door, looking all kinds of cute in scrubs and tennis shoes. "What are you doing here?" She halted midstep. "It isn't Jillian, is it?"

"Jillian's fine." Now he really felt like a jerk. "I just wanted to see if I could buy you lunch." *Because I missed you.*

She smiled and tilted her head, considering. "I'd like that, but I've got another half hour or so of work to do before I can leave. Can you come back in a bit? Or you could just hang out here, if you want. Might get boring, though."

"I'll stay. Just put me where I won't be in the way."

Forty-five minutes later, he was still leaning against a back wall in the main treatment area, and Mollie was scrubbing up to assist in surgery. The patient, a basset hound with a penchant for eating tennis balls, was already sedated, his remarkable X-ray hung up on the wall.

"I am so sorry," Mollie apologized for the third

time. "But someone's got to stay, and with Jillian out, I'm it." She smiled self-consciously and lowered her voice. "I'm just hoping I don't mess up. Jillian's been training me to do more tech work, but this is my first surgery without her here."

"I'm sure you'll do fine." And he was sure. He'd been watching her work, and she had a rare combination of compassion and intelligence that made everyone around her more comfortable. He'd seen her easy connection with animals at the rehab center, but she seemed to get along with her human coworkers just as well. Even when the dog on the surgery table had given her a scare, his heart rate doing something loopy, she had kept her voice calm, her movements controlled. After dealing with the temperamental types so frequently found in the art world—not to mention Angela's near constant histrionics—Mollie's upbeat and competent calm was like a cool ocean breeze, refreshing and restoring.

"All right, let's fix this guy up before afternoon appointments start rolling in." Cassie, an athletic-looking strawberry blonde, called from a doorway. "Sorry about your lunch and for stealing your guide from you today."

"No worries. Is the dog going to be okay?"

Cassie nodded. "I think so. He's just going to be a bit out of sorts for a while."

Well, that was a feeling he could relate to.

Mollie rolled her neck, trying to relieve the stiffness. She'd been on her feet for almost twelve hours now, much of that time spent lifting or restraining animals that didn't understand she was trying to help them. Not to mention the stress of emergency surgery on that poor basset hound. Rambo was going to need to learn more discriminating dietary habits if he wanted to live out all his allotted doggie years.

"That's it, that's the last of them." Cassie hung up her stethoscope, a wan smile on her face. "Thanks again for coming in on your vacation. I couldn't have managed today without you. Janet can handle the front desk in a pinch, and I'm grateful she's willing to fill in…."

"But she's not about to wrangle a Dalmatian into the bathtub for a flea bath."

"No, definitely not." Cassie made a face.

Just the idea of the elderly former librarian doing such a thing had Mollie's lips twitching. She and Cassie were both a little slap happy at this point, exhaustion and low blood sugar taking their toll after a long, hard day. Lunch had been a package of peanuts scrounged from a desk drawer and a can of soda. Cassie had offered to share her protein shake, but Mollie had refused, knowing the pregnant veterinarian needed the nutrition to make it through the day. Now all she wanted was a hot meal and a good night's sleep. But first, she needed to stop by the inn. She told herself it was just to check on Jillian, but she needed to see Noah, too. She wanted to share her day with him, find out what he'd been up to. Just be with him.

A knock at the door startled her back into action. "I'll get it."

Cassie grimaced. "If it's an emergency, tell them I moved away."

As if the soft-hearted vet would ever turn away an animal in need. Bracing herself for another client, Mollie's jaw dropped when she opened the door. Standing there, like the answer to her prayers, was Noah, two pizza boxes in his hands. Overwhelmed with gratitude, she pulled him in, planting a kiss right on his lips. "You are my favorite person in the whole world, starting right now."

He waited for her to lock the door behind him. "A pizza dinner and you're my biggest fan? What would you do for surf and turf, I wonder?"

"Shut up and feed me. I'm starving." She read the labels, one cheese, one with everything. Yum.

"Who was it?" Cassie asked, halfway back into her white lab coat. Her eyes widened as Noah followed Mollie into the room. "Our knight in shining armor, apparently. And just in time. Even the dog kibble was starting to look appetizing."

"Nic was coming into town to pick up some pizza for Jillian, and I remembered that you said you wouldn't have time for lunch. So I hitched a ride and figured I'd add pizza delivery boy to my résumé."

"Well, bless you for thinking of it."

Conversation halted as they dug into the food, eating off of pink paper plates that Mollie had found on top of the staff refrigerator. For several minutes the only sound was the occasional murmur of appreciation.

"Mommy?"

Cassie dropped her slice and wiped her hands. "I'm coming." At Noah's confused look, she explained, "My daughter. My husband drops her off before he starts his night shift with the sheriff's department." She went back up front, returning a minute later with the little girl, a miniature version of herself.

Mollie gave the girl a hug, and then introduced her. "Emma, this is Mr. James. He's staying at the Sandpiper with Mr. Nic and Miss Jillian."

The little girl nodded, her eyes on the food behind him. "Did you bring the pizza? Can I have some, too? I love pizza."

"Emma, it isn't polite to—"

Noah brushed aside Cassie's concern. "Of course you can. It would be rude of me not to share. Which kind do you want?"

"I'll get it for her." Mollie swept the child up into her lap, and slid a piece of plain cheese onto a clean plate. "There you go, cuddle bug." Mollie kept an arm around Emma's waist while she ate, partly to keep her from toppling out of the chair, partly because she liked snuggling the sweet girl. Back when Cassie had been a single mom, Mollie had spent a lot of time babysitting. She'd thought she was doing it just to help out Cassie, but now that Emma had a new stepfather in the picture and two sets of doting grandparents, Mollie was finding she really missed her time with the munchkin.

She always had enjoyed being around children, but that didn't mean she was looking to have her own. At least not anytime soon. Maybe after she'd made a name for herself, really gotten her career going, she could consider it. With the right guy. Her gaze strayed to Noah, her heart thumping a resounding *yes* at the idea. But her biological clock would have to reset itself, because her career trajectory was currently flatlined. It would be a long time before she reached a level where she could feel comfortable shifting her focus from it.

And that was okay. She had her friends, she had Baby and she was having an amazing but short-term fling with a famous artist. She certainly didn't need a committed relationship or a child to be fulfilled; that was the trap her mother had fallen into. No, she'd enjoy being the babysitter, and have her fun with Noah, and keep her eye on the prize. She couldn't afford to get sidetracked, no matter how tempting the idea was.

Mollie's feet were dragging by the time she and Noah got back to the Sandpiper. Clomping up the steps with all the grace of a seasick elephant, she forced herself to keep moving.

"You know, you don't have to walk me in. You should go home and get some rest. We were all up late last night, and you've been on your feet all day."

Mollie shook her head. "I'll go home as soon as I check on Jillian." Last night had been terrifying—

no way was she going to be able to sleep until she saw with her own eyes that everything was okay. They found Jillian in the office she shared with Nic, squinting at what looked like a brochure template on her laptop. Next to her was a large water bottle with the words *Drink Me* scrawled across it. Courtesy of Nic, no doubt. Relief washed over her, Jillian looked as good as ever. Glowing, even. Crossing the room, she gave her friend a hug. "You know, if you wanted a day off, you could have just asked. No need for the drama." She swallowed past the lump in her throat and sat on the edge of a chair. "Seriously though, you look much better."

"I should. I slept until noon, and I've had enough fluids to float the *Titanic*. I swear my feet are going to start sloshing when I walk." She closed her laptop. "Thanks again for covering for me today. I appreciate it. I promise not to let myself get run-down like that again."

"You'd better not. You scared the crap out of us last night."

Jillian sobered. "I know, I don't think Nic's over it yet. He wouldn't even let me go out to get the mail, insisted on doing it himself. Which reminds me, someone called here looking for you." She peeled a pink sticky note off of her desktop and held it out for Mollie.

"For me? Who would call me here?"

"I don't know, but he asked you to call back, said it was important."

The name, George Reeves, was unfamiliar, and

the area code was from out of state. Curiouser and curiouser. She glanced at the clock. It was almost eight; was that too late to call? Of course, if it was important, waiting until tomorrow could be a mistake. Choosing action over inaction, she pulled her cell phone from her pants pocket and dialed.

A few nerve-racking minutes of conversation later and her hands were shaking so hard it took her three tries to turn off her phone.

"What, what is it?" Jillian's concerned voice cut through the roaring in her ears. "Is everything okay?"

Mollie nodded, speechless for the first time in her life.

Noah, looking way too smug, left his perch against the wall and took the phone out of her still trembling hands. "So, are you going to tell us what he had to say?"

"Did you do this?" He must have. It was the only thing that made sense.

"Do what? You still haven't told us what he said. Or who he was, for that matter." Jillian looked from Mollie to Noah. "Can one of you fill me in?"

"That was the owner of a gallery in Atlanta. He saw my work and wants to include it in an upcoming show." Even saying it out loud it still didn't seem real. "He wants to hang my photographs in a gallery. In Atlanta." Nerves tossed her insides like waves after a storm. "Could this be some kind of a hoax?"

Noah smiled like a kid given a second summer vacation. "It's no hoax. George Reeves is the real deal. He's displayed some of my stuff—sold some of it for a good price, too."

Pieces clicked together, and her excitement began to ebb. "So it *was* you. You asked him to do this, as a favor?" She shot out of the chair, pulling her hands away. She didn't want to be touching him right now. Hell, she didn't want to be in the same room with him right now. "Is this some kind of trick, a way to get into my pants? Give me a pity showing, and I'll be so grateful I'll have sex with you?"

"No, of course not."

"Then what, some kind of weird payback because I was nice to you? Because I don't need your pity. Or your favors. I'm going to make it one day, and it's going to be based on my talent. And nothing but my talent." She'd heard of red-hot rage, and now she knew what it meant. Anger burned through her, narrowing her vision and heating her blood. She wouldn't be surprised if she could actually breathe fire.

"Mollie, be reasonable—"

"Reasonable?" She laughed, a bitter, hollow sound. "Oh, Noah, you really don't know me at all, do you? I'm known for a lot of things, but reasonable isn't one of them. A reasonable, sensible girl wouldn't have gone to dinner with you when you were drunk. A reasonable woman wouldn't have offered to be your tour guide on her vacation, or let you kiss her in her friend's kitchen. So you can shove your reasonable up your famous ass." Pivoting, she stormed out of the room.

"Wait, Mollie!"

She ignored him and kept going, down the hall, through the lobby and out the door. She didn't stop until she hit sand, kicking her shoes and socks off on the way. Damn him, she was crying, and she was not a crier. But for a minute there she'd thought this was it; this was going to be her big break. More than that, though, she'd thought Noah understood her, that he got what it was like to have a dream. Obviously not. She was just some chick that he could buy off. No wonder he didn't have many friends, if this was how he treated them.

The glow of a flashlight gave away his presence, and she considered trying to outrun him. But he knew where she lived, and she had a feeling he could be persistent. He'd arranged a gallery showing just to impress her. Who knew what he'd do next?

Noah was breathing hard by the time he reached Mollie. He was in good shape, but running on sand was harder than it looked. The exertion wasn't the real reason his pulse was pounding, though; the betrayal in Mollie's eyes had done that. He'd messed up, big time. He should have asked her before doing anything. Now she thought he was a manipulative bastard, and he didn't blame her.

"What do you want?" Mollie was sitting in the sand, her knees drawn up to her chest like a child. He dimmed the flashlight, letting his eyes adjust to the moonlit night.

"I want to apologize. I shouldn't have acted without your permission."

"Damn straight." Her chin jutted out, but he could still see the tracks her tears had made on her face.

"But you should also know I didn't buy you a spot in the show. I didn't even know he was going to offer you one."

She looked up, confusion clouding her eyes. "Then how? Why?"

"I sent him the link to the rehab center's website, the page with your photos on it. I knew they were good when I saw them on the wall, but I wanted George's opinion. I figured he could maybe hook you up with a dealer, stir up some interest. I had no idea he was going to book you into a show."

"You didn't?"

He shook his head. "No, but I should have. You're really good. I thought maybe I was biased, given how I feel about you, but obviously George thinks so, too."

She frowned, looking up at him, her eyes demanding a straight answer. "You don't think he's doing this just as a favor to you?"

"A favor? George Reeves doesn't do favors for anyone. Trust me, if he wants your work, it's because he thinks you have talent. Period."

She sniffed, and he realized she'd been crying this whole time, silently so he wouldn't hear. Hell. He sat down on the sand beside her, pulling her into his lap where he could feel her quiet sobs. "Don't cry, okay? If you don't want to do the show, I'll just tell him to buzz off."

She punched his shoulder and pulled away from him. "Don't you dare! I'm not crying because I'm mad anymore, I'm crying because it's a dream come true."

"Say what?"

"Happy tears, you idiot. Now shut up and kiss me, before you ruin it."

Now he understood. He palmed the back of her head and pulled her in, his lips seeking hers by the light of the full moon. Slowly, knowing how close he'd come to losing her trust, he kept the kiss gentle. He sampled rather than devoured, nipping at her lips and then soothing them with a flick of his tongue. She whimpered and wrapped her arms around his neck, her fingers tracing patterns along his scalp. Kissing her more firmly, he teased at the seam of her lips, then took the kiss deeper when she opened for him. Seconds turned into minutes, and the crash of the waves was replaced by the pounding of his own heart. She squirmed in his lap, spiking his desire. Lifting her, he turned and laid her on the sand, tracing the lines of her face with the pad of his thumb.

"You're beautiful, you know that? Prettier than anything should be."

"You're not so bad yourself." She tried to sit up, but he stilled her with another kiss. "Let me just look at you for a minute. I want to remember this. I want to remember you with the stars reflected in your eyes."

"Because you're going to leave."

Yeah, he was. But he didn't want to. Not now, and maybe not ever. "You could come with me. To Atlanta."

It was a crazy idea.

But it didn't feel crazy.

She shook her head. "You can't expect me to just pick up and follow you out of the state after knowing you less than a week."

"No, I guess not." So much for that idea.

"But I could come visit you." She offered a vulnerable smile. "I'll be going to Atlanta anyway, for the show. I could stay for a few extra days, let you show me around this time."

It was a start. When she ran out of the inn, he thought he'd lost her, but she was giving him a second chance. They were together for now, and they would be again, on his home turf. "You've got a deal."

Chapter 4

Mollie felt nearly boneless, the sun and sand having once again erased all the tension from her body. Hard to believe she'd been such a basket case just last night. Turning her head to the side, she could see Noah in a similar state of relaxation, spread out on his beach towel looking like every girl's fantasy. The sun had burnished his olive skin to a dark bronze, and his low slung trunks showed off what seemed like acres of lean muscle. Needing to touch, she reached out and traced the top ridge of his six-pack.

"If you keep touching me like that, I'm going to have to roll over to keep from embarrassing myself."

Intrigued, she let her hand drift lower, following the line of hair that started at his navel and disappeared under the edge of his bathing suit.

Noah's breath shot out in a hiss. Then, without warning he scooped her up, throwing her over his shoulder as he stood.

"What are you doing?" She kicked a bit, feeling silly with her head hanging halfway down his back, her only view his butt and the sand beneath his feet. Which, come to think of it, wasn't a bad one, after all. Giggling, she squirmed again, and he just clamped down on her legs more firmly, his step never faltering as he hit the water's edge. "Put me down."

"Okay, but you asked for it."

He dunked them both, letting her slide down his body as they sunk beneath the waves. Weightless, she held her breath, surfacing at the same time he did. Liquid sluiced down his face, his eyes simmering with heat despite the icy water surrounding them. But even that intensity was balanced by a cheeky grin. She loved that he could be sexy and playful at the same time. She loved a lot of things about him, actually.

"What's that smile about?" He wiped her dripping hair off her brow and then landed a gentle kiss on her upturned lips.

"I'm just happy." She was a naturally upbeat person, but today she felt like she was floating.

"About anything in particular?"

"Hmm, maybe," she teased. "I mean, it is a beautiful day."

"Uh-huh. Anything else?"

"Well, I don't know if you've heard, but I have a gallery showing coming up."

He nodded gravely. "That does sound familiar. Sure there isn't anything else?"

"I can't think of anything." He moved to dunk them again and she laughed, "Fine, yes, I'm also happy that I met you, and that I'm going to get to see you again, in Atlanta."

"That's better. I was starting to wonder if you were getting sick of me."

"Not yet. Of course, you're here for another two days, so maybe by then…" She sobered at the thought. Two days wasn't very long, and the show in Atlanta wasn't for another month. Of course, she'd be back to her regular life then—going to school, working, spending time with her family.

"Oh my gosh, I forgot about my family!"

"What about them?"

"I totally forgot to call and tell them about the invitation to the show. I should stop by there and show them the contract. Maybe that will prove to them that my photography isn't just a silly hobby."

"Well, then, let's go see them. You signed off on everything this morning, right?" She nodded. She'd spent most of the morning filling out the forms the gallery had sent over and oohing and aahing over their website. Noah had finally come by and dragged her out of the house, promising she'd have plenty of time to sift through it all later. They'd eaten Cuban sandwiches at Alejandro's again and then spent the afternoon on the beach stealing kisses and acting like tourists.

"Then we might as well celebrate, now that it's

official. I bet Nic keeps some decent champagne. I'll grab a bottle and we can all toast to your career."

"Um, okay." She hadn't taken a guy to meet her parents since high school; this was going to be interesting. And even though Noah probably wasn't thinking of it that way, her parents would.

"You don't have to come, if you don't want to. I could just run by, then come back afterwards."

He shook his head. "No way am I missing out on this celebration. We'll go together."

She swallowed, not seeing a way out. Oh well, her parents would just have to deal. "Let's head up and get changed, then. I don't think I'll be able to pull off a professional vibe if I'm in a bikini."

They ran up to the Sandpiper so Noah could get cleaned up and then headed to Mollie's house. She showered quickly and changed into a soft blue tank and a pair of tan capris. Not exactly high fashion, but compared to her normal cutoffs, it was a step up. She felt good in it, and if Noah's look of appreciation could be trusted, she looked good too. She'd even taken the time to blow-dry her hair and put on some makeup while Noah busied himself filling Baby's food and water bowls. Having a doggy door meant she didn't have to worry about letting Baby in and out, but he did expect his meals delivered on time and in sufficient quantity.

"All set?" Noah was leaning against her counter, looking for all the world as if he belonged right there in her kitchen, in her life. But as comfortable as it felt having him around, she needed to keep her head in the game. Dating him was one thing; making him a permanent part of her life was another. She'd gotten a toehold on success, but it was a long climb to the top. She needed to focus and stay nimble if she was going to make it in the art world. Her career had to come first, not a man.

She gripped the champagne Noah had brought in one hand and her signed contract in the other. "Ready as I'll ever be."

Noah watched the sky turn colors outside the car window as Mollie silently navigated the streets of her hometown. She'd been quiet ever since he suggested going to her parents' house. Did she think this was some kind of relationship milestone he was pushing on her? He wasn't trying to make a statement; he just wanted to be there for her, especially if her parents weren't as excited as she hoped. Heck, he wanted to be with her whenever something important happened. But how could he say that, given everything she'd said about avoiding long-term relationships? He needed to give her the space she needed and hope that in time she realized he would never stand in the way of her dreams. It wasn't much of a plan, but it was the only one he had.

Mollie stopped the car in front of a modest but well-kept single story home. A large oak tree dominated the yard, shading the manicured lawn. A hedge of hibiscus flowers bordered the driveway, and he could smell jasmine in the air. Mollie got out, and he followed her up a cobblestone path to the front door. She briefly knocked, then surprised him by walking right in.

"They don't lock the front door?"

"No one around here does, at least not during the day. Paradise isn't exactly a high-crime area."

Maybe not, but he'd lived in big cities too long to be comfortable with that level of openness. "You lock your door, though, right?" The idea of someone being able to walk in on her made his blood run cold.

She shrugged. "When I remember. But don't worry—I've got Baby. No one's going to bother me."

True, a dog that size was probably better protection than any dead bolt. He was just being paranoid, hating the idea that he'd be leaving in a couple days and she'd be here alone.

"Mom, Dad, are you home?" Mollie led them through a white-tiled foyer, past a sunken living room to their left and into an eat-in kitchen that looked out onto a small family room. A tall, slender woman with brunette hair pulled into a sleek ponytail stood at the counter chopping vegetables for a salad. Obviously Mollie's mother, she had the same ethereal grace and slight build as her daughter. Only the faint lines around her eyes and a few streaks of gray in her hair kept her from looking more like an older sister than the matriarch of the family.

"Mollie, what a surprise. I didn't know you were coming by. Are you and your friend staying for dinner?"

"Um, I don't think so. I just wanted to stop by and tell you and Dad something. Is he here?"

"He's in his office. Dani's in there with him. She wanted his advice about a new case she's working on. Why don't you go drag them out of there, or they'll be talking opening arguments for hours."

"Sure. Noah, I'll be right back. Oh, and this is my mom, Anna Post. Mom, this is Noah James. He's a friend of Nic's and is staying at the Sandpiper this week."

"Nice to meet you, Noah."

"The pleasure is all mine."

Mollie stepped around her mother, stealing a slice of red pepper as she walked by. Sticking her head into the hallway on the opposite side of the kitchen, she said something he couldn't quite hear, then turned back. "They're coming."

She paced back to him, and he almost reached for her hand to reassure her. Not a good move. If she'd wanted to advertise their relationship, she wouldn't have introduced him as Nic's friend.

A movement in the hall alerted him to the arrival of the rest of the family. Mr. Post was broad where his wife was slender, his shoulders nearly taking up the entire doorway. He was average height, in good shape, and had a full head of salt and pepper hair. Behind him was Dani, an athletic blonde who seemed to have inherited her father's strong physique as well as his interest in the law.

"Hey, sis, did you come by to mooch some of Mom's food? I know that's why I'm here." She stopped in her tracks, eyeing Noah like he was another menu item. "Who's the beefcake?"

Mollie rolled her eyes, then plucked a cherry tomato from the cutting board. "That's Noah. Noah, the smart aleck over there is my sister, Dani. You'd think a lawyer would have better people skills, but somehow she keeps winning cases."

The sisters' looks and lifestyles might be worlds apart, but they obviously had a similar sense of humor. And, he saw as Mollie swiped another tomato and tossed it to Dani, a close bond. "Nice to meet you Dani, and you, Mr. Post."

Dani nodded, her mouth full, but Mollie's father came over and offered his hand. "Nice to meet you, too, Noah...?"

"Noah James, sir." The man's handshake was firm, but not so strong it could be considered an attempt to intimidate.

"Are you two staying for dinner?"

Mollie stepped forward, taking control of the situation. "No, Dad. We came by because I have some news."

"News?" Dani's eyes widened.

"Yes." Mollie squared her shoulders, her eyes shining with pride. "I was offered my first gallery showing in Atlanta." She held up the contract in one hand, and the champagne in the other. "So I thought we should celebrate."

"That's awesome!" Dani high-fived her sister, then began pulling champagne flutes out of a kitchen cabinet. "So, does this mean people are going to buy your pictures?"

"Maybe, I hope so." Mollie started wrestling with the wire cage on the champagne bottle.

"Hold on, slow down here." Mollie's father furrowed his brow. "How did this happen? Are you sure it's legit? I've heard of scams, where they make artists pay for a spot and then it turns out the gallery never existed."

"Dad, yes, it's real." Mollie's shoulders sunk, hurt tingeing her voice. "But if the idea of me having real talent is so hard to believe, ask Noah. He knows the owner."

She should have known they'd react like this. Why couldn't they just be happy for her? At least Dani had congratulated her, rather than suggesting it was a scam like her father had. And Mom had that concerned look on her face she wore whenever one of her kids got into trouble.

"The gallery is legit, as is the offer." Noah took her hand, squeezing it in encouragement. He'd only known her a few days and was ready to stand by her. Why couldn't her parents give her the same kind of support?

"Honey, I'm sorry. I didn't mean to doubt your abilities. It's just out of the blue, is all. How did this happen?"

"They saw my work, and they liked it." It stung that her own abilities weren't enough to convince them, but maybe explaining Noah's connection to the art world would help. "Noah's shown some of his sculptures there, and he contacted the owner."

"What sculptures?" Her mom wiped her hands on a dish cloth and went to stand by her husband.

"Noah works as a metal sculptor. His last piece was featured in *Architectural Digest*. You can look up him online if you don't believe me."

Dani pulled her phone out and looked like she was doing just that.

"I thought you said Noah was a friend of Nic's?" Her mom blinked in confusion. "Now he's some famous artist?"

"I did a piece for Caruso Hotels a while back. That's when I met Nic. And yes, I've been lucky enough to be very successful with my art. But I didn't call in any favors, if that's what you're thinking. I just sent the owner a link to some of the photos she's done for the animal rehab center. He liked what he saw and thought she'd do well in his upcoming show. Mollie got this on her own merits. You should be proud of her."

Her dad cleared his throat. "Well, of course we're proud of her. It's not that. We just want to make sure she's thinking it all through." He nodded at her mother. "Right, honey?"

"Of course. It sounds impressive. But what about school and work? Can you just pick up and go to Atlanta like that?"

She held back a sigh, knowing that keeping calm was the only way to win them over. "It's a month away, and I'll only be gone a few days." Maybe longer, if she wanted to spend extra time with Noah. "I'm sure Cassie will give me the time off, and I can talk to my professors about it ahead of time. But I'm not going to let this opportunity go by, no matter what."

Her father jumped back in; they made quite the tag team, those two. "I know you want to do this. It's an honor, I'm sure. But we just don't want you to get sidetracked, that's all. Photography is enjoyable, and it's great that you might sell some of your work. But you need to remember that art isn't something you can count on, long-term."

"Not if I never try, it isn't." She blinked against the tears that had started to form. "And maybe you're right. Maybe I'm not good enough to make a career out of it. But the only way I'll find out is if I do my best and it isn't good enough. This show could open doors for me, get me noticed. Maybe I could even get some magazine work, I don't know. But I'm going to find out. I'm going to go to Atlanta, and I'm going to follow every lead I can and learn as much as I can. And I'm going to stay in school, not because it makes you happy, but because I want to learn more and get better at what I do. Which isn't law or accounting or any of those practical things you keep trying to push on me. I'm sorry, I can't be who you want me to be—I can't be another Dani."

Well, now she'd done it. Her father looked ready to argue, but her mom just looked hurt.

Dani, however, was laughing. "Well, thank God for that! I'm not looking for a clone. In fact, pass me that bottle, Noah. I want to make a toast."

Noah popped the cork with a practiced ease and

handed her the champagne, watching her fill the glasses with an amused smile.

"To my sister, the photographer. May she remember us little people when she's famous one day."

Mollie gave a brittle smile. Thank heavens her sister stood by her. Growing up, she'd never lorded her own success over Mollie, but had treated her as an equal. But Dani's support wasn't enough to balance out her parents' doubts.

As she sipped what was probably very expensive champagne, all she could taste was disappointment. She'd really thought this might finally impress her parents and get them to understand how important photography was to her. But it wasn't enough. It probably never would be. Her father wanted her to do something more lucrative, and her mother wanted her to have stability. What no one seemed to care about was what she wanted. Well, other than Dani.

And Noah, she realized. He'd braved this awkward family drama with grace and had defended her without bulldozing her. Her parents might be trying to control her, but he hadn't, not once. Instead he had encouraged her to chase her dreams. Even knowing that meant putting her career ahead of him.

As much as Noah had worried this might happen, it was obvious Mollie had expected a different sort of reaction from her parents. He could almost understand their concerns, probably from hearing similar ones expressed by his own father year after year. But where he had rebelled, he could see Mollie was just devastated. She had a closeness with her family that he'd never quite managed, and that gave her parents' words more weight. Weight that was crushing her right in front of his eyes.

"I think we'd better leave you all to your dinner. It was nice meeting you." He wrapped an arm around Mollie, her bare arms like ice against his skin.

"You don't have to go—"

"Yes, they do." Dani interrupted her mother, re-filling the glass she'd already drained. "They wanted to celebrate, so let them go do that."

Mollie found his hand, holding it with a death grip that belied her calm tone. "Mom, Dad, I appreciate your concern but I don't think there is anything else to say. I'll send you a postcard from Atlanta."

On that note Noah guided Mollie out of the house, wondering what it was between parents and their children that made everything so hard. He'd certainly never managed to see eye to eye on much with his own, but he'd thought that was because of their strained relationship. The pendulum swung the other way in Mollie's family, but the damage was just as great.

Outside he held the car door for Mollie. As she set her purse on the center console, she frowned, then quickly sifted through the contents. "Hell's bells. I think I left the contract on the counter inside." Her head fell back against the seat, her eyes closed. "I do not want to go back in there."

He didn't blame her after that scene. "I'll go get it, and you wait here."

"Thanks. I just don't want to get into it again with them, you know?"

"I know." He closed the car door gently and jogged back up to the house. Her father answered the door.

"Mollie forgot the contract—I told her I'd grab it while she started the car."

Moving aside, the older man let him by. "I feel like I should apologize."

"You don't need to, not to me. Mollie's the one that's hurting right now."

"Fair enough. But let me at least try to explain. Please."

Noah walked to the counter and picked up the contract, then nodded. The man clearly cared for his daughter, even if he wasn't doing a great job of showing it.

Her father sighed, looking older than he had just a few minutes ago. "It's not that we don't appreciate Mollie's talent or care about her feelings. It's just that we know how hard it can be to make a living doing something so…impractical."

The last sculpture Noah had sold probably cost more than this guy's mortgage, but pointing that out wasn't going to help the situation. "There aren't any guarantees when it comes to a career in art, but respectfully, sir, that's true of many things. There isn't much in life that's a sure thing."

Mollie's mother, who'd been quietly stirring something on the stove, broke in. "It's not just about the money. We didn't raise Mollie to be a snob. When I was a dancer, it wasn't the size of my paycheck that was an issue. It was never knowing if the next part would be your last, never knowing what was around the corner. The uncertainty of it all can wear you down and the isolation can be crippling. It's a hard life, and it can be a lonely one. I don't want that for my daughter."

"With all due respect, ma'am, I think that's her choice to make. She's a grown woman, smarter and stronger than most."

Her father nodded slowly. "We know that. We just want her to be happy."

"I believe you. But giving up her dream isn't going to make her happy, and neither is going against your wishes. If you make her choose, she's going to be miserable either way."

Which was why he was going to be damned sure he didn't put her in the same situation.

"If you want her to be happy, you have to trust her, that she knows what she wants, risks and all. It might not be what you want, but it doesn't have to be, if you love her. Now, if you'll excuse me, I've got a celebration to save."

He let himself out and found Mollie nervously drumming her fingers on the steering wheel. She started the car and cast an anxious glance back at the house. "Were they okay?"

"Yeah. They're fine, just confused. What about you—are you okay?"

"I am now." She took a deep breath, the tension visibly leaving her body. "Thanks for coming with

me. It helped, knowing you were there, that you believed in me."

"Anytime." He always wanted to be there, to have
her back. Maybe now was the time to tell her. "Listen, I know you said you don't have room in your
life for a relationship, that you don't want to sacrifice your goals for love. But just because your mom
gave up dancing when she got married and had kids
doesn't mean it always has to work that way. Having a family doesn't have to mean losing yourself or
giving up who you are."

Mollie's face paled under the yellow glow of the
street lights. "You say that now, but—"

"But nothing." He waited until she'd stopped for
a red light, the streets deserted in either direction.
Reaching out, he stroked her cheek before gently
turning her fact towards him, needing her to see his
sincerity. "I didn't plan for this to happen, and there
are a million reasons it can't work. But I believe in
being honest. And the honest truth is, I'm falling in
love with you."

She couldn't have heard that right. "You're what?"

"I'm falling in love with you." Any hope that he
wasn't serious was dashed by the heated look in his
eyes. "I didn't mean for it to happen, if that helps."

She didn't know whether to laugh or cry. He was
crazy; there was no other explanation. "But you're on
your honeymoon. A week ago, you were going to get
married to another woman, for the love of all things
holy." White-knuckling the steering wheel, she made

the last turn onto her street and pulled into the driveway. Shutting the car off, she turned in her seat to face him. She needed to set him straight, and fast. "So there is no way you could be in love with me."

"But I am." His eyes sought hers. "I know the timing is awkward."

She snorted. "Gee, you think?"

"But that doesn't change how I feel. I think I fell for you that first day when I saw you on the steps of the Sandpiper. You're beautiful, and talented, and you go out of your way to make everyone around you happy. You're the most amazing person I've ever met, and I don't want to just be some guy that you met on vacation."

"I said I'd visit when I'm in Atlanta." Why couldn't that be enough for him?

"I want more."

His eyes had gone dark, his voice thick with emotion. Part of her—okay, a big part—wanted to say the words he wanted to hear, but she couldn't. She was finally getting her career on track, and she owed it to herself to stick with her promises. If she compromised her future to be with him, she'd regret it forever. "Noah… I can't. I'm sorry, I just can't. In a few years, maybe…"

Pain flashed in his eyes, but he didn't argue. "Don't be sorry. You didn't do anything wrong. I'm the one pushing when I have no right to. You told me up front that you weren't looking for anything serious."

"So where does that leave us?"

"We go back to the way things were. No strings, no pressure."

A tightness eased in her chest. She couldn't commit to him, but she wasn't ready to say goodbye, either, at least not yet. "I liked things the way they were." She licked her lips and watched his gaze follow her tongue.

"You did, huh?" His tone was all smoke and whiskey, his features dark and dangerous in the moonlight. And dangerous was exactly what he was.

Before she had time to form her next thought, he'd crossed the tiny distance between the seats, his hand anchored in her hair as his mouth came crashing down on hers. Their other kisses had been passionate; this time he was possessing, nearly bruising as he probed and then penetrated, tangling his tongue with hers. She shifted on the seat, needing more contact, but trapped by the gearshift and center console.

As if sensing her frustration, he undid her seat belt and lifted her up and over into his lap. The angle of the kiss changed, his mouth trailing down her neck, his tongue sending tiny shocks down her spine. She could feel how much he wanted her as she wiggled in his lap, trying to maneuver in the narrow confines. "You were right." She bit off a moan as he bit her earlobe. "I do need a bigger car. Much bigger."

"So you're saying size matters?"

"Definitely." From what she could feel, he had nothing to worry about in that department. "I'm thinking an SUV. A big one."

"How about we just move inside before your

neighbors call the cops on us and Cassie's husband has to arrest me?"

"Neighbors? Oh, right." Her windows weren't even tinted; they'd been totally exposed and she hadn't once thought about anyone seeing them. He had a way of making her forget everything but him. Not good, not good at all. Even if it felt wonderful.

He opened the passenger door for her and she climbed out of his lap, banging her head on the roof of the car. "Damn it!"

"Are you okay?" She rubbed her head and nodded, but she was anything but okay. This was supposed to have been a fling, just a little fooling around before going back to real life. He could work off his rebound energy and she could have some fun before doubling down on her goals. But no, he had to go and say the L-word. Even worse, she'd almost said it back. Then what? As tempting as it was to just go with her feelings, she had to think of her future. If she sacrificed her dreams for him, she'd end up resenting him later. And she wouldn't do that, not to him and not to herself.

Besides, he couldn't really be in love with her. He might think he was, but no doubt he'd be over her by the time his flight landed in Atlanta.

Putting her key in the lock, she opened the door and absently patted Baby when he greeted her. Soon it would be just him and her again.

Suddenly exhausted, she considered their dinner options. "How about I call for pizza, and you find us a movie to watch? I think that's as much of a celebration as I can handle right now."

"That sounds perfect. Just no anchovies." He pressed a kiss to the top of her head and some of the tension of the last hour melted away. He wasn't going to press her; it was going to be fine. They'd have some food, cuddle on the couch, and just enjoy the time they had left. She could do this.

Chapter 5

Noah flipped through the on-demand movie options, looking for a comedy. Or an action movie. Just not a romance. The last thing he needed was to remind Mollie he was in love with her. She'd made it perfectly clear that she wasn't ready to settle down or make a commitment. She had a career to build, and he knew more than most the amount of time and dedication that took. It wasn't that many years ago that he'd been her place, just starting out. He'd had to focus 100 percent on his art to get that first big sale, and then he'd spent the next several years scrambling to keep the momentum going. Work-life balance wasn't something he'd had time to worry about, so how could he blame her for not wanting to take it on?

He couldn't.

She'd been right to shut him down. They were in two different places, going different directions. Which meant, if he really loved her, he'd let her go.

They had tonight and tomorrow, and then he'd be headed back to Atlanta and regular life, one without Mollie. The thought was like a physical pain, but there was nothing to be done about it, other than enjoy what time they had left.

Two hours later, they were curled up on the couch watching a second-rate movie, a half-eaten pizza on the coffee table in front of them. Or rather, he was watching the movie—Mollie had passed out before the first chase scene. In her sleep she was even more achingly beautiful, her long lashes making perfect half-moons against her creamy skin. Careful not to wake her, he stretched for the remote and turned off the movie, a blank screen replacing the rolling credits. He should leave and head back to his borrowed bed at the Sandpiper. But tonight was his last night in Paradise, and if he had the chance to hold her he was going to take it.

Sliding down, he tucked one arm under his head and rested the other across her chest. He could feel her heart beat, ticking away as if marking the time they had left. His own squeezed in response. No, he wasn't leaving tonight. He'd grab every last minute he could.

He lay there a long time, just listening to her breathe before he finally drifted off into a restless kind of sleep. Sometime later, he woke to an elbow digging into his ribcage. Eyes closed, he tried to shift, realizing too late that the couch was a lot smaller than his bed back at the inn. He hit the floor with a solid thunk, Mollie landing on top of him.

"Ow!"

"Are you okay?" He smoothed his hands down her body, not sure what he was even feeling for.

"Yeah. I just bit my lip."

His eyes had adjusted enough to the low light for him to see her gingerly touch her lip with the tips of her fingers. Still on top of him, her face was only inches away from his. Lifting his head he gently kissed the spot she'd touched. "Better?"

"Mmm-hmm." She nearly purred her agreement, and every sleeping cell in his body woke up, alert. She leaned in, brushing her mouth across his, and that was it—he was lost.

He rolled them, bracing himself above her, his hands on either side of her face. Her eyes were heavy with sleep and desire, her lips parted and her breathing heavy. She was by far the sexiest thing he'd ever seen, and he had to have her. Now. Here. Tonight. Nothing else mattered anymore; there was just the two of them in the silence of the night.

As if she'd sensed his decision or just reached the same conclusion on her own, she worked her hands under his shirt, her hands skating along his spine as she tried to free him from the fabric without breaking the kiss. Taking control, he shifted his weight to one hand and tore the shirt off with the other. A sigh of appreciation escaped her lips before she moved to explore more of his now bare skin.

Needing to even the playing field, he edged up the silky tank she wore, the sight of her lacy black bra pushing him one step closer to the edge. He hadn't been this worked up since his teenage rumblings in the backseat of a car, but with Mollie everything was more intense, more real. "If you're going to tell me to stop, tell me now." His voice sounded unrecognizable, more growl than human speech. She reduced him to bare instinct, the desire to mate and possess throbbing through his blood.

She wrapped one long, lean leg around his waist, holding him to her. "Don't you dare stop."

That was all he needed to hear. He found her mouth again, suckling her bottom lip while his hands went for the clasp of her bra. She arched her back to give him better access, pressing her barely covered breasts up as if in offering. He slid the fastener free, but didn't pull the material away. She was a master-piece, and he planned to study her inch by glorious inch. He licked along the ridge of her collarbone, then stifled her gasp of pleasure with another kiss.

At first he thought the ringing in his ears was from his skyrocketing blood pressure. But the sound continued, high pitched and utterly unwelcome.

Mollie's small hands pushed against his bare chest. "You should get that."

Cursing whatever phone gods he'd pissed off he got to his feet and snatched the ringing device off of the coffee table. Glancing at the display, he saw an unfamiliar number with an Atlanta area code and out of habit hit the speakerphone icon. "What?" Whoever it was better have a damned good reason for calling after midnight. Not to mention interrupting the most erotic moment of his life.

A saccharine sweet voice responded, "Is this Mr. Noah James?"

"It is."

"I'm calling from St. Luke's Hospital. We have a patient here, a Ms. Angela Garner. She's in labor and she's asking for you."

Anger coiled in his gut. "Why the hell should I care?"

"She listed you as the father of her unborn child."

"That can't be right. I'm afraid you've made a mistake."

"There's no mistake, sir. The paternity results are right here in the chart."

Mollie could hear every word of Noah's conversation, the sound carrying clearly in the still dark apartment. Tears stung her eyes, but she didn't have the right to cry. She should never have gotten involved with him, and half-naked rolling on the floor certainly counted as involved. Turning her back on him, she pulled down her shirt and then refastened her bra with shaking hands. How could she have let this happen? Getting caught up in the moment was no excuse. Not that her jumbled-up feelings were the issue right now. What mattered was getting him to Atlanta. He was going to be a father. Another woman just had his child. He should be at her side, no matter what had happened between them.

Steeling herself, she stole a glance at Noah. He was staring at the phone in his hand as if he couldn't understand what it was for. She took it from him and spoke to the woman on the other end of the line, writing down the details on the back of a napkin. Hanging up, she handed it back to him.

"Mollie…." His voice trailed off, his expression lost. "I have to—"

"I know." That he needed to leave was the one thing she did understand. "I'll drive you to the airport. I can have Jillian ship your things tomorrow, unless there's something you need to get now."

He shook his head. "No, there's nothing I need."

"Just give me a minute, and we can go."

She managed to make it to the bathroom before the first sob hit her. She turned the water on to mask the sound, not wanting to humiliate herself any further. Dear heavens, she'd practically begged him to make love to her. And only hours after she'd thrown his declaration of love back in his face. Thank God the phone had rung and she'd spared herself that final mistake. Because getting any closer to Noah James would probably kill her. She lost her mind every time she was near him; she couldn't bear to lose her heart, too.

A quick scrub with a wet cloth washed away her ruined makeup, but there was nothing she could do about her red, swollen eyes. Or the dull ache in the center of her chest.

Noah was by the front door waiting for her when she came out. His eyes were hollow, his mouth grim. There was no sign of the fun-loving man she'd gotten to know over the past few days; this man was a hard wall of fear and regret.

Baby whined as she opened the door, sensing something wasn't right, or maybe just confused by the commotion at such a late hour. "I'll be back soon. Don't worry, everything is okay." She hoped she was telling the truth. Hadn't Noah said the baby wasn't his? Better not to ask, since her questions wouldn't change anything. The baby was coming, and it was coming now.

Outside the moon had settled near the horizon, but the stars were as bright as ever, little hard points of light in the summer sky. Night-blooming jasmine floated on a warm wind, its sweetness mocking the bitter ache in her throat.

They drove in silence, Noah furiously tapping on his phone screen, probably making flight arrangements. The highway was nearly deserted, her headlights lighting up the asphalt as they sped by mile after mile of grassland and scrub. Of course, the land was never truly empty, and she kept an eye out for wildlife. The last thing she needed was to hit bobcat or deer trying to cross the road.

Finally, she saw the exit for the airport and a minute later was merging onto the slightly busier road. Even at this time of night, Orlando had a decent amount of traffic, tractor trailers carrying goods to the countless outlet malls and shops, tour buses, and the intrepid citizens who worked the night shift.

"We're almost there. Did you get a flight?"

He didn't look at her, just kept staring out the window, the only sign of emotion the clenched fists in his lap. "Yeah, Southern Air. It leaves at five."

The glowing numbers on the dashboard clock showed it was almost three in the morning. He'd have plenty of time to check in and get through security. And plenty of time to worry. "Want me to go in with you? We could get some coffee or something while you wait."

"No."

So much for that idea. Not that she blamed him. He was worried about his child, and who knew what he was feeling towards his ex? She'd lied about her lies, and now the baby whose loss he'd mourned for was here in the flesh, waiting for him. He had a huge mess on his hands, and having to make small talk with the woman he'd nearly slept with only an hour ago certainly wasn't going to make his night any less complicated. Better to say goodbye quickly and let them both move on with their separate lives. Their holiday interlude had been magical, but reality was rearing its ugly head and no amount of wishing was going to change the facts. He had a baby, maybe even a family, if he could work things out with his ex. And she had a career just starting to take flight. If she could remember that, and not the way his mouth felt on hers, maybe she could say goodbye without embarrassing herself.

She pulled into the drop-off zone outside the terminal, leaving the engine running. He didn't even have any luggage to unload, nothing to slow him down or draw out the moment. Not that she was trying to stall him. The sooner he was out of the car, the sooner she could stop pretending everything was okay.

Noah unbuckled his seat belt, then looked to her, pain and longing warring in those soulful eyes. "Mollie… I'm sorry. I didn't mean for things to happen this way."

She forced a smile to her lips, feeling like her face might crack from the unnatural expression. "Don't worry about me, I'm fine. Just go, be with your son. He needs you." She blinked, refusing to let her tears fall. "And Noah, if there's a possibility you and Angela can make things work, promise you'll try. You said you wanted to build relationships, and you have a second chance there if you want it."

He didn't answer, just brushed a stray lock of hair off her face and then let himself out of the car. And out of her life.

Noah had held on to the anger burning through him during the long, dark drive, using it to keep the fear and pain at bay. But looking into Mollie's eyes, bright with the tears she was trying so hard to hide, had been a torture that no amount of worry about the baby or hatred towards his ex could dull. He hadn't even been strong enough to say goodbye. Now she was gone, and he had to pull himself together.

He picked up his boarding pass, then took his turn in the security line, fighting to get back the numbness he'd perfected during all those goodbyes growing up. He'd learned as a child that there were situations in life you had no control over, and the only way to deal with them was to keep moving forward. But he'd never faced anything so terrifying before. What if the baby, his baby, wasn't okay? Angela's due date was weeks away—how early was too early? He should have asked the nurse when he'd had her on the phone. Hell, if Mollie hadn't been there to write down the name of the hospital, he might not even know where to go. His brain had short circuited the minute he'd heard the word *father*.

Of course, there was no guarantee he *was* the father. Angela could be lying again, for some ulterior motive only she understood. The nurse said there were paternity-test results, but how? He'd never been tested, although she could have stolen some hair from his brush or something. He wouldn't put that past her.

Still, he'd demand another test, one that he could make sure was on the up and up. But even paying for a DNA testing in a private lab would take a few days. What the heck did he do in the meantime? Could he trust anything Angela said? Could he let himself fall in love all over again with a baby that might not be his?

But deep inside, hadn't he always known it was his child? Wasn't that why he'd been so upset when Angela had run off? In his bones, he'd felt a bond with his unborn son, and whatever Angela had said in her note, he'd never stopped loving him.

Overwhelmed, he sank into a chair in front of his gate and automatically plugged in his phone to charge. At least that was productive. Desperate to keep his thoughts off of Angela and the baby, he flipped through some messages, but couldn't keep his mind on the words in front of him. Finally, he gave in and did what he'd been wanting to do since he got the phone call. He opened his wallet and pulled from its folds a black-and-white ultrasound photo. The technician had printed it for him months ago, pointing out the pixelated features of his son. He'd meant to throw it away after Angela's note, but hadn't been able to bring himself to actually do it. Or maybe he'd unconsciously held on to it out of hope, not wanting to believe the unborn baby he'd come to love belonged to another man.

Rubbing the wrinkled paper between his fingers, he realized it wasn't a matter of *if* he would be able to let down his guard and bond with the baby. The picture in his hand that he'd carried with him everywhere for the past four months showed it was too late for that. No, the real question was, how did he move forward from here?

"Is that your baby?" A middle-aged woman in a theme park T-shirt and too-tight yoga pants sat down next to him, her pink carry-on bag balanced on her lap.

Good question. Not knowing how to answer, he just nodded. Maybe she'd take a hint.

"Your first? I remember when I was expecting my first. We didn't have all those scans and tests and such back then. We had to wait until they were born to find out if it was a boy or a girl. Now, my daughter, she had a party when she found out with one of those cakes that you cut into—blue for a boy, pink for a girl. I think it's more fun to wait myself, but at least she knew what color to paint the nursery."

He nodded again and wondered how anyone could be so chipper before dawn.

"So, did you find out?"

"Excuse me?"

"The sex. Is it a boy or a girl? Or are you waiting to find out?"

"A boy." That he knew. It was everything else that he'd have to wait to find out about. If the baby was healthy. Why Angela had lied to him. He rubbed his eyes, suddenly exhausted.

"Are you okay?" The woman's eyes widened. "Oh my, is the baby... Is everything okay? I didn't even think—"

"I don't know." And the not knowing was killing him. "I got the call that my... The mother is in labor, but it's too soon. The due date isn't for another month." He wasn't sure why he was sharing all this with a stranger, maybe because saying it out loud made it more real. He needed to face the facts, and fast.

"Oh, how scary." The grandmotherly woman patted his hand reassuringly. "I'll say a prayer for him, but don't you worry. Doctors can do amazing things these days. A few weeks is nothing to worry about. Your son's going to be just fine, you'll see."

He nodded, swallowing past the lump in his throat. In his hands the grainy lines of the ultrasound blurred and his eyes stung. Damn it, he was not going to cry.

Thankfully, a bored-looking airline employee chose that moment to announce the boarding call for first class. "That's me." He gave a nod to his seatmate and stood.

"Good luck."

"Thanks." He needed all the luck he could get.

The ticket taker was efficient, if not personable, which was just fine with him. Soon he was settled in a window seat in a mostly empty section of the plane. It seemed midweek early-morning flights weren't popular with the first-class demographic. The half dozen other passengers sharing the space looked to be flying for business, whispering into phones or typing on their laptops right up until takeoff. Not a life he'd ever wanted to lead.

He'd worked part-time gigs over the years, made minimum wage doing various odd jobs, but he'd never felt tied to them. And now that he was actually making money as an artist, he could set his own hours, lead his own life. Not that he was doing very well in that regard. He was about to have a baby with one woman and had fallen head over heels with another. And he had no idea what he was supposed to do about any of it.

Chapter 6

Mollie woke to the sun shining in her eyes and a dog butt in her face. She vaguely remembered crashing on the couch when she got back from dropping Noah off. She should have gone to bed, but somehow being on the couch where they'd cuddled just hours before made him feel closer. Maybe that was pathetic, but Baby wasn't going to judge her. That was the great thing about dogs—they never made fun of you or told you to pull it together. Really, he'd just been excited to be allowed on the couch at all. She normally had a firm rule against dogs on the furniture, but she'd also had a firm rule against falling in love. Rules weren't her thing, obviously.

"Go on, move over." Baby grudgingly moved an

inch, probably afraid he was about to lose his coveted spot. "Fine, stay there. But I'm getting up."

She left the big dog sprawled across the cushions while she used the bathroom and brushed her teeth. She avoided the mirror entirely. No good could come of that, not after three hours of sleep and another two of crying. Instead, she finger-combed her hair by feel and pulled on her comfiest sweats. Today was her last day of vacation; maybe a walk on the beach would put things in perspective. That, and a cup of coffee.

She gathered her camera bag and the dog's leash while her old-fashioned percolator heated, filling the air with the world's best aroma. Maybe if she took deep enough breaths she could absorb some of the caffeine while she waited for it to finish. Finally it stopped bubbling and she poured the dark, rich coffee into a thermos with milk and sugar. "Come on, Baby. You can't stay on the couch forever."

The big dog blinked slowly as if considering doing exactly that, before finally clambering down, one leg at a time. She let him do his business outside, then loaded him into the car for the short drive to the Sandpiper. Paradise had a public beach, but she'd gotten in the habit of parking in the Sandpiper's lot and starting from that end. Probably because that way she could raid the big commercial refrigerators before going home. Her own food stash tended towards stale crackers and outdated yogurt more often than not.

She parked at the far end of the lot and skirted the inn itself, sticking to the sandy path that wove through the grounds and down to the beach. Jillian should be at work on a Friday morning, but she wasn't taking any chances. Sympathy from her friend would just send her over the edge. She needed clarity, not company.

The beach itself was nearly deserted, just a few retired fishermen surf casting, unable to stay away from the water where they'd spent the better part of their lives.

She returned their waves as she and Baby walked by, taking comfort in the normalcy of the moment. Her life might feel like it was spinning on its axis, but no matter what, there would always be old men fishing on the beach, as constant as the tides themselves.

She strolled right at the water's edge, where the wet sand was hard-packed and easier to walk on. Baby kept pace, eyeing the chattering gulls but not giving chase. He was a constant, too; she could count on him even when doubting herself. They walked for about a mile, passing the most deserted part of the shore before hitting the public beach area. Ahead, she spotted a young boy tossing a ball and she tightened her grip on the leash.

"Not yours, Baby." The dog had an addiction to fetch, despite his missing limb, and was liable to beg, borrow or steal any ball he came across. He whined pathetically but didn't attempt to pull away.

"Hi! Can I pet your dog?" The freckle-faced child smiled up at her, no fear showing despite the fact the dog probably outweighed him three times over.

Baby whined again and nudged the ball in the boy's hand.

"Sure, if your mom says it's okay."

"Mo-om! Can I pet the dog? The lady said I had to ask you first."

Mollie grinned as a woman around her own age got up from her beach chair, shaking her head at her son's exuberance. "Hi, I'm Gina. This guy," she ruffled his hair affectionately, "is Benji. I hope he wasn't bothering you. He just really loves animals."

"I'm Mollie, and no, he's fine. Baby loves to make new friends. And he especially loves kids."

"Baby?" She smiled. "I guess that's better than Tiny."

Mollie chuckled. "It's probably good I didn't think of that, or I might have gone with it."

"So, can I, Mom? Please?"

"Sure." To Mollie, she whispered, "He's been wanting a dog for ages, I'm thinking maybe for Christmas. I'll have finished the manuscript I'm working on by then, so I'll have more time to spend training a puppy."

"Good plan. You don't want to get into a position where you're overwhelmed."

Gina laughed, her eyes dancing. "I think that ship has sailed. Being a stay-at-home mom while trying to have a writing career is more than I bargained for. Not that I'd change a thing."

"That does sound tough. What kind of writing do you do?"

"I write mystery novels. As much as I love being

home with him, I think it will be a lot easier once he starts kindergarten. Until then, it's…interesting. Yesterday I was in the middle of this gory murder scene and had to stop midsentence to help him use the potty." She shook her head, grinning. "I thought about putting off writing until he's older, but I'd be lost without it, you know? It's just part of who I am."

"How do you manage it?" There she went, blurting out whatever she was thinking. It wasn't any of her business how this woman managed her time. But she talked about writing the same way Mollie felt about her photography. It was a part of her identity, and she couldn't imagine giving it up.

The young mother shrugged and watched her son. "I have a great babysitter, and I get a lot done during his naps. Then when my husband gets home in the evening, he handles the bath and bedtime so I can squeeze in some more hours then." She stroked the dog's fur as she thought. "It's hard sometimes, and I don't get anywhere near as much sleep as I'd like, but it's totally worth it."

Mollie nodded, trying to fit this woman's experience into the mental dividers in her head. Wife, mother, writer. Of course she'd known in theory that plenty of women worked and had families. Cassie certainly managed, but Mollie had somehow drawn a mental line between a scheduled workweek and more creative pursuits. An artist's muse didn't follow a set schedule and she'd assumed someone like Gina would end up secretly resentful of the time she lost to her family. "No regrets, huh?"

Gina grinned at her son, who was now covered in dog slobber and sand. "Never. But speaking of getting it all done, I've got to take him home for his nap. Thanks for letting him make friends with Baby."

"Anytime." Mollie watched the pair leave and then headed farther down the beach. She had a lot to think about and plenty of ground to cover while she did it.

Back in Atlanta, Noah's car was waiting for him in long-term parking, a tiny piece of normalcy in a world that no longer felt like his. The traffic was also normal, which meant it had been nearly an hour and he still wasn't at the hospital. An hour that seemed like forever, on top of the lifetime he'd already spent on the plane. He'd tried to nap in the air, but despite his exhaustion he couldn't stop his thoughts long enough to fall asleep. His brain was a constantly turning carousel, rotating between his anger at Angela, his worry for his son and his heartbreak at leaving Mollie. If he'd had a little more time with her, maybe he could have gained her trust, convinced her that he would never stand in the way of who she wanted to be. As it was, he'd groped her and then run out, flying hundreds of miles away to see another woman give birth to his child. Not the way to convince Mollie he was serious about her. No, he'd marked himself as a drama magnet, and no doubt she was glad to be rid of him.

Finally he spotted the sign for St. Luke's. He wove through the lot, eventually spotting a car pulling out. He snagged the spot, then jogged into the towering steel and glass building. Moving felt good, a way to take some action and burn off the adrenaline souring his stomach. Inside, the icy air hit him like a fist, slamming him with the scents of disinfectant and disease. Damn it, he hated hospitals. Anything medical, really. But none of this was about his likes or dislikes, so he forced what he hoped was a pleasant look on his face and asked the volunteer at the reception desk where to find Angela.

"Third floor, in the west tower." It sounded like the kind of directions you'd get in a medieval castle. But he dutifully took the paper visitor's badge and stuck it to his shirt before heading to the bank of elevators she'd indicated. He passed an enormous fish tank and briefly wondered why it was that all hospitals seemed to have fish. Maybe unconsciously the designers recognized that the fish were trapped just like the patients were, in tightly controlled environments calibrated to their specific needs. A depressing thought, probably not what the hospital had in mind when it added the tank.

On the third floor, he found himself in a yet another lobby, a smaller one with framed pictures of teddy bears on the walls. A frosted glass window led to what he assumed was the labor and delivery area. He rang the bell and a nurse slid the window open. "Can I help you?"

"I'm here to see Angela Garner. Someone called me and told me she was in labor."

"Are you a relative?"

He swallowed hard. "I'm the baby's father."

She nodded and typed something into the keyboard in front of her. "The doctor is checking her now. When he's done, I'll have someone come and get you. It shouldn't be too long."

"Thank you." He flopped down in one of the chairs and absently grabbed a magazine. *The Illustrated Guide to Breastfeeding.* No, just no. He tossed it down and rested his head in his hands.

Minutes passed. An older couple came in, the wife in tears, the husband beaming, his chest stuck out like prize rooster. *I'm the Grandpa* was emblazoned on his shirt in big black letters. Crap, Noah hadn't called his parents. He'd do so later, when he knew what was going on.

The nurse at the desk buzzed the proud grandparents through and then answered the phone. A frown crossed her face for just a second before her features smoothed into a more neutral expression. Speaking softly, she watched Noah, and he felt a premonition come over him. He watched her hang up, unable to move.

"Mr. James, I'm afraid there have been some complications."

Complications? What the hell did that mean?

"The baby isn't tolerating labor, so they're taking Ms. Garner in for surgery. She's on her way to the operating room now."

"Operating room?" A ball of fear solidified in his stomach, settling like lead on the ocean floor. "What? How?" He didn't even know what to ask. Had no idea what to do. He'd been signed up to take a weekend childbirth course, but Angela had left him before it had started.

"She's having a cesarean section. The baby's in distress, so they need to act fast. She'll be under general anesthesia, so I'm afraid you can't go back with her. But if you have a seat, I'll let you know when she's out of surgery."

Holy hell, distress? What did that even mean? "Just tell me, is she going to be okay? Is the baby okay?"

The nurse's eyes softened briefly. "I'll try to get an update for you as soon as I can. All right?"

"Yeah, I guess it has to be." He somehow made it over to one of the chairs lining the wall, then popped up again, unable to stay in one place. Pacing the ridiculously decorated room, he realized just how over his head he was. He needed backup. Instantly, his mind went to Mollie, but that was hardly a viable option. No, there was only one person he could call right now and know they'd pick up.

Taking out his phone, he dialed the number by heart. As he expected, it was answered on the first ring. "Hey, Dad. It's Noah."

Mollie walked on the beach for another hour, the young mother's words stuck in her head. No regrets. Wasn't that what she wanted, a life with no regrets? She'd vowed to stay single and pursue her career because she didn't want to look back and wonder, "What if?" But Gina's words offered a whole other perspective. Mollie had been so focused on her photography she hadn't thought about how many other things she might lose out on. Somehow she'd assumed that a relationship, a family, would all be there when she was ready for them, if she ever was. Like she could schedule a lover the way she scheduled her twice-a-year dentist visits. What if she missed her chance at love, and it wasn't waiting for her when she was ready for it? What if there was a whole other world of regret she'd never really considered? Was she making the same mistake her mother had, closing off one part of herself to fulfill another? At least her mother had her scrapbooks and those old programs—Mollie just had that single photo of Noah she'd snapped on the boat. Would that be enough to satisfy her if she ended up alone in her old age?

Feeling more lost than when she'd woken up this morning, she let her steps take her up into the old inn. Jillian wasn't there, but she could at least get some more coffee and a muffin and hope the sugar and caffeine would kick-start her brain. Murphy greeted them eagerly, barking and bouncing around Baby, but the bigger, older dog was too worn out from their walk to do much more than wag his tail in return. "Sorry, Murphy. We should have taken you with us, I wasn't thinking. Next time you can go, too."

"Go where?"

Mollie turned at the sound of Nic's voice, nearly tripping over Baby, who had collapsed in a heap in the middle of the floor. "The beach. I took Baby for a long walk and now he's too tuckered out to play. If

I'd been thinking, I would have stopped and picked up Murphy on my way."

"Don't let him fool you. I already took him for a jog first thing this morning. He ran three miles, and if he had any sense at all he would be snoozing like Baby. He's just too rock-headed to know he's tired."

Mollie ruffled the border collie's ears, smiling at his goofy dog grin. "Don't you listen to him, boy. He's just jealous that you're in better shape than he is."

Nic laughed and stepped around her to the big coffeepot they kept constantly filled for their guests. "Want some?"

"Do you even have to ask?" He handed her a steaming mug and she helped herself to the cream and sugar. "I don't suppose you have any muffins left over from breakfast?"

"In the bread box."

She grabbed a blueberry one and bit down into pure, sugar-filled decadence. "Yum. I needed that, thanks."

He waved off the appreciation and leaned against the counter, sipping his own coffee. "So, you want to talk about it?"

She swallowed, the sweet muffin turning to saw-dust in her mouth. "Talk about what?"

"Noah leaving, finding out he's going to be a father. Or the weather, your pick."

How did Nic know about any of that?

Seeing the question on her face, he grinned. "Don't worry, I'm not a mind reader. Noah texted me from the airport, asking me to ship his luggage to his place in Atlanta. Naturally I asked if everything was all right, and he explained about the baby."

She tried to force a smile but gave up. "Yeah, it sucks."

"Sounds like it. So, what are you going to do?"

"Do? There's nothing left for me to do. He's gone. He needs to figure out his life, and I'm moving on with mine. End of story."

"Uh-huh." Nic looked less than convinced. "So that's it?"

"Why wouldn't it be? He was only here on vacation. For heaven's sake, he was supposed to be on his honeymoon with another woman. We had some fun, but it was never supposed to be anything more than that."

"So you're not in love with him, then?"

"No."

Nic raised an eyebrow.

"Fine, maybe." She clenched the coffee mug like a lifeline. "But that doesn't matter. He needs to focus on his family now, not me. Who knows, maybe he and his ex will get back together now that he knows it's his baby."

Nic rolled his eyes. "Right, because nothing makes a guy want to give a girl a second chance like finding out she lied to him. Noah is not that stupid."

He had a point. "Even still, he has a kid now. That's got to be his priority."

"And having a child means you can't have a relationship? I'll make sure to tell Jillian we need to get divorced once the baby comes."

"Not the same thing. You were together before you started a family."

"Okay, then how about Cassie and Alex? Should they not have gotten married just because she already had a child? Would that have been best for Emma?"

She opened her mouth then closed it. Emma adored her stepfather and was blossoming with all the extra attention that her new grandmother and aunt gave her. And Cassie had never been so happy. "You're a pain in the butt. Don't you have guests to greet or something?"

"Not right now. And someone has to talk some sense into you. Jillian's at work, so you get me." He softened his voice and gave a wry smile. "Trust me, I've been there. When I met Jillian, I told myself there were a million reasons it couldn't work. But it did. Love is always a risk, but it's one worth taking."

"Wow. I didn't know you were such a romantic. Did you steal that off a greeting card or something?"

"Probably. But it's still true. At least consider it, okay?"

"I'll think about it." She couldn't stop thinking about Noah. But that about him wasn't going to change anything. No matter how much she wanted it to.

Chapter 7

Noah had known his father would come. A man of few words, his dad had simply asked which floor to go to and then hung up. That his mother had come with him was more of a surprise, although maybe it shouldn't have been. Didn't all women get worked up over the idea of grandchildren? Still, his parents usually managed to avoid being in the same room together. They had a tendency to combust when kept in close quarters and Noah felt the tension flooding his system ratchet up a few degrees.

"Have you heard anything?" His mom gave him a hard hug, then stroked his face the way she had when he was a kid.

He shook his head. It had been half an hour since

they'd told him Angela was being taken to surgery. "I'm hoping no news is good news."

"That's exactly right." His father patted him on the shoulder. "These things take time. I can't tell you how long I waited for news when your mother was having you. I was getting ready to punch my way back there when they finally told me you were both okay."

Noah's felt the muscles in his neck relax an infinitesimal amount. "Yeah, the idea did cross my mind."

His mom took his arm and led him to a chair. "Sit, tell us what happened. I thought she'd taken off, that she said you weren't the father."

"That what I thought, too. But when the hospital called, they made it clear that she's saying I am. They took her back to surgery before I could see her, so I didn't get a chance to ask her why she lied or what kind of game she's trying to play now."

His father nodded thoughtfully. "You'll have testing done, I suppose."

"She already did, or so she says."

"And you believe her?"

He shrugged. "I probably shouldn't, but yeah, I do. I'll pay for another test, to be certain, but my gut tells me she's telling the truth this time. So I'm here."

"Of course you are. You're not the kind of person that could turn your back on a woman and child in need, no matter what the circumstances." His mother's confidence in him helped ease the sting of Angela's betrayal.

"I just feel like an idiot."

His father's head snapped up. "Don't even go there. You took her at her word, you stood by her when she said it was yours and you did what you could to track her down even after she left you. Your actions have been honorable. That hers haven't is no reflection on you or that baby."

Humbled, he nodded. He had done the best he could and would have to figure out the rest as he came to it. He started to say "thank you," then spotted someone in scrubs out of the corner of his eye.

"Noah James?"

"Yes." He stood, wanting to take whatever news she had for him on his feet, like a man.

"Your girlfriend is in recovery. She's going to be out of it for quite some time. But I can take you to the NICU to see your son if you'd like."

The breath he'd been holding whooshed out of him all at once. "Are they okay?"

She smiled. "They're both stable. Your son gave us a scare in labor, but his APGAR scores were good and he's breathing on his own. They took him to the NICU more as a precaution than anything else."

"What kind of scores?"

"APGAR scores are a way to judge how well a baby is doing in the first few minutes of life. He passed with top marks."

"And I can see him? Now?"

"Just follow me. Oh, and you're allowed two people at a time in the NICU, so if you want to bring someone back with you..."

He turned back to his parents. "Mom? Want to come?"

She sniffed and wiped a tear from the corner of her eye. "Wild horses couldn't keep me away."

"Dad, you okay out here?"

"I'm fine. Your mother would have me court martialed if I tried to cut in line ahead of her. I'll go find us some coffee or something. You two take your time."

"This way, please." The nurse used her badge to open the heavy automatic doors, leading them through a labyrinth of hallways. Finally they stopped in an alcove next to a glassed-in room. The nurse pointed to a large sink. "First you need to wash your hands up the elbows, removing any rings or bracelets. Then I'll give you each a gown to put on over your clothes."

This whole thing was surreal. He scrubbed as thoroughly as he could, but all he could think was that this was it. He was going to meet his son.

He probably should hold something back, just in case this was all an elaborate plot concocted by Angela. Gut feeling or not. But when they were finally gowned up and ushered into the nursery, he knew it was a losing battle. He let the nurse squirt sanitizing gel into his already clean hands, his heart thumping triple time in his chest. There was no way he could hold back or be logical about this. "Mr. James, this little guy would like to meet you."

The nurse beckoned him over to some kind of space-age plastic crib, with more lights and monitors than he'd imagined could fit in such a small space. His mother took his hand, squeezing tightly when she looked at the tiny baby inside. "Oh, Noah, he's the spitting image of you as a newborn."

The little one had pale skin that looked a size too big for him, but he was awake and alert, watching them as intently as they watched him. The full head of curly hair looked a bit out of place on such a young baby, but what had Noah's breath catching in his chest were his eyes. They were the same ones he saw looking back at him from the mirror every day, the eyes he'd gotten from his father and his grandfather before that. "He's really mine. He's my son."

"Can I hold him, please?" The nurse checked the chart once, then adjusted the wire that led from the beeping machine beside her to a small, heart-shaped sticker on the baby's chest. "He's all yours, Daddy."

Noah slid one hand under the baby's head, relishing the feel of his soft curls, and the other under the diaper-clad bottom. "Like this?"

"That's it."

Trembling with awe, he lifted the baby boy to his chest and felt the hot tears he had been holding back slide down his face. His son. Whatever else happened, he was a father now. And he was going to do whatever it took to stay in his son's life, no matter what Angela tried to pull.

Noah spent the rest of the day just holding his son, letting go only so that his parents could take their turns. He'd even gotten to feed the little guy his first bottle. But now it was time for the seven o'clock shift change and the nurses were about to kick him out.

"Go get dinner or visit your girlfriend. She should be on the postpartum floor by now."

Noah didn't bother to correct the assumption, feeling a pang of guilt for not having thought of Angela earlier. He might never forgive her for her lies, but she was the mother of his child and he could have at least checked on her. "Has she been asking to see the baby?"

The pretty nurse colored, her cheeks flushing as she averted her eyes. "Um, not that I've heard. But surgery can be rough. I'm sure she'll be asking to visit tomorrow, once she's feeling a bit stronger."

Understanding hit him. It wasn't that Angela was unable to visit the baby. She just didn't want to. Which made an awful kind of sense, as much as he hated to admit it. Maybe she was just tired, like the nurse said, but Angela had a bad habit of avoiding anything she thought might be difficult. If that was the case, well, she was going to have to grow up—whether she liked it or not. Starting right now.

He'd wanted to rush right up to Angela's room, but his parents had insisted on getting dinner together before they left. He'd chewed through a soggy tuna sandwich without tasting anything other than his own impatience and was now nursing a cup of lukewarm coffee while his parents shared a piece of chocolate cake.

"Don't make assumptions, son." His father stared him down, apparently picking up on Noah's ill-concealed anger. "She just gave birth, and she had a pretty bad time of it from the sounds of things. You don't know what she's thinking or why she hasn't seen the baby yet."

"Right." It was true he had no idea what she was thinking, but then he obviously never really had. And what's more, he didn't care. All he needed to know was that she was going to do the right thing by the baby and by him. Once he'd talked to her, they could work everything else out through their lawyers. Her daddy's old money would certainly pay for hers and he'd had one on retainer since she walked out on him.

"Your father's right, of course. She may just be having a hard time of it. But I'm willing to say now that I never trusted her. Don't go up there and attack the woman, but be on your guard. I wouldn't put anything past her, not after what she did. The thought of her keeping a son from his father..." She shook her head, her stylishly bobbed and highlighted hair shimmering even under the cheap hospital lighting. "Just don't let her suck you back in. Just because you love your son doesn't mean you have to be with his mother. No good can come of that kind of a marriage."

"One like yours, you mean?" Crap, where did that come from?

"Excuse me?" His mother arched one perfectly arched eyebrow. "What's wrong with my relationship with your father?"

Noah looked from one parent to the other, desperately wishing he'd kept his damn mouth shut. Either the lack of sleep or the shock of fatherhood seemed to have broken the part of his brain that filtered his thoughts before he said them. Crumpling his napkin, he tried to backtrack. "Nothing. I just know you two tend to be…volatile." And argumentative, and stubborn, and sometimes even a tiny bit manipulative.

His mother's eyes widened in surprise before she burst out laughing. She thought it was funny? Were all women crazy?

His father reached over and pecked her on the cheek before turning back to Noah, an easy grin on his face. "Your mom and I fight, but it doesn't mean anything."

Huh? "So it's some kind of game for you?"

"I wouldn't say that," his mother interjected. "Your father and I just have very different views on a lot of things. And we're a bit hardheaded about it. But we never take offense, right, honey?"

"Right. I'd hate to have a pushover for a wife. Your mother keeps me on my toes, battle-ready so to speak. If it wasn't for her, I might have gone soft in my old age. She challenges me, and I like that."

He blinked, his synapses short-circuiting. "Wait, you like fighting with each other?"

His mom shrugged. "I wouldn't call it fighting. We just both like to express our opinions."

Right. Whatever. If constantly disagreeing made his parents happy, well, then, he was happy for them. But it was still crazy, and not what he wanted in a relationship. He wanted someone who had his back and understood him even when he didn't understand himself. He wanted Mollie.

He stood up from the table, shoving any thoughts of Mollie to the back of his mind. He couldn't deal with that right now. But he could go handle whatever drama Angela had cooked up. And by then the NICU visiting hours would have started up again and he could spend the night with his son. "Thanks for the dinner, and thanks for coming. It meant a lot."

"Of course we came. And we'll be back tomorrow, to check on you and visit our grandbaby. Like it or not, you aren't going to be able to keep us away."

A few months ago, the thought of more family time with his parents would have been terrifying, but not tonight. "Good. Now go home. I'll see you tomorrow."

He somehow found his way back to that original waiting room with the stuffed bear pictures on the wall. This time he spoke with more confidence when the nurse at the window asked him his name. "Noah James, here to visit Angela Garner."

The woman buzzed him back, then directed him down a long hallway in the same direction as the NICU. "Postpartum rooms are in that wing. She's in 1102."

He hadn't realized how near she'd been before. Probably better that way. He was still upset, but his parents had been right; some food and a mental break had left him feeling slightly more in control. But just slightly.

At the very end of the hallway, he found room

1102. The door was partially opened, but he knocked anyway.

"Come in."

He eased the door open and walked in, then stopped at the foot of the bed. He didn't know what he'd expected to find, but it wasn't this. Angela was wearing an embroidered robe and silk nightgown, the teal color picking up the green in her eyes. Her heavily made-up eyes. She was in full makeup and her hair was perfectly arranged. But more surprising than that was the random guy sitting at her bedside.

"Noah, you came!" Angela's surprise sounded real. Had she really thought he'd ignore her call?

"They said you were in labor, that the baby was mine."

"Well, of course it's yours, silly."

He fisted his hands in his pants pockets. "You said in your letter that you'd lied, that he wasn't."

"Oh, that. I was just upset. You didn't really believe me, did you?"

"I didn't know what to believe. Or where you were. Or if my baby, if it was my baby, was okay. But mostly, yeah, I believed you because what else could I do? You left, Angela."

Her face contorted into her version of a frown, one that was careful not to cause any wrinkles. "I was hormonal. And you weren't treating me well." She reached over and patted Mr. Polo-and-Khakis on the hand. Who at least had the good grace to look uncomfortable about the whole situation.

"If by treating you well, you mean letting you

spend all my money on whatever you wanted, I guess I didn't. But this is a life you're talking about. Not a disagreement over what movie to watch."

"Fine, you're right. I thought you might get like this. That's why I had the paternity test done. All they needed was your toothbrush. Crazy what they can do these days."

Damn, his toothbrush. He'd noticed it was missing, but had assumed the cleaning lady had tossed it. That Angela would have swiped it had never occurred to him.

"So are we okay now?"

Nothing about what she'd done was okay, but there was no point in pressing her. Changing the subject, he gestured to the third party in the room. "Going to introduce me to your friend?"

Angela flashed a brilliant smile, and he remembered why he'd initially fallen for her. Or rather, been sucked in by her. She was gorgeous on the outside. It was the inside that was the problem. "Oh, yes, Noah, this is Dick. He was nice enough to let me stay with him while I was sorting things out."

Noah just barely managed to stifle a laugh. She'd left him for a guy named Dick? Speaking of names— "The hospital wanted to know if we had a name for him."

Angela's nose crunched in confusion. "For who?"

Noah counted to ten and reminded himself she was probably on a lot of painkillers. "The baby. They want to know what we are naming the baby."

"Oh. Well, I thought you'd want to name him, since it's a boy. All the fun names are girl names."

All right, then. "How about Ryan after my father?"

She nodded absently. "That's fine. Can you come up with a middle name, too? And tell the nurses?"

Yeah, he could do that. "Do you want me to see about taking you down there to visit him? I'm pretty sure I can commandeer a wheelchair if you need one."

She looked at her new boy toy, then back to him. "I don't think so… I'm so tired. And I've got a visitor, I wouldn't want to be rude and leave him all alone while I went traipsing around the hospital."

Noah's jaw dropped. Surely she didn't mean what she was saying. "You don't want to go see your baby, whom you haven't seen yet, because you're entertaining?"

"I said I was tired, too. And sore. You have no idea how hard this all was on me. Besides, I wouldn't even know what to do. I'm sure I'd just be in the way."

He kept his temper in check—she *had* just had major surgery, and who knows how many hours of labor before that? Maybe she just needed some time to rest. But very soon they were going to have a serious talk. Alone.

Mollie had spent the afternoon at her computer, editing images, looking for ones good enough to include in the upcoming show. Tedious but creative, the work was detailed enough to keep her mind off of

Noah, at least mostly. At nine, she finally finished. Wincing a bit, she stretched her kinked-up muscles and realized she was starving. She'd somehow forgotten both lunch and dinner. She'd made real progress, though, so a grumbling tummy wasn't too high a price to pay.

"How about you? You hungry, too?" Baby thumped his tail in response. "Okay, then, let's get some dinner." She padded into the kitchen and filled Baby's bowl with kibble, then added half a can of wet food as a treat. She poured herself a bowl of chocolate-frosted cereal and milk, and then carried it to the tiny kitchen table to eat. Her phone was there where she'd thrown it when she'd come home, the message light blinking. Oops. She picked it up, and saw she had three text messages. One was from Jillian, asking how she was. She texted back, Okay. Call you tomorrow, and thumbed down to the next.

The next two were from Noah.

The first read: Sorry about everything.

The next was a picture of a newborn, with the words: He's okay.

She thumbed back, So glad with shaking hands. Looking at the photo, there was no question the baby was his. It looked like a tiny, slightly wrinkled version of Noah. Which meant he really was a father now. Was he happy? Scared? Was he angry at Angela, or had he looked past her mistakes for the sake of his son?

Mollie set the phone down and stared at it. What

was she supposed to do now? Call him? Pretend she'd never met him? Drown her feelings in sugary cereal?

The phone rang, vibrating on the table. It was Noah. Taking a deep breath, she picked it up.

"Hi, Noah."

"Hey." He sounded good. Tired, but good. "I hope it's okay to call. I saw you had texted back, and I figured I'd take a chance."

"Of course you can call. I'm happy to hear everything is all right."

"Yeah, he's great. His name's Ryan Thomas. He's five pounds, nine ounces and healthy. They're saying he should be able to move to the regular nursery tomorrow, as long as he keeps doing well overnight."

The pride in his voice had her blinking back tears. "I'm sure he will do well. He's a lucky little boy. And Angela, is she okay, too?"

"Um, yeah. Better than expected, in fact. We still need to sit down and talk about everything, though."

She fought to keep the jealousy out of her voice. "That's great. Well, I should let you get back to them, and I've got a ton of work to do before the gallery show. Have a good night."

"You, too. And Mollie, I really am sorry. About everything."

"Yeah, me, too. Goodbye, Noah."

She stared at the phone for another few minutes after hanging up. He was happy; that's what should matter. And it did matter. It just also sucked to know that he was happy there, with his ex and his baby, snuggling and bonding, while she was here eating soggy cereal with her dog.

Worse, she wasn't just jealous because he was with his ex. No, she was actually jealous that Angela was the one with the baby. With Noah's baby. Which was just plain stupid. She'd never felt her biological clock so much as tick, and now, looking at the baby picture on her phone, it was in full alarm mode.

Just the thought of a child should terrify her, even if it was Noah's baby. Especially if it was Noah's baby. Man, love really did mess with your head.

Thankfully, she had the upcoming show to distract herself with, not to mention the summer semester starting on Monday. She had plenty to keep her busy and keep her away from Noah. Maybe in a while she would consider the idea of a relationship, a family, but not right now. Not with Noah. He deserved a chance to figure things out on his own without worrying about her. More to the point, his son deserved all of his father's attention right now. Learning to parent a newborn and hashing things out with the ex would be hard enough without adding a long-distance relationship to the mix. If she cared about him at all she'd let him navigate his new life without any extra encumbrances or demands. And she did care, more than she wanted to. Which meant there was only one thing to do.

She picked up her phone and looked at the picture one more time before hitting delete. Then, her stomach clenching, she forced herself to block his number. They needed a clean break. If he kept calling her, she'd eventually cave and tell him how she felt, and she was not going to pressure him like that. This was the right thing to do, for both of them.

But man, it felt awful. Sliding out of her chair she sat down on the kitchen floor and wrapped her arms around her dog. Thank God dogs didn't have drama. She couldn't handle any more.

Chapter 8

Noah hefted the car seat carrying his sleeping son in one hand and knocked as softly as he could on the apartment door with the other. No way was he risking the doorbell—Ryan had just fallen asleep and he'd rather face a lion unarmed than an over-tired baby. He could hear muted noises on the other side of the door, but after several long minutes and repeated knocks, no one answered. Angela knew he was coming by now with the baby. Noah had been keeping him at his apartment ever since he'd been discharged so that Angela could rest and recover from the C-section. But it had been over a week, and they were supposed to switch off. He'd even paid for a nanny so she'd have help with Ryan.

Maybe that's who he could hear inside, and Angela had gone out for something? If the nanny had just started, she might not feel comfortable answering the door. Either way, he wasn't going to keep standing outside when he had a perfectly good key in his pocket. He let himself in and spotted Angela's favorite designer purse sitting on the entryway table with her keys. So she *was* here. Maybe he'd just knocked too softly for her to hear him. He passed through into the large living room, his steps muffled by the plush wall-to-wall carpeting. Seeing no sign of anyone, he set the car seat, sleeping baby and all, on the floor and headed down the hall towards the back of the apartment.

Angela's bedroom door was open, and he could see her standing in front of the bed with her back to him. "Hey," he called out. "Sorry to barge in, but I was trying to be quiet so I didn't wake the baby."

Startled, she spun around, clutching a folded sweater to her chest. Was she doing laundry? That didn't sound like her; she sent all her clothes out to be cleaned. "Noah, I didn't think you'd be here so early."

"I said after lunch. It's one o'clock."

She darted a nervous glance at the clock on the nightstand. "Oh, I must have lost track of time." Her face was pinched, as if he'd interrupted something and she wished he'd go. Looking around, he realized the normally tidy room was a mess, with clothes thrown on every surface. Two suitcases with trendy logos on them were on the floor beside her, a smaller one on the bed. A sick, dark pain curled deep in his chest.

"What the hell's going on here?"

She smiled just a shade too brightly. He knew her manipulative ways too well to fall for that. "I'm just...going through my things."

"That's bull and you know it. You're packing. Why? Where are you going this time?" He heard the baby fuss outside and panic took over. "If you were planning to take my son away from me, you'll have to do it over my dead body. It's time to grow up, Angela. It's not about you and your temper tantrums anymore. We've got a kid, and he deserves to grow up in a stable family. That means we have to try to get along, no matter how we feel about each other. No running off, and no more lies. He deserves better than your petty schemes."

Her eyes filled, and for once he thought maybe, just maybe, he was seeing the real Angela, not the facade she normally wore. "Don't you think I know that?" She dropped the sweater onto the bed, and wiped her eyes, smearing her makeup. "I know I'm flighty and irresponsible. Maybe it's genetic. My mom certainly never won a Mother of the Year award. And I'm definitely not anywhere near ready to settle down and be the kind of person that has a kid. I mean, look at me. Do I look like someone's mom?"

What she looked like was a confused and spoiled girl trying to play dress-up. He almost felt sorry for her, but the baby in the next room was the one that deserved his compassion. Angela had used up her share long ago. "It doesn't matter what you look like.

The fact is, you have a child, and you need to start acting like it."

"No, actually I don't."

"What the hell does that mean?" He was too tired to play games, and Ryan's cries were getting more urgent. Stalking back down the hall, he went to the kitchen to make up a fresh bottle of formula. And found nothing there but wine and leftovers from the high-end restaurant down the street. Where was all the baby stuff? "Where's the formula? He's due for a bottle, and now is as good a time as any to show you how to mix it up."

"I don't have any. Didn't you bring some?"

He counted to ten silently before answering. "No, I didn't bring some, because I assumed that you would have the basics, like formula and bottles and diapers. But I guess I overestimated you. Again." He shoved a hand through his hair. He needed this to work, and getting angry wasn't going to fix things. "I'll run down to the store. We can finish talking when I get back."

"No." She stood in the kitchen doorway, blocking him in.

"Angela, whatever is going on, we'll work it out when I get back, okay? I'm sorry I yelled, but damn it, this is exactly the kind of thing I'm talking about."

"I didn't buy that stuff because I didn't plan for him to be here."

"Angela, I know the pregnancy was a surprise, but you've had nine freaking months to get used to the idea. That's more than enough time to stock up on some bottles. Hell, you don't even have to fill them. That's what the nanny is for."

She looked down, avoiding his eyes. "She's not coming. I fired her. And before you ask why, it's because I'm not going to need a nanny."

He rolled his eyes. "Please, you don't even have the basic necessities, and you've never changed a diaper in your life."

"That's right, and I don't intend to start." She shrugged, and her eyes clouded a bit. "We both know I wouldn't be any good at it anyway."

What was she saying? "You'll learn. Everyone has to learn."

"I don't. I'm leaving. Dick's flying me to New York City. He has an apartment on the Upper East Side."

Was her boyfriend's yuppie address supposed to impress him? "I don't care if he lives in the top of the Empire State Building. You can't just come and go whenever you feel like it and dump Ryan off on me like you're taking a dog to the kennel." Man, he should have expected this. Too tired to argue, he headed back to the living room to get Ryan. "Fine. When are you getting back? We can work out a custody schedule then."

"That's what I'm trying to tell you. I'm not coming back, and I don't want custody."

Noah stopped, his legs frozen to the floor. "You don't mean that."

"Oh, I do. I mean, he's a cute baby and everything,

but I'm just not cut out for motherhood. And Dick, he needs me up in New York right now."

"And your son doesn't need you?" Rage fought with denial. "You're what? Just going to give him to me and pretend this never happened?"

"If I can." She blinked back a few more tears. "In fact, it's probably best we don't stay in contact—no use picking at old wounds and all."

Grabbing the baby carrier, he stalked for the door. "Don't worry. The only contact you'll have from now on is with my lawyer."

Mollie eyed her suitcase and the black spiked heels sitting beside it. She'd packed and repacked for Atlanta three times, but she couldn't make it all fit. Normally she was a minimalist, but she had no idea what she was going to feel like wearing, and in a fit of desperation had shoved what seemed like every outfit she owned into her only piece of luggage. Which would be fine if she could just get it closed. With her shoes in it.

The sound of the doorbell broke her standoff with the recalcitrant suitcase. "Come in, Mom. I'm back here." Baby scurried to the front door to act as greeter, leaving on her own.

"Aren't you ready? We need to get going."

Like she didn't already know that. "I'm almost done. I'm just packing a few last things."

Her mom walked into the room and then stopped, her jaw dropping open at the tangled mess of clothes spilling out of the suitcase. "Oh, honey! What happened?"

Mollie set her jaw. "Nothing. I just wasn't sure what to bring, so I kept adding things. Be prepared, you know? I may have let it get out of hand, though."

To her mom's credit, she tried to keep her composure, Mollie could see that. But she couldn't help the twitching of her lips or the twinkle of amusement in her eyes. "Being prepared is one thing, but panicking is another. You should have called. I would have come over and helped you pick out what to bring."

She was right. She should have called for backup when she first opened her closet and broke out in a cold sweat. Or at least gone shopping for a new outfit, like Cassie and Jillian had asked her to do. But lately she'd barely had the fortitude to make it through work and school, let alone some kind of girly shopping trip. And asking her mom for packing advice had seemed too close to asking for life advice. Not a door she wanted to open. She'd kept her emotions in check for the last month, but just barely. If her mom started asking her all sorts of questions, she was going to have a breakdown and she absolutely didn't have time for that. "I thought I had it under control."

Her mom checked her watch quickly and then set down her purse. "We've got a few more minutes. Let's see what we can do."

Less than ten minutes later, Mollie watched in bewilderment as her mom easily zipped up the suitcase. Shoes and all. Inside she'd fit three possible outfits for opening night of the show, all better than the ones Mollie had originally put together. And a few pairs of jeans, shirts and underthings. "Mom, you're amazing."

Her mother's cheeks turned a dainty pink. "Thank you, but it was nothing. I've just had a lot more experience packing than you have. When the company I was in traveled, you didn't get much time to get ready, and you were only allowed one bag on the bus. It's a skill you never lose once you learn. Now, grab your stuff and let's hit the road."

Mollie nodded, bending down to give Baby one last hug and kiss before slinging her purse over her shoulder and hefting the suitcase into her hand. Alex would be picking him up to take him to the inn after his shift. The big dog would have a blast playing with Murphy and being loved on by Emma. "I'm right behind you."

They made good time, reaching the outskirts of Orlando in a comfortable silence. Mollie felt herself relax. She'd wanted to drive herself, but the parking costs weren't in her budget. And it was a weekday, which meant Cassie and Jillian were working, as were their husbands. So, she'd asked her mom and prayed it wouldn't turn into an hour-long interrogation session about all the ways she'd messed up her life. So far, so good.

"So, do you have plans with your young man while you're in Atlanta?"

Obviously she'd just been waiting for Mollie to drop her guard.

"His name's Noah, and he's not my young man."

Her mom huffed out a breath while cautiously passing a truck carrying pallets of sod. "Well, I don't know what they're calling it these days. Boyfriend, significant other, partner, whatever. I just assumed you'd be going to see him while you're there. That is where he lives, right?"

Mollie silently counted to ten. *She's only asking because she cares.* "I don't think so. We…we haven't kept in touch, I guess you'd say."

"What? Did you have a fight or something? I know you two didn't have much time together, but he seemed so enamored with you. Your dad and I thought it was all very romantic."

"Maybe, but his ex-girlfriend going into labor with his child was kind of a mood-killer."

"What?" Her mother risked a glance at her before returning her attention to the road.

"Yeah." If they were going to have this conversation. she might as well spill all the details. "He was originally supposed to be in Paradise for his honeymoon." She quickly filled her mother in on the circumstances of the non-marriage and the reason for Noah's proposal.

Her mother's brow furrowed as she processed the convoluted story. "So he tried to do the right thing, even though he wasn't in love with her. I don't agree with that idea, but I can understand his reasoning."

"Right, but then his fiancée ran off a few days before the wedding, leaving him a note saying the baby she was carrying wasn't his. He was heartbroken—

about the baby, not her. At least he was until he got a call that she was in labor and it really was his kid."

"Oh, my goodness. I can't imagine how that felt."

Mollie gripped the armrest of the car. "It certainly wasn't the best night of my life. Or his, for that matter."

"So what happened? Did he get back together with the ex? Is that why you broke up?"

She shrugged, purposely looking out the window away from her mother's probing gaze. "I don't know."

"What do you mean, you don't know? He just left and never called or anything?" Indignation laced her tone. Nothing like a man messing with her little girl to bring out the protective mama bear mode.

Mollie felt her face flush. "He did. He sent me a picture of the baby and told me everything was okay. Then I blocked his number."

"You did what?" Her mother took a turn too quickly and had to tap the brakes. "Why would you do something like that?"

"Um, because he has a kid now?"

"And that changes how you feel about him? Did you think he was a virgin or something?"

"Mom! Please." Mollie squirmed in her seat. "I just think he should be focusing on his son right now, not me. And besides, I'm not looking to start a family, so dating a man with a kid isn't in the cards, not now."

"First off, I think you should let him decide what he has time for. But why don't you want a family?

You've always been so good with children. All the neighborhood kids always wanted you to be their babysitter."

Her heart panged at the memory. She did love kids, but those were other people's kids. "I am just starting my career. I may have to travel or work long hours. There's really no telling. How can I do that and have a family? You couldn't." That last part slipped out before she could stop it, but maybe a refresher on her mother's own history would make her understand.

"I certainly could have if I'd wanted to. I just didn't want to."

"Because you couldn't do both at the same time, at least not well."

"No. Because I never actually wanted to be a professional dancer, and meeting your father gave me the confidence to finally quit."

Mollie stared at her in shocked silence. Who was this woman and what had she done with her mother? "You never wanted to be a dancer?" How was that even possible?

"Nope. Your grandmother wanted me to be a ballerina. Dancing was her dream, not mine. Not that I hated it. It was fun at first and I made a lot of wonderful friends. But my feet always hurt, and I was always dieting to try to stay as slender as the other girls. Plus I got horribly homesick whenever we traveled for special shows. When the spot in the New York company opened up, your grandmother just assumed I would go. I almost did. But your father—

he reminded me that I was an adult and I needed to make my own decisions. If I wanted to dance, he'd support me. He'd even move to New York to be with me. But if I didn't want to, then I needed to tell my mother, 'Thank you, but no thank you,' and find something I did want to do." A smile crossed her face as she pulled the car into the drop-off line at the terminal.

Despite being firmly strapped in by her seat belt, Mollie's stomach lurched as if it had been tossed by a rogue wave, her childhood view of her mother flipped sideways and backwards. "But what about all the scrapbooks? I thought you kept them because you missed dancing so much."

"Those?" Her mom laughed. "Your grandmother made those. When she died, she left them to me. I only kept them around because you liked looking through them so much. Trust me, I never resented leaving that life behind. I like my life, my family and being able to eat dessert whenever I want. But if I'd wanted to stay, I would have made that work, too. Anything's possible—you just have to want it badly enough. Now give me a kiss and go, or you're going to miss your plane."

Trying to balance a baby on his shoulder while shaving was a skill Noah hadn't quite acquired yet. He had the baby part down—Ryan was happily drooling on the lapels of a starched dress shirt—but the shaving part had ended with a good slice almost taken out of his ear. The intelligent thing to do would have been to put the baby down. He had in fact tried that no fewer than five times in the past hour, and each time his son had scrunched up his face and let loose with blood-curdling wails. Colic, the doctor had said, and it happened like clockwork every evening. From five to nine every night, the little guy needed to be held and walked around, or there was hell to pay. Right now it was six in the evening and Ryan was nothing if not punctual. A habit that would undoubtedly be an asset later in life, but was currently less than helpful.

Wiping off the last of the shaving cream, Noah backtracked to the bedroom and slipped on his shoes. Now to get the baby ready, a process in and of itself. Just leaving the house now took more time and effort than some part-time jobs he'd had. Juggling the baby in one hand and the diaper bag in the other, he headed for what used to be a workspace but was now a makeshift nursery. Inside, the matching crib and changing table jostled for space with a drafting table and shelves full of his sketches. Some of his smaller sculptures were perched on top of the small dresser he'd wedged into the closet, and none of it was properly baby-proofed. Now that the second paternity test had come back positive and the court had officially granted him full custody, he was going to have to find a bigger place. One more thing to put on his growing to-do list.

Hooking the bag on the corner of the changing table, he laid the baby down and swapped out the wet diaper for a dry one as fast as possible, wincing at the inevitable crying. "Sorry, buddy, but this isn't my idea of a good time, either." He maneuvered his son's surprisingly strong legs back into the romper he'd been wearing and checked to be sure the million and one snaps were all fastened. "There, all done."

The crying stopped as soon as he got the baby up on his shoulder again, as if there was some kind of altimeter that alerted Ryan's cry center to changes in altitude. He was just grateful it worked. Next for the bag. Extra diapers, wipes, a change of outfit, a bottle with powdered formula, a thermos of warm water, two pacifiers and his cell phone went in the diaper bag. His wallet and keys went in his pocket, and then he was good to go. Definitely his fastest diaper-to-door time so far. This fatherhood thing was tough, but he was catching on.

He buckled Ryan into his car seat and headed downtown, hoping he wasn't about to make a huge mistake. Up until now, their only outings had been to the pediatrician and the grocery store. An art show was on a whole different level, and quite possibly an awful idea. On the other hand, staying home when Mollie was going to be there showing her work would take more self-control than he had. Which was why he was driving through downtown traffic with a baby crying in the backseat.

In front of the gallery, he checked the car with the valet, then struggled to unsnap the bucket-shaped seat from the car. The thing weighed as much as the baby and was awkward as heck, but if Ryan got sleepy, he'd be more comfortable in it. And trying to steer a stroller around a packed gallery wasn't a challenge he was up for. At least one of them was. Noah was in a cold sweat and he hadn't even made it into the building yet.

Aside from the logistics of carting a newborn through a very formal, very adult event, he had no idea what he was going to say to Mollie when he saw her. *Hey, I know you said you didn't want a family, but any chance you changed your mind?* probably wasn't the best way to lead off. No, he needed to be strong and let her know he was there to support her, not put pressure on her. This might be his only chance with her, and blowing it wasn't an option. Squaring his shoulders, he opened the glass door and walked in.

The gallery itself was one he was familiar with; he'd had a few shows here earlier on in his career. The room was long and narrow, divided into separate viewing areas with cleverly arranged screens. The walls and floor were a nondescript white to better set off the artwork. In contrast, the majority of the people swarming the room were in black, the typical camouflage of the well-to-do Atlanta social scene. Picking one person out of the masses that had shown up for opening night was impossible, but he could feel in his bones that she was here.

The first small area held dozens of photos of bugs. *Insects of the World*, the display tag said. Close-ups of beetles fighting over dung hung next to an incredible shot of a grasshopper in midleap. Intriguing. And not what he was looking for. Pushing past a couple arguing the merits of various photo-editing techniques, he moved through to the next cluster of photographs. These were all of orchids, some potted, some in the wild. He lingered a moment over a particularly colorful one until Ryan tried to take a swipe at it. "No, sir. No sticky baby hands on the merchandise. They'll kick us out for sure, and we haven't found what we came for yet."

Ryan gurgled as if he understood, moving his hand away from the framed picture and sticking it in his mouth. Sucking happily, he rested his head against Noah's chest and despite the chaos around them Noah felt his blood pressure lower. Who'd have thought a baby would be what it took for him to keep his head on straight?

Feeling more grounded, he weaved his way through the crowd, scanning the walls for Mollie's work. He was almost to the back of the building when he saw it and stopped dead in his tracks. There, in a simple wooden frame, was the photo she'd taken of the anhinga the morning they'd gone fishing together. At the time, he'd been so entranced with the photographer he hadn't really noticed the bird. But she had—she'd captured every detail, from the outstretched wings to the sleepy look in its eye. If he didn't know better, he'd have sworn he could reach out and stroke the damp feathers. Standing in front of it he could almost feel the heat of the sun and smell the sea air. It was a tangible piece of Paradise, and a gut-wrenching reminder of the real reason he was here.

* * *

Mollie nodded politely as yet another patron asked her about alligators. Blame it on the explosion of nature documentaries or just a severe misunderstanding of geography, but as soon as she mentioned her home state people seemed convinced she must have daily exposure to the reptiles.

"So you've never had one get into your house?" The slightly tipsy blonde took another sip of champagne, her eyes wide at the idea of an alligator infestation.

Mollie resisted the urge to roll her eyes. Tonight was about mingling and being polite. "Nope, they pretty much stay in the water. Just like here. Georgia actually has gators, too, in the southern part of the state."

A vapid nod and the woman moved on, dragging her bored-looking boyfriend towards the bar. Seeing her chance, Mollie limped to the little alcove she'd spotted earlier, between a conference room and the owner's office. The shoes she'd worked so hard to get into the suitcase were torture devices in disguise. Checking that no one was watching, she leaned against the wall and rubbed one aching foot. Wrestling pitbulls for nail trims was easier on the body than an evening in stockings and heels. At least the sequined black dress she'd worn was comfortable, if a bit on the revealing side.

She'd worked the kinks out of one arch and was about to switch feet when the door to the office opened. Great. So much for her little hiding spot.

She slipped her shoe back on and stood up straight. She was already the least experienced photographer in the show; she didn't need to be caught looking like a slacker.

The gallery owner she'd met earlier came out, holding the door for whomever he was speaking with. "It was good to see you again, Mr. James. I hope you enjoy your purchase."

"I'm sure I will. Thank you."

It couldn't be. Mollie's heart skipped a beat, then went into overdrive. He wouldn't have come, not after everything that happened, would he? The voice sounded like him, but the door was blocking her view.

Then it swung closed and he was there. She'd known that he could show up, but she hadn't really believed he would. Otherwise she'd never have had the nerve to come. Seeing him in the flesh had her head spinning and her knees turning to jelly. She grabbed the wall for balance and her wristlet slapped the cement, the noise ringing out in the small alcove.

He turned, and time stopped. For a long moment she just stared, drinking in his presence. He looked a bit thinner, maybe a little tired, but still drop-dead gorgeous. And the man could seriously rock a suit. He looked like a movie star ready for the red carpet, only even more incredible. Because he was Noah.

Noah with a baby in his arms. She shifted her gaze from father to son and was instantly captivated. The little boy was cuter than the picture Noah had sent, with his father's big brown eyes and the sweet-est little button nose. "He's wonderful."

"He is. He's also loud, and he has horrible table manners."

She felt a laugh bubble up, all the reasons she'd fallen for this man rising to the surface with it. He was funny and confident and utterly delicious in every way. Why had she pushed him away? There had been reasons, lots of them, but damned if she could think of any now that he was standing in front of her.

Without thinking, she reached out and stroked the baby's curly black hair, loving the silky softness. Her ovaries might actually be exploding right now in the face of so much cuteness. Swallowing hard, she made herself step back. This wasn't her baby, and Noah wasn't her man. She'd had a chance, and she'd blown it. Big time. "I didn't expect to see you here tonight." Not after she'd blocked his calls and ignored him for the last month.

"I said I'd come and I meant it. I know how im-portant it is to you."

She shrugged. "I just figured you'd probably be busy, with the baby and everything."

"What, this guy?" He stroked his son's head. "He loves art galleries. He's a big fan of yours, actually."

She smiled, knowing he'd meant her to. "Right. I should have realized. Well, are you enjoying the show?"

"Yeah, I'd say so. Your stuff is fantastic, by the way."

She felt her cheeks heat. She'd been on the receiving end of dozens of compliments tonight, but his opinion was the one she'd subconsciously needed to hear. "Thanks."

"How about you? Are you enjoying your big night?"

"It's been…exhausting, actually. I think I'm better at taking pictures than talking about them. I probably ought to head back over there, though, before I'm missed." Not that she wanted to leave him so soon after finding him.

"We'll walk with you."

Walking beside him was like walking back into a dream. Their steps fell into an easy rhythm, just like on their walks on the beach back home. If only they were there now, instead of a room full of pretentious strangers. Too soon they stopped in front of her small display. She pretended to look at the photos she'd seen a thousand times already, anything to keep from looking at him. If she stared too long, she'd lose whatever tiny shred of dignity she had left. No one here wanted to hear her beg him for a second chance.

"That one's my favorite." Oblivious to her discomfort, he moved closer, his arm brushing hers as he pointed to the shot of the anhinga. It was her favorite, too, not because of the composition, but because it was a memento of a nearly perfect day. "In fact, I just bought it."

"You bought it? You didn't have to do that. I would have given you a copy if you'd asked."

"Hey, I have to do my part to support the arts, right? And it would have been kind of hard to ask, given how well you've been avoiding my phone calls."

Ugh. "I know, I'm sorry. I just thought, well, I thought that you needed to have some time to focus on your son. I didn't mean to—"

"Mollie, it's fine." He rested a hand on her shoulder, bared by the halter top of her dress. "I understand, and honestly, you were probably right to do it. I've had to make a lot of adjustments and rethink a lot of things."

Things like his relationship with his ex? The only way to find out was to ask. "Sounds tough. Have you been able to come to some sort of understanding with Angela after everything that happened?"

His jaw tensed, and he looked suddenly looked much wearier than he had a few minutes ago. "I guess you could say that."

An awful thought popped into her head. "Is she here with you tonight?" There was no way she could handle seeing the happy family together. Petty or not, she would rather wrestle one of the alligators people kept asking her about than make small talk with that woman.

"No, she's not with me. Not tonight, not any night."

Was it wrong to feel relieved? Because that was definitely the emotion sweeping over her. And right behind it was concern. "I'm sorry. Is she giving you any trouble as far as visitation goes?"

He looked down at the baby on his chest. "None. She gave me full custody."

Wait, what? "What do you mean, full custody?"

"I mean he's mine, full-time. Angela decided she wasn't ready to be a mother, so she gave me full custody, then took off again. Her new boyfriend has a fancy job on Wall Street and she's not letting him or his money out of her sight."

Mollie felt her mouth drop open. "She chose some new guy over her own child? Who does that? What kind of woman could walk out on her kid like that?"

"I wish I could explain it, but all I can say is that Angela isn't like most women. She's wired differently, I guess, and if she wasn't up to being a parent, well, at least she was honest about it. This was probably the most selfless thing she's ever done, although I doubt she realizes it."

"So you've been taking care of him all on your own?"

"Not entirely. My parents have helped a lot, actually. Having a grandchild around seems to have helped heal some old wounds. We're probably closer now than we've ever been."

"That sounds nice." She smacked herself on the head. "I mean it's nice that your parents are helping you. Not that she took off."

He smiled and reached out and stroked a stray hair off her forehead, then quickly moved his hand back to his side. "I know what you meant, and it is nice, actually. And as hard as it's been, adjusting to being a father, it's also been pretty great."

"I bet it has. Angela's a fool to give him up."

"Well, not every woman wants to be a mother."

She sucked in a breath at implication. "That was

a low blow, Noah. There's a big difference between choosing not to have children and walking out on one."

Noah couldn't believe he'd said that. "Damn it, I didn't mean it that way. Trust me, you are nothing like her."

She seemed to be considering his apology, but an earsplitting wail kept her from replying, proving once again that babies had no sense of timing. "Sorry, he's probably hungry. I need to find somewhere quiet and feed him before he gets any crankier."

Her eyes widened. "He gets worse than this?"

"You have no idea." Ryan could put a siren to shame once he got going. Even the nurses at the hospital had been impressed.

"There's a small meeting room in the back. Will that work?"

He nodded and started walking, moving quickly. There was no point in trying to talk over the baby's cries, which were already inciting some hostile looks. He'd been lucky Ryan had kept quiet for so long, probably distracted from his usual nighttime antics by all the people and artwork. Mollie pushed open a wood and glass door and led him into a small but serviceable conference room. A round table took up the majority of the space, with six comfortable-looking chairs spaced evenly around it. Dropping into one, he dug into a black, messenger-style diaper bag with one hand while balancing the baby in his lap with the other.

"Need a hand?"

"You don't mind holding him for a second?"

"I wouldn't have offered if I did. Here, hand him over." She reached out and Noah found himself placing the baby in her arms.

"Be careful of his—"

"Head? Yeah, I know. Believe it or not, I've done this before." She bounced lightly on her toes, calming Ryan's cries. "At one point, I was the most sought-after babysitter on Paradise Isle."

"I can believe it." She'd certainly worked her magic on his son, who was now watching her in wide-eyed fascination. It seemed she now had both of the James men under her spell. Mixing the powdered formula with the water from the thermos, he made up the bottle quickly, handing it over when she reached for it.

"Here we go big guy, dinnertime." Ryan latched on to the bottle nipple and greedily started suckling.

Captivated, Noah watched Mollie feed his son, not wanting to spoil the moment with small talk. Angela might not have been up to motherhood, but Mollie was obviously a natural. Finally the bottle was empty, and without missing a beat she grabbed a clean cloth from the bag and tossed it over her shoulder before shifting the baby to burp him.

"Okay, I give. You're obviously an expert at this. I'd have pegged you for a total baby lover if I didn't know better."

"I never said I don't like babies. Or kids. But being a parent is a whole lot more than just liking babies. It's about sacrifice and putting their needs before your own."

"You're right, I'm sorry. I promise I didn't come here to try to pressure you into anything."

"Why are you here, Noah? After everything I said in Paradise, and then shutting you out after Ryan was born, what made you come here tonight?" He could hear the sincerity in her voice; she wasn't fishing for a compliment or trying to corner him into anything. She really didn't know.

"I came because I couldn't stay away." There it was, the bare truth. "I know I should leave you alone—I'm a single dad, and you aren't ready for a family. And I want you to follow your dreams and do all the amazing things you want to do. You've got a path you want to take, and I promise, I'm not going to stand in your way."

"I know you aren't."

He let out a sigh of relief. At least he hadn't ruined things, not yet. She was still listening, her eyes on his as she rested her cheek on his son's head. If he could freeze time and capture this moment forever, he would. But then he'd be doing exactly what he'd promised not to do. He couldn't control her or keep her in his life, not matter how much he wanted to. "What I'm trying to say is, I've waited a lifetime to find the perfect woman, and a few more years won't kill me. All I'm asking is that if you ever do decide to try your hand at having a family, you give me a call. I'm willing to wait as long as it takes."

Tears filled her big brown eyes and spilled down her cheeks, landing in his son's dark curls. He wiped one away with his thumb, loving how she leaned into his touch. "Don't cry. You don't have to promise anything. I shouldn't have even asked. I just thought if there was some hope, it would make it easier to be apart. But that's not fair to you. Let's just forget I said anything, okay? This is your big night and I've got you burping a baby in the back room." He moved to take his son. "I'll take him, and you go mingle while you can."

Instead of handing the sleepy baby over, she held on, shaking her head even as she smiled. "No way. You can't make me go back out there. Besides, you had your chance to talk. Now it's my turn."

Mollie couldn't decide if she wanted to laugh or cry, but either might wake the baby sleeping so peacefully in her arms. So she took a deep breath and just went for it. "I don't want you to wait." He started to speak and she cut him off, needing him to hear this. "I don't want you to wait because I don't want to wait."

"You don't?" Noah looked so startled she ended up laughing after all, unable to contain the happiness welling up inside her.

"No. This past month has been a nightmare. I miss you constantly, and I'm tired of that. It sucks."

The corner up of mouth tipped up in a lopsided grin. "You missed me."

"Yes, I just said that. And I hated it. Hell, even Baby missed you. So we have to figure something out."

"But what about your career? Your dreams? As well as the show went tonight, I'm sure you're going to have all sorts of opportunities opening up. I think there was even a magazine editor checking out your stuff."

"Seriously? An editor? That would be amazing."

"It would. But it also means you're going to have to make some big decisions. If she doesn't contact you, I'm sure others will. You're going to have lots of work if you want it, mark my words. And as much of a rush as I know that is, it can be overwhelming, too."

"All the more reason I'm going to need your support. I don't want to do this without you. I realized that on the way here. I've been worried about messing up my career with a relationship, afraid I'd look back one day and wonder what might have been. But Noah, the one thing I know I'd regret would be losing you, letting go of whatever we have going on here. And that's scarier than anything I can think of."

"So what are you saying?" He stepped closer, the baby the only thing between them. "What is it you want?"

"Everything." Stretching onto her toes, she ran her free hand over his jaw, feeling the stubble his razor had missed. "You, a career, I want it all."

He leaned in, his mouth inches away, close enough

for her to smell his cologne over the sweet scent of baby shampoo and powder. "And what about Ryan? I'm not asking you to be his mother, but he and I are kind of a package deal now."

"Even better." She pressed her lips to his in a gentle kiss. "In case you hadn't noticed, he and I get along just fine." Better than fine. She could feel herself falling for the little guy already as he slept on her shoulder. It probably shouldn't be a surprise, given how fast his father had slipped past her defenses.

"I can see that. But right now, he's kind of in the way." Noah gently pulled the baby out of her arms and lowered him into the car seat, buckling it around him. "There, now, where were we?"

"I'm not sure," she teased. "Maybe you should remind me."

"Maybe I should." He cupped her bare shoulders with his hands, then ran them ever so slowly down her body to rest on her hips. "By the way, this dress should be illegal. I think my blood pressure hit dangerous levels when I turned around and saw you in it." He pulled her against him, and bent his mouth to her ear. "I'm still feeling a bit woozy. I might even need mouth to mouth."

Goose bumps rose where his breath tickled her skin. "I think that could be arranged. Better safe than sorry." She turned her head and kissed him then, needing him more than she needed her next breath. His lips tasted like champagne, his tongue like velvet, exploring her as if they had all the time in the world. Tangling her hands in his hair, she wondered how she had ever thought she could walk away from him. "I missed this especially," she murmured against his lips. "I don't ever want to stop."

He sucked her bottom lip between his teeth, nipping lightly before letting go. "Then don't. Let's spend the rest of our lives doing this."

Her heart skittered out of rhythm. "Are you... Did you just ask me...?" No, he couldn't have meant that.

He pulled back just enough to look her in the eyes, amusement crinkling his at the corners. "Was I asking you to marry me? Honestly, I don't know. Isn't it too soon for that?"

Butterflies swarmed in her stomach. "Probably. Maybe."

His hands tightened on her waist. "What would you have said if I had?"

"Oh, no, you don't. It doesn't work that way. If you want an answer, you have to ask. Properly."

His mouth was firm, but she saw twinkle of a smile in his eyes. Without letting go of her, he lowered himself onto one knee. Behind him the baby was still sleeping, oblivious to the anticipation flooding the room. "So help me, if you're about to turn me down—"

"Hurry up, before the baby wakes up."

He rolled his eyes. "I thought you wanted this done properly?"

"I do, but I'm also impatient."

"So it seems." He cleared his throat and reached up to take her hands in his. "Mollie Post, I'm probably exactly the wrong thing for you in so many ways, but I promise to spend my life making yours better, if you'll let me. Would you do me the honor of being my wife?"

She smiled, the tears falling for real now. "I've always wanted adventure and excitement, and I thought that meant traveling the world, reaching new goals. But Noah, nothing could be more of an adventure than creating a life with you and Ryan."

He cocked his head, looking up at her from the floor. "That means yes, right?"

"Yes."

Chapter 9

Mollie grabbed another box full of odds and ends off the garage floor and hauled it over to the back-yard table where she had been sorting since break-fast. It was nearing noon now and she'd barely made a dent. "Are you sure you don't want to just rent some studio space somewhere?" In the month since he'd proposed, she'd floated the idea several times, but he'd turned her down each time.

Noah looked up from the workbench he was build-ing. "I'm not going to rent space just so you don't have to clean out the garage. There's plenty of space for your photography equipment and my tools, and I'd rather work from home so I can see Ryan more."

"Fine." He was right; there was plenty of room in her home, or at least there would be once she finished

going through all this stuff. So far she'd found everything from her third-grade report card to a tangle of
rusted fishing hooks, not to mention the old magazines
that were slowly turning to dust. Why had she kept
all this stuff? "But I hate you for making me do this."

"No, you don't. You love me."

She sighed in annoyance. "Yeah, I do. But I'd still
rather be on the beach, or fishing, or doing anything
else, pretty much." She wiped the sweat from her
forehead. It was a perfect summer day for the beach,
but way too hot to be working outside.

"Anything, huh?" Noah waggled his eyebrows at
her. "I might be amenable to a break, depending on
what activity you had in mind."

She felt her face heat, and not just from the blaz-
ing sun overhead. "Not in front of the baby." Ryan
was in his swing a few feet away, Baby curled up on
the ground beside him. Both were snoozing in the
shade of the big oak tree and not paying any attention to Noah's suggestive comments. "Besides, it's
only a few more days."

"Three days. Three very long days," he muttered,
attacking the sanding with more vigor than was probably necessary.

She felt a moment of guilt, but then he winked
at her, and everything was okay. She knew it was
silly, but superstitious or not, she wanted her and Noah's wedding to be totally different from the one he'd
planned with Angela. Up to and including waiting
until after the ceremony for sex. He'd grumbled, but
finally agreed, warning her that she'd better be pre-

pared for a *vigorous* honeymoon. As if he was the only one who was impatient. Even now, the sight of him shirtless, glistening with sweat while he worked had her wanting to ambush him right there on top of the table he was building. No, he certainly wasn't the only one fighting their urges. But it would be worth it on their wedding night.

Speaking of which. "Did your parents' flight get in okay?"

He nodded, not breaking his rhythm as he worked. "Yup, they sent me a text saying they were on their way to the Sandpiper and are looking forward to the rehearsal dinner tonight."

"Good." His father still made her a bit nervous with his military demeanor, but Noah's mom kept him in check and was turning out to be a wonderful friend. They'd spent quite a bit of time together in Atlanta when Mollie had flown up to go apartment-hunting with Noah. He'd offered to move full time to Paradise, but in the end they'd decided to keep a place in both cities. That way they could go back and forth as they pleased, and Ryan could spend time with all of his grandparents, of which he had an abundance. Mollie's parents were totally in love with the little guy, and of course Noah's parents had been a huge help since day one. Even Angela's parents had made cautious inroads, not wanting to miss out on their grandchild's life despite their daughter's decision.

Yes, Ryan was loved, but that wasn't a surprise. He was as sweet a baby as she'd ever seen; he'd even gotten over his colic after a formula switch. And although nature photography was still her focus, taking pictures of the newborn was quickly becoming an addiction. It helped that he seemed just enamored with her as she was with him, often reaching for her even when Noah was there. And as much as she'd worried that having a relationship or a baby would stifle her career, she'd actually been spending more time behind the camera than ever and had even signed a contract with a statewide magazine for some of her photos.

The only slight regret she had was leaving her job at the animal clinic. It was hard not seeing Cassie and Jillian every day, but now she could double up on her classes and graduate next spring. Living off of Noah's money was a bit disconcerting, but he'd blown off her concerns, saying it was an investment in their future. But she, or rather her parents, had drawn the line at paying for the wedding. They'd been saving for years for a day they'd thought might never come and weren't going to be denied the privilege of orchestrating the big event.

Mollie had asked for a simple ceremony on the beach, but her mom was nearly unstoppable. The final compromise was a ceremony on the beach, with a huge reception afterward back at the Sandpiper. The tents had been rented, flowers and food ordered, musicians hired, and now all that was left was to actually say "I do."

And it couldn't happen soon enough.

Noah stood barefoot in the office of the Sandpiper and pulled at the too-tight collar of his shirt.

He'd ordered the white linen shirt and pants online, and everything fit but the neck. He somehow hadn't noticed that when he'd tried it on the day it arrived and now it was too late to do anything about it. Giving up, he undid the top button and hoped Mollie wouldn't mind. She'd wanted a casual, nontraditional wedding—one undone collar shouldn't be a huge deal. Should it?

"Does this look okay?"

Alex, Cassie's husband, shook his head. "Sorry, I don't answer fashion questions, not about suits and stuff. This is the most dressed up I've been since my own wedding." Alex gestured to the khaki slacks and blue, short-sleeved dress shirt he and Nic, the other groomsman, were wearing. "But if I was going to say anything, it would be to relax. She's not going to ditch you at the altar because your collar's unbuttoned."

Noah swallowed hard.

"Oops, sorry, man. I wasn't thinking. But seriously, Mollie's not Angela. If she didn't want to marry you, she would have told your sorry butt no when you first asked her."

"Good point." Mollie didn't say things she didn't mean, and she didn't play games. She was exactly what he wanted in a woman, which was why he was having such a hard time believing this was real. Just a few short months ago, he'd been a loner who spent more time with a blow torch than with other humans. Now he was surrounded by family and newfound friends. He had a new connection with his parents, was raising a son, and in a matter of minutes he'd have the perfect wife to share it all with. It would have been less shocking to win the lottery while being struck by lightning.

A knock at the door was followed by a mad dash into the room by Emma, Alex and Cassie's nearly five-year-old daughter. A few seconds behind her was Cassie, looking flustered but beautiful in the baby blue maternity dress Mollie had chosen for her two pregnant bridesmaids. "Sorry, she insisted she needed to show Alex her dress. Again. I'm raising a fashionista here."

Alex admired Emma as she twirled in her flower-girl dress and then swept her up for a hug. "Nah, she's just a daddy's girl, aren't you, sweetheart?" Emma nodded, all dimples and curls. "Probably was pining away for me."

Cassie rolled her eyes. "She saw you at lunch." But she was smiling, too, obviously pleased by the close relationship the two had forged. Alex wasn't Emma's biological father, but you wouldn't know it from the way they acted. Funny how that worked. Love trumped biology with them, just as it did with Mollie and Ryan. Somehow the right people had found each other, against all the odds.

The door opened again, this time for Alex's father. "They're all set, son. Let's get this show on the road."

"Mommy, it's time! I have to go get my flowers!" Emma scrambled out of Alex's lap, her devotion to her father paling in comparison to flower-girl duties.

"Okay, let's go." Cassie blew her husband a kiss, then let Emma pull her out the door.

"Where's Nic? He was supposed to meet us in here." Noah hadn't seen his other groomsman since they'd first gotten to the inn a few hours ago.

"I just saw him," his father assured him. "He was helping the musicians get set up, something about having to reinforce the bandstand to support the weight. He was going to run and wash up, then meet us out back."

Noah shook his head. Nic had gone from power suits and boardroom meetings to hammering nails and washing dishes, and seemed perfectly happy about it. But then, life was full of twists and turns, wasn't it?

Together the three men trooped down the hall and out the back door, where they found Nic waiting for them. The back porch had been transformed into a buffet line, where uniformed caterers were setting out an ample spread of summer fare. Down on the lawn, tables had been set up under a tent, with large fans to supplement the sea breeze. And of course there was the bandstand and the dance floor that Nic had built himself.

But that was all for later. First he had to get through the ceremony. The men took the steps down to the beach, where the minister waited under an arbor made from driftwood. Behind it was the ever-changing backdrop of the sea, and although the sun hadn't quite set, a glimmer of a moon could be seen peeking over the horizon.

Taking his place beside the minister, he felt his earlier anxiety ease. Something about the enduring sound of the waves steadied him, that and the people he was now facing, all of them here to show their support. He'd come to Paradise to heal his wounds and found so much more.

The first strains of the wedding march caught his attention, and the crowd turned as one to see the bridal party make its way down the aisle. First Jillian, looking radiant, then Cassie, and then little Emma with her flower basket. After all the petals had been thrown, enthusiastically if not gracefully, the music changed again, and Noah felt his heart skip a beat.

There, at the far end of aisle, was Mollie, and she was the most beautiful thing he'd ever seen. Her simple strapless dress was perfect, no lace or flounces for her. No, she was simple and open and honest, and he was about to be the happiest man in the world.

Mollie made her way through the sand, trying to focus on Noah's face and not the countless people staring at her. Somehow she'd forgotten that she'd be so on display, and it was just short of terrifying. What if she tripped? Or what if people thought her dress was too short or too casual? The sheath had seemed perfect back in Jillian's bedroom a few minutes ago, but maybe she should have worn something more traditional. Panic, an unfamiliar and unwelcome feeling, clawed at her, stifling her.

Her father patted her arm where it was looped through his in a show of reassurance, but her lungs still refused to work properly, and she was practically hyperventilating by the time they reached the front row of seats where her and Noah's families sat.

Little Ryan was in his grandmother's lap, and he cried out as Mollie passed, stretching his pudgy arms towards her. Noah's mom flushed and tried to shush him, but the little boy just cried harder, his face turning red.

Jolted out of her self-induced panic, Mollie stopped and stepped away from her father, moving to take the little boy. "You're right, little man," she reassured him, snugging him to her chest. "You deserve to be up there, too."

Linking her arm back with her father's, she let him take her and Ryan the rest of the way. Somehow the people behind her didn't matter now, not with Noah at her side and Ryan in her arms. She was able to smile and enjoy the rest of the ceremony, and then, so much faster than she'd expected, they were married.

She quickly passed Ryan back to his grandmother, and then she was walking back down the aisle—this time, arm in arm with her new husband. Squeezing her hand, Noah leaned down to whisper in her ear. "You look incredible in that dress, but I'm dying to peel it off of you."

She shivered in anticipation. "You don't look bad yourself." In fact, he looked amazing. The summery white fabric made him look even more dark and handsome, and she knew the loose material hid some seriously hard muscles. "I say we make a quick appearance and then start the honeymoon early."

"It's a deal."

An hour and a half later, it was clear that making an appearance took a lot longer than expected when there were so many people to greet. And both sets of parents had insisted that the bride and groom couldn't leave until after the cake cutting at the very earliest. Which, the caterer had told her, wasn't supposed to happen for another forty-five minutes. Well, that just wasn't going to work for her. She'd talked to everyone she needed to talk to, she'd had an amazing first dance in the arms of her groom, she'd stuffed herself silly with crab cakes and fruit and, darn it, she was done.

Time to take matters into her own hands. Putting down her champagne glass on the nearest table, she scanned the tent for Noah. Not seeing him or Ryan, she cut across the yard where Baby, Murphy and Alex's K9 partner, Rex, were chewing on celebratory dog bones, giving them a pat before climbing the porch steps on the side of the house. Here, some of the older guests had gathered, preferring the Sandpiper's comfortable patio furniture to the folding chairs on the lawn. Noah was there, too, talking to his mother, baby Ryan asleep in the portable swing. Perfect.

"Sorry to interrupt, just need to steal my husband away for a minute." She grabbed Noah's arm and tugged. "Mama James, you don't mind keeping an eye on Ryan, do you?"

"Of course not, dear. I'm having a lovely chat with the ladies I've met. You two go enjoy the party."

Oh, she planned on it. Tugging Noah with her, she took him down the stairs and then, making sure none of the women on the patio were watching, around the building and down a well-mulched path.

"Where on earth are you taking me?"

"Somewhere we can be alone." She pointed to the brick and timber house at the end of the path. "Jillian said the house is finished, and as soon as they furnish it they'll move in."

"Are you serious?"

She pulled on their joined hands, swinging him toward her for a hard, fast kiss. "Like a heart attack."

She took the steps to the front door two at a time, sliding a key from where she'd hidden it in her cleavage.

"Where on earth did you get a key to Jillian and Nic's house?"

She rolled her eyes. "Jillian gave it to me. She knew I'd insisted we wait until we were married and since they won't be moving in for another month, she figured we might want to get a jump on things, so to speak."

Noah stopped in his tracks. "Isn't consummating our marriage in your friend's half-built house a bit…unorthodox?"

"Honey, if you wanted traditional, you married the wrong girl. Now, are you coming or not?"

Noah followed her in, and she locked the door behind him, laying the key on the windowsill before closing the blinds. Turning towards him, her heart pounding, she unzipped her dress in one swift move, letting it fall to the floor. Noah's draw dropped, and she had to stifle a giggle at his shock.

"You weren't wearing anything under your dress."

"Nope."

"You do realize, if I'd known that, we probably

wouldn't have even made it through the vows." He stepped closer, his eyes dark with lust, but she saw love there as well, and her own need increased in response.

"Well, then, Mr. James, now you know. So I suggest you get those clothes off and we make this marriage official."

Growling his response, he tore his shirt off, sending buttons flying.

"Noah, your shirt! We still have to go back for the cake cutting."

"I'll borrow one from Nic. Or go naked, I don't care." He kicked off the rest of his clothes, and she got a glimpse of his perfect body before he was picking her up and carrying her to down the hall.

"Where are we going?" Dizzy, she closed her eyes, and let her other senses take control.

"Whatever room has carpet."

Noah couldn't believe Mollie had set this up, even so far as stashing a box of condoms on the mantel, but he wasn't going to argue. He'd been taking cold showers for too long to turn her down now. But he was too primed to go slow, and hardwood floors might leave them both bruised. The back bedroom had the plush carpet he was looking for. Dropping to his knees, he laid her out in front of him. She was gorgeous, and she was his.

"You know I planned for this to be special, with candles and flower petals and music," he muttered against her neck, loving how she squirmed as he kissed her there.

"I couldn't wait for special," she whimpered, her breathing fast and shallow. "I need you, Noah."

"I need you, too." That was the truth, and with a quick motion of his hips, he gave her all of himself, joining them together the way man and woman had joined since the beginning of time. It wasn't the slow and gentle lovemaking he'd envisioned for their wedding night, but it was raw and honest and real, just like the woman beneath him. He kept his eyes open, watching her fall apart before finding his own release inside her. Panting, he dropped down, rolling off of her when she feebly pushed at him.

"That was incredible." Mollie snuggled up beside him, her hand making circles of gooseflesh on his chest. "We should do that again. A lot."

"Agreed. But as much as I'd like to lie here with you all night, we need to get back for the whole cake thing."

Her hand dropped lower, and his breath caught. "Actually, I was thinking. If we were just a little late, that would probably be fine. It's not like they can start without us, right?"

He rolled her on top of him, unable to resist her logic. Or her body. "Smart *and* sexy—I knew I married you for a reason. Hell, they can keep their cake, I've got everything I want right here."

* * * * *

He stuck his head around the corner of the fasteners
aisle just in time to see a tall brunette stagger into the
revolving seed display. Some of the packets went flying,
but she managed to steady the display before the whole
thing toppled. He took in what probably had been a very
nice silk blouse and tailored trouser suit before she was
drenched in the storm raging outside. The heel on one of
the ridiculously high heels she was wearing had snapped
off, explaining why she was stumbling around.

"Having a bad morning?"

The woman looked up in annoyance, strands of dark,
wet hair falling across her face.

"You could say that. I don't suppose you have a shoe
repair place in this town?" She looked at the bright red
heel in her hand.

Nate shook his head as he approached her. "Nope. But hand it over. I'll see what I can do."

A perfectly shaped brow arched high. "Why? Are you going to cobble them back together with—" she gestured around widely "—maybe some staples or screws?"

"Technically, what you just described is the definition of cobbling, so yeah. I've got some glue that'll do the trick." He met her gaze calmly. "It'd be a lot easier to do if you'd take the shoe off. Unless you also think I'm a blacksmith?"

He was teasing her. Something about this soaking-wet woman still having so much…regal bearing…amused Nate. He wasn't usually a fan of the pearl-clutching country club set who strutted through Gallant Lake on the weekends and referred to his family's hardware store as "adorable." But he couldn't help admiring this woman's ability to hold on to her superiority while looking like she accidentally went to a water park instead of the business meeting she was dressed for. To be honest, he also admired the figure that expensive red suit was clinging to as it dripped water on his floor.

He held out his hand. "I'm Nate Thomas. This is my store."

She let out an irritated sigh. "Brittany Doyle." She slid her long, slender hand into his and gripped with surprising strength. He held it for just a half second longer than necessary before shaking off the odd current of interest she invoked in him.

Don't miss
Changing His Plans *by Jo McNally,*
available September 2020 wherever
Harlequin Special Edition books and ebooks are sold.

Harlequin.com